ᎨᏇ ᎨᏇ ᎨᏇ ᎨᏇ ᎨᏇ ᎨᏇ ᎨᏇ ᎨᏇ ᎨᏇ ᎨᏇ ᎨᏇ

BILLY GASHADE

ᎨᏇ ᎨᏇ ᎨᏇ ᎨᏇ ᎨᏇ ᎨᏇ ᎨᏇ ᎨᏇ ᎨᏇ ᎨᏇ ᎨᏇ

Acclaim for Loren D. Estleman

▼ ▼ ▼ ▼ ▼ ▼ ▼ ▼ ▼ ▼ ▼ ▼ ▼ ▼ ▼ ▼ ▼ ▼ ▼

"Quicksilver dialogue, incisive characterizations, and canny interweaving of observations and events. Estleman's eye, ear, and hand are in perfect sync—you will want to call up your closest friends to read them your favorite paragraphs."
Washington Post Book World on Billy Gashade

"A wizard piece of historical reconstruction, exciting as a gangster film but with a texturing of the characters and the times that rises well above the genre."
Los Angeles Times Book Review on Billy Gashade

"As usual, Estleman brilliantly re-creates a period that may now be dead, but certainly isn't forgotten."
AP Newswire on Billy Gashade

"With a pro's practiced skill, Estleman keeps all the plates spinning through the air with no apparent effort and a hundred different voices."
Boston Sunday Globe on Murdock's Law

"Estleman ranks among the best of current American novelists."
San Diego Union-Tribune

"Prose as picturesque as the Painted Desert. When Page Murdock shuffles the words, deal me in."
New York Times Book Review on City of Widows

"*City of Widows* is a terrific book that seized me by mind and throat and never let go. I loved it. If this book gets its due, it'll sell a million copies." David Nevin, author of the New York Times bestseller Dream West

"I was going to see how *City of Widows* opens and read fifty-five pages. I smelled the horses in Loren Estleman's other

Westerns—they're that realistic and alive—and I smelled them again in *City of Widows*. It's a honey." Elmore Leonard

"Mr. Estleman plays in the majors... and his nervy characters can talk their way home on a double. A good clean game."
NEW YORK TIMES BOOK REVIEW on CITY OF WIDOWS

"Estleman's prose and ability to set a mood are always first-rate." CHICAGO SUN-TIMES

"Estleman's story evokes the brutality and heat of the Southwest through the efficient actions and dialogue of its characters."
KIRKUS REVIEWS on CITY OF WIDOWS

"Master storyteller Estleman—who mines both Western and mystery genres and is the author of the popular Amos Walker private-eye series—weaves a complex plot and populates it with three-dimensional characters whose actions are always slightly unexpected. This is a real treat for Western fans who need a break from the same old same old."
BOOKLIST on CITY OF WIDOWS

"Lean and lively. Estleman brews all these elements together into a potent mix, enlivened by some of the best dialogue in the business. He skillfully mingles reality-based characters with such fictional creations as Poker Annie. As readers have come to expect of this veteran writer, he also displays an eye for detail and gift of description that transcends the genre."
PUBLISHERS WEEKLY on CITY OF WIDOWS

"His research is meticulous, and his writing wastes no words. Highly recommended."
LIBRARY JOURNAL on CITY OF WIDOWS

▲ ▲ ▲ ▲ ▲ ▲ ▲ ▲ ▲ ▲ ▲ ▲ ▲ ▲ ▲ ▲ ▲ ▲ ▲

BILLY GASHADE

Loren D. Estleman

A TOM DOHERTY ASSOCIATES BOOK
NEW YORK

For KEVIN and KIMBERLY,
my children, delivered to me full-grown;
and for DEBI,
their mother, my world

NOTE: If you purchased this book without a cover you should be aware that this is stolen property. It was reported as "unsold and destroyed" to the publisher, and neither the author nor the publisher has received any payment for this "stripped book."

This is a work of fiction. All the characters and events portrayed in this book are either products of the author's imagination or are used fictitiously.

BILLY GASHADE

Copyright © 1997 by Loren D. Estleman

All rights reserved, including the right to reproduce this book, or portions thereof, in any form.

A Forge Book
Published by Tom Doherty Associates, Inc.
175 Fifth Avenue
New York, NY 10010

Forge® is a registered trademark of Tom Doherty Associates, Inc.

ISBN: 0-812-54915-5
Library of Congress Card Catalog Number: 96-27426

First edition: April 1997
First mass market edition: May 1998

Printed in the United States of America

0 9 8 7 6 5 4 3 2 1

Full lasting is the song, though he,
The singer, passes.

—GEORGE MEREDITH

AUTHOR'S NOTE

This song was made by Billy Gashade
Just as soon as the news did arrive.

It's possible that the above lyrics have never been sung by anyone but their composer. Yet in the saloons and parlors of the trans-Mississippi West between 1882 and the turn of the twentieth century, the song in which they appear, "Jesse James," was requested as often as any of today's million-selling hits, and is still a folk staple. Ironically, almost nothing is known of the man who wrote it.

The following is a work of imagination.

PART ONE

A Selection of Hells

CHAPTER ONE

My birth name doesn't matter, although that wasn't always the case. If you've patience enough to page through the New York Social Register—and in my time there were many who built entire careers on doing no more than that—you're sure to come across someone or other who bore it clear back to Peter Minuet.

No, my birth name doesn't matter, and I won't tell it now, even though all my enemies are dead. The truth is I've gone by Billy Gashade for so many years—full four times as many as I answered to the other—that if someone were to address me by the name under which I was baptized I'd keep on walking as like as not.

In any case, neither name displaces much cargo now. If you're the kind of moviegoer who sits through the opening credits instead of going out for Cracker Jacks, you won't find me listed there, despite the fact that I wrote three songs for Gene Autry to sing in *Phantom Empire* and two in *Tumbling Tumbleweeds,* and composed the entire score for a Porky Pig cartoon. Not bad in a Depression year for a man of eight-and-eighty.

I pocketed the cash for this work and let others slap their

brands on it, not because I'm modest, but because any kind of attention sooner or later gets back to New York and I didn't want to take the chance of one of my old blueblood acquaintances recognizing my features in a wire photograph after all these years and spreading the news through the season boxes at the Met that the judge's son is making his living as some kind of Tin Pan Alley songster in Hollywood, California. I don't care a damn what they say, but my father always did, and I respect that dead gent too much to let those hypocrites have the satisfaction of dragging his name through horseshit.

It isn't a bad living at that. There are no summers in Newport or autumns in Europe, but I've a small apartment I find comfortable at Pacific Palisades with a dandy view of the ocean when I stand in the northwest corner of the living room and crank my head, a two-block walk to the bus stop, and at an age when most men require strained turnips and a bedpan I have my health. Not to mention a pretty young blonde named Myra to bring me my meals on those occasional days when I'm too stove up to go out. Her mother, my landlady, carries my rent when the studios aren't calling and floats loans to her oldest tenant when his less understanding creditors come around. But then I've always had the good fortune to make the acquaintance of generous ladies.

You'd know this one. Not so long ago, when pictures didn't talk, she did her communicating with Rod la Rocque, Valentino, and a score of other pop-eyed foreign male leads by means of a black lace fan, usually to their ruin in the last reel. She was billed as Annique Deriger, which if my drawing-room French isn't too rusty translates as Annie of the Erection; and she had her day right up until she tested for her first role in a talkie and her Flatbush accent landed her on her girdle square in the middle of Hollywood Boulevard. Since then, along with a dead husband and property, she's acquired a fair approximation of a Parisian way of speech, which only deserts her when one of her succession of bad housekeepers neglects to clean an apartment she wants to show a prospective tenant, or she encounters a word ending in *r*. Underneath that voluminous gypsy scarf and pound and a half of makeup she's a good old gal with a heart as big as a Tennessee Walker. Daughter Myra's more steely-eyed, with a clearer view of what she wants out of the film trade and how to get it than her mother ever had, but she's sweet-tempered and more patient with an old man's guerrilla ways than most people her age. I think she's been an extra in a couple of programmers over at Fox. I know she sleeps with an assistant director there, and that's more than her mother knows. Women confide in me. Always have.

A deal more than three thousand miles and seventy-two years separates my palm-lined neighborhood from the Fifth Avenue of my youth, where I recall strolling home one day, a boy of sixteen, with my father from his club, and stopping to converse with one George Frederic Jones, a courtroom acquaintance of Father's, and his wife Lucretia. Jones was six feet and bore himself erect beside his birdlike and exquisitely seamstressed wife, who was pushing a perambulator. Its occupant, a grave little girl about a year old in a sparkling white linen dress and a starched bonnet trimmed with pink lace, took no notice of the conversation, appearing to be preoccupied with the gold elk's tooth depending from my father's watch chain, which dangled tantalizingly at her eye level when he stooped gallantly to retrieve the wood rattle that had dropped from her hand to the sidewalk. Ten or twelve years ago I was amused upon reading *The Age of Innocence,* by Mrs. Edith Jones Wharton, to learn that the Pulitzer prize-winning novelist had retained her fascination with such details more than half a century after saying farewell to perambulators and rattles. How different our lives have been. I've known associations whose gold teeth were extracted with a blacksmith's tongs from the jaws of their previous owners; but I am getting my verses mixed up. I'll sing them in their time.

My father was an expert jurist in a court system that routinely awarded the black robes to men who had simply managed to avoid personal scandal. Before that he was a brilliant and dedicated attorney with a firm whose partners had ascended to their positions by arranging not to be stillborn. So much genius and industry might have been regarded as unseemly in the New York society of the middle of the last century but for his celebrated family. That, together with my mother's line, less illustrious but nearly as old, guaranteed him membership in all the best clubs, and by projection the finest of musical educations for his only son.

I don't know how old I was when I first clambered aboard the stool of the Steinway grand in the conservatory of our Fifth Avenue town house, but I am told that at age three I was pecking out the opening chords to "Will You Come to the Bower?" without benefit of sheet music. My parents lost no time in engaging a tutor. One of my earliest memories is fearsome: A child with legs too short to reach the pedals attempts the bridge to the "Moonlight Sonata" over and over while an ancient dragon of a Viennese piano master with a Louis-Napoléon goatee hovers nearby, keeping time with malacca stick raised as if to strike at the first false note. It never fell that I recall, but the implied threat remained, and to this day I am unnerved by men with thick European accents and chin-whiskers.

By the time I turned sixteen—at which point my song begins in earnest—I had performed in a number of successful recitals, and it had long been assumed that my future lay not with the law but with music. Although this was a subject of some ungallant gossip in a class that looked upon any sort of public exhibition as vulgar—this despite the fact that the beginning of the social season coincided with the Academy of Music's first opera production of the year—my parents were undisturbed: "Follow your strength" was a favorite axiom of Father's, and he would no more presume to turn me from the path that was obvious to me than he would have allowed my grandfather, a former head of surgery at New York Hospital, to suggest to him a course in medicine. The complacent belief was that in time I would take my place as a soloist with the great Philharmonic Orchestra.

Fate, however, is seldom complacent.

In May 1863, with the Civil War in full savage swing, President Lincoln proclaimed the military draft to be in effect. The selection process, based upon a list of men of eligible age compiled from the tax rolls and voting registers, began in New England several days before the lottery wheel spun in New York for the first time. The declaration that the draft was unconstitutional, made by a number of politicians and several esteemed judges—with whom Father chose not to include himself, believing the war a necessary horror in which each must take his part—had led to a number of demonstrations and minor civil disturbances in Boston, Massachusetts, and Troy upstate. Therefore the police were out in force when a crowd gathered before the Enrollment Office on the corner of Forty-sixth Street and Third Avenue on the morning of Saturday, July 11.

The event was anticlimactic. Neither the city patrolmen nor a squad of wounded soldiers assigned to assist them in maintaining the peace were so called upon. Spectators remained peaceful, although there was a murmur of surprise when the names of several firemen from the local Black Joke Engine Company No. 33 were drawn. Since firefighters were exempt from service in the state militia, it was assumed they would be spared placement with the Union. Nevertheless the crowd dispersed quietly when the doors closed at six o'clock.

Monday, July 13, dawned placidly enough for me, if unpleasantly warm. In other years the family would some time since have repaired to Rhode Island and the cooling sea breezes of Newport, but this year my mother, never a sturdy woman, was confined to her bed with strict physician's orders to avoid travel of any sort, and Father had chosen to employ the enforced stay in the completion of one of those legal tracts that were always so well received from one of his stature in the profession. This time he had honored me by requesting my assistance, and so I made no complaint about the heat and grime of the city in summer as I struck off on a research errand to the library.

I have ever been curious, an incurable affliction and nearly always personally disastrous. When I was five I climbed by means of a construction of ottomans, pillows, and the works of Sir Walter Scott to the top of an eighteenth-century chifforobe in my parents' bedroom, only to burn my hand badly in the pretty blue flame of the gas jet that had inspired the ascent. Alas, it was not a learning experience. As many times since then as my Need to Know a Thing has landed me in foul soup, I would in my present extremity sooner chase a siren than dine on pheasant. In 1863 I nearly died of this condition.

Brief though the walk was to the library, I boarded a horsecar to avoid exerting myself in the punishing heat. It seemed to me as I paid my fare that the driver, an old campaigner in a battered shako with an inch of cigar screwed into the corner of his mouth, looked me over with more than the customary suspicion of the confirmed urbanite; but then I had been brought up to regard these denizens of the world outside the rails that connected our parlor, the opera house, our friends' dining rooms, and Father's clubs as nothing more than fixtures in the scenery, and so gave his behavior no great thought. However, as I found my way swayingly to a seat I overheard gossip among some of my fellow passengers that set my pulse throbbing.

Reports had spread that members of the city's Irish element, sworn enemies of the Republican administration that had created the draft, had been gathering in saloons and public halls since Saturday to grumble about the situation. Bad tempers and cheap alcohol was not a mix to be considered lightly, particularly when there was usually a derby-sporting agitator from rival Tammany Hall on hand to buy the drinks and keep the conversation from drifting in less volatile directions. Several horsecars on Second and Third Avenues had been stopped that morning by rough-dressed men armed with cudgels and iron bars, forced to unload their passengers, and turned back to their barns with instructions to the drivers to go home from there. Other men had been seen with axes, chopping down telegraph poles in the same vicinity and along Forty-sixth Street. Plainly the objective of these activities was to seal off the Enrollment Office. Trouble was in the air as thick as cinders.

It was a spectacle I was determined not to miss. I got off at the next stop and headed east on foot. As I did so I had no way of knowing that twenty years would pass before I returned home.

CHAPTER TWO

⚜

The rumors I had heard proved true the moment I rounded the corner onto Third Avenue.

There the carriage traffic, normally brisk at this business hour, was halted. A city policeman stood in the middle of the street holding things in check with an upraised hand while a party of laborers in overalls and flannel shirts black with sweat strained to lift a fallen telegraph pole from the macadam to the sidewalk. Impatient oaths arose from the stranded travelers, as might be expected, but it seemed to me that there was an added edge to the cries this day. The work progressed under the supervision of a second policeman, glum and moustachioed, who stood slapping the business end of his billy stick into the palm of his free hand while rotating his helmeted head constantly in search of interlopers who would hinder the operation for reasons of their own. That he was an Irishman was stamped plainly across his features; that his native sympathies and his professional sense of duty were in conflict appeared equally plain to my (admittedly prejudiced) eye. How divided we were then, and it was nothing so simple as abolition *versus* slavery, or an arbitrary line drawn in cold black ink across a paper map. Republicans and Tammany, Irish and Negro, rich and poor, assemblymen and suffragettes, the socially acceptable and the morally unredeemable; had a political cartographer set his pen to a chart of our tiny island of Manhattan it would have resembled a butcher's diagram, with all the sections outlined in angry red.

All this is clear enough to an old man who has seen the best and worst of his species at their most typical, but to a boy of ten-and-six whose most daring recent act was to take the March air in the back of an open phaeton without bringing along a lap robe, an unplanned excursion into the belly of the beast was jolly good sport, a prime anecdote to drop casually into the conversation next time the Reverend Eustace Abernathy's son Reginald brought up the weary subject of his sailing holiday in Puget Sound. Even Thurlow Rainsford, whose treasures included a brown withered scalp said to have been taken by his grandfather from a Huguenot captive during the French and Indian wars, would have to take second chair to the boy who brought a bloody riot still dripping to the circle.

The building, an unprepossessing two-story brick structure officially known as the Ninth District Provost Marshal's Office, was not the scene of pandemonium I had anticipated, although a sizable crowd had converged in front of its doors, blocking the street with their numbers and obliterating the sidewalk. Elsewhere, I learned later, hardware stores were being broken into to procure broadaxes for the continuing destruction of the local telegraph system, the tracks of the Fourth Avenue railway had been torn up with crowbars by the wives of prospective Irish draftees, and Superintendent of Police John A. Kennedy had been identified and bludgeoned within inches of his life by a gang of protesters; but for the moment, thanks in part to a show of force by some sixty police officers cordoned around the building, order reigned at the center of the tempest. As I stood straining to see over the heads of the crowd, the lottery wheel began turning inside, and each name as it was drawn was announced in a clear ringing baritone by a draft official standing atop the front stoop in gartered shirtsleeves and a straw boater.

I was not surprised that I failed to recognize most of the names. Percy Vandergriff's was called, but as he had just returned from Princeton to accept a position as junior vice president in his father's bank, I had no doubt but that he would report promptly with the three hundred dollars required to remove his name from the rolls. This provision, a bone tossed by President Lincoln to the Congress to secure passage of the Conscription Act, was the point of sharpest contention between the measure's supporters and detractors. It was said that it singled out the poor for military service while excluding the wealthy.

Chaos, when it came, arrived all of a piece. After about fifty names had been called, a horse-drawn hose cart with the legend ENGINE CO. NO. 33 splashed in elaborately serifed gilt letters upon its side panels swung around the corner, scattering pedestrians as the wheels ground to a halt in front of the office. This was the company from whose ranks several members had been selected on Saturday to serve the Union. On board were a score or more of firefighters in leather helmets and slickers and boots laced to their knees, carrying hooked axes. At sight of them a police whistle blasted and the uniformed patrolmen closed ranks, joining hands to seal off the entrance to the building.

There was a pause, and then a shot rang out.

At the time I thought someone had been shot *at,* and like many of my fellow seekers after diversion I scrambled away from this latest amusement for my own safety; but I have since concluded that the report was merely a signal for action. Instantly the firemen spilled from the wagon, exposing a bed mounded over with fist-sized rocks, ideally suited for hurling. A window shattered. A second projectile knocked a policeman's helmet askew and he went down, either grazed or seeking cover. Emboldened, the crowd surged forward. I tried to hold my ground, but the pressure from behind was too great. With my feet scarcely touching the earth I was swept with the tide up the front steps. By now I heard wood splintering. The firemen were battering down the door with their axes, bound for the lottery wheel and any draft volunteers unfortunate enough to be standing in their path.

I saw a despicable thing.

A city policeman, sent to his knees by a thrown rock or a blow from an axe handle, his face scarlet from a gash in his brow, attempted to rise, only to be shoved sprawling by a booted foot planted against his chest. The firefighter behind the boot, an ogre with huge red muttonchop whiskers and a great blue-flanneled belly pushing out through the opening in his slicker, braced himself then and swung his axe. The fallen officer thrust up his billy club in time to deflect the blow. However, the axe cut cleanly through the stick and the flat of the blade struck the policeman over one eye, stunning him. I thought that was the end of it, but again the axe came up. The fireman spread his feet. It was clear that he was about to do murder.

I am not a large man, and in that summer of my sixteenth year I had not yet reached full growth. I was lithe, however, and hours of daily exercises at the keyboard had made my fingers abnormally strong. With no thought at all I threw myself into a gap between bodies and caught the axe handle in both hands just as the blade reached the top of its arc. Using the momentum of my spring, I wrenched it from the man's grip before he could react. He stumbled, caught his balance, and turned my way, his face black with rage. I raised the axe and he hesitated.

For an eternity we stood facing each other across a space of three feet while humanity boiled around us, shouting and shoving and tearing at the shutters and flower boxes with which some aesthete of a civil servant had decorated the windows. Then the firefighter's marble-blue gaze flicked beyond my shoulder, and light came into them.

"Shoot the fuzzy son of a bitch, Brennan," he said in a brogue thick with Old Sod. "He's got me chopper."

I thought it to be a trick to get me to turn away, and I was loath to fall for it. At the same time I was acutely aware of two things: That my back was without protection of any sort, among hundreds whose sympathies lay with the man whose murderous intent I had thwarted; and that through schoolboy caprice I had waded chin-deep into a business that had nothing to do with me, in a place where none of the elaborate mechanisms that had seen me safely to my present age were likely to have any effect. I turned; and in that one movement saved my life and changed its course.

I nearly missed seeing the new danger, at that. He was a small, rat-faced fellow, not much over five feet and eighty pounds in a tight-fitting striped suit and child's-sized derby cocked over one eye. He had one of those spade-shaped black beards that I continued to associate with my tyrannical early music tutor, who was by then either retired or dead everywhere but in my nightmares. This man posed a more real threat. He was sprinting straight toward me up the front steps from the sidewalk with a short-barreled black revolver gripped in his left hand.

Pinned to his right lapel was a gold badge in the shape of a shield, of that scroll-encrusted variety that is shriven out to certain municipal employees by the handful. Since the man I had disarmed was one of these, and since he had hailed the newcomer in a tone of friendly familiarity, I took no heart from this discovery, but stepped forward to defend myself.

The sequence of the next several events eludes me after all these years, as indeed it did at the time.

Flame pounced from the revolver's barrel. I swung the axe in a short unsatisfactory arc, not having had time to lift it above my shoulder. I felt the jar when it connected. Fireworks burst inside my head, red and yellow and then black, black. My knees folded. My insignificant role in the New York City Draft Riots was over.

"Michael *J.* Brennan?"

"Himself."

"*Jehosophat* Brennan?"

"The same."

"Well. When this young sprout comes around I'll be asking him what he's got against doing a thing by half."

"*If* he comes around. That potato-eater knotted him good."

"Tupper, if you weren't so good to the girls I'd have Zebulun throw you out back with the slops. You know bloody well I was born in Limerick and ate my fair share of potatoes on both sides of the water."

"Ah, but, Arleen, you're one of the good ones. You never pull a cork before ten and you got the vote out for Jimmy Lynch in the Fourth Ward."

"Not so loud, boyo. Tweed's got long ears."

That this conversation, overheard dimly as through cotton batting, made little sense to me came as no great surprise. I had for some time been passing in and out of a dream state peopled with angels and ogres from my early childhood to times much more recent, and as they kept changing faces, confusion had become my customary condition. I wondered if the echoes of crashing wood and exploding glass would always be with me. When I turned my head, broken pieces seemed to slosh around inside like shards of glass in an earthenware jug.

"You lose, Tupper. It's God's grace you ain't a betting man. It looks like our lad has a brainpan as thick as Bob's bunions. Slide that basin a little closer."

A scraping noise was followed by a wet smacking as of water lapping the sides of a vessel. Something soft and damp slithered across my forehead. A somewhat soiled blossom opened inside my skull, bearing with it a dull brown throbbing. I opened my eyes, squeezed them shut hurriedly against the light as the pain went from brown to bright red, opened them more slowly.

I was lying on a rough mattress in a room papered in yellow. There was a water spot on the ceiling, vaguely swan-shaped. Although the room was oppressively warm, the single narrow window was shut and shaded and a coarse brown blanket covered me to the chin. In the light of a tin lamp burning on the nightstand, a stoutish woman in a high-necked seersucker dress with sleeves puffed at the shoulders sat wringing a flannel face cloth over a basin on the stand. Her black hair was piled high with spun silver at the temples and her face was as pale as bone china under a modest application of rouge. Her eyes, when she turned them upon me, were of a deep shade of mahogany, almost black. She belonged, I was to learn, to that curious race known as the Black Irish, who, lacking the red hair and blue eyes commonly associated with their countrymen, betrayed their geographic origins only when they spoke.

"Welcome back, young sir," she said without smiling. She never did in the time I knew her, but her eyes had a way of puckering at the corners when she intended lightness that made up for the omission. "Are the devil's garters really red?"

I flinched a little at the emerald lilt in her speech; the association was not a happy one. I responded, alarmed at the hoarseness of my voice. How long had it gone unused? I couldn't tell if it was dark or light out. "Am I shot?"

She exhaled, a short blast—redolent with fermented sour mash—in a semblance of laughter. "The ball went wide, Tupper says. You got your headache from behind. Fist or forearm?" She glanced up.

"Fist, and a good thing it was. That big red-whiskered Mick had wrists as big around as beeves."

I had been aware of someone standing in the corner by the headboard, but I knew instinctively if I tried turning my head that far, the pain would make me swoon. The man had no accent that I could determine, which was something of a relief. I was not entirely in the hands of marauding Celts. "The fireman hit me?"

"Not soon enough, I'm sorry to say," said the woman. "It would've gone a good sight easier for you if he'd got you before you made kindling out of Jehosophat Brennan."

"If you mean the man with the badge, I was defending myself. He meant to shoot me."

"Probably he was just out to nick you." This from the man called Tupper. "Brennan hasn't the stomach for murder. It was the wheel he was after. You just happened to be standing in front of it."

A horrendous crash shook the building. The woman winced. "What's keeping them broken soldiers of yours, Tupper? In a little while there won't be anything left to save."

"On their way, old gal. Yours isn't the only disorderly house in the neighborhood."

"What place is this?" I asked.

Her eyes puckered. "That's Shakespeare." To Tupper: "See, I know a little more than what the pictures tell me in *Frank Leslie's Illustrated Newspaper*. Lad, you're a patient at the East River Society House at Twenty-third and First. The physician in residence is 'Doctor' Bridget Arleen McMurtaugh, but you're free to address her as Bridey. Everyone else does except the general here."

The other occupant of the room stepped forward. I jumped at the sight of him, shooting a white-hot bolt of pain to the top of my skull. His face was unlined, but his hair was pure white, long for the fashion of the day, and streaked with filth. His clothes were smudged as well, blue wool with brass buttons and a belt with a U.S.–engraved buckle cinching the tunic; the uniform of a Federal infantryman. Soiled bandages covered his right eye and ear and that entire half of his head from crown to jaw. My first thought was that it had been carried away by a cannon shot.

He bowed his head briskly, his single eye twinkling. "Corporal Templeton Deane," he said. "Late of the Eleventh New York Fire Zoaves, serving with the First Army Corps at Gettysburg. Assigned at present to the Invalid Corps of Volunteers."

"Tupper was a hook-and-ladder man," said Bridey. "It's why they sent him to the Enrollment Office yesterday, to deal with them Leatherheads, and a good thing for you. He skidded a ball past the ear of the man what brained you and ran him off."

"Yesterday!" I sat up—and fell back in agony. Father had expected me at his chambers by noon Monday at the latest.

Bridey bathed my face. "Smooth your feathers, boyo. You've had a fair knocking."

I was loath to ask the next question. "The man with the badge; is he—did I—?"

"Split his gun arm like rotten oak." Tupper's grin wrinkled the grotesque bandage. "He may pull through. We'll hope he does. Brennan's a fire inspector, and Boss Tweed's man. Tammany will hound you to your grave if Jehosophat dies. Maybe even if he doesn't. Once it starts you may damn me to the devil for interfering."

Chapter Three

∽∾

The thought that I had maimed a man, and possibly killed him, made me ill at my stomach and incapable of comprehending the rest of the information Tupper provided on that first meeting. Even when it was explained to me later I found it incredible. A native New Yorker, exposed by my parents from an early age to the tailcoat-wearing gears and diamond-bosomed cogs that ran the machinery that governed our lives, I was now made to realize that they were but parts of a clockwork toy compared to the dynamic forces into whose path I had stepped with a single impulsive act.

It's true that in that third year of the terrible War of Secession the name William Marcy Tweed was still unknown to most of my fellow citizens. Born on the Lower East Side of the city, the son of a Scots immigrant chair maker, he had served as an alderman, a member of the county board of supervisors, and chairman of the Tammany general committee, but except for a single term in Congress he had spent his entire public career in the obscurity of that bureaucratic maze peculiar to our municipality, a conundrum fully as impenetrable to the political layman as a Chinese box. By the end of the decade he would parlay the twin posts of street commissioner and state senator into a pattern of influence-peddling on a grand scale, wresting control, with only an occasional nod-and-wink to the democratic process, of the entire city, and by reflection Greater New York State. At the time I first learned of his existence, he was just beginning to be spoken of as "Boss Tweed," and eager to repair the damage caused by his loss in the last sheriff's election to James Lynch by means of whatever opportunity came his way.

This proved to be the draft riots; and while no one ever successfully tied Tweed to that week of horror, no one questioned the fact that when the smoke blew away and the dust settled, he and that band of cronies who would shortly be known throughout the Union as The Ring stood all alone atop the rubble.

And I, a beardless society sprout with musical aspirations, had injured a Tweed protégé.

On that first day, however, there were more immediate concerns. Hardest to ignore was the din of destruction that continued to drift up from the floor below.

"That would be the breakfront," announced Bridey in response to a prodigiously drawn-out splintering of glass and wrenching of wood directly beneath our feet; and reading the question on my face, explained: "Looters. Jackals. In another few minutes they'll be up here, looking for the millions we hostesses are known to stuff into our mattresses. Damn your eyes, Tupper! Your invalids never had trouble finding this address in the past. You must have told them I sent my ladies to the Port Authority till things blew over."

"Shush, old gal. I think I hear them." The bandaged corporal limped to the window and drew aside the shade. Outside was darkness. I now realized I had spent most of Monday and all of Tuesday in that room, insensible. The judge would be tearing his hair. "You'll learn to trust me yet!" Tupper exulted. "That's the Zoave regimental they're whistling. I taught it to them the whole time I was laid up."

Bridey rose, all rustling seersucker, and joined him at the window. "I hope you taught them to throw away their torches before they come inside. I'd as soon the foxes burned the place down as the ferrets."

"I must get word to my family," I said. "If I could trouble you for a pen and paper."

"Tupper here'll do the writing when it's time," said the mistress of the house, turning. "You'll trouble me for oxtail soup and eight hours flat on your back."

I had begun to protest when my stomach rumbled audibly. The creases at the corners of Bridey's eyes settled the argument.

Two more days passed before I left the agreeable confines of the East River Society House, in the course of which my world had altered irretrievably. The reports that reached me from outside were monstrous, and would have been inconceivable had I intercepted them in the cosseting shelter of my parents' Fifth Avenue town house instead of there in the eye of the cyclone. By the end of its first day, the disturbance that had begun at the Enrollment Office had taken a far more ugly turn. Policemen were hunted down, stripped of their uniforms, and beaten faceless; the homes of private citizens not involved in the protest were plundered and set afire; defenseless Negroes, blamed for the war that had given birth to the draft, were hung by their necks from flagstaffs and streetlamps; and the Colored Orphan Asylum on Fifth Avenue between Forty-third and Forty-fourth streets was torched by a demented mob, its innocent occupants rescued from a hideous burning death at the last minute by volunteers who hustled them out a back door to the nearby sanctuary of the Twentieth Police Precinct. These vicious attacks upon the most vulnerable segment of the population were especially indefensible in view of the fact that black men were as accessible to conscription as anyone, and more than most, few possessing the wherewithal to buy their way out. The Age of Reason was extinct.

Noncombatants were victimized by both sides. On Tuesday, a female bystander and her child were slain by a howitzer blast directed at a throng of demonstrators on Second Avenue. In retaliation, rioters seized the man responsible for the order to fire and tore him to pieces. This was Tupper's own commander, Colonel Henry O'Brien of the Eleventh New York Volunteers. The whole bloody business built to a ghastly crescendo late Thursday afternoon when shots were fired into a company of volunteers on the Upper East Side. With rifles and bayonets the soldiers drove the crowds shrieking to the roofs of the surrounding tenement buildings and over the edge to their deaths.

Revolted as I was by these events, I was not a complete innocent. I readily guessed the nature of the transactions that were conducted under the roof I shared with Bridey McMurtaugh and Zebulun, her huge and laconic black manservant. Indeed, I had been aware for some time that such things went on in the city. I congratulated myself for concealing my pious sense of moral superiority from my hostess. I am embarrassed to relate, however, that at one point my damnable curiosity got the better of me and I inquired as to what arrangements were made for the care of the illegitimate children who were bound to result from so many sexual liaisons.

Bridey, who was spoon-feeding me oxtail soup at the time, paused to daub at my chin with a folded linen napkin. "For some, there's always room in the sweatshops. Why don't you ask your father's friends what becomes of the rest?"

She was by this time aware of who my father was, and was awaiting a reply to a telegram she had sent him informing him of my fate. Although I failed—or refused—to understand the full meaning of her words, I read in her mahogany-colored eyes a subtle condemnation of the values of my class. I was so far insulted as to refuse another spoonful of her rich and greasy brew.

She gathered her skirts and stood. "You're strong enough now to feed yourself, anyway. You'll find fresh clothes in that wardrobe. I had Zebulun air and brush them. The man who occupied this room before you was much your size. I'm sorry to say your own suit of clothes was ruined. Join us below and we'll put you to work. There's a deal of clearing and cleaning that needs doing." She took herself out.

I arose, troubled by her judgment of my people and somewhat ashamed of my anger. She had shown me great kindness, which I supposed entitled her to certain liberties, preposterous as was their foundation. I was clad in only a nightshirt—no doubt the former property of the room's late tenant, who I had been given to understand had succumbed to an apoplectic seizure shortly after paying his first month's rent. This was a sum calculated to overcome Bridey's prejudice against boarders and silence her questions about his motives for not paying a much lower rate at a hotel. The wardrobe, in addition to three shirts, two changes of socks and underwear, and a multiplicity of collars, contained two suits—one plain serge, one checked—high-topped shoes, and a derby hat with a red silk lining, wrapped in blue tissue. I chose the quieter of the suits, which although tight in the shoulders fit well as to sleeves and length of trousers, tried on the hat, and returned it to its shelf when it proved too small, setting my head to aching all over again when I pried it off.

The shoes were snug but serviceable. Just before going out, I put my hand in the right coat pocket and brought out a dozen small rectangular pasteboards pressed in a worn pigskin folder. This was a collection of gentleman's calling cards, all bearing the same name. I put them back in the pocket and left the room for the first time in three days.

Shambles greeted me downstairs. The front door hung on one hinge, its lock shattered and all but one of its panels battered in. Not a single windowpane had survived the attack. Shards of glass and crockery and pieces of plaster covered nearly every square inch of the broad oak planks of the floor. Great ragged cavities yawned between the studs where someone had kicked holes in the walls—whether searching for hidden treasure or for the pure deranged joy of destruction, there was no determining. A number of surprisingly tasteful oil portraits (I had been given to believe that such establishments were decorated solely with cheap reclining nudes and obese nymphs romping with satyrs) had been torn from their hooks and slashed with knives, their gilt frames smashed or stolen. It was a sight to sicken the soul.

From the foyer I passed into a parlor whose curtains had been ripped down, doused with coal oil—the stench was unmistakeable—and set afire. Someone, perhaps a member of Tupper's Invalid Corps, had put out the flames before they could spread to the rest of the room, but the fine Brussels carpet was scorched beyond repair. Here I found Bridey, in a long white apron with her hair tied up in a kerchief, fretting over the ruins of an upright piano. The front panel had been demolished as by an axe and the ivory keys blackened, likely by the same pyromaniac who had set a torch to the curtains. Big quiet Zebulun, appearing embarrassed by the tears shining on his employer's cheeks, shook his great head absently and went on sweeping up the debris.

"O, the bastards, the bloody misbegotten whelps of Jezebel's runt bitch," she was saying, in a chanting tone not unlike that of a heartfelt prayer. "Why didn't they tear me heart out instead? This piano was the only thing my father left me. It was the one thing he wouldn't sell, including his only daughter Bridget. He had it shipped over from Londonderry with the money he made laying brick. It took him five years to set enough aside. O, the purity-spouting, two-faced sons of Grendl out of banished Cain."

"Perhaps I can get it to play," said I.

She turned suddenly, and seeing me there made haste to swipe a forearm across her eyes. "You walk as quiet as a savage Apache. What's a judge's boy know about repairing pianos?"

"I play. And I've watched the tuner at work. There isn't much to it, actually. All you have to know is what to listen for." I approached the keyboard and rippled a forefinger down its length. It was abominably out of tune; several of the ivories gave up only a thud. "Have you a tuning hammer?"

"I've a hammer."

"Too hard. A cork will suffice, and a knitting needle."

"Will you knit me a new instrument?" Her eyes crinkled, but there was a line between them. "Do you really think you can fix it?"

"It depends on whether any strings are broken." I doffed my borrowed coat and turned back my dead man's cuffs.

"Zeb, go up to Charity's room and see if she left her sewing things. Bring them down."

Zebulun went out, returning moments later with a small wicker hamper. Bridey meanwhile had gone to the kitchen and brought back the stopper from a bottle. It smelled of brandy. I rummaged through the hamper, retrieved a needle about eight inches long, transfixed the cylinder of porous material with the point, and tested it by holding the needle as if it were a handle and thumping the cork against the heel of my hand. It was a crude substitute for the precision tool required, but I felt the need to return the kindness of my nurse and hostess in whatever way presented itself, no matter how small.

I removed the ruined panel and was pleased to observe that none of the strings had parted. Evidently the vandals had been interrupted, possibly by the arrival of Tupper's fellow invalids, before the destruction was complete. However, several of the stops were stuck fast, jammed as if someone had pounded with both fists on a number of keys at once. I set to work to free them with blows from my makeshift tuning hammer.

While I was thus engaged, Tupper entered the parlor. He was much changed. The disreputable-looking campaigner of Tuesday night had bathed, brushed his uniform, and changed his dressing. His collar-length hair gleamed white against his deep sunburn and the fresh antiseptic bandages lent him a rakish quality, as of the eye-patched pirates of old. His expression, however, was grim.

"I got this from a derelict on Twenty-second," he told Bridey without greeting. "He had a stack of them. He said a gent in a derby gave him half a buck to hand them out."

She took the stiff sheet of paper he held out and stared at it for a thoughtful moment. "It's a fair likeness. Who drew it?"

"Tammany has journalists on its payroll, why not artists? If Brennan was sound enough to provide a description, it could be a good sign; on the other hand, they might've gotten it from that redheaded fireman."

"What's it say?"

"Forgive me, Arleen, old girl; I forgot." He took the sheet from her and held it out to me. "Tell her, will you?"

The handout, printed on the thick white stock usually reserved for election bills, contained a reproduction from a woodcut made from a drawing that resembled my face not a little, along with a written description and a legend offering a hundred dollars in cash to the individual who reported my whereabouts to the proprietors of Delmonico's Restaurant. I was sought, it said, "for the unprovoked Battery upon the Person of Michael James Brennan, a Fire Inspector of this City, with intent to do Murder."

"Saints preserve us!" exclaimed Bridey after I had read this to her. "There are wharf rats in this neighborhood would slice up their mothers for less than a hundred."

"I don't understand the part about Delmonico's Restaurant," I said.

Tupper lifted his single exposed brow. "You *are* a show pup. Delmonico's is where Tweed hangs his hat. You'll find him there more often than you will at City Hall.".

I returned the handbill to him and buttoned my cuffs. "I must turn myself in."

"The devil you will!" This from Bridey.

"My father will represent me. I have nothing to fear from a judge and jury."

"You'll never see either! Tupper?"

The soldier's domino face was expressionless. "You'll be locked up in a precinct house while they make ready to send you downtown to the Tombs. Long before the paddy wagon comes, a mob will storm the precinct house. You will be dragged from your cell and strung from a lamppost. Commissioner Acton will express his sincere regrets to your family. Mayor Opdyke will announce an investigation. Aside from that you'll be just another victim of the riots, and as dead as Tim Coogan's cat."

Had a man of Corporal Templeton Deane's appearance and demeanor told me of these things a few days previously, I would have known him for a mountebank and given him no more of my time. The events of the past seventy-two hours had unsettled all my preconceptions of the world as an orderly place. When a duly appointed military commander could be beaten to death in broad daylight by his own fellow citizens, no outrage was impossible.

"I wish Father would reply to that wire," I said. "He'd know what action to take."

"Damn! That Johnny Reb saber carried away more of my brains than I thought. I met the boy on the walk." From inside his tunic, Tupper drew a yellow telegraph flimsy and gave it to me.

MY BOY
YOU ARE IN GREATER DANGER THAN YOU KNOW STOP ARRANGING PASSAGE FOR YOU TO FRANCE UNTIL SITUATION CHANGES STOP I PERCEIVE YOU ARE IN CHRISTIAN HANDS AT PRESENT

YOUR FATHER

"Christian hands, Tupper," preened Bridey after I had read the wire aloud. "Pipe that. And me father excommunicated."

Tupper was grave. "Don't change your money to francs just yet, young fellow."

I inquired what he meant.

"Tweed may know your name by now. If he doesn't I wouldn't bet a copper against a double eagle he won't by the time that tide goes out with you on it. Your throat will be cut before you're halfway up the gangplank."

"Still, the old boy's right about new scenery."

We both looked at Bridey. She laid a finger beside her nose.

CHAPTER FOUR

Casting back over the terrain of my life, its summits and valleys, I find it appropriate that my departure from New York and from the only life I had ever known should have been conducted under circumstances that would shame the producer of a tenth-rate melodrama.

Before providing details, I would tell of my parting gift to Bridget Arleen McMurtaugh, gracious proprietress of the East River Society House and the lady who found time amid a great turbulence to return an impudent boy to health and strength. Having managed to repair the piano while Bridey was upstairs preparing to implement the plan she had yet to share with either Tupper or myself, I wiped off the keys with a rag soaked in kerosene, drew up the stool, and, after loosening my fingers with a few simple exercises, launched into Chopin's Waltz #3 in A Minor. To be sure, it was an ambitious selection for an instrument that had been used so hard, and which likely had been long past due for tuning before that; but it was a favorite of mine, and after such an unaccustomed time away from my practices and so many mortal blows to my complacency I needed reassurance that my skills had not deserted me.

My fears were groundless. After an awkward beginning, my fingers found the proper chords from memory alone. Chopin will not be put off by inferior equipment. Very soon I was transported. Climbing, gliding away, then climbing again toward the crescendo, I was unaware that I had attracted an audience. Without pausing I slid into a tune from my childhood, one better calculated to please the heart of the mistress of the house. I had barely begun when a voice, pure but untrained, the clear and guileless falsetto of a young girl, picked up the verse behind me:

> *Through streets broad and narrow,*
> *she wheeled her wheelbarrow,*
> *crying, "Cockles and mussels, alive, alive, oh!"*

> *Alive, alive, oh!*
> *Alive, alive, oh!*
> *Crying, "Cockles and mussels, alive, alive, oh!"*

I continued through "Molly Malone" with Bridey keeping pace—she knew all the verses, even the most obscure—and finished to a double ovation. When I turned, she and Tupper were both in the room, the soldier leaning against the door frame. Bridey flicked at both her eyes.

"I've not heard that played in more years than you've been on this earth," she said. "Are you so sure you haven't a bit of the Old Sod in your family past? Perhaps a free fumble behind the stables with a groom named Murphy?"

I shook my head. I can truthfully say that at that moment I was ashamed of the fact for the first time. "I had a governess whom I liked very much. Enid was her name. She taught me the song. She said no child in Dublin learned his numbers until he could recite 'Molly Malone' from start to finish. Father fired her for filching drinks from the whiskey cabinet."

"A native failing. Even so it was a small enough price to pay for your first music lesson. How is your head? Will it travel?"

I replied that it would, although it remained sore.

She nodded curtly. "Drucilla Patakos is more sister to me than friend; has been since we slept in doorways and nicked turnips off pushcarts to eat. She married well and took off for California, but the odds caught up with her in Kansas. Indians butchered her man and cut her up fair. She's running a house in Lawrence with a Creole who calls himself LaFitte or some such fancy frog name. She wrote me last year. Here's my answer." She removed a sealed envelope from the pocket of her dress and gave it to me. "Tupper helped me get the words down. It says you'll work hard in return for a roof and found. Don't make Bridey out a liar."

I looked at the envelope, which contained no address. "I'm going west?"

"There are worse places," Tupper said. "There must be. Just don't press me for names."

"How will I find her?"

Bridey exhaled. "Ask the nearest wharf rat, bullwhacker, or saloon swamp. Unless Dru's changed her method of doing business, any one of them will give you directions you could follow in the dark."

"When can I return home?"

"When Tweed dies, or his fortunes change. He's a Scotchman, remember, and a politician to the bone. He never forgets a favor or a wrong. He may seem to, but it's just the grudge going underground. Them that's thought otherwise ain't here to share their wisdom."

I felt bleak. Save for the annual trip to the Continent, I had never been so far from home, and then I had been accompanied by my parents and at least two family retainers to lessen the shock of new surroundings. This journey proposed to insert a thousand miles between me and familiar things, with no indication as to how much time must pass before we were reunited. "When do I leave?"

"Tonight."

"So soon?" It was evening. I had expected to spend the night and depart sometime the next day.

"It may already be too late," Tupper said. "Tammany has more spies than the Confederacy has fleas. They'll be searching house to house before we know it."

Bridey said, "There's the eight-fifty to Chicago, and then no more trains till morning. Just time to get ready if we don't dawdle."

I stood. "Won't they be watching the stations?"

"Like sparrow hawks," she said. "But they're looking for a young man."

Something about her words, and the puckering of the skin around her eyes, put me on my guard; but I was too much in her debt, and perhaps too wary of the answer, to question her further.

What transpired during the hour that followed I still find repugnant to relate, after a lapse of more than seven decades. I am, however, far too close to the Great Truth to dissemble at this juncture.

I was then beardless, and more delicate of feature than time, exposure, and the circumstances of my life would render me. With my short hair covered by a sturdy bonnet of the type designed to protect against cinders, and a broadcloth cloak concealing my masculine attire, I'll warrant I might have passed for a young woman in the shadows of a railroad platform. The "improvement" was not accomplished without a great deal of resistance on my part. Bridey threw up her hands at last and threatened to cast me out to find my own way through the hazards awaiting me. It was Tupper, the professional man of violence, who made me see reason.

"You know Dumas?" he asked. *"The Count of Monte Cristo?"*

I replied somewhat stuffily that I had read that great adventure in the original French, although the relevance of the conversation escaped me.

"After all those years of imprisonment, do you seriously believe that Edmund Dantes would have refused to trade places with Faria's corpse had his friend been a woman?"

"I cannot help but think that I am hiding behind skirts," said I, after mulling this over.

"What do you think you've been doing since Tupper fetched you here, all filthy and trampled?" Bridey flared. "Jesus, Mary, and Joseph! Why you men set such store by your precious trousers is beyond my grasp. What you carry there leads you into every manner of a fix, and all for what's inside a woman's skirt! Yet you call us weak. It don't signify."

I had never been spoken to with so much earthiness. That the speaker should be a woman made my cheeks hot. I made no more protest, lacking the words.

"No rouge, Arleen," put in Tupper. "We want to deflect interest, not attract it. A trackside seduction might cause complications."

She shrugged and put away the pot while I sent a silent message of gratitude to the corporal. He winked his good eye.

We squeezed into an enclosed hansom for the ride to the

Fourth Avenue station. The streets were quiet, eerily so for our metropolis of four hundred thousand souls at that hour on a fine summer evening. Here and there, peeping around the leather curtain, I spotted physical evidence of the revolt that was even then still winding down in various parts of the city: the boarded-over windows and charred front of an abolitionist newspaper office, a gaslit gleam off the polished barrel of a rifle in the shadows of a doorway where a homeowner stood guard against roving bands of looters. As we turned the corner onto Fourth Avenue, I saw a sight that haunts me still: the corpse of a black man in laborer's overalls, dangling from a rope made fast to an awning post in front of a darkened clothier's, the rounded shoulders, lowered head on the broken neck, and drawn-up legs describing a question mark three feet above the sidewalk; the terminus of a tragic query.

I changed then. Although I would see horrors as bad or worse in the weeks and years to come, none would have as profound an effect upon me as that lonely tableau, gone from my sight in a moment, but branded in my memory for all time. Often in recent years I have seen it afresh, particularly whenever a self-ennobled Northerner born since the war has held forth within my hearing on the depredations visited upon the black race by godless Dixie. I have met only contemptuous disregard when I explain that the first Negro I had ever seen lynched was in New York City.

Civilian pedestrians were few and moved furtively. Squads of soldiers in uniform, some with bandages and slings identifying them as members of the Invalid Corps, but most without such encumberances, patrolled the streets openly, rifles at the ready. Tupper, veteran that he was, pointed out the insignia of the Twenty-sixth Michigan Volunteers and the Seventh and Sixty-fifth regiments of the New York Militia. Rumor had it that with Robert E. Lee's army reported broken at Gettysburg, Secretary of War Stanton had ordered five more regiments of the Army of the Potomac to report to New York and put down the insurrection. When I asked if that meant the war was over, Tupper pulled aside the curtain on his side of the coach and spat out the window.

"I watched fifteen thousand of Lee's men hurl themselves against our artillery on Cemetery Ridge for an hour. No sooner had we mowed down one line than another sprang up, charging through the smoke with bayonets fixed, to be mowed down in turn, line upon line. Of that fifteen thousand, not a hundred made it to the top of the ridge, every man jack of them full of piss and fire and ready to fight hand-to-hand. Broken?" He spat again. "Not as long as there's a Virginian still standing with blood in his boots."

The station was more crowded than the streets, evidence that an exodus was in effect, at least among those with means to quit the troubled city. There were soldiers here as well, and policemen in numbers to prevent further uprooting of the rails by those bent on extending the pandemonium. Still other vigilants were present, these more sinister to my own predicament. In the arched entrance from the street, and at each end of the westbound platform, men in derbies and tight suits stood studying closely the faces of travelers and well-wishers through wreaths of blue cigar smoke. One or two held a square of stiff pasteboard and consulted it from time to time as the throngs passed.

"Chin high, my girl," whispered Bridey at my side, thrusting an elbow into my ribs as we approached the waiting cars. "Ladies of good family don't skulk about with their eyes on the ground like a common tart."

I obeyed, feeling the color rise in my unrouged cheeks—and locked gazes with a derby man standing by the caboose. My heart stood in place as hard interest came into his eyes—then resumed beating when his moustache came up on one side and his right eye closed in a lewd wink. I flushed deeper still and looked away quickly.

Bridey exhaled, the closest thing to a laugh she knew. "Don't take on airs. Them ballot-boxers ain't particular as to what they take between the sheets. Last year when half my ladies were down with the grippe I fobbed off a scrub-drudge with one good ear and two teeth in her head on an alderman. He came back."

Mortified, I said nothing. I truly hated her then, if only for an instant.

At the steps to the car I raised my foot, only to be boosted aboard by Tupper, who handed me the carpetbag Bridey had packed with a change of shirts and other necessaries, including a hundred dollars in cash, which I swore I would repay. Shielding the movement with his body, the wounded soldier pressed

something cold and smooth and solid into my other hand.
"Something to tide you over."

I swiftly secreted the object under my cloak.

"Good-bye, Maisie, dear, and remember me to Uncle Liam."
Bridey raised her lips to kiss my cheek. When I bent forward she
whispered, "Don't write, don't wire. If anything changes I'll let
you know. And think of a name. You can't use the old one."

"I've thought of one." I handed her a card from the folder in
my suit pocket.

She stared at it uncomprehending, then showed it to Tupper,
who laughed shortly and told her what it said, standing close to
make himself heard over the train's whistle. Listening, she
scowled. Then, for the first time, something came to her lips
that I can only call the phantom of a smile. It was my last image
of her.

The card read:

Billy Gashade

Entertainments

CHAPTER FIVE

Every seat in the day coach was taken. The brass racks were
stacked high with parcels and portmanteaux, and in the
dreary orange glow of the lamps sixty passengers sat hunched
beneath the burden of their own weariness. The air stank of perspiration and stale defeat. It was in every sense a refugee train,
making ready to propel a shipment of frightened and disillu-

sioned souls into an uncertain night. This intelligence, that I was
not alone in my situation, should have given me solace. Instead
it filled me with despair. What had I in common with these
wretches? I was the scion of a distinguished family, and by all
rights on this summer evening belonged home, reading my
Browning or practicing an étude, perhaps looking forward to
Sunday morning, when Cook would bring buttered scones and
a pot of steaming coffee to my room. When would I know these
things again? Nothing I had heard or read of the country where
I was bound included any mention of such benchmarks of civilization.

At that juncture the thing from which I was fleeing seemed
not so formidable after all. Really it was no more than a misun-
derstanding, one which a generous contribution to Tammany,
and perhaps an endorsement from my father, must set right. Encouraged by these reflections, I think I would have turned
around and gotten off the train but for what happened at that moment.

I was standing in the middle of the car and in an ideal position
to scrutinize the two men who entered at the rear from the next
car up the line. One, tall and beefy, his great belly prying a gap
of striped shirt between vest and trousers, pawed at the backs of
the seats on both sides as he lurched my way, swiveling his big
derby-hatted head to peer into the faces of the seated passengers.
Those who were alert enough to return the gaze quickly averted
their eyes, so intense was his expression. Without warning, he
stopped and snatched the hat from the head of a young man dozing not half a dozen seats from where I stood. When the young
man blinked up at him, he muttered an oath and lumbered on,
dropping the hat on the runner.

His companion, moving more slowly behind him, was identical in height and girth, but carried himself with so much more
gravity, leaning heavily on a gold-headed stick, that he gave the
impression of outweighing the other man by a hundred pounds.
His paunch—solid, prodigious, counterbalanced by the backward tilt of his shoulders—was contained in the black wool of
a superbly tailored suit far too heavy for the season, although he
didn't appear in the least uncomfortable, perspiring not at all in
a starched collar and soft hat with the brim turned down jauntily
on one side. His face, above a fine auburn beard chased with sil-

ver, was pale and unremarkable but for the eyes. These were large, dark, and set deeper than any I had ever seen, and seemed to burn steadily like embers in the belly of a black iron furnace. They were predatory in the extreme.

I had no doubt that I was in the presence of Boss Tweed. I was as certain of it, in fact, as I was that the man walking in front of him bent on identifying every passenger in the coach was the same red-whiskered fireman whose axe I had confiscated before he could swing it upon a defenseless policeman, and which I had employed in my own protection against his superior, Fire Inspector Michael "Jehosophat" Brennan—Tweed's own man and the only plausible reason he was here in the company of a witness capable of pointing out Brennan's attacker.

The firefighter stopped directly in front of me. His breath was strong with whiskey and bad teeth. Beneath my woman's cloak I closed my fingers around the smooth polished handle of the pistol Tupper had pressed upon me. My pulse thudded between my temples.

Abruptly, with a gruff attempt at some lesson of manners half forgotten, he fisted the brim of his derby, raising it a fraction of an inch, and bustled past without once having looked me full in the face.

The disguise Bridey had engineered had held fast!

I was denied the luxury of immediate relief; for without the obstruction of the fireman's ungainly form, nothing remained to separate me from the source of all my troubles.

Time cannot measure how long Tweed and I stood there while he turned the searching, speculative heat of his gaze upon me. He seemed to see clear through to the roots of my hair. His expression, what there was of it, evolved from bland curiosity to keen suspicion to perplexity, and finally bemused resignation, as of the philosopher who has spent the better part of a potentially productive day contemplating the unknowable, consoling himself at last with the certainty that where he has failed to go, none may visit. At this point a set of admirably manicured fingers lifted his hat entirely from his head, which was bald to the crown.

"Your pardon, miss," he said, rolling his *r*s slightly in the Scots fashion. Inserting his expansive rear into the space between two seats, he made what room he could for me to pass.

Galvanized suddenly, I slid through, brushing the front of his person hard enough to jostle his heavy gold watch chain—terrified lest I disarrange my cloak and expose the man's suit I wore underneath.

I managed to avoid this disaster and hurried on to the end of the car, feeling those incendiary eyes upon my back until the whistle shrilled again, indicating that the train was preparing to leave the station, whereupon a shifting of the floor told me he had turned and moved on.

Witnessing my approach, an elderly man with white handlebars rose from the rear seat, tipped his hat, and graciously offered me the place he had vacated. I shook my head quickly and went through the door to the platform between the cars. Here, out of sight of my fellow travelers and shielded from the loiterers at trackside by shadows, I tore off the bonnet and cloak and stuffed them inside the carpetbag. I tugged the pistol from the waistband of my trousers, thinking to do the same with it, then thought better of that plan and shifted the weapon to a more comfortable position in front of my left hipbone. I was still in Tweed's New York, after all, and far from "out of the woods," as my late benefactors might put it.

The next coach was less crowded. I found a window seat near the front and space overhead for my bag and, bone-weary suddenly, collapsed in a heap into the horsehair upholstery. On the other side of the glass I spotted Bridey in her light wrap and broad-brimmed hat tied with a scarf under her chin and beside her Tupper in his infantry uniform with his kepi canted over to the side to make room for his head bandage. From this little distance I noticed for the first time how small Bridey was; the crown of her hat barely cleared her companion's shoulder. Strange to reflect that the most powerful personality I had known aside from my father should come in so tiny a parcel. Another sixteen years would pass before I saw the phenomenon repeated, in the person of young William Bonney.

The pair were searching the windows of the train, apparently hoping to catch sight of me. For the third time the whistle sounded and the train lurched into motion. Their eyes moved in my direction. I raised my hand to wave—and immediately withdrew it, slumping down in the seat, as Tweed and his flame-whiskered accomplice came into sight farther down the platform. They, too, were watching the windows, the fireman's face all grimace and darting glances, Tweed's composed and without expression, the embers of his eyes fixed steadily at window level, letting the train do the work. As I was carried into their field of vision, I distorted my features by yawning broadly and pretending to rub the sleep from both eyes with my fists. I could not be certain that the subterfuge worked, but as the train kept picking up speed I assumed that I had, for the time being at least, "dodged the bullet." I believed then, and I believe now, that the man responsible for tending the flow of money and services that kept the machinery of the city in motion was capable of having the train stopped and searched thoroughly, and to the devil with the schedule.

Many hundreds of miles would roll away beneath the wheels, however, before I ceased to expect that I would be removed at the next stop, and yet the next, to face Tweed's retribution. The memory of those days is still potent. Even today, whenever a streetcar slips its cable or congestion ahead forces the taxicab in which I am riding to slow down or brake, I become acutely agitated. Dead these fifty years and more, the Boss of Tammany haunts my dotage.

It would be false to claim that the experience was entirely negative. Despite my longing for the comfortable and predictable life I was forced to leave behind, and trepidation over my uncertain prospects in a place—a direction, actually—about which I knew nothing beyond hysterical tales of Indian atrocities and bandit outrages, I could scarcely contain my excitement. The adventurous yarns of Dumas and Victor Hugo (to say nothing of a number of cheaply printed pamphlets concealed in an unlocked pantry by an Australian majordomo named Halliard) had made me eager to experience at firsthand the great vulgar world without.

Like Melville's Ishmael, I was seized with wanderlust. I could not then know that I shared the condition with nearly a third of the nation.

The pull was strong indeed to survive the rigors of travel across country in 1863. After the war, Cornelius Vanderbilt, like Tweed the son of poor parents, would acquire the New York Central Railroad, employ his self-made fortune to annihilate most of his competitors and merge their operations with his, making it possible to ride the same car directly from Manhattan to Chicago; but in those final days before the rise of the great robber barons of the Industrial Age, the same process required changing trains no fewer than fifteen times, with interminable waits on hard depot benches in between, and worse to come west of the Windy City.

On one such bench, in the decidedly flat and singularly undiverting town of Indianapolis, Indiana, I was roused from a half doze late in the evening by a mountainously fat man in a gray striped suit smelling of mothballs, who deposited himself beside me amid an audible settling of chins and buttocks-flesh. After fixing me for some little time with a glare that had perhaps been described to him one too many times as hawklike, he cleared his throat and said:

"Where sits the knights' master? By what name is he called?"

"I beg your pardon?"

"Come, man! Who keeps the sword of the covenant?"

I sat up, clutching at the handle of the carpetbag in my lap and cursing myself for my lack of foresight. Finding the pistol uncomfortable and thinking it no longer necessary to keep close to hand, I had transferred it from my trousers to the bag. "I think you have me confused with another party," I said. "My name—"

"Not *your* name, confound it! Are you not of the Circle?"

"To what circle are you referring?"

For a moment he remained still, glaring in a way that I might have found disconcerting had I not but lately known a gaze far more impressive. Divining at length that he had failed in the effect he sought, he muttered something unintelligible, pushed himself with a grunt to his feet, and waddled off to give his attention to the chalkboard containing the day's schedule of trains. Five minutes of that, and then he consulted a turnip watch on the end of a chain clipped to his handkerchief pocket, swept a glance around the sparsely populated interior of the train station with the air of an obese bird of prey, and took himself out the door.

No sooner had he departed than a pair of men who had been smoking cigars in the corner by the ticket window came over to where I sat. Both had on slouch hats and ankle-length dusters— the attire of the seasoned traveler, easily maintained and useful in protecting faces and clothing from the ravages of dirt and blowing cinders—but aside from that they bore little resemblance to each other. One, whom I judged to be in his twenties, was moon-faced and clean-shaven, and affected a splendor of dress not often seen in railroad depots, including a beautifully embroidered vest and tooled boots with flaps on the toes to prevent scuffing. The other, twice his age and sallow, wore a rumpled suit with a soiled collar and chin-whiskers in need of trimming.

"Stand up, please," directed the younger man.

He spoke politely, but I was slow to comply, being weary. By the time I rose, his companion's face was white with anger. "Inspect him!" he barked.

With a swiftness that made resistance impossible, my arms were flung up by the elbows and a pair of practiced hands stroked and patted my clothing from armpits to ankles.

"Nothing, sir."

"Name," demanded the man with the whiskers.

Intimidated by the turn of events, I very nearly gave my true name. "Billy Gashade."

"Proof."

I produced the leather folder and held out a card. He made no move to accept it, drawing on his cigar and letting the smoke drift into my face. His eyes were small and hard. After a moment his companion took the card, read it, and showed it to his superior, who glanced at it, then removed the cigar and flicked ashes to the floor. "What kind of entertainments?"

"I am a musician." In truth I had pondered over that advertisement and drawn a sordid conclusion.

"What tunes do you know besides 'Dixie'?"

This bizarre query left me dumb for an answer. The burring *r*s of the older man's Scottish intonations, so reminiscent of Tweed's, had convinced me that Tammany's long arm had reached me at last, but I could find no place in the hypothesis for this reference to the anthem of the Confederacy.

Now he replaced the cigar and stepped close. He was slightly taller than I, and the hot tip burned within inches of my right eye. I cringed away. "These Copperheads are getting younger by the day," he said. "I expect they'll be changing diapers in Elmira before the fighting's over."

"What were you and Major Johnson discussing just now?" inquired the other, not unpleasantly.

"Major Johnson?"

"The fat man. The conversation looked intense."

"He mistook me for someone else. He asked questions I didn't understand." *Like you,* I added silently.

"What sort of questions?" rapped the older man.

"Questions that made no sense, about knights' masters and keepers of the sword."

The moonfaced man stroked his smooth chin. "The sword of the covenant?"

"Yes. He wanted to know if I was with the Circle. He left when I asked what he meant."

"Pah!" A ball of poisonous smoke stung my eyes. "No one's that ignorant. Search his bag."

The other man opened the carpetbag on the bench where I had left it, rummaged through the contents, and removed the pistol. "Sir."

Triumphantly, his companion seized the weapon, a handsome nickel-plated European revolver of the five-shot variety with ivory grips, and examined it. A furrow appeared between his eyes when he noticed the engraving on the backstrap, which read: "To T.D., Jr., from T.D., Sr.; The Union Unsundered."

"Who did you take this from?" he asked.

"I did not take it. It was given to me by a friend. His name is Templeton Deane. He is a corporal with the Invalid Corps."

"Do you expect me to believe that?"

"Sir, the things Johnson asked him are part of the Circle's identification ceremony. If they'd never met before, it's possible he made a mistake."

"It is if we take this whelp's word that's what they talked about."

"It's a *secret* ceremony, sir; or they flatter themselves it is. If this young fellow were a member he wouldn't divulge any part of it to strangers."

The other fell into a silent contemplation of the revolver. The younger man regarded me with a mild expression, which I was only then beginning to consider more sinister than the other's scowl. He had pale eyes without discernible brows and his lips, full and curved gracefully, turned up at the corners like a cat's. "How old are you, Billy?"

"Eighteen," I lied, not wishing to be taken for a runaway.

"Indeed. I'd have guessed younger. Where are you from?"

"New York City."

"Bound where?"

"Kansas." Feeling a sudden need to dissemble, I added, "City."

"I'm from Chicago myself. I work there. Jack Fabian. I'm a captain with the Pinkerton National Detective Agency. This is my employer, Allan Pinkerton."

Incredible as it seems now, none of these names held any significance for me at the time. No one could have convinced me of the importance they would assume.

I ventured a question of my own. "What is the Circle?"

He nodded. "You do come from far away. The Knights of the Golden Circle is a secret society of Confederate sympathizers. Their aim is to hinder the Union here in its own territory. Mostly it's an excuse for grown men to play at pirates. Now and then they leave off the secret handshakes and coded messages and take up arms. Something of the sort took place here a couple of months ago. That's when we came on the case. We answer only to Mr. Lincoln."

"What do you do?"

"Just now we're following Johnson. It's easy duty. He's hard to miss when he's on Circle business. The rest of the time he's a barber."

"I assure you, I have no Confederate sympathies."

"If you haven't and you're eighteen, why aren't you in Union blue?"

This harsh question, breaking Pinkerton's long silence, took me unawares. I stammered out that I was on my way to visit my aunt.

"That's no answer."

Fabian was soothing. "What's your aunt's name, son?"

"Drucilla Patakos." I had run out of fictions.

The sensuous lips turned up another notch. "I believe I know your aunt. I've visited her establishment a time or two on Pinkerton business. However, the last time I was there it was still in Lawrence, not Kansas City. Has she relocated?"

Thus caught in a falsehood, I said nothing. Pinkerton threw down his cigar and crushed it out with his toe. "We'll ask this whelp some of the same questions in Chicago. We tend to draw straighter answers there."

"I think it would be a waste of time, sir. Young Mr. Gashade knows nothing we can use."

"Then we'll take him there on principle."

"It would be just our luck to have Johnson make some sort of move while we're gone."

The older man's tongue bulged his cheeks in a scouring movement, as if the cigar had left a foul taste. "Perhaps you're right, Captain."

"Of course I'm right. The fellow's a musician, not a spy. What instrument do you play?"

"The piano."

Fabian asked his superior for the revolver. When Pinkerton hesitated: "He's headed for Jayhawker country, sir. It's no place to be without a smoke-wagon."

Pinkerton handed it to him. Fabian offered it to me, butt foremost. When I reached to grasp it, he spun it around, bringing the muzzle into play. I stopped, paralyzed. Again he rotated the weapon. This time he held it by the very end of the barrel.

"You've just had your first lesson on life on the border," he said. "When a man offers you a pistol, make sure his finger isn't inside the trigger guard. Go ahead, take it."

I did, and threaded the barrel down inside my belt. The Pinkerton man nodded approval. "I'm in Lawrence often on agency business. I look forward to dropping in at Drucilla's and hearing you play."

The pair left, presumably in pursuit of the fat barber.

CHAPTER SIX

New York, New York
23 July, 1863

Dear Son,
In the week that has passed since the tragic events of July 13–16, little appears to have been resolved. The Irish

newspapers, in particular the *Tablet* and the *Metropolitan Record,* continue to trade accusations as to who was responsible for the disturbance, the Republican government in Washington or certain unassimilated Irishmen loyal to Tammany Hall. Meanwhile many parts of the city remain in ruins, and pledges of funds totaling $12,000 from such as A. T. Stewart and Leonard Jerome (whom you will perhaps remember as the "Uncle Leonard" who presented you with the hobby horse carved in Austria on the occasion of your seventh birthday) promise to make little progress toward clearing away damages and claims now estimated to exceed 1.5 million; and in any case will probably find their way into various personal pockets long before they reach those most in need. A Committee of Merchants for the Relief of Colored People Suffering from the Late Riots, whose members include numerous Irish repelled by the behavior of some of their countrymen, has begun to collect donations, but many are agreed that they will have to work swiftly, as the period of shame and expiation among New Yorkers is notoriously brief.

Although some hysterical reports tally the deaths above a thousand, more reasonable assessments place the figure closer to five score. The feeling in the clubs is high that in spite of the several investigations that have been announced, few if any of the true criminals involved will actually be brought to justice. The district attorney, Oakey Hall—familiar in certain quarters as "Elegant Oakey"—is a Tammany man through and through, and an outspoken opponent of the draft.

Michael J. Brennan, the man with whom you fought before the Enrollment Office, is rumored to be in stable condition at St. Vincent's Hospital, but direct inquiries to that institution are turned away with the explanation that details concerning the patients' health are restricted to members of the immediate family. As this is not the policy of most hospitals, one can but assume that a conspiracy to obfuscate is in effect.

The man Tweed has been on view in Delmonico's Restaurant almost constantly since the riots, holding court at his customary table in back. Despite his association with those principles which sparked a now-unpopular revolt, his power increases daily. It has been bandied about that that great unlettered horde of immigrants whose ballots maintain the Tweed ring were sufficiently impressed by Tammany's challenge to the Lincoln administration to redouble their support, saturated as they are from birth with the mystery and ceremony of the Church of Rome. A more earthy interpretation counters that the wholesale plundering which went on in the city at the time of the troubles has enriched the graft. In either case the Scotsman's star is decidedly on the rise, and sources in the courthouse where I adjudicate inform me that if Tweed carries out his threat to prosecute "the person or persons responsible" for the attack upon his man Brennan—some sort of relative, I am told, by marriage—acquittal will be impossible.

And so, my dear son, I must counsel you as I have been counseled, to take no action at present. I am assured by one of my more reliable (if less clubbable) informants in the enemy camp that the sun is not privileged to shine upon the same dog's backside the entire day, by which I take him to mean that circumstances are bound to shift in our favor if we can but possess our souls in patience.

The McMurtaugh woman, who has agreed to forward this letter, refuses adamantly to divulge your whereabouts to me lest I attempt some rash act that will lead the wolves to your threshold. While I disapprove of both her assessment of my prudence and the immoral way she makes her living, I sense that she holds your best interest at heart. This one thing we share.

Your mother asks me to send you her love, and to remind you to stay clear of noxious weeds, which irritate your sensitive skin. My sole request is that you conduct yourself in a manner that will not shame you to relate to me upon our reunion. Awaiting that event I remain
                                        Your loving father

The letter, creased and scuffed all over from the many hands through which it had passed and its shifting position in one canvas mailbag after another, bore my father's familiar and precise calligraphy, yet it found me strangely detached, as if I were read-ing a missive addressed to someone I knew but slightly. In truth, I was not the person for whom it was intended. I had taken my first step away from that individual when I reached up to wrench the axe from the hands of the murder-bound fireman, and each one since—my stay at the East River Society House, my face-to-face encounter with Boss Tweed aboard the train to Chicago, my conversation with Allan Pinkerton and Captain Jack Fabian in the depot at Indianapolis, and most especially my first two weeks in Lawrence—had carried me that much farther. I missed my strong and resolute father, my distracted and often ailing but always affectionate mother, the hum and whirr of the city on the Hudson, but these people and this place that had circumscribed my world for all but the last twenty-one days of my life had al-ready begun to soften at the edges, like a childhood dream so vivid in the dreaming that I could no longer separate it from the memory of real experience. And the realization that they were slipping away so swiftly made me bleak. To this day a letter ad-dressed to me in a familiar hand fills me with the kind of dread that most people who are unaccustomed to receiving telegrams feel when a messenger from Western Union rings their bell.

The party who had brought me the letter from the Lawrence landing, though I had known him scarcely two weeks, was a good deal more real to me at that juncture than the man who had sent it. A short man, thick in the torso, with the bowed legs and rolling gait of the lifelong mariner, he wore a visored cap of the fashion worn by Mississippi riverboat pilots and an absurd long military greatcoat over a red-and-black-striped shirt and duck canvas trousers, the last indescribably filthy and stuffed into the tops of stovepipe boots that gleamed with a blue-black vengeance. The boots were the only items of apparel he paid any attention to, and when he propped them on a table or porch rail while sitting, the soles and heels showed evidence of having been recovered many times by cobblers of widely varying de-grees of skill.

His face was as dark as any Negro's, but the undersides of his wrists were fair, demonstrating that he had not been born to the pigment but had acquired it through years of exposure to the sun. When he grinned—which he did almost perpetually—his teeth stood out in his snarl of black beard like oyster shells in a

bed of Spanish moss. His full name, as he confided to me over
a cup of the vile rum, as thick and black as molasses, that he preferred above all other forms of libation, was Robert Leslie
LeFleur. Everyone who knew him called him Panama Bob.

He was born thirty-six years previously on the French-held island of Martinique, had taken to the sea as a cabin boy at age ten,
and captained his first craft at nineteen. For ten years he had
smuggled slaves from the west coast of Africa to New Orleans,
eluding ships of the British Navy whose masters were trained to
identify and confiscate slave vessels and hang their crews from
the yardarms for violating the international embargo, until an incident at sea "showed him the light," after which he became a
dedicated abolitionist. As he explained it:

"Off the Canaries, it was. We caught the eye of a man-of-war
a week past, and thought we shook it as many times as I have the
fingers, but then a fog would lift or we'd crest a wave and there
she'd be, all sprit and sheets to the wind, coming on like Jesus
at the temple, and us with a hold full of niggers. It was our necks
if they boarded.

"It wasn't my idea, nor anyone else's I could name. It just
came up, and we took a vote. Over the side they went. Sixty-
three there was, men and women, and didn't they put up a
squawk when they saw what we were about. Some of those
bucks were strong as rhinos—we picked them for strength, you
see, good field hands commanding the highest price—and it
took three good men to put one over, chains and all. Sometimes
when the wind blows right I still hear them wailing, I see those
dark heads bobbing in the wake.

"I did terrible things, Billy"—to him I was always *Bee-lee*—
"damnable things, things worse than that. But it all stopped that
day. It wasn't the wailing and carrying on that did it, either, or
even any of those we put over the side. It appeared one of the ne-
gresses we threw in belonged to this one buck, and before it
came his turn he fought his way to the rail and threw himself in
after her. Not to save her; he must have known if he even got her
back on board we'd just turn around and pitch him back in. He
wanted to be with her, that was all. He wanted it so bad he put
himself over before his turn. She was away back by then. I
greatly doubt he even got close before they both went under.
Blacks don't float for *merde*, you know; not for shit or tin coins."

He paused to relight his pipe, a penny corncob with a mended stem. We were sitting on the front porch, and, soporific in the afternoon heat, I was mesmerized by the sight of an enormous horsefly perched upon his right cheek. No amount of movement of his head or facial muscles would shake it off, but then Bob appeared in no great haste to be rid of it. He was the laziest human being I have ever met, and one of the most evil.

"By the time the limeys pulled alongside," he went on, "there wasn't a thing on board to tie us to the slave trade. Or almost. They asked about the bedding straw in the hold and we told them we'd delivered a load of goats to the Canaries and were off to the Azores for lemons. Mind, they didn't believe a word of it, but they needed proof to hang us, and they weren't half going to haul us all the way back to the Canaries to look for goats. The Brits are hell for keeping the calendar.

"Right about then this runty second mate let out a whoop and fished a Bible out of the straw, one of that hidebound kind the missionaries gave out. I said it was mine. The captain, a skinny old crane with blue veins in his beak, thumbed through it and handed it to me and told me to read from it."

"Did you know how to read?" I asked.

"Oh, I had my letters and could chart a course through a cargo manifest. But only in French. It was an English Bible." He put his head back and blew a smoke ring, enjoying the moment. The blue oval hung on the sultry air for an improbable length of time, then drifted streetward. "The last ship I took before my captain's papers came through was a sealer out of Baltimore. The master was a Presbyterian, and a deacon in the church during the off season. Sundays he insisted every man aboard sit still for Scripture. Being a seafaring man he was more than passing fond of chapters seven and eight of Genesis. He read from them six Sundays out of ten for two years. I'll wager there wasn't one of us who sailed with him didn't know it forward and backward by the time we reached port. I opened the book and said:

" 'In the six hundredth year of Noah's life, in the second month, the seventeenth day of the month, the same day were all the fountains of the great deep broken up, and the windows of heaven were opened.

" 'And the rain was upon the earth forty days and forty nights.

" 'In the selfsame day entered Noah, and Shem, and Ham,

and Japheth, the sons of Noah, and Noah's wife, and the three wives of his sons with them, into the ark;

" 'They, and every beast after his kind, and all the cattle after their kind, and every creeping thing that creepeth upon the earth after his kind, and every fowl after his kind, every bird of every sort.

" 'And they went in unto Noah into the ark, two and two of all flesh, wherein is the breath of life.' "

This passage he delivered without hesitation in the clear, ringing chant of a veteran of the pulpit, drawing curious stares from more than a few passersby on the sidewalk below the porch. Listening, I felt a deep burning shame, as if by merely providing him with an audience I had made myself an accomplice to a great blasphemy.

"The British captain said no more, but left after poking his beak into my cabin aft and the forecastle and galley. For the rest of the day the man-of-war trailed us, but it was gone come dawn. I have carried that Bible ever since. It taught me the rest of what English I now know, and a great deal more." Again his voice rose to a chant. " 'And when thou sendest him out free from thee, thou shalt not let him go away empty; Thou shalt furnish him liberally out of thy flock, and out of thy floor, and out of thy winepress; of that wherewith the Lord thy God hath blessed thee thou shalt give unto him.'

"That is how I came to be in this great free state of Kansas," he said, knocking out his pipe against the sole of a boot. "Certainly I couldn't continue in my former profession, and so I became a Jayhawker and an *entrepreneur.*"

This term, which he pronounced in the French manner, with obvious relish, was as close as he ever came to explaining his function; for I never saw him do anything around the establishment operated by his partner, Drucilla Patakos, beyond take naps and diminish its stores of rum and tobacco in wondrous volume. When he became restless he would black his boots and walk down to the ferry landing to see who came in and what they brought with them. (That was where we had met, the day I alighted in Lawrence for the first time and accompanied him back to the house.) If he felt energetic he might pick up the mail.

For cleaning and maintenance Drucilla employed a maid named Isabel, who I suspected had performed other services until she grew too old and stout to bring in sufficient capital to justify her continued residence, and the odd handyman around town, who more often than not took his pay in trade. Drucilla herself kept the books, scratching the credits and debits precisely in their columns in the light of the single lamp she kept burning in her room at the top of the house. She seldom left it, and the thick curtains that covered the windows were never opened. There were sound reasons for this eccentricity, as I shall presently explain.

Lawrence was just nine years old when I came to it, but in contrast to the monotonous succession of raw log and clapboard hamlets through which I had passed since leaving the Chicago sprawl, it had a look of permanence about it, from the brick and frame and stone buildings that lined its orderly streets to the earthworks that surrounded it, erected as high as seven feet in places as protection against border ruffians. Proud it was, declaring its abolitionist principles on signs advertising the Free State Hotel and the city's two newspapers, the *Herald of Freedom* and the *Kansas Free-State*. Meanwhile that state, like the nation itself, was more or less evenly divided upon that very point, with the predominantly pro-slave Missouri border only a day's ride to the east.

Such was my safe haven in August 1863, the Year Kansas Bled.

CHAPTER SEVEN

I had been in residence—if keeping to the ground-floor parlor with my carpetbag close at hand can be spoken of as "in residence"—in the house at 98 Massachusetts Street for fully two hours on my first day in Lawrence before I was allowed to meet my hostess. It was a fine three-story brick colonial with a well-tended flower bed in front, an iron-railed balcony encircling the building on the second level, and heavy wooden shutters reinforced with iron on every window, which Panama Bob told me had been added after border vandals raided the town in 1856, hurling torches through the windows of homes belonging to prominent abolitionists. A gently curving staircase with an Oriental runner and an elaborately carved newel post swept into a spacious foyer, with a curtained archway leading into the parlor to the left. This was a good-sized room rendered small by a superabundance of furniture and decorations: upholstered rockers, straight-backed chairs, overstuffed settees, pedestal tables, music stands, ottomans, and cabinets of china commanding nearly every foot of floor space, with a handsome pump organ occupying the place of honor against a long wall hung with painted fans and square and oval portraits in gold-encrusted frames. Every flat surface was covered with a shawl, and upon every shawl stood a forest of vases, candles in holders, and pictures on stands. The atmosphere, in a country most often described by returning excursionists as wide and open and empty, was suffocating.

Instructed by the austere, bell-shaped Isabel to wait there while she carried the letter of introduction I had brought from Bridey McMurtaugh to her mistress, I entertained myself for a time with a number of books and periodicals, treated myself to a tour of the gardens of Versailles and the canals of Venice through the magic of the Stereoscope, dozed in a wingback chair pinned all over with doilies and antimacassars, and to restore my circulation paced carefully among the bric-a-brac, studying the paintings of dogs and pilgrims and bewhiskered elder statesmen depending from the picture rail. At length, bored beyond measure, I took the stool before the pump organ, adjusted it for my comfort, and, after executing the scales a number of times until I became accustomed to the operation of the treadle, played from the sheet on the tiltboard in front of me. It bore no title or any other legend, just chords that seemed to make no sense when I read them, but which came alive in the playing; a strange, exciting composition I had neither played nor heard before I attempted it that day. It was novel and original—not quite brilliant, perhaps, but unforgettable once encountered. I played it all the way through with the intention of repeating it, only to be dissuaded before the final note ceased to resonate by the sudden appearance of Isabel at my elbow.

"Madame will see you now."

I followed her out of the parlor and up two flights to an unlit corridor whose features I could barely make out, the window at each end being cloaked in heavy velvet curtains of either deep red or black. There I nearly collided with the maid when she stopped abruptly before a door near the end of the hall and tapped softly on a panel. A voice on the other side bade her enter. She didn't, but merely opened the door and stood aside. I stepped into pitch-blackness.

The room was not as dark as that, as I saw when my eyes adjusted themselves to the change; but with the windows swathed and its only lamp turned down to an orange glow, its larger contents, including a four-poster bed and corner wardrobe, were but solid blocks of shadow and the walls were invisible. The effect was of a dying star in a limitless universe, or if not that a universe made up entirely of limits, created and defined by them, as is a coffin. Far from brightening the atmosphere, the low oil flame directed attention to its gloom.

"Close the door, please."

I obliged the unseen speaker, completing the sense of isolation. A minute dragged past, possibly less. Then the flame came up, illuminating first the glass chimney and then a globe-shaped area the size of a cantaloupe. Now I saw that the lamp stood upon a small writing desk equipped with a brass inkstand. A creased sheet of paper lay unfolded on its top, which I supposed was the letter I had brought. The hand resting upon it, small and dark—although not as dark as Panama Bob's—wore an enormous garnet ring on the index finger. Darkness above that, and then a smear of reflected light on the frontal bones of the face of the woman seated at the desk with her chair turned to face me. I saw the corner of a mouth, downturned and pulling a sharp crease from it to the base of a nose with a slight, strong curve, an eye with a heavy lid, an arch of brow, as thick and dark as a man's. All else, including the entire right side of her face, was obscured.

"Bridget. She is well?"

Her voice was deeper than that of some men I had known, and she had an accent that returned me instantly to the winter I had spent touring the Mediterranean with my parents, measuring equal value to vowels and consonants. I answered in the affirmative.

"I am glad. I have close relatives in Athens who mean less to me."

"I owe her my life."

"As do I. And she hers, to me. More times than either of us can count. Which I think cancels the debt."

This made me uneasy. Was she preparing to turn me away? I knew not a soul in the whole of Kansas. What remained of the money Bridey had given me, after meals and various bathhouses, would not pay my fare back to New York, even if it were safe for me to return.

"Was your journey unpleasant?"

"At times," I replied. "There were many delays. We were stopped twice by Union troops and once by Confederates, each looking for the other."

"Were you frightened?"

I hesitated, then nodded. "Often."

"Are you always this candid?"

"I was taught to regard honesty as the first of virtues."

"You will find the opposite to be true here on the border." She glanced down at the letter. "Bridget says you are gifted musically. I am inclined to agree. Do you know the name of the piece you played just now?"

"No."

"I was told it has none. Had you ever heard it before?"

I said I had not.

She seemed gratified by this response. She nodded very slightly, then drew a deep breath and released it. "The man to whom I was married claimed to have written it for me. He was a good violinist, but not always reliable in the things he said. You are the first person I have had the courage to ask if it was original."

"I have never come across it before today, and my training has been extensive."

To this she showed no reaction; suspecting, perhaps, my eagerness to say what pleased her. "I suppose Bridget told you he was killed?"

"She said you were set upon by savages."

"Savages, yes. Not Indians, although some of them were painted and wore feathers to leave that impression. They were Missouri trash, and whiter than I. Gareth had too much to drink in Kansas City and let slip how much cash we were bringing along to see us through to San Francisco. They followed us across the river and fell upon us as we made camp. Gareth's throat was cut before either of us knew we were not alone. I fought, but there are only so many times you can be slashed with the knife that took your husband's life before you will lie still and let them do to you what they like.

"They left me for dead. It was an easy mistake. Robert thought I was a corpse when he found me."

"You were rescued by Panama Bob?"

"The inspiration was not his. He bent over me, searching what clothing remained on me for valuables. I slid his belly gun from under his belt, placed it against his groin, and whispered that he had straddled his last woman if he did not agree to take me to a doctor. The nearest doctor happened to be in Lawrence."

Appalling as I found this narrative, I was yet the same curious youth who had interfered in an affair not his own in the city of his birth, and thus set in motion the circumstances which had brought him west. "If you came here with nothing—"

"Nothing except five hundred dollars in gold double eagles in a sack hidden in a barrel of flour. The murderers threw off the barrel while they were ransacking our wagon, but did not think to sift through its contents. This was of some assistance in persuading Robert to comply with my request."

"Surely, in your condition, he could have overpowered you and taken the gold."

"You have taken him for a shorter-sighted scoundrel than he is. People often do. By this time I think he saw possibilities in our partnership if I survived. If I did not, the five hundred was his for the picking up. The gamble paid off for us both. He has made many times that amount in our years together."

"And you?" I was bold enough to ask.

She lowered her eyelid almost demurely. "Scoundrels are more useful than you know. In his time he has shown himself well worth every cent he has stolen from me." Stirring, she refolded the letter and returned it to its envelope. "I cannot afford to employ a man to do nothing all day so that he can play the organ at night. Isabel requires help with the heavy cleaning, and there are repairs to be made and errands to be run. The room next to the kitchen is vacant. You will have clean linen weekly and three meals by the day. We shall discuss salary once you've shown you are worth these things. Isabel will show you the room."

I turned to go. Remembering that I had not thanked her, I turned back just as she reached over to lower the lamp's wick, and saw the right side of her face for the first time. It was slashed cruelly from the ear to the mouth and from the hairline to the chin in a ragged, livid X, and amateurishly stitched. Healing, the skin had puckered at the edges, pulling her lip up into a grimace that exposed teeth and tugging down the lid of her right eye—bisected by the vertical gash—into a grotesque caricature of a wink. There were other scars, mercifully disappearing into her high black lace collar, and all were white against the natural olive hue of her skin, like maggots. The result was a torn and tragic mask, barely human.

Involuntarily, I gasped. Instantly her hand went to the damaged half of her face and she drew it back into darkness. I saw the pain in her good eye when it fell upon my revulsion, which I was unable to dissemble in time. The unimpaired side of her visage went rigid with controlled fury.

"Is there something else?" Her tone was as cold as metal.

I shook my head and let myself out quickly.

My room was tiny but clean, containing a narrow cot, a chest of drawers with a brick substituted for a shattered leg, and a washstand with a small mirror above it suspended from a nail. It had no window, and had probably served originally as the pantry. The nights were hot, almost unbearably so Mondays and Thursdays, when the cookstove was stoked and banked for the next morning's baking. My native modesty was an early casualty. That Monday night I slept without a nightshirt for the first time in my life, lying naked and awash in perspiration on top of the sheets.

I had little time for homesickness. Isabel—housekeeper, cook, and now head of the household staff—kept me busy chopping and splitting wood in the backyard, filling and carrying in buckets of water from the pump, scrubbing the windows inside and out (with the exception of those on the top floor), feeding the chickens that scratched inside the fenced-off area behind the house and raiding their nests for eggs, and buying supplies and provisions at the mercantile nearby, called simply the Country Store. In between these regular chores, I replaced the odd broken hinge, pounded home the occasional rebel nail, and cleaned and refilled the lamps. These operations were time-consuming, as I had scarcely held a hammer or a screwdriver in my life, and poor Isabel was forced to take on the added duties of nurse to my swollen thumbs and burst blisters.

The food was unadventurous but hearty: salted ham, boiled potatoes, steamed greens, and white biscuits that flaked apart at a touch, smothered with gravy and heaps of melting butter and washed down with pots of scalding coffee, followed by peach cobblers, mincemeat pies, and strawberry shortcake. My appetite, indifferent at best in New York, became robust due to increased exercise, and I gained weight rapidly, which is not to say that I grew fat; I was a reedy youth to begin with, and still growing. At night, exhausted, I became senseless the instant my body made contact with the mattress and slept without dreaming straight through to dawn, when my day would begin all over again with morning chores and a breakfast of eggs, sausages, corn bread, and pancakes with honey.

Manhood came to me during this period. Stimulated by the motion of the axe and the weight of the water buckets, the muscles in my back and shoulders took on definition and strained the shoulders of my blue serge when I donned it in the evenings to play the organ. And I felt a man's desires.

The four women who shared the house with Drucilla and the maid were bound by a city ordinance regulating the conduct of women of their calling never to appear below the second story less than fully clothed, with all buttons fastened and ankles and bosoms decently covered. My duties as handyman without portfolio took me to every floor, and it was my fate to stand for no small amount of feminine sport, which in the hands of women whom society has already declared outcast can devastate the sensibilities of a burgeoning male.

For helping me to resist bewitchment I was grateful to my father, a man of the world whose jurist's-eye view of human frailty had given birth to the frankest and sternest advice a man could provide for his son. At the time it seemed that he had foreseen everything, and even now I can detect only merit in his proposed mechanism for the prevention of surrender and disgrace.

However, not even Father could prepare me for what went on at 98 Massachusetts Street while western civilization crumbled around it like so much wormy bread.

CHAPTER EIGHT

The *inventory*—for such was the term Panama Bob employed in reference to the women who resided on the second floor at Drucilla's, enamored as he was with the *entrepreneurial* life—was at its low point when I discovered it. Serena, who held greatest seniority after Isabel and Drucilla herself, was away visiting her brother in a Baltimore hospital, where he was recovering from injuries received at Gettysburg. Another, Zoe, had deserted the profession for the Church, which Bob assured me was a common nuisance, "whores spending as much time as they do staring up." Two more had wed soldiers with the Tenth Missouri Volunteers and were following that body south behind General Sherman. The reformed slaverunner was confident, however, that Drucilla would soon find more applicants than she had rooms in which to put them up. "War widows," he confided, grinning despicably in his tarry beard.

Of the four women who remained, Ada, a fleshy, motherly sort with sunset-colored hair caught behind her head with combs, busied herself the day long darning the hose of her fellow residents and lecturing them good-naturedly upon such practical matters as the importance of not powdering one's neck too close to the collar of one's dress to avoid frequent laundering; Carmel, pale, black-haired, and slender—nearly translucent by lamplight—spoke with a soft and cultured Southern lilt that cracked upon occasion, when she would deliver an oath more suited to a Biloxi alley than a plantation ballroom; Rachel, a tall octoroon with haunted eyes and a pronounced addiction to snuff, held herself aloof from the others, a mode of behavior not calculated to win their admiration, particularly in view of the fact that she was known to receive black freedmen at the back door when she wasn't engaged with a white customer in the parlor; and Veronica, the youngest and freshest, upon whom Isabel doted, contrary to her habitual attitude of reserved contempt for the world and its population, dressing the girl's strawberry-blond hair in the sausage curls then fashionable among young ladies of the local aristocracy and outfitting her in frothy dresses of pale blue and champagne pink trimmed with lace.

Veronica. Close to my age, bright, feral-eyed, and determined after the manner of the indisputably spoiled to satisfy her basest desires at the moment they occurred, this tiny creature caused me more vexation than the other three combined; but not, as it turned out, my undoing. That dubious prize went to another.

Saturday nights were busiest. Lawrence was a recruiting center for the Union Army, and when the guards deployed to protect the enrollment office fell out, with no place for them on the duty roster until the following Monday, the foyer and parlor became a sea of Federal blue. Isabel carried their names and calling cards upstairs to her mistress, who considered them and arranged assignations in order of rank. Those who were forced to wait were made as comfortable as possible in the seats available while the maid passed among them with glasses of brandy and trays of sandwiches. I performed requested tunes on the organ, and in so doing learned a great deal about the musical preferences of men stranded far from home and family.

I expected that their tastes would run toward the bawdy and boisterous, and indeed there were those who fulfilled that expectation; but their suggestions were shouted down almost invariably in favor of the sentimental and, as the evening wore on and the liquor had made the rounds several times, the mawkish and maudlin. Complying, I wondered idly what the gentlemen's bordellos back home would make of "Aura Lee," "The Riddle Song," and "The Gypsy Laddie." To be sure, when these homely ballads of love and faith and purity had reduced every man within earshot to helpless tears, someone would call for a "right rouser," and elicit no protest. In this category, "The Arkansas Traveler" was the clear favorite, followed closely by "Jeannie with the Light Brown Hair." On those occasions when the group's spirit became martial, the selection was less likely to be the belligerent "Rally 'Round the Flag" or the righteous "John Brown's Body" as the melancholy and pensive "Darling Nellie

Gray," about a slave girl sold away from her lover's side. What they sang about in the barracks I cannot say, but I came to conclude that with physical fulfillment so near—literally, the distance of a single flight of stairs—these trained and experienced men-at-arms found the security to indulge themselves at long last in reflections on what they had left behind.

Carmel, she of the spectral complexion and Delta drawl, sang between her upstairs appointments, disclosing a choir-trained voice and what amounted to an inexhaustible memory for lyrics, no matter how obscure. She stood close to the organ without moving, hands clasped below her bosom, the scent of her personal blend of lilacs and jasmine (with the slightest hint of the camphor she and the others employed to prevent inconvenient pregnancies) drifting my way, and to this day I find that I cannot play "Wondrous Love" or "Lucy Locket" without detecting that delicate combination; or pass a scent shop that features it without hearing one of those tunes in my head. She had a lovely voice, which worked to rob her favorite gutter expressions of their intended effect. Raised in song, it never failed to subtract, for some little time, the bleakness of combat from the haggard faces of her listeners.

This was Saturday. Sundays we closed, and on weeknights business was sporadic, the clientele checkered. It was then, when the troops were confined to the post, that I learned how well known Drucilla's establishment was outside the city of Lawrence. Although hardly the only disorderly house in this community of twelve hundred, it was the one located closest to the eastern limits, and as the first encountered by visitors from across the border, the one most familiar to Missourians traveling west.

"Look livesome, Bee-lee," was Panama Bob's advice to me the first time one of these individuals was shown into the parlor with me at the keyboard; whereupon the former slaver left the room, to return a few minutes later carrying a single-barreled shotgun, which he leaned conspicuously in the corner near where he sat drinking from his ubiquitous cup with a bottle of black rum at his elbow.

This ostentation wasn't entirely superfluous. The stranger who had prompted it, a long, bony specimen of the great outdoors, with the raw neck and knoblike knuckles of the lifelong farmer, wore a shining black slicker—for it was raining heavily—over a curious knit pullover buttoned to the neck, and although he surrendered his hat to Isabel, muttered that he would keep the coat. This was unconventional, as the atmosphere in the overfurnished parlor was close and the weight of the oilcloth on his shoulders must have been uncomfortable. I divined immediately that he was "packing iron," and unwilling to expose his weaponry to the strangers present. His untrimmed hair and day's growth of beard aged him, but I placed him in his early twenties. His eyes were older.

It appeared that he had stated his wishes to Isabel, for when that grave lady returned he rose from the edge of the hard seat where he had placed himself and accompanied her through the curtains. His spurs clanked when he walked. Leather creaked.

"Freebooter," spat Bob when he had gone. "Pro-slave Missouri murdering trash. I cannot think why she countenances it."

"Who, Drucilla?" I went on playing.

"Any of them. A whore who lies with a pig hasn't far to go to touch bottom."

"How are you certain he's from Missouri?"

"He has the guerrilla stink all over him. Did you mark that business with the slicker?"

"He is armed, of course."

"Show me a man who is not. This one didn't leave anything behind. I want his horse. Any animal that can haul that much iron across the river on a wet night like this could pull boxcars. What's that you are playing?"

"A fugue. Bach."

"Well, I don't know what language that is, but our cutthroat friend seemed to like it."

"I noticed he was watching my hands."

"He was watching everyone's hands. That's how you know a killer."

"I thought it was the eyes."

He showed his startling teeth. "You have read too many of the penny dreadfuls. Eyes do not kill."

"Perhaps he didn't care for the music after all."

"He cared. It would surprise you to know how simple a brute is, and what may tame him. I know of one, surrounded by enemies, who hesitated to whip his horse through a gap that might have saved him because he feared to trample a stray dog. His death was messy."

"A horse? I thought all your adventures took place at sea."

"It is a story I heard," he said.

I had no opportunity to pursue the point, for he left the parlor shortly thereafter, and when I asked about him the next morning I was informed by Isabel that he had saddled his horse and left during the night. When he returned some days later, exhausted and covered with mud and dust, he was uncommunicative, but after some sixteen hours' sleep and an enormous breakfast he was again his convivial, anecdotal self, although he made no reference to where he had been or what he had done, nor would he be drawn out on the subject. Ada, ever the fount of information on the doings of the household, told me over her darning egg and needle that Panama Bob's frequent unexplained absences were a point of much discussion among "the ladies," some of whom held the opinion that Drucilla had a rival on the Missouri side of the border.

"And what opinion does Ada hold?" I asked, mocking her habit of referring to herself in the third person.

"Ada's older and less romantic. For Drucilla to have a rival, she'd have to be interested in Bob to begin with, and you'd easier breed a Kansas mare with a barnacle than get them two together over anything more tender than a cash box."

"Then where does he go, and what does he do once he gets there?"

"I'd only be guessing. I've not seen Bob with his drawers down—he likes 'em young and skinny, thank the Lord—but I'm thinking if I did I'd not be shocked to see his limbs are bright scarlet."

This was not as enigmatic a remark as she may have intended, thinking me an ignorant Easterner. In fact I had overheard a great many conversations in the day coaches and depots on my way west, and had gleaned something of the long history of raids and counterraids into each other's territory launched by the pro-slave Missouri night riders and the abolitionist Kansas "Jayhawkers." There were men on both sides who took advantage of the breakdown in law and order to settle private scores and carry away plunder. These jackals were known universally by a colorful and sanguinary nickname.

"Bob's a Redleg?"

I could not see her expression, bent over her work as she was; but the hand holding the needle hesitated between stitches, then resumed moving with a fresh purpose. "I'll never get through my sewing for all this jabber. I thought you came for the bedding."

I gathered the soiled sheets and pillowcases from her iron-framed bed and carried them out back, where Isabel was scrubbing the laundry in a great cauldron designed for scalding hogs; the amount of washing to be done among even that reduced workforce having long since outgrown an ordinary wooden tub. I was filled with thought. My initial judgment of Panama Bob's character—that he was a blackguard masquerading as a soul reformed—was correct, and I should have felt some satisfaction. However, I had experienced at firsthand the special horrors of wickedness done in support of a creed, and found it more distasteful than blind, unthinking evil. LeFleur the unregenerate pirate and slaverunner would have been easier to accept than Bob the Bible-quoting night rider, espousing by day the virtues of freedom for all and looting the homes and businesses of known or suspected pro-slavers under cover of darkness for his own aggrandizement. Very possibly he had committed murder: The story of the man gone to a bloody death for love of a dog had sounded like an incident witnessed rather than a rumor heard. I thought it conceivable that Bob had been among his slayers.

There was no one in whom I could confide my feelings in this matter. The issue in this part of the world was heated, and I could not be sure of a sympathetic ear. Drucilla alone, on the evidence of our discussion on the day of my arrival, might have handled the situation with reason and logic, but I was quickly made to understand that our meeting in her quarters was unprecedented, and would not be repeated. Isabel, who brought her meals and carried out the chamber pot, was the sole resident allowed regular access to that darkened room. Even Panama Bob visited there by appointment only. Its occupant seldom ventured out during the day, and never appeared below the top floor before dark. On hot nights when sleep was slow in coming, I would hear the squeak of a floorboard outside my room or the scrape of a chair, and I would know that the mistress of 98 Massachusetts Street was abroad in the house, carrying a lamp from room to room, surveying her monarchy at the only hour during which she felt secure enough to expose her ruined face outside her self-enforced exile. After many years spent searching my soul I can say with confidence that it was not fear of her deformity that prevented me from getting up and opening my door when I sensed her presence just outside it, but respect for the privacy of the only person who had shown me charity west of Bridey McMurtaugh's East River Society House.

At other times I showed my gratitude in a way less passive.

Some nights, when the last customer had drifted out the door on a cloud of personal satisfaction and the "inventory" had retired, I would produce the stained and yellowed sheet of music that had greeted me the first time I sat at the organ and play, as softly as the instrument allowed, the composition left by Drucilla's slain husband. I was certain that its strains reached clearly to the top of the house, where its subject sat at her writing desk entering the evening's transactions in the ledger and waiting for the hours to grow small, and yet I received neither word nor signal that she had heard; which I took to mean that she did not disapprove. I never played the piece at any other time. Indeed, though I know it by heart, I haven't played it in twenty years, not since the news reached me that Drucilla was dead.

When I state that she was my only source of charity, I am not forgetting the contribution made by the women of the second floor, which carried a price. As the sole male on the premises apart from Bob, who had sampled the charms of all save the matronly Ada—with special attention to the octoroon Rachel, whom he seemed to have convinced himself he was freeing, if only a little bit at a time—I was their "meat," particularly desirable because of the shared view that I was a virgin, and the first such in the vicinity since Shiloh.

Subtlety was not a weapon in their armory. A visit to an upstairs room to deliver clean linens or to unstick a swollen window was invariably a fresh lesson in the mysteries of the female anatomy, as I was forever "surprising" the occupant in an advanced state of deshabille, despite conscientious knocking at the door. I learned, among other things, that Carmel had a small tattoo on her right hip that she thought was a pineapple, but which I, being familiar with that overemployed symbol of Victorian hospitality, should have thought more closely resembled a this-

tle; that Rachel—cool, distant Rachel—was the same even but-
terscotch color all over, with the exceptions of her palms and the
soles of her feet, which were pink—and that Veronica spent
most of the money she earned ordering lacy black undergar-
ments from a company in New Orleans, whose catalogue
Panama Bob had brought with him across the continent for the
purpose of starting fires.

This youngest of Ada's "ladies" had been such a reliable customer that the firm had sent her, free of charge, a sampling of its
most popular scents with its last shipment. These she insisted on
daubing upon inaccessible parts of her person and asking my
opinion of their value. This I declined to do, but it would be less
than honest of me to assert that I was not tempted. She was an
extremely pretty girl, well formed in the slightly overuphol-
stered fashion that passed for feminine beauty in those innocent
days, and framed to perfection in the best artifice of Beechlove's
Parisian Stays & Garters, Ltd.

Honesty eludes me yet. I did not decline. I fled.

Out of her room and down the hall, still carrying bunched
under one arm the blue-and-white counterpane I had brought,
fresh from an outdoors airing, for Veronica's bed. Down the hall,
and into a near collision with Ada, who curled her fleshy arms
around me, cooing and whispering phrases of motherly comfort, and drew me into the sanctuary of her room.

CHAPTER NINE

෴

This was Thursday, August 20, 1863; a date that many another who survived to tell of it would remember for reasons
other than a boy's first experience with the physical act of love.

As I lay, thoroughly spent, in Ada's slumbering embrace in the
old gold light of a late-summer Kansas afternoon, another young
man, only ten years my senior, with Quakerish long hair and
the sparse beginnings of a ginger-colored moustache, was
preparing, at the head of a column of three hundred men, to
cross the border from Missouri and destroy whatever illusions I

retained that I lived in a Christian country. His name was William Clarke Quantrill.

I had heard the name exactly twice since coming to Lawrence, both times in the form of a jest. Once, awaiting my turn at the counter of the Country Store behind an enormous farmer in dirt-smeared overalls and thick-soled boots laced up to his knees, I overheard the farmer inquire of the clerk, Jim Perine, if he had seen anything yet of Captain Quantrill.

Perine, a long-faced, stoop-shouldered man who never smiled when I was present, lowered his left eyelid in a solemn wink and replied, "No, but yesterday's receipts came up three cents short, so I expect he's been in."

The farmer hoisted his sack of flour and went out past me, shoulders shaking.

On another occasion, as I was sweeping the steps in front of Drucilla's, a portly, white-maned gentleman in a frock coat, whom Panama Bob had pointed out to me as a Judge Carpenter, paused in mid-stroll at the end of the block to observe a bearded fellow unloading a crate from the back of a buckboard in front of Palmer's gun repair shop. Cupping his hands around his mouth, the judge cried: "Watch your back, Ed! Quantrill's behind you!"

The man swiveled, face expressionless, with the crate balanced on his shoulder. He burst out laughing at the sight of a scruffy yellow dog raising its leg to urinate on the wagon's left rear wheel.

"Sorry, Ed!" called the judge. "Honest mistake."

Bob, who made it his business to know every affair not connected with the day-to-day drudgery of keeping Drucilla's house prosperous, explained to me that the rumor had been abroad for months that the Missouri guerrilla chief was planning to attack Lawrence, slaughtering prominent Jayhawkers and burning the city to the ground. For a time armed guards were stationed at all the roads leading into town, but when nothing happened after several weeks the panic subsided and people began to joke about the threat they believed had passed. The guards were withdrawn, and Lawrence resumed its routine as a backwater of the war.

Quantrill's hatred of Kansas was legend. At age twenty-six, having pursued the variant careers of Sunday school teacher, horse thief, and gambler, this Ohio native had nursed a grudge for the state since his expulsion in 1858 for stealing from his fellow Johnson County settlers. Another story, believed by many to have been invented by Quantrill himself, held that his older brother had been murdered in a raid led by Senator Jim Lane, the Jayhawker chief later responsible for the burning of Osceola, Missouri. Whatever the story's truth or lack of it, the sack of Osceola was reason enough for the embittered irregulars who rode with Quantrill to harbor a loathing for Lawrence—home to Senator Lane, whose rawboned frame and head of flame-colored hair were celebrated locally with the fervor reserved for the native son who had distinguished himself in the world.

Commissioned a captain of partisan rangers by no less an authority than General Sterling Price of the Confederacy, Quantrill commanded a cavalry of 150, hardened campaigners all, their souls afire with the will for vengeance, plunder, and death to any abolitionist who crossed their path. An equal number of men led by Confederate Colonel Holt joined them at Lone Jack, and together the forces crossed the border south of Kansas City at five o'clock in the evening. Above their heads snapped the black flag of the damned.

I knew none of this at the time, of course; and if I gave any thought to the man Quantrill at all, I suppose I considered him a half reality at best, largely an ogre fabricated for the purpose of frightening children lest they stay up past their retirement hour or neglect the greens on their plate. No, as I lay partially dozing in the arms of Ada (who snored, I am unchivalrous enough to report, like a teamster), smelling of her not inconsiderable ardor, my reflections were those of discovery. So this, I thought, was what all the stir was about; the low whispers between husband and wife that ceased abruptly when a child entered the room, the sniggering speculation of filthy little boys on a street corner, the indecent jests and bellows of coarse laughter shared by grown men in rooms filled with smoke and ferment, out of ladies' earshot. After so much anticipation, I found it oddly unsatisfying, somewhat depressing, and, to one of my fastidious temperament, untidy in the extreme. And I felt that I could not wait to experience it again.

I was watching Ada's face when her eyes opened. She blinked away the blurriness, recognized me, frowned, and remembered.

I smiled tentatively. She disengaged an arm, fumbled on the nightstand for the decorative watch she pinned to her dress when she went downstairs, held it close to her face, mewed, and threw aside the covers violently. I watched uncomprehending as she stooped and slid something out from under the bed. When she hiked up her nightdress and squatted on the chamber pot, I swung my feet to the floor and put on my clothes quickly. Not a word had passed between us from the moment she took me into her room until I let myself back out into the hall.

Thus was my initiation to the pleasures of the flesh. Women to whom I have related its details are usually unsympathetic. I am told that the aftermath is not often different when the man is the seducer. In any case, I have been with many women since, and knowing from experience the sting of being cast to one side immediately upon conquest, I have tried always to make the coda as tender as the overture. However successful the result, it is a scrap of wisdom I owe to Ada, who little realized what she had wrought in her fever to beat her younger, prettier rivals to the finish, and who I suspect would not have cared had she known.

Am I guilty of hindsight when I maintain that I felt an impending Something when I descended the stairs that evening to take my place at the organ? Very likely. An old man's recollections are not entirely to be trusted. Yet I distinctly remember noticing the way the hairs on the backs of my hands stood erect when I ran through the scales, and feeling acute discomfort for the first time at being forced to sit with my back to the parlor entrance. I found myself glancing back over my shoulder often. Hindsight perhaps. The fact remains that I was watching the curtains when the tall, bony young man came through whom I had last seen the night Panama Bob disappeared on his most recent mysterious excursion. Tonight he wore a duster in place of the oilcloth slicker, and this time he was not alone.

Fiends I have known in plenty, and yet I never met a man I feared at first sight as I feared this new stranger. In attire there was nothing to mark him from the usual customer who drifted in of a weeknight: slouch hat with a broken brim, canvas coat darned and patched all over and fraying at the cuffs, ticking trousers reinforced with leather along the inseam, dusty boots run-down at the heels and nearly worn through at the toes. His face was another matter. Fine-skinned if deeply burned, the fea-

tures even and recently shaved, it belonged on the shoulders of
a marble statue but for the eyes. These were pale, startlingly so
in their dark setting, and stared straight ahead without blinking,
seeming to see everything while making contact with nothing,
and giving nothing back. The eyes of a corpse, and not one who
had surrendered its shade peacefully. Behind them raged the fire
that burned without consuming.

I was playing, I remember, "Sally in Our Alley," much to the
delight of the local visitors, whose preferences varied in a backward direction from those of the soldiers. Colonial songs were
greatly prized, possibly because they invoked thoughts of the
gentler times of their grandfathers, or at least a time when the
enemy was foreign—a Brit, nothing less, who wore a scarlet
coat and honked through his nose like a gander when he spoke—
and less likely to be a close relative from a slave state. Carmel
being engaged upstairs, a number of the men had gathered
around the organ and raised their not entirely incompatible
voices in an approximation of Henry Carey's lyrics. Some of
them tended to rush the melody, while others lagged behind,
and as it required concentration not to fall into their bad habits
I lost track of the two newcomers until I heard a voice close to
my ear.

" 'Bonnie Blue Flag.' "

The request was a whispered sibilant, and affected me as
would a venomous snake dropping from the ceiling to my shoulder. I missed a beat, let two more go by before I picked up the
chord, and shook my head without taking my eyes off the music
sheet. I knew without looking that the man who had placed the
request was the man I have just described.

" 'Bonnie Blue Flag.' " This time the whisper was accompanied by a metallic click.

I smelled sharp oil and felt the cold of the steel behind my
right ear. The stranger was standing behind me and to the right,
with his body twisted to the left, shielding the pistol from the
others, who were declaring that if it weren't for Sally they'd
rather be slaves and row a galley.

I was in a quandary. I had no doubt, based on the stranger's
frightening appearance, that he would not hesitate to squeeze the
trigger if I ignored his demand to play the rebel march. At the
same time I held no illusions that the boisterous good fellowship

of these Kansans and Free-Staters would not turn to violence before the first verse was out. Their initial inclination would be to tear to pieces the same musician whose skills they were now celebrating so loudly.

"I don't know it," I said at last.

"You got thirty seconds to learn. After that you won't have brains enough to finish that piece you're playing."

I longed for Panama Bob and his shotgun; but I had not seen him since morning, at which time he had already made serious inroads in his day's allotment of rum. Ada had told me it was ever thus when he returned from a protracted absence: "Three days flat on his arse to each one in the saddle. That's the count, and there's no changing it."

"You are one stubborn bluebelly," said the man with the pistol.

I shrank from the blast I knew was coming. Then a new body blocked the light from the corner lamp. I thought at first it was Bob, and turned my head that way in relief. My heart went sour when I recognized the gaunt young man who had come in with my tormentor.

"It's no good, John." His voice was thin, with the clear high twang of the Missouri hill country. "There's four of them to a man."

"Brings the odds just about even," said the other, but after another moment the hammer snicked back into place and the muzzle was withdrawn. Deliverance flooded my veins.

The pair left, and the rest of the evening was uneventful. Exhausted by the day's momentous events, I retired as soon as the last customer was out the door, unaware that the next day would be the longest of my life.

I couldn't know at the time, but as I turned out the downstairs lamps the bloodshed was beginning. At around eleven P.M. the main body of guerrillas swept through the village of Gardner on the Santa Fe Trail, firing buildings and shooting down the half-dozen or so men who came running to put out the flames. Four hours later they kidnapped a boy in Hesper and forced him to agree to guide them through the well-bottom blackness of a moonless night to Lawrence. In the gray light of dawn, the column trotted bold as brass down the main street of Franklin, four miles to the east. There they were spotted by a handful of citizens who mistook them for Union cavalry, and thus failed to report their presence. When they were two miles from their destination the Missourians galloped into the barnyard of the Reverend Snyder, a Federal officer on leave who commanded a company of colored troops in the field. He stepped out, rifle in hand, into a wall of bullets. The band set fire to the house and barn and left him writhing in a muck of dirt and blood.

Stopping at the Lawrence city limits, they were intercepted by two scouts Quantrill had sent in the night before, who reported that all was quiet. These were the two men I had encountered in Drucilla's parlor.

Four hundred Union soldiers were camped north of the Kansas River outside town, separated by the ferry from a few dozen more on the Lawrence side. Quantrill dispatched a detail to take possession of the ferry and prevent the enemy's main body from crossing. The others were slaughtered in their tents.

I awoke to a rattle of gunfire, which I have since decided belonged to the action described above. I was groggily reaching for my trousers when my door burst open. Panama Bob, barefoot with his braces dangling and no shirt on over his stained and faded long underwear, rushed in gripping a long-barreled revolver with an enormous bore. Around his narrow waist he had buckled a belt with a scabbard containing a curved saber, its handle chased with gold.

"Your pistol, Billy! Where is it?"

"In my bag," I managed to stammer. His great Gallic eyes were wild, his black hair and beard more tangled than ever. I felt myself in the presence of an aroused and cornered beast.

"Put it in your hand and come with me! Hurry!"

"But who—?"

"The Philistines!" With that he was gone, crossing the kitchen with long loping strides.

I finished dressing quickly, inspected the charges in the cylinder of the five-shot, and went out behind him. Ada and Rachel, in their dressing gowns, were huddled in the foyer by the open door, and I was aware of Carmel and Veronica standing on the stairs. From outside came a din of splintering glass and drumming hooves, punctuated by pistol reports and a hellish scale of unearthly, high-pitched shrieks: the rebel yell. I went outside.

Massachusetts Street was in uproar. A plunging, rearing

stream of men on horseback filled it from end to end, whooping
and quirting their reins across their mounts' withers, twisting
this way and that in their saddles to shoot at men and windows.
Some carried torches, some waved sabers. To a man they were
dressed in the butternut gray of the Southern Confederacy. I saw
campaign hats and kepis, ostrich plumes and gold braid and the
black flag on a staff. They shattered panes, punched holes in
watering troughs, riddled signs, and shot at everything that
moved. No sooner had I appeared on the porch than the lantern
hanging above the discreet sign that identified the house as Drucilla's exploded not a foot from my head. I ducked as a shower
of glass pelted my shoulders and went down inside my collar.

"Over here, Billy!"

Bob was crouched in a corner behind the railing, using a small
dogwood growing on the other side for cover. The barrel of his
pistol rested atop the railing. I joined him, keeping low.

"Rebels?" I asked.

"Worse. Bushwhackers. Captain Q's black devils, or I am
damned."

"How can you tell?"

"I get one and show you."

Before I could stop him, he rose, extended the arm holding the
revolver, picked his target, led it, and fired. A horseman sweeping past the steps back his head and cartwheeled out of
the saddle, landing in the strip of grass between the porch and
the street. Bob made a triumphant noise in his throat—a growl,
really—shouted, "Cover me!" and scampered down the steps.
While the enemy thundered past an arm's length away, the reformed slaverunner made a brief examination of the fallen man,
then belted his pistol and backed up the steps, dragging the man
by his Sam Browne belt. A rider, spotting him, shouted a curse
of indescribable filth and took aim at him with a bone-handled
revolver. Before he could fire another horseman came between
him and his target. In another moment he was swept out of ef-
fective range, and Bob was back behind the dogwood with his
trophy.

The whites of Bob's eyes glittered in his dark face as he studied me. His chest heaved. "Is that what you call giving cover?"

"It was all too fast," I said.

"The next time a fellow shoots at me I will ask him to slow

down." With a final exertion, he turned the dead man over on his back between us. I was astonished to see a beardless face, spotted with acne on the chin and forehead. He was not much older than I. His blue eyes were open, but they saw nothing and would never see anything again.

Bob wasted no time looking at the boy's face. He seized the front of the gray tunic in both hands and tore it open, exposing a mass of ruffled white linen peppered with blood.

"Guerrilla shirt." He sat back on his heels. "You'll not see a fancy rig like that on any honest man-at-arms. Most of them never wore anything but homespun before they joined up. It's the first thing they buy once they get their hands on plunder." He hawked noisily and spat into the ruffles. Then his head flew apart.

It was as sudden as that. One instant his face was before me, and the next it was a red smear. Something stung both my eyes; I tasted salt and iron on my lips and spat it out in an automatic reaction. Much time would pass, and with it many a bar of coarse brown soap and several layers of skin, before I felt that I had cleansed myself of the last of Panama Bob's brains. He slumped forward across the corpse of the boy he had killed, and I looked up, my face dripping, into a pair of eyes as dead as the boy's.

I knew the man at once, though he stood on the porch against the red glare of the morning sun and had exchanged his worn canvas and ticking of the night before for the belted gray coat and single-striped trousers of a Confederate officer. Under the broad brim of his hat, pinned up on one side and decorated with a plume, were the icily classic features of the man from the parlor. Smoke was still twisting out of the end of his revolver when he turned it upon me.

"I reckon you'll be playing 'Bonnie Blue Flag' next time on a harp," he said, drawing back the hammer.

"Step to the ground."

The low, Greek-inflected tones drew those empty eyes toward the open front door, and mine just behind. There, in the full light of day, stood Drucilla Patakos, in a handsome embroidered dressing gown with the stock of Panama Bob's shotgun pressed to her ruined right cheek. The sun's searching rays brought the scars into brutal relief.

The man assessed the situation at a glance. "There's right

around three hundred of us," he said. "What you fixing to do once you empty that barrel?"

"It will not be any concern of yours, since I intend to empty it into you."

"Too thin, old lady. I'm calling your hand."

Hooves rataplaned up to the porch. The lanky young farmer I had seen on two previous occasions swung down from the back of a racing bay. He, too, had switched to rebel gray, but of a much simpler design, without insignia or frivolous ornament. He wore two pistols on his belt and a saber in a scabbard. Standing on the bottom step he glanced quickly from the woman with the shotgun to the guerrilla on the porch. "I wouldn't, John. She ain't bluffing."

"Balls, Frank. You couldn't take a pot with a hogleg."

A shot rang out very close. I'm ashamed to say I wet myself, for I thought the report belonged to the weapon pointed at me. In fact, both he and his friend were looking away from Drucilla and me, at a resplendent figure leaning down from the saddle of a tall blue roan to peer under the roof of the porch. Long-maned and heavily bearded, he wore his hat at a dandyish angle and a scarlet sash around the waist of a tunic with captain's bars on the shoulders. I counted three pistols on his person—two in the sash, a third gripped in his right fist pointed skyward and smoking— and had the impression there were others I didn't see. I assumed that so flamboyant and abundantly armed a figure must belong to Quantrill himself. I was wrong.

He spoke quietly, and I realized for the first time that the street was quiet. The slaughter had abated temporarily. There would be more, so much more; but even the devil must pause betimes for breath.

"No women killed or harmed, that was the order. Which part do you find unclear, Lieutenant Thrailkill?"

"It ain't the woman I want, Captain. It's this key-plunking son of a bitch."

The bearded man appraised me, not missing the pistol in my hand, which I myself had forgotten. It wasn't likely to assist me in any case. "Sergeant James?" He looked at the farmer.

"He's no threat, Captain. Plays the organ at Drucilla's."

Now he looked at Drucilla. "You prize him so, madam?"

She said nothing. The shotgun remained steady.

"Plays well, does he?" he asked Sergeant James then.

The farmer surprised me by grinning. Then he surprised me a great deal more. "Bach. Sir."

"Bach?"

"Yes, sir."

The captain appeared to consider. Then he thrust his weapon into the sash with the others. "Bring him."

PART TWO

Nocturne for Night Riders

CHAPTER TEN

As it was with the New York draft riots, casualty reports connected with the sack of Lawrence by Quantrill's raiders were exaggerated hysterically. The world may never know how many men died—all the victims were male, by decree of the commander, who thought himself chivalrous—in that community between the hours of five and nine A.M., when the last of the invaders departed. None of the accounts I've read make mention of the young guerrilla shot down by Panama Bob in front of Drucilla's, and since most of them point to a former preacher named Skaggs as the only Missourian slain, I have come to doubt all the statistics cited by "experts" who were not present that day. I do know that a mass funeral took place there on the day following the attack, and that throughout the rest of the war a double row of naked chimneys and broken sections of scorched brick wall were all that remained of the business district.

Gone were the Eldridge House and the Johnson House, hotels and popular meeting places for the Free-Staters; the Country Store was burned to the ground as well, also Palmer's Gun Shop, the latter with the occupants still inside. When the kegs of black powder stored in back went up, they took the roof with them, along with every window on the street not already broken by gunfire. Several stables and granaries went to the torch, for no apparent reason other than that they burned so easily. I am told that for days afterward a cloud of smoke hung above the settlement like the black pall of doom.

Mayor Collamore was dead. So too were State Senator Thorpe and editor Josiah Trask of the abolitionist *State Journal,* gunned down in front of their wives when they came out of their houses to surrender. Judge Louis Carpenter, who had jestingly pretended to mistake a stray cur for Quantrill, was shot down like a dog in his home. Dozens more, strangers to their assailants, died for the crime of being male and of age in the Jayhawker capital of Kansas.

Ironically, Senator James Lane, whose Redleg raid on Osceola, Missouri, had inspired the assault, escaped harm by concealing himself in a nearby cornfield until the danger had passed. Guerrillas searched his house, questioned his wife, and rode away after leaving their compliments. It was that kind of war.

All of my information regarding the aftermath of the grisly events of August 21 came to me secondhand, and long after the fact, for I was not there. This was not Drucilla's wish. She did not lower Panama Bob's shotgun when the showily dressed captain instructed Sergeant James and Lieutenant Thrailkill to bring me along; instead, she moved it slightly to bring the captain within range of its broad pattern. The hand that wore the garnet ring did not quaver.

"The young man will stay," she announced. "You will not carry him away so that you can murder him in private."

The man on horseback lifted his brows. Then he laughed—a genuine, deep, guttering sound that issued from the base of his chest and carried to the watching guerrillas, all of whom joined in, with the notable exceptions of Thrailkill and James. But for their silence it was as if someone had told a Homeric off-color joke at a gentlemen's smoker.

Suddenly the captain stopped laughing. Just as suddenly, before anyone could react, he drew the revolver he had recently shoved under the sash about his waist, cocking it in the same motion, and fired.

A townsman I knew by sight but not by name, middle-aging

and running to fat in a dusty morning coat and wire spectacles, cried out, clutched his abdomen with both hands, and fell from the section of boardwalk between Drucilla's and the house next door. Evidently hoping to escape attention, he had emerged from the neighboring shallow doorway and begun inching toward the narrow passage that separated the two buildings. The man in the saddle had made no sign of noticing him until he put a bullet in the fellow's stomach. Lying in the street, the wounded man pitched and rolled, groaning and kicking with both feet.

"Maddox," said the captain.

A bearded guerrilla sitting his horse near the suffering man leaned down and shot him through the head. The wretch arched his back, then slowly subsided. He lay still.

One or two of the watching Missourians sniggered.

The captain levered the device attached to his revolver to extract the spent powder from the two chambers he had fired recently. "Captain Anderson, madam," he said, pausing to touch two fingers to the brim of his hat. "Some of the boys call me Bloody Bill, and I guess I've earned it even if I don't answer to it. I have never busted a cap on a man in private in my life. If I intended to kill this young man I would have shot you just now instead of that sneak, and finished the job at my leisure. You would have died with your finger on the trigger."

"What do you want with him?" Her voice was even. I could not tell if she were dissembling, or if her past experience with border killers had so hardened her to the sight of a man's death in cold blood that it left her unaffected. As for me, it seemed the more of it I saw, the less I was prepared for it. The fact that I had not had breakfast was the only thing that kept me from retching.

"An army, madam, requires three things to remain an army: God, music, and the will to fight. The damn Union has given us all of the last we need, and we have more preachers in our ranks than General Lee has whiskers. We are rotten short on music. Corporal Taylor's squeeze-box doesn't answer, and Lieutenant Yeager's mouth organ is an abomination before God. We have a piano at headquarters and a trunk full of good Southern music going to waste."

"What are you offering him in return for all this entertainment?"

"His life. It's poor enough coin in these times, but it's all we can spare. Everything else goes to Richmond."

"You lie as easily as you do murder, Bloody Bill."

The look in Anderson's eye told me that he had run out of words. I rose to my feet, Templeton Deane's pistol dangling from my hand. "I will go."

"Don't be foolish, Billy. It is a secessionist trick." The shotgun had begun to sway. Soon she would find it too heavy to hold.

"Thank you for the hospitality of your house, Mrs. Patakos. It's time for me to move on."

She was silent for another moment. Then, slowly, she lowered the shotgun.

Anderson began replacing his charges from a pair of leather pouches he drew from his tunic. "Thrailkill."

The guerrilla kept me covered. "He's still heeled."

I offered him the butt of the revolver. After a pause he holstered his weapon and reached out to take it. I rotated the pistol.

Now he was staring down the muzzle. He bent his elbow to redraw, stopped. It was his own uncertain swiftness against the velocity of powder and ball.

Fast as thought, Anderson spun his own cylinder buzzingly with the heel of his hand and "threw down" on me. On the street a dozen or more hammers crackled in reply.

Again I spun the five-shot, and this time I slid my hand down to the end of the barrel.

Thrailkill hesitated, then took hold of the grip. When his grasp was secure he tore it out of my hand viciously.

Someone whooped. Laughter Gatlinged through the mob of killers. Even Sergeant Frank James grinned. Looking quizzical, Bloody Bill Anderson took his pistol off cock and returned his attention to the fired chambers. "You're rusty, Lieutenant," was his only comment.

The humiliated guerrilla thrust my revolver into his belt, wheeled, and stamped down the front steps in search of his horse, shoving James out of the way.

Beyond doubt, executing the border spin against John Thrailkill was the most foolhardy thing I had done since leaving home. I had been practicing the maneuver in private ever since it was shown to me by Captain Jack Fabian of the Pinkerton

National Detective Agency, and in the rush of the moment I had surrendered to the impulse to demonstrate how well I had learned it. In the course of things I had made an enemy for life.

I was allowed, under the close supervision of Sergeant Frank James, to roll my few possessions into a borrowed blanket—for the carpetbag was too bulky and awkward to carry on horseback—and say my farewells. My reception varied according to whom they were said.

Ada, distracted by the turmoil but still glowing over her conquest, smiled self-satisfaction at the flush that came to my face when I spoke to her, and pinched my freshly scrubbed cheek. "Sweet boy, listen to Ada's advice: Don't fire first unless you're in the field."

Veronica was openly hostile and left the parlor abruptly when I entered it. She had started the race as the favorite and was not of that breed that accepts defeat with grace.

Rachel was either haughty to the end or acutely conscious of her mixed blood in the presence of so many rampaging proslavers, for she did not come to her door when I knocked.

Of that crew, only the marble-skinned, raven-haired Carmel was cordial. The contest for my virtue had been a lark to her, nothing more, and we had shared too many a successful parlor concert for her to express anything but sweet sorrow at my leaving. She curtsied in the best Southern fashion and kissed me upon the cheek.

Isabel, stoic tyrant of the mop and dustpan, received my words of parting with a granite face. She appeared unmoved by the events of the morning. Panama Bob's death seemed not to concern her except perhaps for the fact that now she would have to clean up the mess herself. In her way, she was as ruthless as Quantrill.

Drucilla had retreated to her third-floor sanctum. When a full minute went past without an answer to my knock, I turned to go. Just then the lock snapped and the door opened inward six inches. The left half of her face alone was visible. Her eye went from me to the guerrilla sergeant standing behind me and back to my face. "Yes?"

"I am going now," said I.

"Yes."

"I am sorry about Bob."

Nothing changed in her expression.

"I wanted to thank you again before I left. But for you—"

"Yes."

The door closed. The lock snapped to.

"Women." James hooked his thumbs inside his gun belt. "Once they get started you can't shut them up."

Massacres do not cease for the sake of a hostage. I was escorted from Drucilla's to a house around the corner and shut up in the potato bin in the cellar with a guard posted outside while the raid continued. There in the humid darkness, accompanied by the smell of earth and vegetable decay and the occasional inquisitive rummaging of a rat, I sat on the end of a barrel and listened to the shots and cries from outside. What became of the people who lived in the house I did not know, but I suspected the worst. Later I learned that, far from a random and unplanned act of vengeance, the attack on Lawrence had been organized to the last detail and carried out according to a strict time schedule, with squads of guerrillas assigned to particular sections of the city, equipped with maps upon which the homes and businesses of individuals singled out for special punishment had been clearly marked. Quantrill himself had led the group that searched Senator Lane's house, and his parting request to Mrs. Lane to give his regards to her husband reflected a kind of restraint for which he was not generally known.

I did not mourn the loss of Robert Leslie LeFleur, *alias* Panama Bob; although I did feel responsible for his death. He was a thoroughgoing scoundrel, and if he indeed felt remorse for the black slaves he had drowned to spare his neck, as he had claimed, that same conscience had not seemed to plague him for the wrongs committed by the Redlegs with whom he rode. Murder and pillage in the name of freedom from chains did not strike me as more noble than similar injustices performed for the sake of states' rights. However, to remain idle with a weapon in one's hand while a man with whom one has lived and broken bread is slain horribly is not an act to look back upon with pride. True, I was confused and upset, and my brain was still saturated with sleep. Was the situation so different from the one in front of the New York Enrollment Office, when I had stepped forward without thinking to save the life of an unknown policeman, and then struck without hesitation to save my own? Had the horrors to which I had been exposed since that day broken my courage, rendering me unable to take decisive action when the danger became personal? These were not thoughts designed to comfort a boy trapped in the vile dark with visions of Bob's exploded head for company. I could still taste his gray matter upon my tongue, musky and sharp, like iodine.

Sunk in these reflections, I knew not how much time passed, and failed to notice when the hellish noises from the street began to fade. I came out of myself only when the hatch above my head was flung open and daylight gushed in, dazzling me.

I was aware of a number of figures standing between me and the light, but I could not tell how many, nor make out details of their faces or costume. Then one of them trotted down the short flight of rotting steps, kicked the barrel out from under me, sending me over onto my back in a pile of black dirt and desiccated potatoes, and snarled in John Thrailkill's voice: "Stand for Captain Quantrill, you Jayhawking son of a bitch!"

CHAPTER ELEVEN

In the matter of making the actual acquaintance of men and women whose reputations precede them—of being bitterly disappointed as opposed to finding all my expectations fulfilled—my score sheet is nearly even. Greta Garbo and Buffalo Bill Cody in person were even finer physical specimens than either their photographs or their legends suggested, while Sheriff Pat Garrett was a tall, stoop-shouldered gawk with a hook nose and an Adam's apple the size of a croquet ball, and none of the costly perfumes with which Lola Montez drenched herself, gifts of Austrian emperors and vice presidents of Mexico, could disguise the fact that she smelled like a coyote bitch in season.

William Clarke Quantrill—Antichrist, Death Angel, Avenger of Osceola, Slaughterer of the Innocents; call him what you will according to your sympathies—belonged to the category of disappointments.

When I first saw him he was a shadow against the sun, and even when I had ascended to ground level and stood before him he remained vague and largely without feature. He stood at average height, a slender figure in his tailored Confederate coat, belted at the waist and reaching to mid-thigh, with captain's bars on the high collar. He wore his reddish hair long and brushed back over the tops of his ears, and in the shadow of his tasseled campaign hat his complexion was fair beneath a smudge of dust and spent powder, his moustaches sparse and darkened with wax. His lids overhung his eyes, which were murky and indirect; dreamer's eyes, and not at all what one expected of a self-appointed seeker after retribution. The strongest impression I received was of a scent, faint but definite, underneath the mingled odors of horse and perspiration and sulfur, of violets.

I have looked in vain for a record of Quantrill's life that mentions the violets. I now believe I am the only man living who knows of them, and of the thin glass phials he carried inside his coat so that, riding at the head of his odoriferous column, he had only to reach inside and crush them to his chest to deliver himself from the stench of his own fellow guerrillas. These many years later, violets remain my least favorite fragrance, associated with sweet corruption.

"He's disarmed?" he asked, without looking away from me.

"Yes, sir. I took this off him." Thrailkill held out the ivory-handled revolver.

Someone snorted. I recognized Sergeant Frank James among the group. The lieutenant gave him a poisonous look.

Quantrill glanced at the weapon without taking it. He returned his attention to me. After an awkward moment Thrailkill put it back in his belt.

"Did Anderson happen to say why he wants this boy?" asked the guerrilla chief.

James spoke up. "Sir, he said we need somebody to play the piano back at headquarters."

A smoke-filled silence followed this information. My eyes began to sting.

Finally Quantrill stirred. He slid a pair of kid gauntlets from under his belt and pulled them on, taking care to press the ma-

terial tight between the fingers. "Make sure he understands the
prisoner is his responsibility."

"Yes, sir," James said.

"Personally I detest music."

"Yes, sir!" barked Thrailkill.

"What o'clock is it, Sergeant?"

James produced a watch from inside his tunic and popped
open the face. "Quarter of nine, Captain." He snapped it shut and
put it away.

"Tell the men to mount up. We're leaving." Quantrill turned
and, surveying the smoldering ruins of the buildings across the
street, astonished me by slipping into Latin:

> *"Impia tortorum longos hic turba furores*
> *Sanguinas innocu, non satiata, aluit.*
> *Sospite nunc patriâ, fracto nunc funeris antro,*
> *Mors ubi dira fuit vita salusque patent."*

In that barbaric arena, surrounded by creatures whom Panama
Bob had correctly identified as marauding pagans, I could not
have been taken further aback had a hydrophobic dog raised its
lathered and bloody chin and quoted Shakespeare. As if quizzed
by a tutor, I voiced an automatic reply:

> *"Nil sapientiae odiosius acume nimio."*

Quantrill's head snapped around. Interest flared in his eyes for
the first time; interest, and something else that until I knew him
better I would hesitate to name, but which in another I should
have called jealousy. He banked the fires quickly. "A scholar,"
said he.

"Merely a student," said I.

"Lieutenant, see that this man is treated with the courtesy reserved for a captured enemy officer."

"Hang him?" Thrailkill was eager.

"Not that kind of officer. I mean make him comfortable."

"Yes, sir."

When Quantrill left, the lieutenant snapped at James to carry
on and stalked away. The sergeant took my arm and we started
off down a street clogged with rubble and dead bodies in heaps.

I spotted Jim Perine, the clerk from the Country Store, sprawled atop one of them, one eye clotted with blood and his toes poking through a hole in his left sock. Flies had begun to convene in great glittering clouds.

"That was Roman you two was talking," Frank James said proudly. "I know a line or two myself. My pa was a Baptist minister and a man of learning. That old man was hell for Bach. I didn't catch none of what you said, though."

I translated Quantrill:

> *"Here the wicked mob, unappeased,*
> *long cherished a hatred of innocent blood.*
> *Now that the fatherland has been saved,*
> *and the cave of death demolished,*
> *where grim death has been, life and health appear.*

"It was a Royalist inscription, popular at the time of the Bourbon Restoration in France. It was a colorful choice." My voice sounded shallow in my ears. I was fighting to keep down my bile. Already the day was growing hot. Soon the corpses would begin to turn.

"What was that you said back?"

"It is from Seneca. 'Nothing is more disagreeable to wisdom than too much cunning.' "

He laughed, a short high bray. "That's the captain down to the ground. Always lets on to know more than he does. I'd bet a silver dollar to a horse turd he didn't feature a word."

"Why do you follow him if you do not respect him?"

"On account of he hates Yankees even more than I do."

We crossed Massachusetts Street in silence. The roof of the Eldridge House, a few doors down from Drucilla's, collapsed with a noise like a great tree falling, sending up a geyser of sparks and flaming debris. I was gratified to see that the house where I had spent the past three weeks was untouched. It appeared that unlike New York, where such establishments had been prime targets for vandalism and looting, on the border they were treated as neutral territory. In time I would come to regard those evenings of sentimental music in the parlor, and the pleasures upstairs, as a furlough for combatants weary of the killing fields.

"I daresay neither you nor your commander hates as deeply as Lieutenant Thrailkill," I said then. "He seems to abhor the universe."

"Well, he's got better reason than most. This here's your horse. Sorry I couldn't catch you a thoroughbred."

I recognized the sergeant's muscular bay hitched to the rail in front of the City House hotel, which remained intact, beside a swaybacked gelding with shaggy fetlocks and a milky eye. A worn blanket had been flung over its back, but nothing else.

"Where is the saddle?" I asked.

"Same place as the spring-wagon with the fancy red wheels. You're lucky you got a horse. It was Thrailkill running the show you'd be afoot, and barefoot besides."

"I haven't had much riding experience."

"Well, you come to the right place to get it."

Despite its truculent reputation, Quantrill's command was a miracle of military discipline. Every man was in his saddle with reins gathered by the time I finally got a leg up over the gelding. Bloody Bill Anderson, in charge of the division that included Thrailkill and James, trotted his roan to the end of the block and waited, pocket watch in hand, for the others to fall in, which they did with a minimum of confusion, considering that their saddle pouches and blanket rolls bulged with what was euphemistically referred to as the spoils of war. I saw silver candelabra, yards of gold chain coiled like lariats, and bolts of brightly printed fabric stashed behind cantles and bundled and strung from pommels. One red-whiskered corporal had tied a dozen white geese together by their feet and slung them across the throat of his saddle, their heads dangling like pompons from their wrung necks. A bellow of command, picked up and carried by relays to the rest of the column, and we were in motion. I rode sandwiched between Frank James and the rest of the division, hanging on tight to the rope hackamore with all my worldly *accoutrement* in a duvet tied at the ends with cord and balanced across my lap, a prisoner of a war for which I had no taste and in which I had no personal stake, and which a scant month earlier had seemed a thing as remote as an uprising in Russia. I had never felt farther from home, nor more abandoned by my God.

And then I felt ashamed; for as we moved down that street of glowing timbers, of bodies spread-eagled on the boardwalks and draped like quilts over the hitching rails, I saw the smudged, sweaty faces of widowed women and orphaned children staring out with vacant eyes at the moving column from alleys and through the windows of the buildings left standing, and knew myself fortunate to be alive. They were as dead as their husbands and fathers, many of them doomed to wander the place of their former happiness and security, gaunt shades of what once they were. And I knew then that any calculation of casualties, no matter how accurate, was only half the truth, that no battle ends with the last to die, and that no war takes place so far away from him who hears of it that he is unaffected by it. It scars us all as deeply and permanently as that part of Drucilla's face she turned from the light.

Lawrence was no longer the proud and orderly place I had come to at the end of July; nor would it be again, notwithstanding new construction and improved fortification. Its landmarks were in ruins, the surrounding corn and wheat fields intended to support it through the long winter set to the torch. In weeks its streets, once so well kept, would fill with beggars. All this was reversible and would be corrected in time. What could not be fixed was its stubborn Jayhawker heart. It had been torn out by the roots, spat upon, and trampled, and the watchworks that replaced it would not answer. This was Quantrill's legacy, and that of the war that spawned him: the murder not just of a city, but of the bumptious pioneer will upon which it was built.

Lawrence was dead. I was alive. I could not help but wonder which of us was the more fortunate.

Chapter Twelve

ର୍ଯ

As fate would have it, I was not to see the guerrilla headquarters or its piano for some time.

We were less than a day's ride east of Lawrence, moving at an easy canter to spare the horses, when one of the men

Quantrill had left behind to watch the back trail came galloping up on a lathered gray and reported breathlessly that Union troops were five miles to the rear. In less time than the most pessimistic predictions had allowed for, troops of the Eleventh Kansas Volunteer Cavalry out of Emporia had linked up with the Federals who were stranded when Quantrill took the ferry and were coming on hard under Colonel Preston B. Plumb. A number of stragglers at the rear of the guerrilla column were already in skirmish with the pursuers; the snap and pop of sporadic gunfire could be heard to the west. The commander's single-word order bounced back through the ranks like a ricocheting bullet: "Disband!"

Frank James quickly inspected the loads in each of the .36 Navy Colts he carried in a pair of scabbards attached to his saddle, then returned them to their sheaths. "It's every hog to its own tit, youngster," he said, gathering his reins. "Come or get lynched."

"But I am not a guerrilla!"

"That don't signify to the Eleventh Kansas. Them boys is mad as yellow jackets about now. If it's betwixt them and the border and it ain't wearing Lincoln's blue, they'll string it up or ride right on over it."

"Where are we going?"

"I'm going home. You don't have to come, though you'll be giving up the best corn bread in Missouri for a short trip from a high limb if you don't. Personally I don't give a possum's ass what you do, but as I got on Johnny Thrailkill's black side to save your scalp I figure I got to make the invitation. I damn sure ain't waiting for them Kansas boys to show up while you're deciding."

I was in turmoil. Sore from the ride and sickened by the events of that morning, but light-headed after nearly twenty-four hours without food, I was hardly in a state to make a lightning decision that was bound to affect my life. I don't know what I would have told him had not the clear ringing note of a bugle, warped by wind and distance, reached me at that instant from the direction of the sunset. I had a sudden, sharp vision of the Negro I had seen hanging from an awning post in New York, his head lolling from his broken neck.

"Which way?" I asked.

James grinned. "Where the Yankees ain't. Hang on!" Taking the ends of the hackamore from me, he tied them to his saddle ring and raked the bay's flanks with both spurs. It whinnied and bolted, and behind it the gelding, which would have pitched me off if I weren't hugging its neck with both arms. Around us the column had broken in three directions, some of the riders casting aside their heavier plunder in the interest of speed. For all that, it was an orderly rout. I remember thinking that if the enemy's *irregular* cavalry was this well organized, the Union would be a much longer time putting down the rebellion than was commonly believed back home. Then I noticed that we had turned, placing the sun directly to our left.

"Isn't this north?" I shouted.

He ducked to clear the low-slung limb of a sycamore. "Was last time I looked."

"That's Federal territory!"

"Where's the last place *you'd* hunt for Johnny Reb?"

At dusk we camped in a stand of trees at the top of a small hill. I was exhausted, for we had ridden hard for an hour and my tail-bone was without feeling; but James handed me a canvas bucket and his canteen and told me to walk down to the narrow creek at the foot of the hill and bring back water. "Don't wander off, now," he said. "These woods is full of two-legged coyotes'd slice off your pecker for a pipe."

When I returned, panting from the exertion, he relieved me of the bucket and handed me a hard biscuit. The surface was as sandy as granite.

"Soak it from the canteen before you bite into it. That is, unless you like spitting teeth."

The water softened the biscuit to the consistency of harness leather. The hinges of my jaws ached from chewing, but I ate every last morsel, to ease the feral clawing in my stomach. I asked if there was more.

He finished watering the horses and produced another biscuit from inside his tunic. "Just this, and it's mine. I'd fry up some bacon, but I can't risk a fire. Here." Reaching into the tunic again, he took out a dark oblong the size of his thumb, sawed off a piece with the bone-handled knife he carried on his belt, and held out the piece.

I took it and examined it, then tried to return it. "I don't chew tobacco."

"Didn't ask if you did. Chaw on it anyway. It'll give your juices something to work on besides your own gut." He put away the knife and tobacco plug and sat down on a moss-covered rock to eat his biscuit. "I guess you'll live on less before this war's done. Folks in Jefferson City was down to eating wallpaper when that son of a bitch Frémont declared martial law."

The tobacco was vile, as I was certain it would be: brackish and bittersweet to such a point that my stomach tried to reject the biscuit I had eaten. The juices backed up and filled my nasal passages, making my eyes water. Inadvertently I swallowed some and got up, retching, to purge what remained of the plug. I leaned heavily against a tree, hacking and sputtering and wiping my mouth with the back of my hand.

Frank James chuckled. "You put me in mind of my little brother. He's about your age; couldn't stomach the stuff neither. Last time I was home he begged for me to put in a word for him with Captain Quantrill. I said, 'Now, what kind of a guerrilla would you make? You can't even stick a piece of chaw in your mouth without heaving up your guts.' Well, he's got our ma's stubborn blood. I expect he'll be chawing and spitting like a muleskinner when I get back."

"Is that where we're going?" I felt dizzy and pale. I was afraid to abandon the support of the tree.

"Clay County, Missouri." He licked the crumbs from his fingers and cut himself a plug. "Poorest farm country you ever did see. Our pa never could raise hell on that plot of land we got. I reckon that's why he went to California and got himself dead. It was just too slow the other way."

"I thought you said he was a minister."

"That's even slower than scratching in the dirt. Preachers' kin lives on what the flock gives them. A piece of pigshit don't go no farther in Clay County than anywheres else. He went to dig for gold and dug his own hole instead. Pneumonia, they said."

"Your mother and your little brother work the farm alone?"

"We got us a stepfather. There was another one in between, but he hurt my brother's arm and I stuck him with a hay fork and he went away. Doctor Samuel, this one is. I never seen him do no doctoring, so I don't know if he's any good at it, but he's a fair enough farmer. Better anyhow than our pa ever was. This one grows things."

"What does he think about your riding with Captain Quantrill instead of staying home and working the farm?"

"Oh, he's for anything that's against the Yankees. So's everyone else in Clay County. It was a choice of go to the devil or turn Yankee, there ain't a man or a woman there wouldn't grow horns."

I pushed myself away from the tree at last and turned. "I'm a Yankee."

He spat a glittering stream and wiped his mouth. "That's because you don't know better. Where you from?"

"New York City."

"No shit. Where's that?"

"A long way from Clay County."

That was the end of the conversation. We spread our blankets on the ground and wrapped ourselves in them against the cold night air; for along with destruction and slaughter, Quantrill's horde had brought winter's first chill to the State of Kansas. Before drifting off, Frank James slid one of the Navy Colts from its scabbard on the saddle he was using for a pillow and laid it on his chest with his right hand closed around the butt.

I had thought that my first night ever on the stiff cold ground would be sleepless, but I was more tired than I was sore and hungry. I dreamed that I was back in my comfortable bed in my father's town house, awakening from a nightmare that I had been banished to a barbaric land. I waited for the soft knocking that told me Cook was outside my door with my breakfast on a tray. Instead a booted foot kicked my ankle and I opened my eyes to total darkness.

"On your feet, youngster," Frank James said. "It's coming on first light."

I rose staggering, stiff in the back and legs and shivering in the raw damp. My breakfast was not scones and coffee but a long icy draught from my keeper's canteen, intended to fool my gnawing stomach that it contained something more substantial. I watered the horses while James scuffed about, eradicating all signs of encampment, and then we were riding, guided by the first blade of metallic light in the east.

By dawn the pain in my insides had grown so sharp I feared my condition was serious. I had never before experienced true hunger of the life-threatening kind, had not imagined that it actually hurt so that one could think of nothing else; and I wondered what must it be like to go for days in such a state. Thirty-six hours only had passed since my last meal, I had had a biscuit in the interim, and I was in agony. I thought of the beggars I had passed so many times in the doorways and alleys of my home city, their heads wrapped in scarves and their grubby fingers protruding through holes in their gloves, and knew I had earned a week in Purgatory for each open palm I had passed without leaving a coin. Perhaps this was that penance.

The sun was above the trees when salvation arrived, though I failed to recognize it. We were riding down a shallow decline ending in a boggy marsh when James drew rein suddenly and leaned over to grip the gelding's makeshift bridle.

"Sing out if you lay eyes on anyone."

He took off at a canter before I could question him. Soon the marsh closed in behind man and horse, and for a quarter of an hour I was alone with the whistling birds and the occasional rustling from the direction of the bog. I nearly fell off my horse when a flock of grouse exploded from the tangle with a noise like a locomotive charging out of a tunnel. I remember wondering, when I recovered, if they tasted like partridge.

Presently my companion emerged from the underbrush, leading the bay and holding his campaign hat cradled in the crook of his free arm. As he drew near I saw that the hat's inverted crown was filled to the sweatband with blackberries.

"Bears live on this shit," he said as I dismounted and dug in with both hands. "You never hear of no bears starving to death. Slow down, now. You'll bloat up and bust like a horse. They don't know when to stop neither."

My fingers—and, I was sure, my face as well—were stained purple by the time I stopped eating long enough to speak. "I wondered why you didn't shoot those grouse."

"I didn't want to risk the shot. Anyway, we can't build a fire for the smoke. You can get mighty sick eating raw bird. They carry grubs and shit."

When we had both eaten our fill, he tied up the remaining berries in a bandanna and hung it from the horn of his saddle. "Ma might make a pie." He mounted. "We'll be eating grits and fatback by sundown."

We had swung east at morning, and crossed the Missouri border below Kansas City around noon. James said we'd go on to Independence, stake out a spot where we could see the ferry landing, and if no Union troops were in sight we'd cross the Missouri River and head straight north for Kearney and the Samuel farm nearby.

"Home," he said. "The air smells better already. In Kansas I hold my breath the whole time."

The road to Independence was hardpack, with dense forest on both sides. Our hoofbeats echoed off the wall of trees, the echoes feeding upon themselves and multiplying, as if we were a dozen instead of just two. The effect was mesmerizing; which may help to explain what happened next.

The road was too narrow for two horsemen to ride abreast comfortably, and so we had formed an Indian file with the guerrilla in front. Something pricked the back of my neck, I slapped at it automatically, and looked down at the smashed mosquito in my palm. When I flicked it away and looked ahead again, Frank James and his bay were gone.

I blinked like a child at a conjuring trick. That a horse and rider could just disappear without my seeing or hearing them was a phenomenon outside my experience and understanding. Yet the road in front was empty, and when I turned to see if they had somehow fallen behind I saw nothing but a ribbon of beaten clay with the branches of the trees latticed overhead, forming a natural tunnel. And the beat of my gelding's hooves came back and mocked me like malevolent spirits chuckling in the shadows.

And then I was not alone.

Thirty yards farther on, the road broadened where trees had been cleared for some civilizing project that had probably been cut short by the war. Just beyond where it began, moving like ghosts, noiselessly and with unearthly precision, two horsemen from one side and three from the other came out into the road from the thick cover and turned their animals to face me. They were dressed in blue, and each man held a side arm in his free hand.

"Well, I'm damned," said one as I drew rein before them. "Look what the wind blew up from the south; and us with all these pretty trees to tie a rope to."

CHAPTER THIRTEEN

The speaker was a six-stripe sergeant with the largest pair of handlebars I had ever seen, swooping past his ears and up at the ends on a level with his kepi. All of his companions sported facial hair as well, though none so impressively, and this together with an unmistakable look upon their sun-stained features identified them as veteran campaigners. I had perceived the identical quality in the visages of the men who rode with Quantrill: of having passed through a fire that had left their bodies intact while burning away their humanity. I saw little difference between them and the dumb resigned war-bitten faces of the horses they straddled.

"You see, boys," resumed the sergeant, "that's what I dislike most about Missouri: You can't walk in any direction without stepping in a mess of muleshit, and you can't step in a mess of muleshit without kicking up a bushel of secesh maggots like what we got here."

"I am no secessionist," I said.

"Shut your cake-hole and get them hands in the air."

I complied, protesting that I was unarmed.

"Horseshit. There ain't a one of you guerrilla trash don't pack more iron than a sow's got tits. Pat him down, Syke. Day's half shot already and we got us a lot of necks to stretch before we lose the light."

"We ain't got time to stretch even one, Sarge." The man mounted at the sergeant's right had a lean, simian face half-shadowed with beard. "We got to be in Kansas City by dark."

The sergeant let out a lungful of air. "That's a disappointment. Things have sure gone to hell when you can't take a minute to strangle a grit-eating bushwhacker. Well, hell." He raised his pistol and sighted down his arm.

A high-pitched shriek tore through the alley between the trees. A cloud of startled birds took to the air with a panicky chatter and a whoosh of wings. The horses pitched and reared. The sergeant hauled back on his reins, almost losing his grip on his weapon.

A hundred feet beyond, Frank James sat aboard his racing bay in the center of the road. His reins were clamped between his teeth and he held a Navy Colt in each hand.

"Yellow rebel trick!" cried the sergeant, turning his horse to meet this new threat.

While the others followed suit, I leapt to the ground and led the gelding up the bank into the trees. From there I had a clear view of what I like to call the Battle for the Independence Road.

The five were still turning when James galloped straight at them, coattails flying, muzzles flashing, a grinning Angel of Death charging through the smoke of his own fire. The Union men returned fire, but as they were still in the midst of regrouping none of them had time to take aim. The man called Syke cursed shrilly and clawed at his shoulder. Another man fell out of his saddle, and still another lost his kepi, but I could not tell if he was hurt. The smoke was as thick as cotton by the time the opposing sides met. For an instant I could not see what was happening. Then the guerrilla came out the other side, leaning back on the reins and heeling over to turn the bay. While the Union riders were untangling themselves, he leaned forward, dug in his spurs, and vaulted the bank not ten feet from where I crouched holding on to the gelding's hackamore.

At the top he stopped long enough to leather his revolvers and take the reins from his teeth. Then, with a significant look in my direction, he took off through the woods, keeping his head low to avoid the boughs.

I mounted and followed, kicking into a gallop when a rattle of belated reports sounded from the road. I could hear the pistol balls skipping through the branches overhead.

We rode hard for two miles. Then, in a broad clearing rutted with the overgrown furrows of an abandoned field, James stopped to let his horse blow. I stopped alongside.

"Won't they keep coming?" I was gasping for breath.

"No. They got wounded to see to, and Kansas City to make before sundown. That kind don't put theirselves out if they don't have to. It was just our sore luck to stumble right on top of them. My fault. I let down my gate when we left Kansas."

"But you knew they were waiting for us. That's why you left, to circle behind them."

"I guessed. It was a likely spot for what they had in mind. I should of seen it sooner."

"You used me as a decoy."

"Had to. They heard us coming, though they didn't know how many we was on account of the echoes. I needed something to keep them occupied. Lucky that sergeant's a talker."

"I don't mind telling you I was terrified."

"Don't never stand still for it, that's my advice. If you come on hard enough and fast enough, folks will generally clear you a path. Nobody wants to die when you come down to it."

"I'm not angry for what you did," I said. "You could have kept going after you left the road."

He cut himself a chew and offered me the plug, shrugging when I didn't take it. "Don't set yourself up too high, youngster. I didn't join up with the captain to turn tail and run when I see Yankees." He returned the tobacco to his tunic and took up his reins. "Also I aim to hear me some more of that Bach." He clucked the bay into a walk.

The sun was close to the horizon, spreading molten copper light over the swelling country below, when Frank James leaned down from the saddle and unlatched a whitewashed wooden gate bearing a sign whose hand-painted legend read:

SAMUEL FARM

NO TRESPASSING
HUNTING
PEDDLERS

"Are you expected?" I asked.

"Nobody's expected me anywhere since 1861."

As if in confirmation, drawing within sight of an L-shaped one-story frame house with a corral and barn standing nearby, we were greeted by a thick-waisted, brown-haired figure in a simple dress standing on the long front porch with a twin-barreled shotgun raised to her shoulder.

"Around here we pay attention to signs!" the woman called out in a voice surprisingly strong and full of timber.

James drew rein, signaling for me to do the same, and cupped a hand around his mouth. "You're getting old, Ma! I remember when you could pick a coyote out of a dog pack at a thousand yards."

"Alexander Franklin, is that you?"

"I asked you not to call me that in front of company, Ma."

"Who is that with you?"

"Well, promise me you won't blow him out from under his hat and I'll introduce you."

She lowered the shotgun. "Come ahead, then."

We approached at a walk. James swung down before the porch and mounted the steps to embrace his mother, who rested the shotgun's butt on the boards and patted his back with her free hand. When they parted, she studied him from head to foot. "You've been forgetting to eat. How do you expect to kill your share of Yankees if you will not keep up your strength?"

"Why don't you rustle up some of your fatback and corn bread and put me right? I been bragging on your cooking to Billy here for sixty miles."

Now she turned her attention to me. A large woman with a straight back, she gave the impression of having been weathered by care and hard work rather than age—for I placed her close to forty, although she could have passed for older—with graying hair and sharp lines in her broad forehead and at the corners of her eyes. I had the suspicion that if she untied the black ribbon that held her hair in place behind her head her face would collapse. As she turned, I realized with a start that she was in a family way; the swelling in her abdomen beneath the plain dress was slight but unmistakable. I averted my eyes. Pregnancy in those days was a thing to be endured behind closed doors.

Her gaze remained on me, bright and wary. "Who is Billy?"

I removed my hat, an old sweat-stained felt with a flop brim, borrowed from Drucilla Patakos' store of male garments left behind by their owners. "Billy Gashade, ma'am."

"Say something more."

I searched my brain. "You have a handsome farm."

"I don't like the way he talks."

"It ain't his fault, Ma. Billy's from New York City."

Her grip tightened on the barrels of the shotgun. "Yankee?"

"I brung him from Lawrence. He's a prisoner."

"You brought a Yankee to our home?"

"He plays piano, Ma. Wait'll you hear him."

She slapped his face. The noise was like a pistol shot.

"The Yankee militia was here in the spring," she said without emotion. "They claimed we were carrying information to the guerrillas. They tied a rope around your stepfather's neck and hauled him up in that tree four times to get him to talk." She pointed at a heavy-trunked pecan in the yard. "When he refused they kicked him on the ground and broke his ribs. They called me names I would not call a nigger, and me carrying your stepfather's child. Then they rode out to the field where your brother was plowing and slashed him with quirts. Last month, with Reuben still bedridden and your brother in Kearney buying flour, they came back and arrested me and put me in jail in St. Joseph."

"How'd you get out?" He stroked his cheek, which bore the red imprint of her hand.

"They let me out when they saw it wasn't going to do any good. They knew when they put me in I wouldn't say anything. They just wanted to bring me down. That's the Yankee way. They respect neither women nor honor. And now you've brought one to our house."

"Billy ain't one of them, Ma. Captain Anderson seen that himself or he'd of let Johnny Thrailkill blow his brains out when he was busting to."

"Bill Anderson stopped him? Bloody Bill?" She looked at me now with curious interest.

" 'Bring him.' Those was his exact words."

"Were," she corrected. "I did not give up an hour after supper every night for eight years teaching you grammar to hear you speaking like Jayhawker trash."

"Yes, ma'am."

She was still studying me. "Well, he knows enough not to step down uninvited."

Frank James risked a grin. "I reckon even a Yankee respects a Southern woman with a scattergun."

"Tell him to step down. I cannot cook with a crick in my neck."

I alighted from the gelding, grateful to be on my feet once again. In addition to sores on my backside, I had developed an irritation inside my thighs from the rough material of the blanket and the salty lather shed by the horse.

"Your brother will be along directly," Mrs. Samuel said. "He and Leander are out with the team, pulling stumps."

"Ain't the doctor up to it yet?"

"Isn't. He is a slow healer. You will find the basin out back. Wipe your boots before you come through the kitchen. I will not have you tracking Kansas into my house." She looked at me. "I apologize for my inhospitality, Mr. Gashade. Prisoner or not, you are here at my son's invitation. You will be treated as a guest." Swinging the shotgun under her arm, she turned toward the door. "It's good you're home, son."

"You'll never know how good, Ma."

We led the horses to the barn and rubbed them down with burlap sacks hanging on the stalls. Frank pitched hay down from the loft with a three-tined fork that might have been the one he had used to drive his first stepfather from the farm, and we carried our belongings around to the back of the house. There we found a young black woman in a faded print dress with her hair tied up in a kerchief pouring water into a blue enamel basin on a plank laid across two sawhorses. When she finished she curtsied before each of us, then hung the bucket on the spout of the pump nearby and went inside through the back door.

Minutes later, scrubbed, buttoned, and our boots duly wiped on a straw mat outside the door, we followed her. We were in a spacious, immaculate kitchen, with broad pine floorboards scoured white, a black iron stove with a warming oven on top, and a square painted table with a red-and-white-checked oilcloth and ladderback chairs all around. The young Negress was setting the table with blue china and Mrs. Samuel was at the stove, stirring a pot. The mingled smells of hot grease and warm bread reawakened the dormant gnawing in my stomach.

When we entered, a tall, spare, white-bearded man, many

years Mrs. Samuel's senior, came forward from the opposite doorway and switched hands on his cane to shake Frank's hand. His gray homespun shirt was buttoned to the throat and he wore his woolen trousers supported not with braces in the manner of a farmer or a store clerk, but with a broad brown glossy leather belt.

"I hear you gave those Jayhawkers what-for," he said by way of greeting.

"I never will feature how news travels twice as fast as a good horse."

That ended the conversation between stepfather and stepson for a while. The two appeared ill at ease in each other's company, without being hostile. Frank introduced me briefly. Dr. Samuel nodded with what seemed genuine courtesy, but did not offer his hand. I saw that he had a house pallor, yet the leathery look of his face told me he was accustomed to being outdoors. I thought of his ordeal at the hands of the militia. Many a healthy Easterner would have died from a lesser shock.

We were just sitting down at the table when the back screen swung open and a youth about my age walked in from the yard. He wore dirty overalls over a stained shirt and his longish brown hair was slicked back with water from the basin. I recognized his mother's fineness of feature, but the disconcerting directness of his gaze—apparently a James family trait—was developed to an even greater degree than his mother's and his brother's. A handsome boy with a girlish complexion, a proud lift to his chin, and something of a whiff of brimstone about him which at the time I attributed to his daylong exposure to the sun while clearing his late father's land for crops. It was a scent that would never leave him until his last days, when its absence would prove fatal.

But his grin was as bright and guileless as any boy's when he laid eyes upon his brother. "Buck!"

Frank leapt to his feet with a rebel whoop and bounded around the table to seize the youth's hand. After a minute or so of horseplay, pummeling shoulders and attempting to lock their arms around each other's head—cut short by a sharp word from their mother—the brothers, farmer and guerrilla, stood side by side facing the table. Frank said, "I want you to meet the pet Yankee I brung you."

"Brought." Mrs. Samuel passed a bowl of steaming boiled potatoes to her husband.

Frank ignored the correction. "Jesse, this here's Billy Gashade, from New York City. Billy, this here's my baby brother, Jesse James."

CHAPTER FOURTEEN

M rs. Samuel was as good a cook as advertised. Unaccustomed as I was to the rich, heavy food of that region— pork slices dripping with fat, biscuits swimming in gravy, and pies of every description—I filled my plate twice and mopped it clean both times with spongy corn bread. After supper Nettie, the Negro maid, washed the dishes while the rest of us retired to the well-appointed parlor. There, under clouds of smoke from Dr. Samuel's cigar, I sat at the piano, a fine old upright with inlaid ebony panels and polished brass pedals, and played a host of songs from a dog-eared stack of sheets tied together with ribbon, which Mrs. Samuel took from a cedar trunk. These included such standards as "Amazing Grace," "The Blue Tail Fly," and that exquisite medieval folk ballad "Barb'ra Allen," which had also been a favorite at Drucilla's among those whose parents had left ancestral homes in England and Ireland to settle the area. There were others with which I was not familiar, such as "The Gospel Train" and "The Hunters of Kentucky," a rousing celebration of the Battle of New Orleans that had accompanied Mrs. Samuel from her Kentucky birthplace after she wed the Reverend James.

And to show my gratitude to Frank for having saved my life on the Independence Road, I played "The Bonnie Blue Flag." I thought it significant that this was the only selection of the evening to which the assembly did not give voice, listening instead in the heavy silence of their own reflections. I was learning that the closer one moved to the actual fighting, the less likely he was to hear others sing of its glories.

Young Jesse had a particularly good voice, light but broad-ranged, and indescribably sweet during those passages where he overcame his natural self-awareness. His brother's was deeper but confined to a single half octave, and their mother, a contralto, dropped out on the high notes. Dr. Samuel had no ear at all and hummed when he didn't know the lyrics, which he frequently did not. Of that family, I felt its youngest member had the best chance at a career in music, provided he received the proper training. I have always believed that the world lost a good tenor when Jesse James took to robbing stages instead of appearing on them.

One song that was not to be found in the stack, and which I was never asked to play in all the time I spent with Confederate sympathizers, was "Dixie." I now attribute this to the song's Northern origins, to its composition by a Yankee named Daniel Decatur Emmett in New York, and, somewhat confusingly, to its popularity in Richmond. Along the border there existed a native distrust of the rebel capital and of all things Virginian; and if the anti-abolitionist element in Missouri chose to stand with the Old Dominion against a common foe, as had the Irish with England in the time of Napoleon, this did not erase the common feeling among these simple farmers, many of whom had never owned nor even seen a slave in the flesh, that Jefferson Davis and his West Point generals held themselves above the ordinary run of soldiers with dirty fingernails who fought and bled for the "land o' cotton."

Many years later this information enabled me to spot a fraud. In my early days in Hollywood, the bistros teemed with colorful old characters cadging drinks from gullible listeners with their blood-and-thunder "personal" accounts of life on the old frontier. One white-stubbled scarecrow, wearing a moth-eaten Confederate greatcoat and shouting "Dixie" at the top of his lungs, was rescued from a sordid walk-up speakeasy on Yucca Avenue by an executive producer at RKO, who hired him as technical advisor on a Civil War film on the strength of his boast that he was the last surviving member of Quantrill's Raiders. My attempts to discredit him based on his fondness for a tune despised by all true guerrillas were failures: Telephone calls to the executive producer went unanswered, an assistant director kept me waiting in his outer office for two hours, then listened to me for five minutes before glancing at his watch and announcing he was late for a luncheon appointment with John Gilbert. A letter to Will Hays, president of the Motion Picture Producers and Distributors Association of America, brought a polite reply that since the employment of a bogus night rider did not violate the Production Code he was not in a position to do anything about it, but asked me to keep an eye on the project and report "anything of an indecent nature." At this point I abandoned my crusade. Sometime later a writer with *Photoplay* unmasked the charlatan as a retired streetcar conductor from Ohio who before his sixty-fifth birthday had never ventured west of Cincinnati. The unpleasant publicity frightened off the bankers, the production was shelved, and the executive producer took a job in radio. All because the people in charge chose to ignore the wrong old man.

I should point out that this prejudice against Virginians did not extend to Robert E. Lee, whose framed lithograph occupied a place of pride in the James-Samuel household between an age-varnished miniature of one of Zerelda Samuel's Scottish ancestors ("Zerelda" being the mother's Christian name, and one of frequent recurrence in the family) and Dr. Samuel's diploma from the Kansas City School of Medicine. Like many of her neighbors, Mrs. Samuel, who boasted a great-grandfather from the pluckier Virginia of the American Revolution, considered General Lee a noble throwback to the spirited men and women who led the first fight for independence. I have seen two wars since those days of North versus South, and read of many more, and none has shown so many sides.

My first evening in Missouri was a success. Frank slapped me on the back, and this time the doctor shook my hand. Mrs. Samuel unbent so far as to apologize for having to put me up in the barn for lack of room in the house. "I will have Nettie bring you blankets. The nights here are capricious in late summer."

Jesse said nothing. His eyes spoke volumes. Plainly, it had been a long time since music had been heard in that house, and longer still since he had been able to behave as a boy of sixteen, as he had during the roughhouse with his brother Frank, whom I never heard him address by any name other than "Buck." My

memory of Jesse at this time is of a shy youth, awkward and un-
sure of himself in the presence of strangers, yet one who seemed
older than his years. As much as I had seen and been through
since leaving behind my life in the East, I sensed that bleak
scenes and personal hardship were to him a part of the natural
order. His whipping in the field, the abuse of his mother, and his
stepfather's torture were not unique in the county of Clay. He
was and always would be just outside my ken. Friendly we
would be, but we would never be friends. All this I suspected
within minutes of our first acquaintance.

I slept well that night. The blankets brought to me by the
black girl, together with the sweet-smelling hay in the vacant
stall where I made my bed, insulated me against the dampness
of the night and cushioned my sore muscles. With my belly full
for the first time in days I drifted into a warm black void. Months
would pass before I dreamed again of home, by which time its
details had acquired the pastel, unreal quality of an illustrated
Alice.

> *"We are a brand of brothers, and native to the soil;*
> *fighting for the property we gained by honest toil.*
> *And when our rights were threatened,*
> *the cry rose near and far:*
> *'Hurrah for the Bonnie Blue Flag that bears a single star!*
> *Hurrah! Hurrah! For Southern rights hurrah!*
> *Hurrah for the Bonnie Blue Flag that bears a single star!' "*

In the bronze light of midday, with the gold and emerald belts
of wheat and corn stretching to the hardwoods that crowned the
hills to east and west, the evening's melancholy was forgotten,
and stripped to the waist, the muscles in his lean back working,
Frank James shoveled shit through the back door of the barn
into a big pile outside and sang of war's glories. In the yard I
sank the axe into the chopping block and bent to scoop up some
pieces of split maple that had rolled off the heap and collected
around my feet. I was becoming an adept at the chore of chopping wood.

"What do you do with the manure when the pile gets too big?"
I asked.

"Well, the corn that made the meal that went into that

bread you been eating didn't just grow from sun and rain and please-God."

"Oh."

"Everything a farm produces it uses." He fished a red bandanna from his hip pocket and mopped his face. "The shit goes into the corn, the corn goes into us, the shucks go into the horses and come out shit."

"What about the cobs?" I grinned.

He showed me his teeth back. "You been here three days. Don't tell me you ain't seen the inside of the outhouse by now."

Had anyone told me a week before that I would soon be living with one of Quantrill's bushwhackers, much less enjoying my stay, I would have assumed he'd been into Panama Bob's rum. My days were filled with hard work and substantial food prepared by a cook as good in her way as any chef in Manhattan; my evenings were spent at the piano, where at Frank's request I worked the fugues of Johann Sebastian Bach in among the sentimental compositions of Stephen Foster and rough-hewn Ozark ballads by anonymous but gifted illiterates dead since before Yorktown; my nights were pleasant oblivion, thoroughly earned for perhaps the first time in my life. I imagined myself to be growing lean and muscular, my voice deepening. It was a fact that when I scrubbed my face over the basin in the backyard I encountered cottony wisps on my cheeks and upper lip that told me I would be borrowing Frank's razor before long. In this I was more precocious than Jesse, who watched me stroking my face with envy in his whole carriage. Despite his twelve-hour days working in the sun with Leander, the Negro farmhand employed by the Samuels, his skin remained fair and fine on the underside of his jaw and across the top of his forehead where his hat rested, and he had yet to sprout his first whisker.

His jealousy was misplaced. When it came to life in that open country he excelled in areas where I could hope to be no more than adequate.

His horsemanship was one. Frank and I looked up from our toils to see Jesse racing in from the far field aboard one of the mules he and Leander had hitched to the wagon that morning: Head down, back hunched, his knees drawn up to his chest, he whipped the old gray jack up over the last hill and into the yard, where at the last second he leaned back on the reins and leapt off. He hit the ground running and stopped six feet short of the barn.

"What'd you think?" he asked his brother. He was out of breath, his face aglow.

"I think you better not let Ma catch you riding old Pete that way. They're eating mules younger'n him in Vicksburg."

"You know what I mean. I can ride as well as any guerrilla, and you know I can shoot."

"Can you chaw?"

"Cut me a plug and I'll show you."

Frank winked my way. "I ain't real sure there's going to be any more guerrillas, Jess. We done broke up after Lawrence. There's going to be hell to pay from the Yankees when we bunch up again."

"When you do I'm bunching right up with you. If you try to leave me behind I'll just follow you."

"If you try it you'll cross your own trail so many times you'll meet yourself both ways."

"Buck, there isn't a man alive who can throw me off his scent."

"You're a good tracker, for a fact."

"I'm the best you ever saw."

"It don't signify if you are. The Yankee army ain't hard to track." Frank tipped me a grin. "What you say, Billy? If I show up at headquarters with this sprout, is the captain going to strip me to my boots and run me over the border on a splintery old rail or what?"

"What are you asking him for? He's a Yankee, and greener'n gooseshit to boot."

That took the starch out of me, for I thought I'd done a fair job of assimilating in a short amount of time; but then there is no deceiving the child of pioneers. As rough as my outer skin became in later years, frontiersmen to the manner born frequently guessed my origins. In the places and situations God had in store for me, that intangible thing my father always spoke of as good breeding would often work to my detriment.

"He's green, all right, but he knows enough to keep his yap buttoned about things he don't know from a squirrel's ass, which is more'n I can say for a certain baby brother."

"Who you calling baby, you horsetail-faced monkey?" Jesse shot back; and in another moment the James boys were grappling in the dust and manure inside the barn.

"Stop that right now! I thought I raised two sons, not a pair of razorback hogs."

Fascinated by the spectacle of two healthy hillmen locked in combat who knew more than a thing or two about wrestling, I had taken no notice when Dr. and Mrs. Samuel rattled into the yard on the seat of the family buckboard and braked to a halt. Immediately the boys broke off and climbed to their feet, brushing the debris from their clothes.

"Ma, I didn't expect you back by daylight," Frank said, striding out to meet them. "Did you pick up some Levi Garretts?"

"Never mind your damn tobacco! What if we were the militia? You'd both be strung up like hams by now. I'm surprised you've lasted this long with no more sense than you've acquired serving with Captain Quantrill."

Zerelda Samuel continued in this vein for another minute, lifting the dark skirts she wore into Kearney to climb down from the buckboard. The cloak she had donned to disguise her pregnancy had collected dust in the folds, testifying to a hard ride from town. Dr. Samuel kept his seat—preferring to wait there, evidently, for his wife's decision to go inside the house rather than stand around supporting himself upon his cane. I listened in silence, struck dumb by the intensity of her diatribe. I had never heard her curse before that day. Her sons were equally cowed. I shall forever retain that picture of Bloody Bill Anderson's loyal sergeant, who scant days before had been up to his elbows in slaughter, and his brother, whose name would one day sear across the Western states like a flaming brand, standing with heads bowed while an irate woman enumerated their sins against intelligence. I fully believe I am the only man living who saw them so.

"What happened in Kearney?" Frank's question, dropped meekly into the ringing stillness that followed the censure, was as a pebble come to rest atop a rockslide. It had the curious effect of tranquilizing his mother, who replied in a tone of icy calm.

"They are posting these all over." She drew from beneath her cloak a cylinder of stiff paper, which Frank unrolled, then read aloud from the text printed upon it. The words were black and smudged, but they might have been written in letters of fire for the information they contained.

CHAPTER FIFTEEN

Among my small collection of souvenirs from my early days on the frontier is a brown and flaking document, disintegrating along the folds, headed "General Order Number 11." I here record its main provisions, which had the devastating effect of an artillery barrage directed against the homes and businesses located in four Missouri counties in the summer of my sixteenth year—and, by projection, upon the history of the Western United States for the next two decades:

Headquarters District of the Border,
Kansas City, August 25, 1863.

1. All persons living in Jackson, Cass, and Bates Counties, and in that part of Vernon included in this district . . . are hereby ordered to remove from their present places of residence within fifteen days from the date hereof.

Those who within that time establish their loyalty to the satisfaction of the commanding officer of the military station near their present place of residence . . . will be permitted to remove to any military station in this district, or to any part of the State of Kansas, except the counties of the eastern border of the state. All others shall remove out of the district. Officers commanding companies and detachments serving in the counties named, will see that this paragraph is promptly obeyed.

2. All grain and hay in the field or under shelter, in the district from which inhabitants are required to move, within reach of military stations after the 9th day of September next, will be taken to such stations and turned over to the proper officers there. . . . All grain and hay

found in such district after the 9th day of September next, not convenient to such stations, will be destroyed. . . .

> By Order of Brigadier General Ewing.
> H. Hannahs, Adjutant General.

"What's it mean?" asked Jesse when his brother had finished reading.

"Confiscation."

Four pairs of eyes swung upon Dr. Samuel, who rarely spoke up on any subject of importance. The head of the household sat stiffly erect on the buckboard seat, face taut, his knuckles white on the crook of his cane.

"Confiscation is the legal term," he went on. "The military calls it requisitioning, or commandeerment. However you say it they mean to claim the western district from the citizens of Missouri. Some of the grain and hay will be used to feed Federal troops and their stock. The rest will be sold back to us at three times its value and the profit will go into the Redlegs' pockets. Some of the houses and barns will be used to quarter officers and horses and supplies. They will put the torch to the others. General Ewing means to eliminate those places where guerrillas may find concealment and rest, if it means starvation and exposure to hundreds who never raised a hand against the damned striped banner.

"That's the Yankee way," he finished, averting his eyes, as if embarrassed by the attention he had drawn.

"He is right," said Mrs. Samuel. "It is just an excuse for looting. Posting their intentions doesn't change anything."

Frank rerolled the document and bent it in the middle with his fists. "I reckon this is the payout for Lawrence."

"It doesn't mention Clay County," I said.

Now I became the attraction. My presence appeared to have been forgotten.

"That don't mean it don't touch us," Frank said.

I felt shamed and foreign. New York, with its self-contained town houses, neighborhoods, and immigrant communities—four hundred thousand individuals sequestered upon an island seven miles long and three miles wide, yet cordoned off into independent units as thoroughly as the hundred principalities of

Europe—was a far cry from this country of cousins. Prick the skin of one, and hundreds bled.

Mrs. Samuel said, "The militia will be back here with blood in their eyes. They will take this to mean the Federals are behind them. This time they will not be content with abuse and torture. They will ransack the house and barn and ride down the rows with sabers."

"This time we'll be ready," Jesse put in. "I'll take off the head of the first Redleg that sets foot on our property with a double load of buckshot."

His mother shook her head. "You will not be here to do that."

"I'm sixteen, Ma. I'm not going to crawl down some hole and hide like a rabbit."

"Of course not. You have Cole blood in you, and no member of my family ever ran from a fight with right on his side. You are going with Frank."

Frank lifted his eyebrows. "Where am I going?"

"You are going back to Captain Quantrill. Do not pretend you don't know where he is. Guerrillas always have a plan."

"When was you ever a guerrilla?" Her older son was amused.

"Were. I was born a guerrilla, of guerrillas. My great-grandfather was one before there was a name for it. Your father taught you to turn the other cheek, like Jesus, but it was I who read you the story of Jesus at the temple. He was the first guer-rilla."

Jesse said, "What will happen to you and the doctor here alone?"

"We will let them search the farm. The God-fearing have nothing to hide. They know from the last time your stepfather will tell them nothing even at the end of a rope, so they will not try that again."

"You can't be sure of that," Frank said. "A yellow dog will go after the same porcupine before his snout is through healing."

"Not if he is shot first." Zerelda Samuel raised the double-barreled shotgun from under her cloak.

"You took that to town?" Frank was grinning.

"She took it into the dress shop," said Dr. Samuel. "She had it with her in the changing room."

"Hell, Ma, why don't I leave Jesse here and take you with me? The captain can send half the boys home for Thanksgiving."

She shook her finger in his face. "Don't blaspheme."

Still grinning, he shook his head. "Sprout, I reckon you're in. I sure hope you can shoot Yankees the way you pick jars off a fence."

"The first fight we get into I'll shoot one for each of the welts on my back." Jesse's brow was dark.

"Shoot one for me while you're at it," said Dr. Samuel.

Now Jesse smiled, but there was still no mirth in him. "I'll shoot four for you. That's how many ribs they broke."

Frank said, "The first time you get inside gun range of a Yankee trooper, you'll be bare-ass lucky to come away with your hide. They don't just stand there like turkeys."

"Neither will I," his brother assured him.

Mrs. Samuel looked at me, and her eyes warmed. "Billy, you are free to leave anytime you choose. This is not your war."

"Ma, what am I going to say to Captain Anderson when he asks what become of the piano player? My mother let him go?"

"Tell him he broke away. God didn't give Billy music to see him slain on a battlefield for a cause that means nothing to him."

"He didn't give it to him to see him swinging from some old sycamore neither. He won't get two miles before some abolitionist bastard hangs him for a secessionist or some ignorant bastard hangs him for a Jayhawker or some just plain bastard hangs him for the shade. I seen a lot of necks but I never seen one looks so easy to stretch as Billy's."

"If he stays here the militia will hang him," his mother pointed out.

"I will go with Frank and Jesse."

Once again I became the center of the small gathering. This embarrassed me. Then as now, the only time I felt comfortable under public scrutiny was when I made music. "Forgive me for speaking out of turn," I said. "I don't covet being talked about as if I were not present."

Frank had cut himself a plug during the discussion. Now he nearly choked on it laughing. "You're no guerrilla nor ever will be," he said when he recovered. "Jesse ain't, but he's so mule-headed he won't fall down the first ten times he gets shot, and that's what makes a guerrilla. First time you get shot, you won't be able to think of nothing to do but die."

"I don't plan to fight. As Mrs. Samuel said, this isn't my war.

My weapon is the piano. That's what Captain Anderson wanted me for in the first place."

"I was just joshing when I said that. He won't remember you. Anderson carries six pistols at a time. He don't check the loads. When he wants to know is there a live round in a chamber he points it at the nearest Yankee and jerks the trigger. See, he counts Yankees cheaper than the ball and patch and powder and cap. He sees you, maybe he wants to hear you play piano, maybe he wants to see if he remembered to reload. That's why they call him Bloody Bill."

"Does Captain Quantrill encourage that?"

"Hell, for all I know he *taught* him that."

"Don't you want to go home, Billy? Your mother must be sick with worry." Mrs. Samuel rearranged her cloak to cover the shotgun.

"My mother has been sick for as long as I can remember. My coming home won't make her well."

"That isn't what I asked."

"I want to go home," I said. "Trouble is waiting for me there, but that's not the reason I won't go back. If I do, I'll be living in my father's house, taking music lessons my father paid for. When I have learned enough to make my living as a musician, my first appearance will be arranged by a friend of my father's."

"Runs you from pistol to finish, does he?" Frank spat a stream of brown juice at the base of the woodpile.

"Only because I have never tried to run on my own. The trouble I got into was the first thing I have done in my life that was not his idea. Until recently I thought it was a mistake. If it weren't for that I wouldn't be doing what I'm doing now."

"It was a mistake all right. There's plenty worse jobs than chopping wood but if I had my choice I'd watch somebody else chop it for me."

"All my life someone has chopped wood for me, cooked for me, dressed me and washed my clothes. All the time my country was ripping apart at the seams I was complaining to my valet about the crease in my trousers. I didn't know the significance of being alive until I saw my first dead man hanging from an awning. Look." I showed him my palms.

Frank took one and rubbed his thumb over the fresh blisters.

"Them ain't nothing. A little goose grease'll take the sting right out of them."

"I don't intend to do anything with them. I want to feel what it's like to have calluses." I took back the hand. "My father judges men for his living. I wonder how he would judge me if I were to go back now and take up my life exactly where I left off."

"You cannot live for your father," said Mrs. Samuel.

"I cannot live because of him, either. Or I shouldn't. I don't know how else to put it. I don't think I could stand to watch my hands grow soft and smooth as if I'd never swung an axe or hoisted a sack of grain to my shoulder or pointed a pistol at a man."

Frank looked down, then walked two yards to the corral and scraped manure off his boot heel onto the bottom log of the fence that enclosed it. "I reckon I just don't feature you, Billy. I seen more men hung than I got buttons on my underdrawers, and the onliest thing I ever got from it was a bucket of glad it wasn't me up there dancing on top of the weather."

Mrs. Samuel put a hand on my shoulder. "Frank and Jesse's father proposed to me in a convent. I never looked back."

"When do we leave?"

Jesse's impatience was obvious, as was his resentment that someone else had claimed center stage. I had already observed in him a strong need to be the object of everyone's consideration. It would be the pattern of his life until he was no longer in a position to change.

"Don't saddle up just yet, Jess. We still got wheat and corn to get in and a heap of wood to chop for winter."

Mrs. Samuel said, "Leander will see to that. If he requires help we will hire a temporary hand, perhaps a boy from one of the families that have been turned out. We shall have our pick of those soon."

"What's the matter, Ma, we getting on your nerves? We got two weeks."

"The Yankees have never been true to their word in the past, written or spoken. There will be troops crawling all over the county by the end of the week. If you leave within the hour you should be across the Middle Fork by nightfall. By Friday you will be in Arkansas."

"What makes you think we're headed that direction?" Frank asked.

The look Zerelda Samuel gave her son might have been one she had used when he was slow to grasp a lesson after supper. "Everyone in this part of Missouri knows Quantrill winters in Texas."

"Everyone except General Ewing," remarked Dr. Samuel; and for once he had the last word in a family discussion.

CHAPTER SIXTEEN

T exas!
        The very name was exotic to a native New Yorker, as remote-sounding as Babylonia and Old Cathay, and filled my imagination with heroic figures and images: Davy Crockett, Jim Bowie, and Colonel Travis defending the ramparts of the Alamo; running battles between the Texas Rangers and Comanche Indians; Sam Houston and the victory of San Jacinto. Those two syllables were synonymous with the deeds of tall men with big guns and knives and eyes like shards of flint in faces burned brown by the sun. All through our preparations to leave and during the journey through the breathtaking steep green Ozark hills of southern Missouri and Arkansas and the plains and creeks of the Indian Nations, I had visions of vast deserts and brilliant sky, of ferocious sandstorms and acres of cactus and painted savages on horseback with scalps fluttering from their lances.

The reality was far different, although hardly less dramatic.

Our leave-taking was brisk and, considering that one of us was a boy going off to war for the first time, not overtly sentimental. Zerelda Samuel divided a salted ham three ways, baked biscuits, and wrapped them in greased paper and oilcloth, and these we stored in our blanket rolls. She embraced her sons affectionately but with no great display of emotion, and when she took my hand to wish me well I felt no diminution of the warmth she had shown Frank and Jesse. Dr. Samuel shook our hands, reminded Jesse of his promise to shoot a Yankee for each of his broken ribs, and told him he had to sit the dun mare high if he didn't want to be pitched off the first time the horse put its foot wrong. Jesse said he would, rolling his eyes to indicate that he had heard the same advice many times before. As we rode out of the yard the couple stood on the porch waving at us with their hands at shoulder height as if they expected us home the next morning. I gathered that partings were nothing new for them, and that the demands which recent events had made upon their human feelings had taught them the importance of conservation.

I never saw either of them again in the flesh, but I have only to close my eyes to summon Zerelda Cole James Simms Samuel sharp from behind the occlusion of decades: erect, intelligent-eyed, resolute. She was everything my mother was not, and possessed many of the qualities a son looks for in his father. The brothers James could have sprung from no other stock.

Three days out we crossed the Red River into Texas. The water was too deep for wading. I had never swum a horse before, and the gelding sensed my fear. Halfway across, the current struck us and tried to turn us around. The horse's head went under water. It came up screaming and spluttering and I lost my grip on the bridle Frank had donated from the tack at the Samuel farm to replace the hackamore. I slipped beneath the surface, but I was able to grab a fistful of mane and haul myself out of the depths. I had water in my eyes and could not tell which direction we were swimming. Then the water exploded close by, something reddish-brown struck the gelding on the opposite side, turning it crossways to the current, and an arm in a sleeve soaked black with water stretched out and grasped its bridle. I got my free hand up and under the harness on my side, and between the four of us—Frank James, his veteran bay, the gelding, and myself—we kicked and clawed our way to the point where the horses made contact with the gravelly bottom on the south bank. I hung on tight and allowed myself to be pulled up the incline and onto dry land, where I knelt gasping and vomiting water from my lungs.

"You are a bucketful of green," observed Frank when I flopped over onto my back and looked up at him standing tall and dripping against the Texas sky. "You're mighty lucksome the river's so low."

"That's low?" I hawked and spat. The water stung inside my nostrils.

"You ought to see it come spring." Shielding his eyes with a hand, he studied the sun's position. "This ain't camp. We got fifteen more miles to cover, and only four hours of daylight to do it in."

As I dragged myself back into my borrowed saddle, I glimpsed Jesse astride his stepfather's dun mare. He looked triumphant. I had begun to realize that competition was the only scale by which this child of three generations of pioneers measured his relationship with his fellow male creatures.

That part of the Lone Star State did not differ appreciably from much of the country we had been traveling through since leaving Clay County. Green, rolling, and heavily wooded with sassafras and spruce and black walnut and magnificent sequoias, the last towering as high as two hundred feet and as big around as houses at the base, it contrasted severely with all my expectations. I confess that I had little concept then of the state's great size, or of the fact that any territory as large as all of Western Europe must encompass as many different kinds of topography, vegetation, and climate. Thus the adjacent communities of Sherman and Mineral Springs, to which we were headed, bore no more resemblance to the storied settlements of San Antonio and Amarillo as London bore to Madrid, and Madrid to Berlin.

Mineral Springs was a place of uncommon beauty, compromised somewhat by the presence of tents, smoldering campfires, and the blight that accompanies large assemblies of men in a close setting: stiff "long-handled" underwear suits jittering on lengths of rope stretched between trees, heaps of rubbish, and a long slit trench at the far edge over which men squatted with their trousers down to their ankles to void themselves. Beyond all this climbed steep rocky slopes carpeted with hardwoods and evergreens, with the crystal waters of the springs glittering down cuts gouged in the limestone millions of years before the first Indians laid eyes upon them. We had just moved within sight of the tents when a rifle cracked close by. Frank drew rein and signaled for Jesse and me to do the same.

"Get them hands in sight!"

The disembodied voice was nearly as sharp as the report. Jesse and I raised our hands.

Frank kept his where they were. "Jim Younger, that you?" he shouted.

There was a pause, then: "Frank?"

"Well, who else'd come riding smack-dab into your sights a mile after he seen the sun flashing off your rifle?"

"You never did! I got the sun behind me!"

"You don't know the sun from the moon, you cross-eyed son of a bitch."

A handful of pebbles skipped and skidded down a steep limestone slope twenty yards ahead and to the left, and a figure separated itself from the rock, a thick torso balanced on bowed legs in a Confederate uniform with a long-barreled rifle braced against one raised thigh. The face beneath the sail-brimmed hat was a dark oval against the sunset.

"I reckon I ain't so cross-eyed I don't know the moon's got no business being in the same sky with the sun," said the man. "Who's that with you?"

"My brother Jesse and Billy Gashade. He plays piano."

I began to think my tombstone would bear that inscription.

"Which one plays piano?"

Frank produced his plug and sawed at it with his knife. "Does it matter?"

"Not to me. I don't know piano music from a washtub falling downstairs. Throw me a chaw, will you? I'm out and the captain won't let us go to town."

"Where's that dollar you bet me I wouldn't get out of Lawrence alive?"

"Crawling under a boardwalk till the fighting's over don't count."

"Chew grass, you turd-kicking bastard." Frank put away the plug and took up his reins. "You going to shoot us or let us pass?"

The man spat, then rubbed the spittle into the rock with the toe of one boot. "You scared a cross-eyed man shoots better than you think?"

"I'm scared you'll draw a bead on Jesse and blow my ass off. Where's your brother?"

"How the hell would I know? I stopped tagging after him when I got my first hard-on."

"We're coming ahead, Jim."

"Come if you're coming. It's staring into ugly faces like yours crossed my eyes in the first place."

We walked our horses past the rock. When I looked back, the sentry had blended into the hillside once again. "Aren't you afraid he'll shoot you in the back?" I asked Frank.

He leaned over and shot a stream of tobacco into the grass beside the trail. "Jim Younger's just about the best friend I got, next to his brother Cole. And the best rifle shot in Missouri."

We were passing the first tent when I had one of the surprises of my life. A woman stepped out through the flap carrying an enormous dead rat by the tail and threw it into the road. My gelding shied and I choked up on the reins to keep from falling off. The woman, a gourd-shaped Indian in a plain blouse and dark ground-length skirt with her hair in braids, stared at me with bottomless black eyes as I rode past.

Farther on we saw more women, scrubbing laundry in large wooden tubs, stirring kettles suspended from makeshift tripods over open fires, and sitting on canvas stools before their tents, smoking cigarettes and sewing buttons on shirts. Most were white, but several were Indian and a few were black. Many wore men's hats and coats. One or two had on muslin shifts only, with round-toed boots too big for their feet, and the sun behind them showed that they wore no underclothing. I felt my face growing hot and avoided their knowing eyes when they looked up at the three newcomers riding past. I guessed their function.

A cry, shrill enough to cause Frank to jerk one of the Navy Colts partway from its saddle scabbard, turned all our heads in the direction of a tent several yards ahead, where a young woman stumbled out through the flap, barefoot and clutching the ruins of a garment to her chest. She wore nothing above the waist. Running with her head turned to look back over her bare shoulder, she would have collided with Frank's horse had he not yanked back on the reins, emitting an ear-splitting whistle through his teeth as he did so. Startled, the woman looked in front of her, saw the hazard, and tried to stop. She lost her footing and fell into an undignified sitting position on the ground, losing the torn garment and exposing a pair of small breasts with large brown nipples. The sight set my pulse hammering. Ada had lit a fire back at Drucilla's that I knew would continue to smolder into old age.

When I looked back at Jesse, his face was averted and as red as rouge. It gave me some small satisfaction to learn that I had the advantage over him in this one area.

An instant later a familiar ogre emerged from the tent and took two long strides toward the half-naked girl before he saw us and stopped. Instinctively, Lieutenant John Thrailkill reached for the big revolver in the holster on his hip, then changed directions when he recognized Frank and hooked his trailing braces over his shoulders. He wore no shirt over his long underwear, which clung like a second skin to the lean sinew of his arms and torso. His classic features were blurred somewhat by his disheveled hair and a two-day growth of beard, but his dead pale eyes were clear.

"Thought you'd deserted," he said.

Frank ignored the taunt. "I see you're still hell with the ladies, Johnny."

"It ain't what you think. I wanted her to model, but she thought I wanted something else."

The young woman got to her feet and stood with eyes downcast, clutching the tattered cloth to her chest. It had been a blouse, a becoming one printed with flowers. She had long straight black hair like an Indian's, but her features were fine and the skin of her breasts was blue-white.

"Women," Frank said appreciatively. "They're each one different, and all the same. I never seen one so eager for it she wouldn't stop to unbutton a pretty piece of cloth like that there. Especially not with a war on and goods so dear."

"They get queer notions. They think nothing of dancing bare-ass in front of the whole camp, but ask them to take their shirt off in a tent so you can paint them and they fight like a badger." Thrailkill put a hand to his face and took it away to look at it, and I saw a row of angry red scratches on his cheek for the first time. "I reckon I got impatient."

"Hell, Johnny, I don't care what you do with them in your tent. I just don't want you scaring my brother."

"I see you brought more than your brother." The empty eyes turned my way. "We ain't got no piano here."

"You got something else that belongs to Billy, though. That pretty pistol he loaned you."

"I ain't got nothing don't belong to me."

"Sure you do. You just forgot. As I recall it was his decision to let you have it for a while. He damn near gave you the business end of it, and you with your jaw hanging down past your balls."

One of the half-undressed women watching from the tents cut loose with a loud guffaw. Thrailkill threw her a look that choked it off.

"He wants it back he can come get it." He turned his eyes back upon me. It was like looking into a pair of open graves.

"You shouldn't be that way, Johnny. Captain Quantrill won't like it. Any more'n he won't like hearing how you treat your models. You know how soft he is on women."

"Maybe what Quantrill likes or don't like don't matter no more."

Frank straightened in his saddle. "That's foolish talk even for you."

Thrailkill turned his way, and it seemed to me he grew taller. "Things ain't what they were when you lit out. There's been a whole new shuffle since Lawrence. A fresh king's on top."

"And who might that be, you?"

"No. Not him."

This was a new voice; or perhaps, when we looked at the man standing in front of the tent across from Thrailkill's, not so new after all. Bloody Bill Anderson looked up at us from the revolver he was wiping with an oily rag. The other five he wore in various holsters and slings were clearly visible with his coat off.

Chapter Seventeen

𝕵𝕻

They said two women were the cause.

The situation was more complex than that, of course. Money, jealousy, and conscience were also involved.

Fletch Taylor, one of the fiercest of Quantrill's lieutenants, had defied the custom of dividing plunder equally among the men, claiming for himself six thousand dollars in United States currency taken from Lawrence. Appeals to Quantrill were useless; the guerrilla leader, who lived for revenge, was sated temporarily and not inclined to take interest in a squabble over finances. Captain Anderson, commanding as much loyalty as Quantrill, and whose blood lust was even more pronounced, stayed aloof from the dispute while news of the inequity spread through the ranks like a cancer.

Others, sickened and disillusioned by the bloodbath in Kansas, had deserted for their homes or places with the regular army. William H. Gregg had pulled out with a substantial number of followers to join General Jo Shelby's brigade in Louisiana, and it was rumored that Cole Younger, a Quantrill man almost from the beginning, was considering a Confederate post. Those who remained were undecided whether to stay with the status quo or throw in with Bloody Bill. All that was required was a shift to one side of the scale or the other.

After Lawrence, Quantrill had acquired a mistress, one Kate King, who in a kind of common-law ceremony of marriage took on his middle name of Clarke. The pair were often absent from the day-to-day military life at Mineral Springs, pursuing their dalliance. At about the same time, Anderson had reported his desire to marry in nearby Sherman at his earliest opportunity. Quantrill, who seemed to think himself the only guerrilla privileged to permanent female companionship, ordered him to put off his wedding until after the war, whereupon Bloody Bill declared his intentions to pull out for Sherman, and issued a blanket invitation to as many of the men who cared to accompany him to get their gear together.

This was the situation when Frank and Jesse James and I entered the guerrilla camp on the eve of September 1863, never realizing that we were scaling a powder keg until we were sitting on top of it.

Much of our information came courtesy of the brother of the fellow who had challenged us at the edge of camp. After taking our leave of Lieutenant Thrailkill and Captain Anderson, we spotted a man standing up to his knees in a pool of crystalline water down the hill from the first cluster of tents, twirling a length of stout cord with a bent pin attached. Frank watched in silence while the weighted end arced up and out and disappeared into the water with a gulp.

Then: "Them better be Yankee fish you're hooking, Cole Younger."

The man, whose back was turned toward us, didn't flinch, but reeled in the cord slowly with a practiced winding motion of both hands. "I'm safe, then. I ain't hooked a one since before noon."

"Maybe if you washed your feet before you waded in, they'd still have a appetite."

"Maybe if damn fools didn't keep yelling fit to scare a crazy wolf, we'd have catfish for supper instead of Texas rattlesnake. How the hell are you, Frank? I heard you deserted."

"I heard the same thing. Bet we both heard it from the same place. I thought Johnny might simmer down a little after Lawrence."

"He'll simmer down when they pat him in the face with a spade. Me, I had my fill and then some. I'm getting out."

"I heard that too. What you fixing to do with Shelby you can't do with this bunch?"

"Walk on my hind legs, for one. I'm sick of slanching around like a wormy dog." He coiled the cord neatly and resumed twirling, feeding out a little more with each pass until the makeshift hook whistled out in a flat circle eight feet from his head. Then he let fly. This time the end plunked beneath the surface three yards beyond where it had landed the time before. Again he commenced reeling it in. "I seen Thrailkill plug a man full of holes hiding in a cornfield on the edge of Lawrence with a baby in his arms. Left him dead with the baby still there squalling. I picked it up and took it into town and gave it to the first woman I come to. She spit on me. No woman ever spit on me before," he added.

"You shoot her?"

"Why? She didn't do nothing I didn't do to myself when I agreed to ride into that damn town."

"You felt that way, how come you didn't shoot Thrailkill?"

"I didn't get to him in time to save that poor bastard in the cornfield. Anyway you ain't done much when you've shot a man that's dead already."

He'd snagged something. He jerked the cord taut to set the hook and hauled it in hand over hand. In another moment he held up the ugliest fish I'd ever seen, twelve inches long and black, with tentacles sprouting like whiskers from each side of its working mouth. It flapped desperately, splashing him with water from its fins and tail.

Frank whistled. "That's an elephant. I wonder what's the record around here."

Holding the fish by the gills, the man in the water worked the hook out of its mouth. He stood studying it for a moment, then with an underhand flip threw it back into the water.

"Not hungry, I reckon," Frank said.

"I ain't et all day. I ain't so bad off I need to bash in some poor slippery cat's brains to make my dinner. Not tonight anyhow." He looked down at the coiled line. Without hesitation he threw it in after the fish, turned around, and waded toward dry land.

Sturdily built like his brother, but taller and more evenly proportioned, Cole Younger sported a handsome set of chestnut-colored chin-whiskers, perhaps in compensation for the thinning of his widow's peak, though I judged him to be no older than Frank James. (He was in fact several months younger.) He was in his shirtsleeves—plain homespun, no guerrilla ruffles—and shapeless tan trousers rolled up to his knees, and wore no hat. I never knew him to wear one afterward, no matter the weather; there was a belief at the time that covering one's head encouraged baldness, and as he had a keen interest in scientific theory I always suspected this had something to do with his decision. Once out of the water he stooped to pick up a worn pair of stovepipe boots and dingy gray stockings, but before he put them on he came the rest of the way up the bank and reached up to shake Frank's hand. Such scrupulous observation of the courtesies was so rare in my recent experience that I goggled. Here, I thought, was something new in night riders.

"Jesse. I heard a parcel about you from your brother," said he when the other James was introduced.

Jesse murmured a greeting of some kind. He seemed to be in awe of the big man, and I assumed that Frank had told him at least as much about Younger as he had told Younger about his brother.

Jesse James and Cole Younger. I have pummeled my memory for something dramatic about that historic first meeting. All I saw was a boy and a man exchanging polite words.

Frank said, "This here's Billy Gashade. You two got a thing in common, Cole. Billy's old man is a judge."

He turned friendly eyes on me. "What jurisdiction?"

"The eighth District Court of Manhattan," I said.

"That's a long way to travel to fight for the South." He sounded mildly surprised.

"Oh, Billy don't fight. He's a musician."

His smile upon receiving this information was reserved but warm. He had a wide, thin-lipped mouth that seemed always ready to smile or frown; a blank canvas waiting for the first stroke of the brush. "The organist at Drucilla's. I heard. Do you play any other instruments?"

"The piano," I said.

"Sorry to hear it. I found a guitar in Lawrence and I been looking for somebody to play it ever since, to make me feel less the damn fool for carrying it all this way."

"Hell, learning the guitar's got to be easy after the piano," Frank said. "It's just five strings against eighty-eight keys."

"Where is your father's bench?" I asked Younger, changing the subject.

His smile faded. "Six feet under some of the best topsoil in Missouri. Federals killed him last year."

"I'm sorry."

"Not half as sorry as the Yankees," said Frank. "Judge Younger backed the North. They made one fine fair Johnny Reb out of Cole in one night."

Younger sat down on the ground and began pulling on his stockings and boots. "You're welcome to ride with me to see Shelby, Frank. The regulars need good cavalry."

"Your brother going?"

"Jim likes it here. Bloody Bill promised him a commission. Shelby's got more lieutenants than he needs."

"I reckon I'll stick for the same reason. I been in it too long to start taking orders from a shavetail with pimples on his dick." Frank leaned over and spat tobacco.

"Suit yourself. When the Yankees catch you and hang you I'll send flowers to your old ma."

"Well, don't pick 'em just yet. You get any of that Kentucky sippin' I heard Fletch Taylor found in the cellar of the Eldridge House?"

"I been saving a bottle for a special occasion."

"It's my first Texas sundown. If that ain't occasion enough, I don't know what is."

Cole Younger stood and stamped his heels into his boots. "I reckon it is, at that. My tent's this way." He started walking, and we coaxed our horses into his path.

Seated that night on the ground before Cole Younger's tent, eating salted ham and biscuits and passing around a plain unlabeled bottle of mellow rye whiskey—not my first taste of hard spirits, but certainly my most substantial to date, warming my insides and lifting my thoughts free of the gravity that chained my body to the earth—I learned most of what I still know about the men who rode with Quantrill and Anderson. It was a story as old as Homer yet as fresh as the Union and Confederate blood staining the ground at Chancellorsville and along the Shenandoah.

I know not to whom he told it, or whether he was telling it to anyone at all. At the time I assumed it was for the benefit of the newcomers, Jesse and myself, but upon reflection I wonder if he was attempting to fit together the pieces in his own mind, and if the rest of us were merely eavesdropping. He sat with his legs crossed Indian fashion, staring into the small fire he had built to ward off the evening chill and moving only when his long-stemmed clay pipe required recharging. His voice was low and pleasant, changing pitch as the narrative demanded, in the old storytelling tradition.

As he related, most of the men with whom he had spent the past twelvemonth held personal grudges against the North and those who had allied themselves with it. Cole and his brothers, James, Robert, and John, the latter pair still too young to take up arms, had been deprived of a father when Union militiamen robbed and murdered Judge Henry W. Younger in retaliation for his son's guerrilla involvement. Shortly after the murder, Cole's sister and a female cousin were incarcerated in Kansas City by order of James Walley, a militia captain. Walley accused them of espionage, but in fact he was angry over having been scorned by the sister at a dance. When the ramshackle jailhouse collapsed, crushing the cousin to death among others, rumors flew that the building had been undermined deliberately to prevent the

Younger girls from testifying against Walley. Another of the women who died in the disaster happened to be a sister of William Anderson, thus setting that individual on the violent road that would lead him to the sobriquet of Bloody Bill. Accident or otherwise—and I heard too much testimony afterward to disregard entirely the accusation that the hand of man was involved—this tragedy had within the space of a few minutes created two enemies whose acts of vengeance would plague the Union for years.

John Thrailkill's reasons to hate the Yankees were as good as anyone's and better than most. I scarcely credited it at the time, but before the war he had been an artist, and a good one. Engaged to marry a beautiful girl whose family sided with the South, he was locked away in his rented studio laboring with his brushes and easel to make his paintings salable to support them both when militiamen paid a call upon her at her father's home. When they left, the invalid old gentleman was dead, the young woman violated and out of her head with grief and shame. When Thrailkill finally emerged from his artistic exile, he found his fiancée laid out in her prettiest dress on the sofa in her parlor, she having slit her wrists and bled to death in her bath. After kissing her cold lips, the young man swore to avenge her and her father. At the time I met him, he had slain eighteen of the twenty men who had been present at the time of the murder and her disgrace, and if the blood he had spilled had quenched his fires in any way, the flame at the start must have been prodigious indeed.

"It's difficult to believe that two more deaths will restore his humanity," said I at this point in the story.

Cole looked at me over the bowl of his pipe. "Seen any of his paintings?"

"Does he still paint?"

"Sometimes late at night I get up to use the latrine, I see a lantern on in his tent with his shadow jumping around. That's when he works, never outside during daylight like I hear he used to. I seen just one of them, when he went out and left his tent flap crooked. I don't know what his pictures looked like before the war. Maybe they was all like that, but I doubt it or he'd of gone up like a plugged barrel long before he did."

"What did it look like?" I asked.

He shook his head. "I can't tell it so you'd see it. I just hope

I never dream nothing like what I seen on that canvas. I reckon he does, though, all the time."

Jesse's eyes were fixed upon him, pupils wide and shining, like a child's during a bogey tale. "What does he do with the paintings?"

"Burns 'em, I suppose. Or buries 'em. There sure ain't room for them in his traps when we move on."

"Why go to all the bother of painting them just to destroy them?" Jesse asked.

Frowning, Cole knocked out his pipe against a flat rock next to the fire. "I read this piece once in *Harper's,* about getting things out of your skull before they have the chance to fester. Maybe that's what he's doing. I know I sure wouldn't want to walk around with a thing like that stuck under my hat."

"Dogs!" Frank moved his shoulders up and down and reached for the bottle. "I wisht you had a piano in your tent. I'd like to go to sleep thinking about Billy's Bach instead of them paintings in Johnny Thrailkill's skull."

"Your mind made up against that guitar?" Cole was looking at me. "I'd as lief not pack it all the way back to Missouri. I'll bust it up before I let some Yankee find it and pluck out 'John Brown's Body' or worse."

Perhaps it was the whiskey. Perhaps, like Frank James, I preferred to insert something physical between my dreams and the dark visions that came out through the bristles of Lieutenant Thrailkill's brushes. In any case I told Cole I'd give the guitar a try. As he got up to look for it, I heard Jesse sigh. Plainly he resented the interruption. I wondered if the young would-be guerrilla dreamed, and if his dreams had the power to terrify him. Nothing else appeared to come close.

CHAPTER EIGHTEEN

Here my narrative accelerates. The primary responsibility of the storyteller is to hold the interest of his audience, and while lengthy periods of physical and intellectual stagnation are as much a part of war as destruction and death, it would serve no purpose to recount in extended and redundant detail the long flyblown days and stale sultry nights that stretched unbroken between the horrors that continue to season my dreams. Sufficient to say that there is little more diverting in a sticky summer night spent in the open, prey to mosquitoes and chiggers, than is to be found inside a moldy tent in winter, with rain leaking in and two healthy Missouri farmboys sleeping within arm's length, passing gas and snoring loud enough to wake Gettysburg's fifty thousand dead.

The days were hardly better. In effect, with Union troops turning over every rock and leaf in Missouri and Kansas for the men responsible for the Lawrence outrage, we were in hiding, counting upon the Texas alliance with the Confederacy to protect us from retribution. As a result, we were inactive, which was not a situation calculated to rest lightly upon the shoulders of men who had gathered around the standard of the black flag to ride, fight, plunder, and kill. With no enemy within reach, the guerrillas' natural disposition turned inward. Fights broke out daily, challenges were issued and accepted. The object of a squabble might be a missing poke full of coins, a razor borrowed and not returned, or the affections of one of the female camp followers. Broken jaws and gunshot wounds were treated with frequency at the "hospital tent"—two soiled cots overseen by a former St. Louis intern denied a license to practice medicine for reasons of drunkenness.

By and large, these sporadic eruptions were welcome distractions from unbroken days and nights of boredom. There were card games and horse races, shooting contests, and betting; but these things required energy, and each day spent apart from the war that raged in the East drained the stores like coal oil leaking from a neglected barrel. *Morale,* a term of French origin just then beginning to seep its way into the military lexicon, was low, and getting lower by the day. Desertions were reported on a regular basis.

Late in September, Bloody Bill Anderson left Mineral Springs for Sherman, completing the breach between him and Quantrill. Frank, Jesse, and I rode with the men who accompanied him, a number comprising nearly half the remaining command. The change of scenery was a relief. We left the tents behind and took up permanent quarters in the Christian Hotel, where the three of us shared a room.

By this time I had begun to conquer the guitar. The instrument, enameled red and bearing the initials W.G.B. burned into the wood on the back, had six strings rather than five, and I had spent the better part of the first week learning how to tune it properly; but by the end of the second I was plucking out "Amazing Grace," earning for the effort an angry bruise on my upper left arm one midnight when Frank James flung a boot at me in the darkness of the tent and requested I put the damned thing down and go to sleep. Although I still had much to learn, when I slipped the hand-tooled leather strap across my shoulder, my fingers flocked to the frets and strings like birds to a telegraph wire. After the first month I discarded the chip of firewood I had fashioned into a pick. The calluses on my fingertips had grown thick enough to take its place. I was fast forming a bond to rival my lifelong relationship with the keyboard.

Meanwhile, dissension and *ennui* among the men boiled over into the surrounding communities. Fletch Taylor—acting, it was charged, upon orders from Quantrill, who quarreled frequently with the authorities in Texas—led a band of guerrillas to a house north of Sherman and robbed and killed one Major Butts, a Confederate officer. Quantrill, reversing himself under pressure, suggested turning Taylor over to the regular army for court-martial, but Anderson, with whom Taylor had ridden from Mineral Springs, refused to betray the guerrillas' oath of self-government. He had the major's widow escorted into town for her own protection and put her up at the Christian Hotel.

The situation fermented and festered. On Christmas Day, guerrillas loyal to Quantrill charged into Sherman, firing their pistols at whatever targets tempted them, chasing pedestrians off the boardwalks, and riding into stores and public buildings, destroying merchandise and terrorizing employees and patrons. One group, acting with single-minded deliberation, galloped into the lobby of the Christian just as Mrs. Butts was coming downstairs to investigate the commotion and shot the ornament off her woolen cap. Laughing, they turned their horses and rode back out.

A citizens' committee appointed by the town complained to General Henry McCulloch, commander of Confederate troops in the area, asking him to capture and punish the men involved in the attack. With the pressure building, Captain Anderson rode into McCulloch's camp and officially accused Quantrill. In March 1864, William Clarke Quantrill was ordered to report to the general's office and placed under house arrest.

On the last day of March but one, I elected not to leave the hotel room when Frank and Jesse invited me to go walking with them. Things had quieted considerably since the incidents of Christmas—grown soporific, in fact—and with nothing but the guitar and Jesse's personal Bible for entertainment, I was feeling depressed and lethargic. Early spring was a time of awakening in New York, beginning with the raucous frivolity of the St. Patrick's Day parade and quickening with the first warm breezes from the harbor and the height of the theater season, when cabriolets and broughams filled the streets and Fifth Avenue became a sea of high silk hats and ladies' floriated chapeaux. By contrast, March in northeastern Texas was merely wet. Dirty gray skies rolled down almost to the ground, releasing sheets of gluey water like fly paste and churning the streets into troughs of yellow-brown mud knee-deep. Mildew formed on everything, and the quest for dry feet took on all the fanatic importance of the search for the grail. I had not received a letter from my father since Lawrence. I was certain he had written, but I was equally certain his letters had been returned in lieu of a forwarding address. General McCulloch had shut down the post office in Sherman, decreeing that henceforth only military communications would be allowed between the territory under his jurisdiction and the East. I was suffering from a severe head cold, and I was more homesick than ever.

Abetted partly by a medicinal draught from a bottle Frank had purchased in a local establishment of a whiskey he called "Texas tanglefoot"—not by any means to be confused with the smooth, aged spirits we had shared in front of Cole Younger's tent on our first night in Mineral Springs—I drifted from my funk into a deep sleep. When I awoke it was dark. I coughed, stirred, and thought at first that the cold had settled in my chest, realizing but slowly that the weight I felt there was real.

I smelled fresh whiskey. Evidently one of my roommates, most likely Frank, as I had yet to see his brother drink anything stronger than the bottled water from the springs, had returned heavily under the influence, crawled into bed heedless that it was already occupied, and gone to sleep with an arm draped across my chest. I struggled into a sitting position, groped on the nightstand until I found the box of lucifers placed there for the purposes of lighting the lamp, and struck one on the bedrail. The white flare blinded me at first, then as the sulfur burned away and the flame turned yellow, I saw a slender naked arm stretched across the quilt, and beyond it, nestled into the hollow between my neck and shoulder, a head with an abundance of long black unfettered hair. Neither the arm nor the hair belonged to any guerrilla of my acquaintance. As I stared, waiting for the clouds to clear, the head lifted and a pair of dark pretty eyes regarded me in silence.

The flame stung my fingers. I gasped and dropped the match, then slapped desperately at the sheet lest it smolder. While I was thus engaged, another match flared. A hand lifted the glass chimney of the lamp on the nightstand. The hand holding the match started the wick glowing. Frank James's face, demonic in the light from below, floated in the darkness surrounding it. "Happy birthday, youngster. Sorry I didn't get time to wrap your present."

I looked from him to the grave young woman lying against me. She was the same one who had fled from John Thrailkill's tent the day of our arrival at the guerrilla camp. I knew without investigating that she was naked beneath the quilt we shared. Now I looked back at Frank. "How did you know?"

"You told me the date. You wouldn't remember doing it. You was drinking that good Kentucky rye of Cole's. Wonder how he's getting on with Shelby? From what I hear there ain't a dime's worth of difference betwixt him and Captain Quantrill." He shifted the plug in his mouth, found the cuspidor at the foot of the bed, and used it. "Don't get too attached to the filly. Johnny's bound to miss her come morning."

"What am I supposed to do with her?"

He grinned. "You're seventeen now, pard. I reckon you'll come up with something."

"Is Jesse in on this?"

"Jess has a stick up his ass over this kind of thing. He don't hold with it. There's a load of our pa in that boy."

"I can't," I said.

Just then the dark-haired girl slid her hand under the quilt and grazed her fingers down my bare torso. Our faces were inches apart. No smile came to her lips, but her eyes reflected the light from the lamp. Her hand stopped, fondled. I took in my breath.

Frank withdrew into the darkness. "Where are you going?" My voice was strained.

"Little brick house on the west end of town. I know somebody there." The door opened to the hall.

"What are you going to do?"

I heard the grin in his tone. "Celebrate your birthday, what else?"

Alone with the young woman, I fumbled at the nightstand, found the glass tumbler I had set there, and drank. I choked and coughed. Someone, probably Frank, had poured out the water and substituted Texas tanglefoot. As I recovered, gasping, the girl took her hand from under the covers and held it out.

"Can I have some?" Her voice was shallow and breathy, a little girl's snared in a woman's body.

I handed her the glass. She drank off half the contents in a long draught and gave it back. Her dark gaze met mine. She seemed to flush a little, but it may have been the effect of the spirits.

"What is your name?" I asked her.

"Nowata."

"Are you an Indian?"

"I'm half Cherokee."

I took a careful sip from the glass. The whiskey warmed me and calmed my nerves. "Which half?"

She smiled then for the first time.

The war came back with the fury of a mad beast suddenly set free.

On the night of my seventeenth birthday, March 30, 1864, as I lay with Nowata, William Clarke Quantrill overpowered the two Confederate soldiers assigned to guard him, locked them in the clothespress of the room where he had been held, and made his escape.

Alerted by General McCulloch, with whom he was cooperating at present, Bloody Bill Anderson ordered his men to mount up and pursue his former commander.

Quantrill, riding at the head of the small band that had remained loyal to him, fled into Missouri, where he eluded his persecutors and entered upon a series of minor but violent skirmishes that would continue to make his name synonymous with war at its worst.

Anderson, by contrast, aligned himself more closely with the regular Confederate Army, coordinating his command with that of General Sterling Price in a series of devastating raids against Union forces in Missouri.

Although I accompanied the guerrillas on these forays, I saw little of the actual fighting, riding at the rear of the column with the women and other noncombatants, including the young boys and stove-in soldiers who fetched water and performed other necessary chores: repairing boots and harnesses, carrying supplies, trapping and shooting game and preparing it for consumption, driving the ammunition wagons. When we camped, I produced my guitar, played requested tunes, and introduced a few that were unfamiliar to the company. The selections I chose from Vivaldi quickly became favorites, but Liszt left my listeners cold, and they were positively hostile to anything by Rameau, whose bold experiments in dissonance had found little more approval in the French salons of the eighteenth century. To be fair, I must point out that I was playing their compositions from memory, upon an instrument I had yet to master. However, the same was true of the Scottish mountain ballads I attempted to reproduce after hearing a few bars hummed by those members of my audience who asked me to play them, and these seldom failed to spark applause or an impromptu jig. Unsophisticated though these fierce fighters and their women were in the area of musical criticism, I found gratification in their acceptance even as their displeasure mortified me.

Billy Gashade, read the packet of calling cards I still carried in my pocket; *Entertainments.*

A number of the Missourians I had known since the beginning had passed almost beyond my ken.

Anderson, far up front directing murderous flank attacks at the Federals to divert attention from Price's frontal assault, was a source of rumors and legend as farfetched as if his exploits were taking place in another hemisphere and reported in relays, growing with each retelling. At Pilot Knob he was encircled by enemy forces ten times his strength, but slashed his way to freedom with bayonets and sabers; at the Missouri River he charged a Union encampment and forced the troops into the swift waters, where most of them drowned. Homer would have found few heroes in his repertoire to stand beside Bloody Bill as he was described to us at the rear.

Cole Younger, some said, was in California, utterly disillusioned with the war and with his failed efforts on behalf of General Jo Shelby to recruit mercenaries in Mexico for the rebel army. When next he loaded his pistols, it would be for no cause but his own.

John Thrailkill was particularly active, and the stories that drifted back from the fighting, of women and children cut down by his shot and steel, of villages razed and Negroes lynched, curdled the blood. I did not care to see what fearsome paintings sprang from his twisted soul during this period.

What little news I received that I regarded as truth came from Frank James. I had my own tent now, left by a deserter, and he visited often, to enjoy a chew without having to listen to one of his fellow night riders boasting of his prowess and to hear me play. Although I had heard wild tales of his feats fighting at Anderson's side, he seldom spoke of himself, preferring to pass on bits of gossip and share glowing reports of his brother Jesse's performance under the command of Lieutenant Fletch Taylor.

"He's a scrapper," Frank was fond of saying. "Even Bloody Bill says he's the keenest and cleanest fighter he's got. He don't swear nor drink nor pay attention to lewd women. I reckon that's where he finds the energy."

For two weeks in August, Frank did not come around. We were in Carroll County, a wild place of thistles and thorny locust trees forever scheming to reclaim the land from the farmers who did battle with them every day with scythes and axes; combat with militia and Union regulars had been heavy and hot along the Ray County line, and rumors of victory, defeat, and casualties had been contradicting one another furiously for days. I feared that my friend and sometime protector had fallen. Then, on the anniversary of the Lawrence raid, a gaunt, hollow-eyed specter of Zerelda Samuel's firstborn shambled into the light of my fire and stood swaying before the camp stool where I sat picking my way through "Tenting Tonight." His beard was untrimmed and the front of his faithful knitted pullover was caked with something that in another place and time I should have assumed was mud.

"Jess," he said; and without waiting for a response, turned and shuffled back into the shadows.

I followed, of course. He had tied his racing bay, panting and flecked with foam, to the picket line, and despite his clear exhaustion was in the saddle by the time I joined him in the torchlight. My gelding was already saddled—standing orders whenever the war was in full cry—and though I lost no time in mounting, I had to kick the horse into a brisk trot to catch up with him. I had brought my guitar without thinking. Not knowing what else to do with it, I slung the strap across my shoulder.

We covered perhaps two miles. The distance seemed greater in that wild country with no moon and only dusty starlight to guide us around chuckholes and low saplings. At long last we stopped within sight of a small log cabin with a smear of light in a greased-paper window. After a moment spent in silent scrutiny of the building and the clearing that surrounded it, Frank slid one of the Navies from its scabbard and fired it twice at the sky. Again we waited while the echo of the reports growled among the distant hills. Then a fresh crack of light appeared to the right of the window—a door opening—and a muzzle flashed vertically, followed an instant later by the crash of a rifle. Frank scabbarded his pistol and coaxed his tired mount forward. I fell into step behind.

"Who's that with you?"

Our challenger, dimly outlined on the cabin's tiny front porch, wore bib overalls with a piece of twine holding them up on one side where the strap had broken. The light from indoors made haloes in the dents on his bald scalp. An ancient flintlock musket rested on its buttstock with his hand holding the barrel.

"He's with me, ain't he? Any change?"

"Nope. That boy's a goner for certain."

"The hell with you, Rudd," Frank flared. "You're a good Christian and I thank you for all you done, but the hell with you."

Rudd said nothing. We dismounted, handing him the reins, and went inside. A rag rug lay on the dirt and there were a few sticks of furniture and a fireplace for cooking, but aside from that the lone room appeared empty and uninhabited. Frank led the way around a worn quilt hung from a rope strung across the end.

Jesse James lay on an old feather mattress in a bed made from pine planks. Flies crawled on his face in the light of a lantern hung from a nail in the wall. Where the counterpane had slid down, a slash of white bandage slanted up over one shoulder, Roman toga fashion. His skin was pale and appeared clammy.

"Jess?" Frank's tone was a murmur.

Jesse didn't stir. His eyes remained closed.

"Minié ball ripped a hole in his chest big as a barn door on the twelfth," his brother said. "That cork-pulling sawbones didn't give him till the end of the first week. Takes an hour to get a bowl of broth into him. He'll swallow; he just won't wake up. I tried talking and singing and yelling. I don't want to shake him. Sawbones says it wouldn't do no good anyhow."

"I'm sorry."

He looked at me. In the illumination from below, his face was deeply etched, with shadows hammocked in the pockets. He looked three times his age. "Play for him, will you, Billy? Jesse likes your music."

"On the piano," I said. "I'm still learning the guitar."

"That don't matter. If fingers was all there was to it, any teamster ever handled a six-hitch rig could make music. It don't come from the fingers." When still I hesitated, his face grew hard. "I don't like to call in markers. I figure you owe it to me for the Independence Road."

I slid the guitar around. "I cannot promise anything."

He brought me a wobbly cane-bottom chair, and I played for Jesse: "Amazing Grace," "The Bonnie Blue Flag," "The Gospel Train"; as many of the tunes from Zerelda Samuel's cedar trunk as I could remember, along with those I had learned since and those I had brought with me from New York. I played deep into the night, started awake in the gray wash of dawn, and resumed playing. Jesse remained motionless.

The doctor, a young man in everything but outlook, with hands that shook slightly and broken blood vessels in his cheeks, came to examine the patient shortly after sunrise, shook his head, returned his instruments to his cylindrical bag, and spoke to Frank on the other side of the hanging quilt. Frank's voice rose harshly above the guitar music. To avoid listening, I concentrated upon my fingering. I was tired and hungry and sore from my night on a chair not designed for sleeping. I counted ten fingers on one hand. I closed my eyes and went on playing.

". . . the Hunters of Kentucky."

Jesse's singing voice was scarcely a whisper. I opened my eyes, half certain I had dreamt hearing it, and met his gray-blue gaze.

I cried Frank's name. He came running, followed closely by the doctor, who looked into Jesse's eyes and measured his pulse against a battered steel watch. Again he shook his head, this time in disbelief. For all that he seemed no less grave than before.

After the doctor left, Frank and I went outside while his brother rested. Rudd, who apparently had slept on the porch, was busy drawing water from the well in the yard.

"Jesse's strong," I said. "He'll recover."

"I know it." He cut himself a chew.

"I doubt it was anything I did. He'd have awakened sooner or later."

"Maybe not."

I slung the guitar behind my back. "I'm tired. I guess I'll go back to my tent."

"Leave it."

I waited. He was leaning on his forearms on the porch railing, shifting the plug back and forth in his mouth. "Go back to New York. Go to California, like Cole. This ain't your war. Never was."

"I want to stay." Even as I said it, I realized it was untrue.

"You ain't listening. You been sucking this tit too long. Hard enough feeding them that pull their weight."

I watched Rudd carrying the wooden bucket toward the house, throwing out his free arm for balance. "It's going to get bad, isn't it?" I said. "Worse than it's been."

"Leave the gelding. You need a horse can outrun the militia when you stumble smack into them like you're bound to. I don't reckon Jesse will mind too much if you borrow the dun mare."

"What's going to happen?"

"What do you care? You'll be in New York. Or California." He spat a brown stream over the railing.

"I care."

"I know it."

"Thanks." I stuck out my hand.

He regarded it, then extended his across his body to take it.
"One thing you need to remember about that mare."

"I remember. Sit her high."

He grinned.

PART THREE

Ballad of a Wanderer

CHAPTER NINETEEN

❧

Frank James was prescient. It did get worse.

On September 27, 1864, Anderson and 225 guerrillas pulled Union troops off a passenger train in Centralia, Missouri, lined them up on the station platform, and forced them to strip to their underclothing to provide the night riders with disguises for future activities. Bloody Bill, it was reported, stalked up and down the line of captives like an officer reviewing his troops, then turned to John Thrailkill and said, "Muster 'em out." Thrailkill and Arch Clements, another Anderson lieutenant, shot down the first four prisoners without help. The rest of the guerrillas assembled then joined in. When the acrid smoke cleared, twenty-four soldiers of the Army of the Potomac lay dead.

It was not the most heinous act to take place in that darkest theater of the war, but it was among the most widely reported, and its grisly details unhinged the reason of some Northern campaigners who had hitherto displayed nought but cool logic under fire. Upon learning of the outrage, Union Major A.V.E. Johnson later that day made two costly mistakes. First, he divided his command, leaving part of his mounted infantry to secure the town of Centralia while he took off in pursuit of Anderson with a reduced force. Second, upon catching up with the guerrillas in open country, he ordered his men to dismount.

John Thrailkill was credited with leading Johnson into the ambush, allowing the company to pursue him, seemingly a lone fugitive, to a grassy hollow where a portion of Anderson's force stood around watching their horses graze. No sooner had the Yankees dismounted than the guerrillas leapt into the saddle with a rebel yell. Thereupon the rest of the command charged over a hill, shouting and shooting and outnumbering the enemy nearly three to one. Johnson's company was virtually annihilated. Only the men dispatched to the rear to hold the horses escaped.

Major Johnson was an early casualty. Reports identified his killer as a seventeen-year-old guerrilla recently returned to active duty after recovering from a war injury. Jesse James was his name.

News of the Centralia massacre and the battle that followed reached me in Abilene, Kansas, a greenwood settlement a hundred miles west of Lawrence consisting of a post office, a hotel, a blacksmith shop, and a mercantile store where the male residents gathered to drink whiskey and wonder aloud at the deranged fantasies that had brought them to this desolate place. I confess that I knew little more of my own reasons for coming, other than that the farther I traveled in the direction of the setting sun, the fainter grew the din of war. There in the flat, sparsely grown scape of the Great American Desert, the struggle to wrest a living from the granite soil was far more dramatic and personal than the clash of men and ideals taking place only a two-day ride to the east.

Back in Missouri I had traded the gelding to Rudd for a slab of bacon, a gunny sack full of dried beans that rattled like buckshot when I loaded them aboard the dun mare, cooking utensils, and a small sack of Arbuckle's coffee. The mare was strong, and war had trimmed it down and sharpened its instincts; we had attracted enemy attention just once, when a band of militia spotted us near the Kansas border, and we had eluded them easily, outrunning them on the flat and losing them in a stand of trees. I remember wondering, as pistol balls clattered among the branches behind me, what my old horror of a childhood music tutor would think if he saw me then. *"Pianissimo,* young master," he might say, gesturing downward with his stick; "we are running away from the Yankees, not charging up Cemetery Ridge."

I had stopped in Lawrence overnight, and almost immediately regretted coming there.

Although it was late morning when I arrived, the streets were empty. The mare's hoofbeats echoed off the fronts of the boarded-up buildings as off the walls of a canyon. Curtains moved in windows, but when I looked at them they were still. Furtive fluttering movements behind the crumbling walls of burned brick buildings left to fall on their own ceased when I turned my head their way. The busy, boastful farm capital I had first seen barely more than a year before was gone. This was a broken place haunted by frightened phantoms.

At first I failed to recognize Massachusetts Street. Thinking I had miscounted my blocks, I turned the mare and retraced my steps to the corner, where the sign assured me I had not. The absences of the Eldridge House, Palmer's Gun Shop, and a half-dozen other establishments whose names I had already forgotten left blanks in the skyline that altered the shape of the neighborhood nearly beyond recognition. Further, the street where I had lived for three important weeks had bespoken life in its every detail, from the flower boxes in the windows of the houses to the sparkling display windows and bright awnings of the storefronts, whereas these blank board faces and weedy overgrown foundations suggested nothing so much as a cemetery lot filled with the remains of people whose survivors had themselves passed on or moved far away, leaving none to care for the mausoleums and markers.

Stopping before Drucilla's, I sat still for a full minute, fighting the urge to sink my heels into the mare's sides and canter on. The house was untouched. The windows were intact and uncovered, the discreet sign still swung from its staples under the eave of the front porch; yet I knew without checking that I was viewing a corpse whose soul had fled. On a warm morning in the last week of August, the windows should have been open—all but those on the top floor, where Drucilla kept her twilit exile—and Isabel, grim maidservant and *majordoma* of the establishment, should have been visible through them, charging from room to room straightening slipcovers, shaking out dust mops, and just generally storming through the daily exercise required to make the house glitter from attic to basement. The building was sealed tight, and if any activity took place there at all, it was far too subtle to have anything to do with that resolute old dragon.

I dismounted, tied the mare to the hitching rail in front, and climbed the steps to the door. As highly as I regarded the august disfigured lady whose personality still clung to the brick and gingerbread, I had other business that precluded my going off to preserve my memory of the house as it had been in happier times.

My first knock went unanswered. When after a minute the door remained closed to my second attempt, I tried the latch and found it open.

A trapezoidal patch of sunlight lay on the floor of the foyer. In the grayness to the right of the staircase leading to the second story stood a small boy holding a pitchfork with a shattered handle, the tines pointed at me. He was barefoot and his clothes hung in rags. His eyes were huge and hostile and terrified in a face smeared with dirt.

"I am looking for Drucilla," I said. "Does she still live here?"

For answer, the boy jabbed at me with the fork. As six feet separated us, I did not move. He was seeking only to keep me at bay.

"Are you alone here?"

He jabbed again. His breathing was loud and sibilant. I could not tell if he understood my words.

"He ain't alone."

I peered up at the staircase landing. The woman standing there was barefoot as well, in a faded housecoat that she held together at her throat. Her dark shoulder-length hair was streaked with gray and needed combing, had needed it for at least a month. She held a large-bore pistol braced against her right hip with the hammer cocked.

I raised both my hands. "I used to live here. My name is Gashade. I was asking your boy about Drucilla Patakos."

"He ain't my boy."

It occurred to me that she might have seen me through a window when I was hitching up. The mare looked too healthy for a

war-ravaged city whose residents could barely take care of themselves.

"I am not a guerrilla. I am looking for an acquaintaince, nothing more." For emphasis I spread my coat, revealing my lack of
weapons.

"It don't matter. We got nothing to steal. We busted up all the
furniture to burn last winter. I had a house," she added. "Bushwhackers put the torch to it and killed my man. This boy was just
here when I come to get in out of the rain. I don't know his
story. There wasn't nobody else around. You can't take nothing
from me or him ain't already been took."

I believed her. Her tone was without life, producing words
with the grim tired inevitability of factory machinery. She resembled the buildings of the town, boarded over and left to the
weather.

"I wondered if any letters had come for me," I said.

She was silent. Then: "In there." She waggled the pistol barrel in the direction of the parlor.

I took a step over the threshold. The boy jabbed at me, then
moved back the same distance I had advanced. I came in the rest
of the way and turned toward the room where I had earned most
of my keep.

For the second time that morning, I felt that I had turned the
wrong way. The curtains had been pulled down, the organ and
carpet and most of the furniture was missing, and the floor was
caked with dried mud. I could not picture this barren room as the
place to which so many men had gravitated, lonely and needful
and far from home, in search of a respite from their wretched
condition: That corner, where a rat or a squirrel had gnawed a
hole in the wainscoting; was that indeed the spot where a griz-
zled sergeant with buckshot burrowed in the side of his face had
wept aloud at the end of "Darling Nellie Gray"? More immediately, I saw nothing that resembled the bundle of correspon-
dence I had come there hoping to find.

Or perhaps I did.

The fireplace, a narrow brick arch of the design then popular,
was heaped with ashes spilling untidily onto the hearth, as if
new fires had been kindled atop the remains of the old with no
cleaning in between—an intolerable state of affairs were Isabel
still in residence. I approached the heap with a sinking in my vi-

tals, slid a poker from among the implements leaning against the chimney, and crouched to turn over the layers of calcined paper and unburned sections of molding that covered the grate. Some of the sheets retained their original shape, although the heat had turned the cursive white while blackening the surface upon which it was written. I recognized my father's hand, my old name; a phrase, "despondent by the day." Putting aside the poker, I reached out with both hands and attempted gently to lift the burned leaf. It crumbled into cinders.

"Find your letters, did you?"

When I came back through the foyer, the woman had descended the stairs partway. Now she leaned on the railing with both hands, one of which still held the revolver, although she was no longer pointing it. Her eyes were alight, triumphant.

I said nothing, but kept walking toward the door.

"Fires don't start by theirselves!" She laughed. "Paper's the thing!"

Something stabbed me in my lower back. I whirled. The boy was on the other side of the staircase now, the broken pitchfork in his hands. I saw in his face the same expression worn by the woman. I felt blood trickling into my trousers. In a rage, I seized the handle of the fork near the tines and twisted it, breaking his grip. He leapt back, hissing like a cat, and flattened himself against the curve of the staircase. His eyes were as wide as dollars.

I stared back for a long time, breathing hard. Then I threw the fork clattering into the opposite corner, turned, and went out. As I hastened down the steps of the porch, reaching back with one hand to grope at my injury, I heard the woman shouting.

"See what it's like to lose all you got! Just see!"

My wounds, as I discovered when I stopped to wash them at the Kansas River, were superficial. The boy had been too timid or in too much of a hurry to put his weight behind the weapon. The worst of the three punctures was less than a quarter of an inch deep. I flushed them out with water, rubbed them with a piece of the salty bacon to purify them, and applied a patch cut from the tail of my spare shirt with sticky tree sap, as I had seen Frank James do after a saber had slashed his thigh at Pilot Knob.

I felt no anger toward the woman or the boy, nor did I pity

them. And I knew then that I had changed. Not grown; for one who has lost the ability to feel sorrow for those who are made to suffer through no fault of their own cannot be said to have advanced in his journey through life. Too many had died, too many had lost limbs and friends and family to the monstrous obscenity through which we were traveling for me to expend what remained of my humanity upon any one individual. In time, perhaps, I would begin again to share the pain of my brothers and sisters, and there commence the odyssey back to where I had started. Until then I could not return home, for fear that if I tried, I would find that place not to be my home at all. When that bundle of ashes had fallen apart in my hands, it had been a bridge collapsing. It would take much time to rebuild, and what I found at the end when I had rebuilt it would depend upon what sort of man I was when I started back.

On the riverbank I built a fire, cooked a piece of bacon and some beans in Rudd's rusty old skillet, then used the skillet to make coffee. When I finished cleaning up and packing, the mare's head was pointed west. I mounted and rode in that direction.

CHAPTER TWENTY

Abilene, when first I saw it, was not the place it would become in three short years. Then, the coming of the Union Pacific Railroad along the south bank of the Smoky Hill River, and the ballooning postwar cattle trade that would make a Mecca of every railhead between Chicago and El Paso, would render unrecognizable the little farming community where I stopped to rest and replenish my supplies on my way to the frontier. I found there a ragged cluster of a dozen or so log buildings on a prairie road, where the arrival of a stranger on horseback was entertainment sufficient to bring the residents to their doorways to study the phenomenon. I sensed, as I tied up before the mercantile and mounted the boardwalk, that the guitar slung behind my back might as well have been a live ostrich or a third arm for the interest it attracted. A number of the local men had followed me on foot along the walk and formed a knot in front of the door through which I was forced to make my way in order to gain access to the building.

The interior was dim, lit only by the sun coming through the small front window, with a floor made from half-sawn logs, merchandise stacked on shelves, a plank counter at the back, and a partition to the right with an opening cut through and a number of tables and chairs visible beyond. There, I assumed, drinks were served, discreetly separate from the mercantile side and the wives who browsed among the goods offered there. As I made this discovery, a plan began to form in my mind. I prayed I had the sand to pull it off.

The man behind the counter, lanky and sheathed in a white apron from neck to knees, lifted his thick brows as I approached. I suspected his curiosity was not directed so much at me as at the crowd I was towing behind me. Presently he smoothed back his black patent hair with the heels of both hands, swept a knuckle at each of his waxed moustaches, and asked what he could do for me. Plainly he had concluded he was in the presence of some great visiting personage—Secretary Seward, perhaps, or Charles Dickens at the least. As I drew near, however, and he became aware of both my youth and my somewhat travel-worn appearance, both his brows and his moustaches fell.

Quickly, before he could ask what was the meaning of this queer procession, I produced the scrap of soiled paper upon which I had scribbled my list of provisions. "A ham if you have it, sir, or two pounds of bacon if you do not. A sack of coffee, three pounds of flour, and a dozen fresh apples."

He hesitated, glowering, then slid a tablet in front of him, wet the tip of a stub of yellow pencil with his tongue, and totaled the purchases. "Buck twenty-three," he said. "I'm fresh out of ham."

I assumed a regretful expression that was not all the result of artifice. "I haven't even the twenty-three cents. However, I have a proposition to offer, if you can spare thirty seconds to hear it."

"Proposition." He tasted the word. "That better be some kind of U.S. currency."

"It can be."

He glanced sourly at the crowd that had gathered in his little store. I could read his thoughts. No man wants to take the chance of looking the fool before people he must face daily. "No."

"You have not heard the proposition," I said.

"All I want to hear is silver clinking on this here plank. If you can't do that, get going. I don't give credit to drifters."

"Aw, hear him out, Floyd," came a voice from the group behind me.

"What's thirty seconds?" came another.

Floyd's brow darkened. "Higher'n you can count, Gunderson." For a moment he was silent. Then his gaze lit upon a brown glass jug at the end of the counter. The label, printed black on manila, read:

DR. BEAN'S WORMER
For Permanent Relief from Ringworms,
Cutworms, Tapeworms, Roundworms, Pinworms,
Flatworms, Whipworms,
Hookworms, Seatworms,
and Filariasis

With one motion he hooked the jug up by its handle, upended it, and balanced it upon its cork on the counter. The contents, a glutinous mass, began to ooze down the side of the container toward the cork.

"You got till it settles." He folded his arms across the bib of his apron.

I slid the guitar around to the front, trying to keep my eyes off that migratory sludge as I explained to him, with carefully chosen hyperbole, the benefits of music to the alcohol trade: how a sentimental ballad (strumming a few bars of "Barb'ra Allen") can turn a man reflective, ordering drinks to sharpen a pleasant memory or deaden a painful one; how a sprightly quadrille ("Cindy") can erase his troubles, lifting his spirits and inspiring him to call for a round for the house to celebrate; how a patriotic march ("Hail, Columbia") can remind him of his proud national heritage and raise his freshly filled glass to the Founding Fathers; finally, how a song from one's own former homeland can return him to a place and time of innocence, thus mellowing the flavor of the rawest red whiskey.

For the last, presupposing an Irish origin for Floyd, I selected Bridey McMurtaugh's favorite, "Molly Malone," singing:

> *Alive, alive, oh!*
> *Alive, alive, oh!*
> *Crying, "Cockles, and mussels—"*

"Time's up." The counterman snatched up the jug and set it back down on its base.

There were angry protests, which Floyd stilled by reaching beneath the counter and slamming a two-foot section of iron bar onto its top. Evidently this bit of persuasion had been used to settle arguments before, as with a chorus of muttered halfhearted obscenities the group broke up and began drifting toward the door. I followed, crestfallen. I think now that I was less disappointed by the prospect of being forced to leave without the provisions I so desperately needed as by the knowledge that my first serious attempt to become a professional musician had been soundly rejected.

In front of the building, I found my path blocked once again as the group of horn-handed men in threadbare overalls boiled past on both sides and turned to confront me. I could not tell one anxious bearded sunburned face from another; work and weather and hopes worn as thin as their clothing had sculpted them all as alike as rocks in a canyon.

While we had been walking, they had all been talking at once, each trying to attract my attention ahead of his fellows. Now, as I offered it to them, they fell silent, shifting their weight from one foot to the other and avoiding my gaze. At length one of them, a big fellow with the rounded shoulders of an ox and hands the size of gunny sacks, swept off his shapeless felt hat and stood kneading it as he spoke. His drawl was as slow and thick as sour mash.

"Mister, I ain't heard 'Lubly Fan' since I left Alabama. I sure would—"

" 'Froggie Went a-Courtin'!" piped up another, a long drink of water with an animated Adam's apple.

There followed a cacophony of song titles, and again I was assailed by a mix of Eastern and Southern dialects, flattened by their distance from home and roughened by cursing at horses

and mules hitched to plows and harrows. To quiet them, I slid
my guitar back around and began strumming "All Hail the
Power of Jesus' Name," which I thought just the thing to placate
these simple God-fearing tillers of the soil. Indeed, they stopped
jabbering and backed away to give me room to play and air to
breathe.

And as I played, a remarkable transformation occurred. That
circle of worn and dirty faces, so similar when first I saw them,
drew inward, subsiding into forgotten expressions, so that by
the time I reached the final bars each countenance was separate
and singular, and tied to its place of origin: Here was the great
State of Alabama, honest and enduring; there was Maine, coura-
geous, pragmatic, and Puritan; over there, Illinois, Ohio, and
Michigan, and the oaken strength of the Northwest Territory;
and all those other places left behind in the rush to conquer new
worlds, and lost in the dust and desolation of the discovery that
a plot of earth in Kansas is pretty much like all the rest, worse
than some, and in any case no repository for dreams of grandeur.
I had come upon a pack of dumb brutes and uncovered a group
of men.

I did not stop there, but went directly into "Lubly Fan," then
"Froggie Went a-Courtin'," and as many of the asked-for tunes
as I could recall, adding a few from my expanding portfolio and
occasionally helping out a supplicant who could remember neither the name nor the lyrics of the one he wanted, and so
hummed a chorus until I found it on the strings. The light that
dawned on his face upon hearing the first notes was precious to
behold. I felt as a missionary must feel when he sees some be-
nighted soul embrace the Word.

All this was too much for the counterman, who came out to
find the entrance to his establishment obstructed by a musician
and his enraptured listeners, the latter sprawled upon the bench
outside the door and leaning against the posts that supported the
porch and seated on the boardwalk with their legs dangling over
the edge. He spun upon me, his moustaches bristling, and
slapped the palm of his free hand with the iron bar gripped in the
other.

"Just saying you ain't welcome ain't enough for some, looks
like," he said. "Some folks need to have it spelt out." He drew

the bar across his chest for a backhand swing. I shrank away, raising the guitar as a shield.

"Floyd, I see you ain't changed. You ought to take some of that wormer you buy by the barrel for a quarter and sell by the gallon for a dollar. Something's eating your guts for sartin."

Here was a voice to stop a riot or a stampede. I had never heard one to rival it and have not heard one since, though I have sat in the front row when Caruso sang in San Francisco and once pawned my guitar to hear Richard Mansfield deliver the soliloquy from *Richard III* at the Standard Theater in New York. Not quite a bellow, this; that implies exertion on the part of the speaker, and it came out too naturally for that. It was loud enough to drown out a herd of cattle, yet it sounded effortless, and left no room for doubt that it would be understood and heeded.

Certainly this was true in Floyd's case, for he froze on the spot, bludgeon cocked, eyes searching for the source of the interruption. Presently they settled upon the man standing in the middle of the street, one hand holding the reins of a buckskin horse some sixteen hands high, with shaggy fetlocks the size of melons and a mane that nearly swept the ground.

Man and horse were built to scale. Towering well over six feet in scuffed Wellingtons and a coat too heavy for the season that swung below his knees, he was a white-bearded length of gristle under a pearl-gray hat of the style referred to, for reasons that eluded me, as a "Wide-awake," with a brim almost as broad as his shoulders. It was plain to see from the dark, grainy texture of his skin that he was no stranger to the great outdoors. I placed his age around sixty.

One feature he possessed that I could not help staring at was an enormous goiter swelling above his collar. The inflated growth was nearly as large as his head and made him look for all the world like a two-hundred-pound bullfrog.

"Well, Bridger," Floyd said, much of the conviction gone from his tone, "I guess this ain't your affair."

"I know it. But I'm a meddlesome old coot. I come too late to hear this boy play, but he can't be so bad he needs his brainpan cracked open with a big old piece of metal."

"He's spoiling my business!"

"You run the only store in town. They'll be back. I'm asking you to put aside the bar."

When still Floyd hesitated, the man he called Bridger sighed heavily and unfastened with one hand the single button that closed his coat. The right side dropped away, exposing the leather-bound hilt of a knife at least fourteen inches long on his belt, its broad blade sheathed in a scabbard covered with Indian beadwork.

It seemed to me hardly the best weapon to select at a distance of not less than twenty feet, but it had its effect upon the counterman, who lowered his arm, muttering something I assumed was a curse in German. I closed my eyes at my own stupidity. Instead of "Molly Malone," I should have chosen *"Eine Kleine Nachtmusik."*

Bridger caught the eye of the man from Alabama. "What do you say, Yarbo? Should I of let Floyd put a window in the lad's skull, or can he get anything out of that box that don't scare half the game out of Dickinson County?"

A chorus of denials from the others overtook Yarbo's negative.

Bridger nodded. He seemed to take genuine satisfaction out of having made a just decision. "I'm partial to 'Greensleeves' myself. My first wife liked it a heap."

Recognizing a request when I heard one, I turned my attention to that old troubadour's favorite. To my chagrin, my hands were shaking too badly to make anything but a mess of the melody. I looked at him with an expression I knew was tragic.

The anticipation in the weathered old face set like the sun. "Well, it's got a parcel of notes." To Floyd: "Last time I went to Saint Louie this direction, I didn't see three people in your place. Seems to me you'd be a sight better off paying this boy to gather crowds inside." He buttoned his coat, chuckling softly. "Just a dumb notion, mind. I notioned myself right out of my own trading post on the Black Fork of the Green River."

Floyd glowered down at the boardwalk, swinging the iron bar idly at his toe-tops. "Can't pay," he said without looking at me.

I said, "Two meals a day and a cot will suffice. I'll earn my travel expenses in tips."

"That'll come to twice nothing. Last time a nickel showed it-

self here, folks rode clear in from Uniontown to get a look." He
went inside.

And so I joined the musical profession, with Jim Bridger, the
greatest mountain man and Indian scout of them all, as my first
booking agent.

CHAPTER TWENTY-ONE

J

In the fall of 1864 the war was still there, but it had not much
longer to run. Events began moving rapidly the moment I was
no longer intimately associated with them. As with anything that
is flying apart, shreds of war information reached me in Abilene,
carried by travelers on their way west.

One month to the day after the Centralia massacre, Bloody
Bill Anderson fell. Reports said he was leading his column along
a road half a mile north of Orrick, Missouri, in the southwest
corner of Ray County, when he was ambushed by Union infantry, who riddled him in their crossfire. They then lopped off
his handsome bearded head with a saber, dragged his body by its
ankles through the streets, and impaled the head atop a telegraph
pole to serve as a warning to his fellow guerrillas.

Soon afterward, General Sterling Price, deprived of his best
flank commander, withdrew his troops from Missouri. Without
the protection of the regular Confederate Army the raiders who
had served with Quantrill and Anderson were forced to disband
permanently. Six months later, inside a modest brick courthouse
in a town named Appomattox in Virginia, General Robert E.
Lee surrendered his saber to General Ulysses S. Grant, bringing
the Civil War to its conclusion. After four years, the great silence
that ensued was as a void in the air following the prolonged
clangor of a thousand great bells.

It was shattered one week later when an assassin's bullet
ended the life of President Lincoln at Ford's Theater in Washington City.

Despite that tragedy, there was celebration in the North that
the long nightmare was over. Although I raised my glass along

with the Union sympathizers gathered in Floyd's saloon annex when the surrender was announced, I had seen at close hand the hatred and bitterness attending the conflict, and knew that it would require more than a formal declaration to close the gaping wound that divided our republic. News of the president's murder confirmed my suspicions. A great deal more blood would stain the hands of North and South before they joined.

Meanwhile I was a success. Men did not come to a saloon to drink. If whiskey were all they wanted, they could purchase a bottle for far less than they paid for the same amount by the glass and consume it at their leisure in the comfort of home. When in Abilene they passed through that door from the mercantile side, they sought a neutral place where the hard work and heartbreak of grappling with the land for their existence could not follow. They came for the cool dimness, the company of other men who shared and understood their travails, the strong drink—and the music. Afternoons, evenings, and particularly Saturday night, when they left their fields early to come to town for supplies and to clear their souls for church the next morning, I took my place on a chair near the plank bar and played the guitar and sang. My voice, while not gifted, was pleasant, furnishing a welcome change from the braying of their mules and the disconcerting clang when a plow blade struck yet another rock to be prised up and carried to the edge of the field. When, courtesy of the odd transient who brought with him the lyrics of a new song from the metropolises in the East, I presented them with a melody and words they had not heard before, they pummeled my back and bought me drinks and behaved as if I had tapped into a secret underground spring that would irrigate all their properties and make them rich.

The late Stephen Foster's "Beautiful Dreamer" was just such a discovery. Released from among the composer's papers after his death the previous year, this bucolic selection set my listeners' faces aglow and quickly became the tune requested most frequently, as much as a dozen times in an evening. I still find myself humming it when my mind goes drifting, of all the thousands of refrains that are stored there.

In spite of the fact that I was responsible for the steady flow of business to the saloon side of his establishment, my relationship with Floyd remained cool, bordering upon hostility whenever I helped myself to a bowl of rabbit stew, chicken soup, or a slice of ham from the table he arranged daily for his customers. His senior partner, I learned, was Charles H. Thompson, the community's chief developer and tireless promoter, who was usually away in St. Louis or Kansas City, attempting to interest investors in his self-styled Eldorado. Thompson had introduced the free lunch to Kansas after the fashion of saloons in New York, Chicago, and San Francisco, about which he had read in *Harper's Weekly,* but his partner, whose duty it was to prepare the food and pay for it out of the meager monthly profits, disliked the idea intensely. That I, a nonpaying customer, should benefit from it, irritated him further. I ignored his black looks and partook heartily.

On my first full day there, I inquired when Mr. Bridger might drop in. I was grateful to him for helping me land my position and looked forward to treating him to a better rendition of "Greensleeves" to make up for my erratic attempt of the day before.

The counterman, who was busy placing a number of rat traps behind the foodstuffs on the shelves behind the counter, grunted. "You got plenty of time to practice. He left for Saint Louis at first light."

I asked when he would be back.

"Who the hell knows that? *Bridger* don't know. Six months, a year. Never, maybe. When he heads back West it might not even be through this part of the country, and then as like as not he'll probably get his scalp lifted by some damn injun. The time to expect that rawboned old son of a bitch is when he's standing square in front of you." Just then the spring trap he was setting out snapped, catching his thumb and sparking a cry in German that was no doubt vile.

I withdrew, sharply disappointed. I felt that I owed the great frontiersman his one request, and it dissatisfied me to think that he might go on the rest of his life believing me unequal to it.

At that time, I took the fact that Jim Bridger was a great frontiersman on faith. Before I met him I had never heard his name, but he was old, he had the look of a man who knew his way around rough country, and the bloodcurdling tales I had heard about life in the Western territories assured me that the very act of growing old there was in itself a great panegyric. Later I would hear the whole story, and know that I had been privileged to meet a man without peer, both in his own lifetime and beyond it.

Until then I subsisted. Floyd's parable of the nickel that was celebrated in the region for its rarity was not as much of an exaggeration as I had hoped. Popular though my music-making was, the gratuities that came my way were seldom tangible. My hand was shaken, my back slapped. If I accepted every third drink offered me, I would have been in worse shape than the occasional tragic soul who camped upon the porch since before dawn waiting for the establishment to open, hugging his knees lest he shake himself to pieces for want of liquid stimulation. Although I squirreled away what coins I was able to lay hands upon, hoping to collect enough to outfit myself for my intended journey west, the fraying of my collar and cuffs and the holes in the soles of my boots reminded me by the day that if I did not soon pay attention to them I would finish up barefoot and indecent. I commenced to wonder if I would ever get enough ahead to leave, or if this drab community where so many dreams had languished represented the end of the line. These were burdensome thoughts for a boy of eighteen.

I'd passed that mark almost without noting. One year earlier, thanks to Frank James, I had laid to rest my seventeenth in the sweet, fierce company of Nowata, the half-bred Cherokee romantic interest and sometime artist's model of Lieutenant John Thrailkill, and learned a number of things that could not have been taught me by any of the debutantes to whom my parents would have introduced me had I stayed in the city of my birth. This day began before dawn, when my slumber was interrupted by Floyd's rummaging among his baking utensils, which he habitually threw into a pile behind the stove in the cramped kitchen where I slept. (Very early in our arrangement I came to miss the relative privacy of my little pantry at Drucilla's.) I went outside, washed my face in the Smoky Hill River, in which splinters of ice floated, took a brisk walk to restore circulation to those portions of my anatomy grown numb from their contact with the floor through the thin straw pallet that served as my bed, breakfasted upon ham, potatoes, and coffee in the saloon, and was halfway through my morning guitar practice before I remembered the date.

I fancied that I appeared older than my years. I had grown an inch in the past twelvemonth—assuming my sleeves and the legs of my trousers had not shrunk—I was leaner, and when I stood away from the razor two mornings in succession, the shadow upon my cheeks accentuated the bones in a way I flattered myself was handsome. Once again I pledged to grow a beard as soon as I could be certain it wouldn't be one of those spun-sugar absurdities that made a young man resemble a boy in costume for a church pageant. My voice had dropped a full octave. Two or three of my regular listeners had commented favorably upon the change, which had taken place over a period of a month, with none of the grotesque breaks and squawks that often accompany that passage, and one of the farm wives who patronized the mercantile made so bold one day as to compliment me upon my singing, which she had overheard one afternoon while trying on straw hats from a recent St. Louis shipment. She was half her husband's age, and I thought I detected a note of cautious flirtation in her tone. It has since been my observation that youth and a pleasant singing voice present powerful challenges to the sacred oaths.

In spite of such diversions, my outlook during the first spring and summer of peace was not cheerful, particularly as the heat grew oppressive, accentuating the conviction that I was shut in in a close room without air. On one such day toward the end of July, I was perched upon my chair in shirtsleeves, my collar limp with sweat, strumming some lifeless melody in competition with the buzzing of a soporific fly, when one of my listeners came forward and said, " 'Rally 'Round the Flag,' please."

"I don't play war songs." I continued playing without looking up. I noticed he wore ornate boots with tooled shanks and protective flaps over the toes. A vague memory stirred at the sight, but I hadn't the energy or the inclination to ponder it. Of course he was not a native; a pristine pair of boots in Abilene could only be on their way to some other destination. Likely he was one of those scavengers swarming southward with official documents in their carpetbags empowering them to seize property from former secessionists for their personal aggrandizement. I had no sympathy for these carpetbaggers, and hoped this one would go away before I was forced to air my views upon the subject.

He dropped a coin into the cigar box I kept optimistically

open on the end of the bar. "You choose, then. Anything but that dirge you are playing. Your talents are wasted upon it."

I glanced with annoyance toward the copper I expected to find in the box, only to see the gold glinting off a five-dollar piece. It was more than I had collected there in the past month. Startled, I looked up—and recognized instantly the moon face, pale, browless eyes, and gracefully curved lips of the young man who had taken me for a secessionist in the train station at Indianapolis on my way west from New York. Was it only two years ago?

"You remember me," he said. "I'm flattered."

"You were with that sour detective fellow. I've forgotten your name."

"Jack Fabian. Mr. Pinkerton is abrasive, I agree. Still, there are advantages to working for him. He's in Chicago while I am here. That's one."

"I thought you worked in Chicago."

"Not anymore. I've been operating out of the Kansas City office since April. At present I'm on my way to Texas."

"You are dressed for it," I said ironically. Under his linen duster, he wore a tan twill suit with a striped vest—ideal for a Sunday row, but less than suitable for a hard ride across the Texas plain.

He ignored my gaucherie in a way I found conspicuously well bred. I caught myself wondering about his origins. "I seem to remember your saying you played the piano," he said.

I rested my hands upon the guitar. "Where I have been, they burned all the pianos to keep from freezing to death. Your war has been ruinous to culture."

"*My* war. Does this mean you are a Copperhead after all?"

"Sides are not the issue. It doesn't matter to an orphaned child which flag flies above his father's grave."

The corners of his lips curled upward in their catlike way. "You've learned much since Indianapolis, Billy Gashade." Something about the manner in which he pronounced the name suggested that he knew I had not been born to it.

I made no response. Outside the sun was going down; more customers had begun to shuffle in from the mercantile. The Pinkerton man stepped closer and lowered his tone.

"Quantrill is dead."

"I hadn't heard." I felt nothing. The guerrilla chief and I had met but once, and he had not impressed me.

"It happened two months ago, in a place called Smiley in Kentucky. Union cavalry tracked Quantrill and his band to a barn and shot him off his horse when he tried to escape. The rest of his guerrillas surrendered, except for a few. One of those who did not was Frank James."

His pale eyes were fixed on me as he imparted this information. I met his gaze. "Who is he?" I asked.

After a pause he moved his shoulders. "The agency has a warrant for James's arrest for the murder of a Kentucky Militia commander named Barnette. The incident took place after Appomattox, and so is not sanctioned by the articles of war. Our information is he and the others fled to Texas after the death of their leader. I am tracking his brother Jesse as well, and a guerrilla lieutenant named John Thrailkill." He described the three, down to Frank's auburn beard, Jesse's blue eyes, and Thrailkill's classic jaw. "I was wondering if they passed through here."

"I saw nobody who looked like that."

"I thought not." He sighed. "They would be avoiding civilization. According to our informants they are on their way to meet up with Cole and Jim Younger in Mineral Springs, do some recruiting, and return to Missouri. Lee's surrender meant nothing to them. They intend to continue murdering and plundering until they are stopped."

"That will not be easy," I said. "According to what I have heard."

"It would be a good deal less difficult without the protection of their friends."

Under his deceptively mild scrutiny, I picked out the opening bars of "Kingdom Coming" on my guitar.

His lips curled farther. "Good choice." Reaching into a vest pocket, he produced a card and another gold coin and placed both in the cigar box. "You can wire me at this office if you should see any of the men I described. Someone will forward the communication. The agency is offering a reward of five hundred dollars for information leading to their capture."

"For one or all?"

"That point is negotiable," he said. "Short of extortion."

"What if they are not captured, but are killed instead?"

"The result is the same. All our client wants is to be rid of them."

"Your client?"

"The people of the United States of America."

"The Union I knew was not disposed to post human bounty," I said.

"The Union you knew was seriously injured at Fort Sumter. It took a mortal wound at Shiloh and died at Gettysburg. We buried it at Appomattox."

"Thank you, Captain Fabian. For your contribution." I reached over and flipped shut the lid of the box.

"We are old acquaintances, Billy. Call me Jack."

"I prefer not to."

He took off his slouch hat, creased the crown between two fingers, and replaced it. "Then I shall call you Mr. Gashade. What is a name, after all? One changes it as readily as his shirt."

He left, and I was told later that he mounted a blaze-faced black tethered in front of the building and rode west leading a chestnut loaded down with packs. Alone that night, stretched out on my pallet, I examined his card in the light of the lantern I used for reading. It contained, in addition to the name "J. T. Fabian" and an address in Kansas City, a single, wide-open eye with an accusatory arched brow, and beneath it the legend:

"WE NEVER SLEEP."

Chapter Twenty-two

Floyd clamped each of the gold coins in turn between his teeth and studied the results. His expression was as somber as if they had shown themselves to have been made of lead.

"Nobody's had any gold around here since Jed Oxley pried out his fillings to pay for a plow," he said.

"Will it cover my outfit?" I inventoried the items spread across his counter against the list I had made by the light of my lantern the night before: flour, coffee, apples, beans, bacon, a canteen, halter leather to secure packs and make repairs, two flannel shirts, two pairs of whipcord trousers, a blanket, a corduroy coat, and a good pair of riding boots. It had been my pleasure to watch the counterman's moustaches droop when I added the five-dollar pieces to the bent and tarnished coppers and nickels I had hoarded away over the course of a year.

"You got change coming." It was clear he was loath to surrender the point. I never met a man more disgusted by his own honesty than Floyd. I assume he died penniless, and I doubt he was very much surprised. "You headed for China, or just Africa?" he asked.

"Both, perhaps. After I have seen all of this country. I'm off for the frontier."

"What you want to go out there for? All that's there is injuns and rattlesnakes."

"Have you been there?"

"A man don't have to go to the North Pole to know it's cold." He balanced my change in the palm of his hand and squinted one eye. "I could let you have an old Colt for the difference. The action's so loose you got to hold the cylinder back against the frame or the firing pin won't engage, but it beats spitting in some red buck's eye when he's cutting your throat."

"I am done with pistols. I'll take the chance."

"You'll get scalped."

"I'll wear a hat."

"How you figure to get food when your cash runs out?"

I slapped the guitar. "I shall sing for my supper."

Snarling, he tipped the change into my hand. "I was starting to get used to you. I ain't heard a complaint about that noise you make in a week."

"Why, Floyd, are you saying you'll miss me?"

"Go to hell."

I left Abilene with no plan other than to follow the Smoky Hill River, putting in at Fort Harker by dark, and there find out about the situation to the west before venturing farther. I had no map and only a vague sense of the geography through which I would be traveling. Reckless though this may sound in our day of detailed highway routes and auto club directories, there was nothing else for it then. Maps in those days were difficult to obtain, and so unreliable (based as they were upon speculation and hearsay) that to have one proved more often a hindrance than a help. The entire central section of our continent from western Kansas to the border of California was usually drawn as an enormous blob labeled the Great American Desert, and was said by some to contain all manner of curiosities and hazards, from quicksand seas the size of New Jersey to two-headed cannibals and snakes that took their tails in their mouths and rolled downhill. The only way to cross it was to proceed to the next dim light of civilization and then the next, picking up information at each place about the next day's ride.

Fort Harker, when I came to it, was still in the early stages of construction. Muleskinners and bullwhackers hitched their teams to fresh-sawn logs and whipped and cursed them to the top of a hill overlooking the river, where army engineers sharpened the logs with adzes at both ends and sank them into the earth to form a stockade. Stripped to the waist, their backs brown and glistening, they put me in mind of Egyptian slaves raising the pyramids at Giza. The oaths with which they performed their labor, however, were decidedly Anglo-Saxon in origin.

An Irish sergeant who acted as foreman of the crew, prematurely white-haired, with muttonchop whiskers and a pattern of blue-black spots beneath the skin of his right cheek that I attributed to the shotgun barrel of a Confederate LaMatte pistol, directed me to a corner inside the stockade where I could spread my blanket. That night, as I sat cross-legged upon the blanket playing before a small fire I had built of twigs and bark that had fallen from the cut logs, the sergeant came over and asked if he could join me. I informed him that it was a free country and that since the heat coming from the other side of the fire was going to waste anyway, he was welcome to have a seat.

He lowered himself carefully, making the faces that went with having a stiff back, and rolled a cigarette. "Nice," he said of the piece I had just finished. "It ain't English, I hope?"

"It's German, as a matter of fact. I got it from a farmer in Abilene, who learned it from his grandfather. It's about a man who takes his own life because he believes his wife to be untrue."

"Sad."

"The farmer had occasion to remember it. His wife hanged herself in their cabin while he was outside plowing his field."

"Was she untrue?"

"No. Merely tired."

"That can do it." He lit his cigarette with a stick from the fire. "Headed west?"

"Yes."

"Texas?"

"I don't know."

"Everyone's going to Texas, seems like. Some to Mexico. There's a revolution going on down there, as if four years of that up here wasn't enough. Lord, Lord." He shook his white head. "You want to watch your topknot. One of our patrols seen dog soldiers as close as Larned."

"Dog soldiers?"

"Renegade Cheyenne, answering to nobody or nothing. Ever since Chivington give Black Kettle what-for at Sand Creek they been hot as hornets. Savages."

I played through the silence that followed this pronouncement. Then: "I should think the troopers at Fort Larned would be able to contain these dog soldiers."

"You can't contain what you can't catch. Injuns is all yellow. They won't fight when they can run."

"If they're so cowardly, why does the army bother to build forts?"

"They ain't forts, they're fences. Being yellow, injuns take out their mad on women and children and pilgrims traveling alone, like you. We build these here fences to put the women and children and pilgrims inside so they can keep their scalps."

"The stage is coming," I said, "and after that the railroad. Your fences can't protect all the women and children and pilgrims they will bring."

The sergeant grinned around the cigarette clamped between his teeth. "The red bastards can't run forever. When we finish putting up fences they won't have no more *room* to run. That's when we start picking them off, like flies on horseshit."

I studied his face in the firelight, all pouched shadows and polished bone and buckshot beneath the skin like spots of mold. I said, "I'm turning in now, Sergeant. Thank you for warning me about the dog soldiers."

"It's early yet. I'd admire to hear that piece again about the farmer's wife that hung herself."

"No, in the song it was the man who took his life."

"I liked it better when it was the woman. A man that would pull his own cork on account of he found out his woman was peddling her ass ain't no kind of man in my book..He should of pulled *her* cork. There's something worth singing about." He got up with a grunt and flicked his cigarette into the darkness. "Sleep fast, young fellow. One night's all you get. This ain't the Palmer House."

Left alone, I considered Captain Jack Fabian's dry eulogy for the innocent nation slain in the war. Something had expired in me as well: the faith in the basic goodness of man that would have been troubled by the sergeant's philosophy of hate. I slept well in spite of him.

When the first steel rays lanced above the horizon, I fixed myself a breakfast of bacon and coffee and went to the picket line to untie the dun mare. I asked the man who was guarding the horses, a trooper with a face like a grave monkey, how far it was to Fort Larned. He told me if I headed south I would reach the Arkansas River by midmorning; following it west would bring me to the fort by nightfall. When noon came and went and I had not come within sight of the river, I decided either the distance had been greatly underestimated or I was lost. The heat was punishing. When I found the river at last I let the mare drink and got down on my stomach to fill my canteen. When the ripples on the surface of the water smoothed out, I saw three fearsome reflections staring back at me.

Startled, I looked up. In the river near the opposite bank, three horses stood up to their knees drinking. Their riders, nearly naked, had smooth, hairless torsos and were painted to the waist in broad swaths of black and vermilion. All three cradled long-barreled rifles across their laps.

Back in 1932, during dinner at William Randolph Hearst's preposterous castle at San Simeon, I chanced to hear the diamond-plated wife of a studio mogul seated near the end of the long table declare that she regretted the purchases she had *not* made more than the ones she had. I reflected that this was definitely true in the case of the old Colt I had elected not to buy in Abilene. However, if I had indeed bought the pistol, I most certainly would have grabbed for it at the moment I saw that trio of Indian warriors, and been shot down for my trouble. As it was I

merely placed my palms against the ground and pushed myself
to my feet without taking my eyes from the newcomers.

For a time after I rose, there was no movement save the rush
of the water and the four animals drinking. Then one of the Indians turned his head slightly in the direction of the man
mounted nearest him and spoke. The other laughed shortly, then
raised his rifle to his shoulder and pointed it at me.

The crash of the report was like a physical blow. I staggered,
certain I was hit. Then I saw the Indian who had aimed at me
reel. He dropped his rifle into the river and would have fallen in
after it had not the man next to him grasped his arm and pulled
him upright. The stricken brave was wounded on the right side,
the blood smearing his paint. Yipping like an angry terrier, the
third Indian wheeled his horse, braced his rifle along his right
forearm, and snapped a shot toward the opposite bank. The others turned as well, bounding their horses up and over the bank
and galloping away toward the south. The wounded man had recovered himself enough to ride, but from the angle he was leaning, it was clear he would not have his seat long.

Dazed by the sequence of events, I turned—and ducked immediately behind my mare for protection. A rider was bearing
down hard upon me from the north aboard a tall buckskin whose
long mane and tail fluttered behind it like black fire. He did not
slow down as he came near, but swept past me at full gallop,
shrieking at the top of his lungs and swinging his long rifle in
one hand above his head like a club. Man and horse hit the water
with an explosion. They were nearly across the river when the
man drew rein and stood in his stirrups, waving the rifle and
shouting what I assumed were imprecations at the departing Indians, for he spoke in gutturals and consonants which for me
held no meaning.

At length, apparently satisfied that they were not coming
back, the man lowered himself into the saddle, turned his horse
in the current, and started back in my direction. Now I recognized his long coat, so incongruous in the heat, his scarred, high-
topped Wellington boots, and the great sweeping brim of his
gray sombrero. More to the point, I recognized his gristly, white-
stubbled face and the goiter on his throat, so like the sac of a har-
rumphing bullfrog. As he kicked the buckskin up the bank on my

side of the river, I saw by the glint in his small steely eyes that he knew me as well.

"Mister *git*-ar man," greeted Jim Bridger, reining in to look down at me. "I sure hope after going to all this trouble I can count on you being all practiced up on 'Greensleeves.' "

CHAPTER TWENTY-THREE

♪♪

Injuns ain't yellow." Bridger used his clasp knife to whittle slices off a wild onion into the skillet where our bacon and beans were frying. "Some are, I reckon, just like some whites. They ain't no better nor no worse'n the rest of us, and they ain't all one way or all t'other. They don't like things starting out like this and winding up like that. That's the reason them three taken off when one got shot. That weren't cowardly. That was just plain good sense. Nobody but a fool fights when he don't know what he's fighting."

"A sergeant at Fort Harker told me they only attack those who can't defend themselves."

"White-headed jasper? Buckshot in his cheek?" I nodded. "That'd be Mulcahy. He's got balls as big as boulders and brains the size of these here beans. He wouldn't know a *Wōhksēh'hētăniu* from a digger Pawnee."

"All the same, I am grateful to you for rescuing me from those dog soldiers."

"Who said they was dog soldiers?"

"The sergeant—"

"Them weren't renegades. The whole damn Cheyenne Nation's on the prod, and they're all of them as fired up as any of the dogs. That bloody mess at Sand Creek last fall killed any chance of peace with Black Kettle." As he spoke, he became agitated. The knife moved faster and faster. Some of the onion shavings fell outside the pan.

"Chivington," I said, echoing the name I had first heard upon the lips of Sergeant Mulcahy.

"*Colonel* Chivington, he calls himself. Bloody butcher is

more like it. Some of them he kilt was sucking their mother's teats. There's yellow for you."

Profiled in the firelight, the cords in his neck stood out and the growth on his throat appeared more puffed-up than ever. I considered that so much tension was dangerous for a man in his sixties, even for one as hearty as he. Leaning back against my saddle—we were camped fifteen miles upriver from where we had encountered the Indians, in a stand of dogwoods whose branches shredded the smoke of our fire and whose trunks deadened its glow lest we attract the attention of more hostiles—I pulled over my guitar. I played "Greensleeves," of course, this time the way it should be played, or at least as well as it can be without a mandolin, as it was originally intended. A few bars into the sylvan melody, Bridger's entire body began to slacken. His shoulders relaxed, his tendons retreated, he settled back on his heels. The deep lines in the weathered old face smoothed out.

"My first wife was rotten partial to that song," he said, using the blade of his knife to turn over the thick bacon slices. "She was a Flathead, which is a civilized tribe. They make the best wives. I'm powerful sorry I doubted your ability to play it."

"How many wives have you had?"

"Three."

"All Flatheads?"

"No, the second was Snake. If you can't get a Flathead, you can do heaps worse than a Snake. They're gentle as a kit fox when they're gentle and full of piss and vinegar when you want them that way. Sometimes when you don't. One time she brained me with the blunt end of a splitting maul. I was out for six days."

"Did you divorce her?"

"No, she died. The Flathead died too. I sure hope the Arapaho I'm married to now keeps her health. I don't think I could go through another injun wedding ceremony. Grub's ready."

I put the guitar aside and held up my tin plate while he scraped food from the skillet. A slice of the bacon and some of the beans fell into the fire and he cursed. "Better hold it a mite closer. This child's eyes ain't what they used to be up close. Not for far neither. Time was when I could see signal smoke ten miles before them army shavetails could pick it up with their damn glasses.

Don't never get old, son, that's Bridger's advice. Oncet you're there they ain't no place else to go but dead."

I could see he was brooding, so I tried to cheer him by complimenting him upon his cooking. I didn't need to exaggerate. I could not see how the mere addition of some wild onions he had picked along the trail could so transform the meals I'd been eating since leaving Abilene. Indeed, I've never sampled cooking to compare with the old mountain man's, and I've dined in the best restaurants our two coasts have to offer.

He shook his head. He ate directly from the skillet with his fingers, and a more fastidious eater you've never seen with a knife and fork. He made me ashamed of the utensils I was using. "You ain't et spaniel the way a Sioux woman can roast it in a clay pot buried in buffler shit. Melts in your mouth like sweet lard."

"*Cocker* spaniel?"

"Well, mostly. Them injun barkers ain't too particular what they mount."

The talk shifted to our immediate plans. I asked him about Wyoming, where he was employed as chief of Indian scouts at Fort Laramie with the rank of colonel.

"It's sweet country if you like wind that won't quit and rain coming down like iron stoves and heat so hot you can fry bacon on the back of your neck and cold so cold you piss icicles. But you can ride for a week without passing a thing on two legs and that suits this child."

"This one too. I've just been through a war, which is about too many people fighting for too small a plot of ground."

"Wyoming ain't for you." He took a gulp of scalding coffee from his battered cup.

"Why not?"

"That *git*-ar's your hunting rifle. The saloon's your range. With Red Cloud all painted up for war in the Big Horns and Black Kettle the same in Colorado, everybody that likes his scalp is doing his drinking at home. You'd best bide your time in Kansas till the army flushes them out. I'm on my way to meet this carpetbagger colonel named Carrington to do just that. It shouldn't take long, provided I can talk him out of this foolishness of dragging a wagon train with him everyplace he goes. You got to catch up with injuns if you want to force a fight. Otherwise they trickle away into cracks and holes like spring runoff." He chuckled then, a dry rustle in his swollen throat. "Just a dumb notion, mind. I notioned myself right into a Blackfoot arrow trapping the Missouri in thirty-two."

"One of your notions kept me from starving in Abilene," I said. "I have had my fill of Kansas for a while. What is the situation in Texas?"

"That's like asking what's the situation in South Americky. Which part?"

"The Southwest. I've been to the Northeast."

"Mexicans, Comanches, and Apaches. The first ain't got nothing to put in your *see*-gar box and the rest'll cut off your balls and wear 'em for earrings. Either way there ain't much future there for a man in your trade. You might try Fort Riley."

"Where's that?"

"You must of passed it on your way to Abilene. It weren't much to look at then, I expect. They beefed it up since for the same reason they're building these others, to guard the overland stage and then the railroad, if they ever get started on it. Talk is they're getting a new commander, one of them ninety-day generals from the late unpleasantness. He's a young fellow, I hear, and likes his fun. He's sure to put up an officer's bar where you can work for scrip. Some carpetbagger kind of name. I disremember it just now."

"If you think it's best." My disappointment showed in my tone. To reverse directions now symbolized for me a regression in time, when what I wanted most was to put the past behind me.

"Don't take it so bad. You're young, you got time to walk around the world twicet and stop for noon dinner besides. All I got to look forward to is another arrow in the right place this time, or a hunnert and sixty acres of dirt in Missouri if I ain't that lucky. The plow's all there is when you can't read sign no more. Care to trade?"

I said nothing, depressed not only by my own prospects, but by the old mountaineer's self-pity as well. They were a dour lot, these veterans of the frontier.

Suddenly he smacked his knee, startling me with the noise. "Custer!"

"I beg your pardon?"

"George Custer. That's the name of the fellow that's set to take over Fort Riley. You ought to give the place a whirl. Talk is he's headed for tall things."

CHAPTER TWENTY-FOUR

At age nineteen, George Wymore, a student attending classes at William Jewell College in Liberty, Missouri, found a curious kind of immortality. On February 14, 1866—St. Valentine's Day—he walked around a corner into a fusillade of bullets and was dead when he hit the ground, the first fatality of the first daylight bank robbery in American history.

A few minutes previously, two men wearing slouch hats and dusters walked into the business office of the Clay County Savings Association, drew revolvers on Greenup and William Bird, father-and-son employees of the bank, and stuffed a grain sack with cash from the vault. After shutting up the two employees in the vault, the pair joined ten of their confederates guarding the street outside, mounted their horses, and rode out hard, firing their pistols at windows and the sky and yelping like wild dogs. It was at this point that the hapless Wymore stepped from the obscurity of undergraduate academia into history. When a young physician with ancient eyes examined the body later, he declared each of its four wounds fatal. This represented a quality of marksmanship unheard of before the war, and while the victim's friends and family mourned his loss, the newspaper-reading public swiftly concurred on the specific arena that had turned out sharpshooters of such skill and daring.

The amount reported stolen was also unprecedented: sixty thousand dollars. Rumor held that the editors of the St. Louis *Missouri Republican,* while setting the story in type, argued over how many zeroes the figure entailed. Of course this tale was apocryphal. Four years of casualty counts had educated an entire nation upon the configuration of thousands.

A group of hastily deputized citizens mounted upon their own

horses and armed with personal weapons, referred to as a
"posse"—after the Latin term *posse comitatus,* meaning "force
of the county"—tracked the bandits to a country church, paint-
less with paper tacked over the missing panes in its windows,
where bill wrappers bearing the bank's name told them their
quarry had stopped there to "split up the take." After that they
lost the thieves' trail in a fierce blizzard.

That the men involved in the raid were former guerrillas was
accepted without discussion. Much time would pass, and several
more thousands would disappear into grain sacks, before names
were publicly applied to the faces behind the bandanna masks
they wore. For my part, I suspected who they were as soon as I
heard of their noisy method of retreat. The remnants of the band
that had followed the black flag of William Clarke Quantrill and
Bloody Bill Anderson had not changed tactics since the sack of
Lawrence.

I remembered Jack Fabian's report that Frank and Jesse James
and John Thrailkill had been on their way to Texas to meet Cole
and Jim Younger, planning to return to Missouri and their old
habits.

News traveled slowly across the prairie. By the time I learned
about Liberty, I had been at Fort Riley several months, wondering what had persuaded me to stop there for more than a day. It
was November, not my favorite month by twelve; and November is a particularly miserable time on the Kansas plain, when
the great sweep of emerald grass has gone the dead brown of
beetles' wings on a dusty windowsill and the first raw winds of
winter blow straight down from Canada, chilling equally the
townsman in his woolen muffler and the trapper in his buffalo
coat. Unlike the bitter, flinty cold of December and January,
which numbs the skin upon contact and flees on pins and nee-
dles in the presence of a warm fire, November's cold is damp
and cloying, and separates itself from one's spine reluctantly,
like a leech being pulled away from its host. In the sutler's store
where I spent all my time when I wasn't huddled in my unheated
lean-to outside the stockade, many a liquid cough and snuffling
intake of breath told me I was not alone in my wretchedness.

The knowledge was cold succor. The store, a poorly chinked
log hovel, was overheated to compensate for the imperfection,
giving the occupants the choice of loitering near the walls and

shivering in the draughts that whistled through the holes between the logs or moving closer to the center and suffocating in
the soporific glow of the pig-iron stove. The air was thick with
the mingled stenches of unwashed wool, tobacco juice, raw
whiskey, and urine, the last from the corners beyond the lamplight where drunken troopers relieved themselves into the sawdust when they were too unsteady to walk outside. A clapboard
partition separated this room from the officers' bar, a slightly less
feral atmosphere from which the click of colliding billiard balls
announced an additional diversion for the men who commanded
other men. Admission to enlisted men and nonmilitary person-
nel was by invitation only. I had found the officers of Fort Riley
a distinctly unmusical lot, and so I played for those troopers and
noncommissioned officers who upon rare occasions were moved
to contribute a creased and stained rectangle of the post currency known as army scrip to my cigar box. The scrip was re-
deemable for goods at the store, and so kept me from starving.

I had by this time acquired a second instrument, to whose re-
course I turned when the guitar had ceased to draw a reaction
from the stupefied relics of human refuse who had drifted into
the service since the cream of the nation's youth was sacrificed
to the soil from Richmond to Bull Run. The banjo had been
among the personal possessions left behind in the barracks by a
trooper who had deserted while out on patrol, whose sergeant
had offered it to me rather than throw it out or lose it at poker. I
had taken to it more quickly than I had to the guitar, and through
its more impudent sound discovered life in a number of tunes I
had hitherto employed only as a bridge between greater crowd
pleasers. It was singularly suited to an Irish drinking song taught
to me by a former Killarney resident who told me he had enlisted
in the U.S. Army during a campaign to fill the Union register in
Ireland, then learned while his ship was anchored in New York
Harbor that the city Enrollment Office was paying a hundred
dollars to each new recruit, whereupon he jumped overboard,
swam to shore, and enlisted again. Shortly after teaching me the
song, he deserted.

He had company. Post life for the most part was hardship and
boredom, and with the fighting ended in the East and South the
ranks filled with filth and degenerates, fortune hunters, adven-
turers, men sought for crimes committed under other names,

and no small number of disillusioned rebels, who "lit a shuck" for home or the various frontier towers of Babel as soon as they were issued clothing, a weapon, and a mount. Those who remained included hard-drinking Irishmen, misfits from the East like myself, pederasts, cardsharps, and confidence men, many of whom hung around only to prey upon their inmates. Morale was low. Fistfights occurred daily; troopers were sent to the guardhouse on a regular basis for drunkenness while on parade; and there were dark rumors that the fort's new commander was a *dilettante* and a notorious "welsher" when it came to paying off his poker debts. Although the circle to whom these wagers were owed contained such forgiving types as his wife, his younger brother, and a number of friends of long standing, the unpaid markers were a point of harsh conjecture among the perverts and putative murderers who discussed them in low tones with sidelong glances whenever the commander hove in sight.

His gaming practices aside, the C.O.'s credentials were sterling. A splendid figure in tailored uniforms who affected the sail-brimmed hats and fringed buckskin coats of the frontiersman, with coppery locks flowing to his shoulders in defiance of the hostile Indian's predilection for handsome scalps, he had, for courage and audacity in the fighting at Blue Ridge, been promoted from first lieutenant to major general, at age twenty-three the youngest man ever to attain that high rank. Although he had been forced to surrender that brevet position at the end of the war to assume the rank of lieutenant colonel, he continued to be addressed as "general" according to the military custom and held himself as if he had not stepped down at all. In residence at Fort Riley for just over a week, he had through strict adherence to the manual of arms and swift punishment for offenses against the code of conduct—slovenly appearance at muster, for instance, meant lugging a heavy length of tree trunk upon one's shoulder around the parade ground for as long as twenty-four hours; two lengths for a second offense, and a saddle and full kit for a third—established himself as a man to obey before God and government. He was probably the most admired man I ever came to know—and the most poisonously hated.

Coincidentally, I was reflecting upon all this as I picked my way through the Irish air when an erect figure stepped in front of me, very nearly clicking his heels to get my attention, and I

ooked up into the callow, wispily moustachioed face of Lieu-
enant Myles Moylan, the commander's adjutant.

"Mr. Gashade, I am sent to ask if you are not too busy if you
would care to join General Custer in the officers' bar."

George Armstrong Custer was seated in a chair near the par-
or stove that warmed that scarcely more genteel side of the es-
ablishment, idly scratching one of his four great greyhounds
behind the ears and balancing a glass of what appeared to be
emonade upon his right knee. I'd heard he was a teetotaler,
though I had hardly credited the information based upon what I
had observed of the army's bibulous ways, and wondered how
much of this abstemious display was a pose for the ranks; later
learned that the leader of the newly formed Seventh Cavalry
had no capacity for liquor whatsoever and, being Custer, had
chosen sobriety over looking the fool. The other three dogs lay
or sat about his feet, one of them industriously licking its geni-
als. They were gaunt, stupid creatures with narrow heads and
long curved snouts like rats', and were forever getting lost on the
prairie when their master took them out upon his beloved hunts
for deer and buffalo, forcing him to dispatch a patrol to find
them and lead them home. I detested them thoroughly, and as a
ule I like dogs.

For a full minute after I presented myself before him, the general said nothing, watching me and scratching the dog at his
side, which rolled its eyes and grinned dementedly, showing its
eyeteeth. Custer was then about twenty-six, but his prominent
bones, deeply sunken blue eyes, and the heavy, horseshoe-
shaped moustaches whose weight drew his skin taut made him
ook older. His celebrated curly hair was receding, twin horns of
pink scalp appearing alongside his widow's peak.

"Gashade," he said suddenly. His voice, a clipped, clear tenor,
actually made the glasses ring behind the bar. "A name of French
derivation, is it not?"

"I believe it is," I replied.

"Civilized people, the French. Terrible soldiers. Bonaparte
used up the best of them. I expect the current Bonaparte will
ind that out soon enough. What was that tune you were play-
ng just now?"

"A carousing song. The man who taught it to me said the
Royal Irish Fusiliers played it to taunt the French troops storm-

ing the beach at Tarifa, Spain, in 1811. The Irish turned back the attack. Perhaps you were right about the French."

"Does it have words?"

"Yes."

Custer stretched out a leg, hooked a vacant chair with his ankle, and scraped it toward me. "Sing it."

I thought of refusing. The Boy General, as he was referred to by those who were unaffected by his not inconsiderable charm (when they weren't calling him names less printworthy), seemed not to have recovered from the meteor-swing that had carried him overnight from shavetail to the top of the ranks; plainly he expected everyone within his orbit, soldier and civilian, to snap to his command after the example of his dogs. However, the officers' bar was heated more evenly than the enlisted men's, and I was no longer diverted by the curious sensation of roasting upon one side whilst freezing upon the other. I took the seat, placed the banjo in my lap, strummed the melody, and raised my voice above the popping in the stove:

> Let Bacchus's sons be not dismayed,
> But join with me each jovial blade;
> Come booze and sing, and lend your aid
> To help me with the chorus—
> Instead of Spa we'll drink brown ale,
> And pay the reckoning on the nail,
> No man for debt shall go to jail
> From GarryOwen in Glory!
> No man for debt shall go to jail
> From GarryOwen in Glory!

I played and sang it through from start to finish, all seven verses, inserting the chorus after each. Doing so extended my time by the stove, as if by soaking in as much heat as possible I could store it through the night in my clammy quarters. The significance was not lost upon me that with each change of location since leaving New York I had descended a full stage in sleeping arrangements, going in three short years from coffee and scones in a four-poster to a discarded army blanket in an abandoned corn crib, with a pint of raw whiskey to prevent my blood from freezing in my veins. Perhaps that was why I feared to quit Fort

Riley. My next berth might be a shallow doorway or the naked ground of the prairie, where I would be prey to coyotes and hostile tribes. For hostile they all were now, from Oregon to the Gulf of Mexico, the Sioux and Arapaho and Cheyenne and Comanche and Apache nations having declared war upon the railroads, the telegraph, pioneers, cattle companies, and the U.S. Army.

I must say in my defense that I tried no one's patience. In fact, by the third refrain, nearly everyone within earshot had joined in to sing "From GarryOwen in Glory"—the half-dozen officers present, the white-coated corporal serving drinks behind the bar, and a number of men on the other side whose bodies could not follow their voices through the door that separated them from officers' country without facing discipline. Custer alone held his silence. It was impossible to tell what was going on behind that monolithic countenance, all hollows and ridges with his eyes burning like blue-gas flames in the shadows.

"A carousers' song indeed," said he, when I had finished and the members of my impromptu choir were congratulating themselves upon their harmony. "What is Spa?"

"Mineral waters, General." I had nearly addressed him as *sir.* "I'm told the song originated in Limerick, which was famous for its springs."

"Do you agree that hard liquor is superior to the healing waters of Mother Earth?"

"Not having sampled such waters, I wouldn't know." I rose and shouldered my banjo and guitar. It was clear I'd overstayed my invitation.

"Where are you going?" he demanded.

"To bed. It's late, and I have been up since reveille."

"Why? You are not employed by the garrison."

"Your bugle doesn't know that, sir." There it was, curse him. "It's as loud for a civilian as it is for a soldier."

He stopped scratching the greyhound's ears. The dog looked at him, then lowered itself to the floor with a prolonged sigh. Custer applied the same slow, pensive stroking to his moustaches. "Would you consider teaching that song to the regimental band?"

I opened my mouth, then shut it. Then I had to open it again to speak. "I wasn't aware there was a regimental band."

"What is that? W-what is that?" Agitated, he began to stutter. "There is no glass in the west windows of the married officers' quarters, either; Libby and I have had to stuff them with rags to keep out the cold. But glass is coming, and so is a band. I shall start you on trooper's wages tomorrow. You will continue to draw pay while the band gets set up and until they have the tune down. Do not try to draw it out, mind. Out you go when the job is done."

"Does it include quarters?"

"You will bunk in the barracks. You are not Paganini. You will be issued a blanket and clothing, and you will dine with the men at mess."

"I accept."

"Of course you do. Perhaps a good drinking song is what's needed to make a regiment of this vermin. Lord knows the Temperance League would starve here. Lieutenant!"

"Yes, sir!" This time Moylan really did click his heels.

"See that Mr. Gashade gets what he needs."

"Yes, sir."

That night, stretched out upon my plank bunk in the cavalry barracks with a stove at either end, flanked by a trooper whose sinus condition rattled the windows and a corporal masturbating under his blanket, I crossed my arms behind my head and wriggled my toes, luxuriating in my good fortune. I only hoped that Frank and Jesse James and John Thrailkill never found out I was working for the Union.

CHAPTER TWENTY-FIVE

*We are the boys that take delight in
Smashing the Limerick lamps when lighting,
Through the streets like sporters fighting,
And tearing all before us.*

*Instead of Spa we'll drink brown ale,
And pay the reckoning on the nail,*

No man for debt shall go to jail
From GarryOwen in Glory!
No man for debt shall go to jail
From GarryOwen in Glory!
We'll break windows, break the doors
The watch knock down by threes and fours;
Then let the doctors work their cures,
And tinker up our bruises.

(Chorus)

We'll beat the bailiffs, out of fun,
We'll make the mayor and sheriffs run;
We are the boys no man dares dun,
If he regards a whole skin.

(Chorus)

Our hearts, so stout, have got us fame,
For soon 'tis known from whence we came;
Where'er we go they dread the name
Of GarryOwen in Glory.

(Chorus)

Johnny Connell's tall and straight,
And in his limbs he is complete;
He'll pitch a bar of any weight,
From GarryOwen to Thomond Gate.

(Chorus)

GarryOwen is gone to rack
Since Johnny Connell went to Cork,
Though Darby O'Brien leapt over the dock
In spite of judge and jury.

(Chorus)

An unregenerate crew, those fusiliers; but they and their Homeric Connell and O'Brien had nothing upon the men of the Seventh, as drunken and belligerent a gang as ever served a lemonade-sipping commander. Punishments for intoxication while on duty and brawling were meted out with all the predictability of the spoonfuls of castor oil the post surgeon issued to the long line of malingerers who appeared before him each morning, feigning every variety of illness from Blue Balls to smallpox, to avoid work assignments. At times the men "walking the Ring" with logs upon their shoulders outnumbered those on parade drill. Desertion continued to be a problem throughout the stiff winter of '66 and muddy spring of '67: Offenders, when captured, were stripped naked and paraded across the compound before their fellow soldiers, with their heads shaved and the livid letter *D* branded upon their left hips, to the jeering accompaniment of "The Rogues' March" provided by the regimental band. When their sentences in the stone guardhouse were finished, they were put outside the stockade with neither money nor horse nor provisions, no matter if the sun were shining or a great door-battering blizzard were pushing the drifts to eighteen feet and snapping off trees like birthday candles.

At that, I imagine they felt themselves well shut of Fort Riley. The work was hard, the commander a martinet, the boredom paralyzing, and the food—bitter saleratus flour, spoiled meat, concrete hardtack, and watery soup—was barely acceptable. Vegetables and sugar were impossible delicacies associated with Easter and Christmas, and scurvy was a common complaint. There wasn't a full set of teeth or an uninflamed case of hemorrhoids in the ranks. I was told the general himself stationed a sentry outside the outhouse to warn him when anyone approached, particularly an officer's wife, that he might refrain from groaning until she had passed; and now that I pause to read that, I realize it's the first I've seen on paper about Custer's piles. I should think it would go a long way toward explaining his behavior at the Washita and Little Big Horn. However, there I go again, placing the lyric ahead of the melody.

The monotony, at least, found respite late in March 1867, when Major General Winfield Scott Hancock—"Old Eagle Eye," "Hancock the Superb," "The Thunderbolt of the Grand Army of the Potomac," "Old Bull Nuts," call him what you will according to your experience of him—arrived at Fort Riley with twelve hundred men and a pontoon train, assembled four companies of the Seventh Cavalry and one company of the Thirty-seventh Infantry, and set out in April for Fort Harker at the head of a column of fourteen hundred, not counting a colorful band of Delaware Indians acting as scouts, guides, and interpreters, with their faces painted for war and bandoliers of ammunition strung across their naked chests. The expedition was bound eventually for Fort Larned, there to meet with a delegation from the Cheyenne, Arapaho, and Apache nations to request safe passage for the Overland stage and employees of the Kansas Pacific Railroad, who had by that time lain track to within a few days' ride of Fort Riley. In actuality (so went the talk in the barracks and at the sutler's), the excursion, complete with regimental band blaring martial airs and bicolored guidons snapping above the ranks of men in brass buttons and fringed white gauntlets, was intended to frighten the Indians into submission with the largest show of military force yet exhibited upon the plains. Farther north, where the real fighting was taking place, Colonel Carrington (abetted, one assumed, by the scouting *savvy* of Jim Bridger) was holding the Bozeman Road against Red Cloud's Sioux, flush with their victory over Captain William J. Fetterman, who had gone down with his entire command of seventy-nine men southwest of Fort Phil Kearny last December. In selecting Black Kettle's Cheyenne to look on his works, it was said, the Thunderbolt was in effect demonstrating solidarity with the demonic Chivington and the massacre at Sand Creek.

"The Sioux'll thank Old Bull Nuts, and that's for sartin," declared one old campaigner on the eve of the expedition, throwing in his cards and leaning back to strike a match on the sutler's stove. He was a side-whiskered trooper with a vivid inverted V on the sleeve of his tunic where a sergeant's chevron had been. He claimed to have fought the Comanche as a Texas Ranger before heading north to join the Union. The Seventh was full of liars, but none with a scar like the one that bisected his face from the right side of his forehead to the left corner of his jaw.

The man to whom he had surrendered his hand, a tall jasper hard on thirty with ringleted hair longer than Custer's and a set of silken moustaches that would have made a Chinese mandarin envious, raked in the chips on the table with his left forearm, retrieved the deck, and shuffled. A new arrival attached to Hancock's brigade of civilian scouts, he was a ripe dandy, fitted out with a big sombrero, buckskin trousers, knee-length boots with Mexican spurs, and a Zouave jacket of scarlet and black fastened with gold frogs. Cinched about his waist was a yellow sash with a pair of ivory-handled .36 Navy Colts thrust down inside.

"They're bound to fight sometime," said he, dealing. "We'd best do it now while we still remember how."

"Tell that to Fetterman's ghost. Three." The former ranger discarded three pasteboards.

The dandy dealt him replacements. "Fetterman was a horse's ass. Mr. Stanley?"

The third member of the party, a mild-looking fellow, tidy in his dress and habits, replied that he would stand pat. Henry Morton Stanley's soft Louisiana mode of speech belied his British birth. He had joined the campaign as special correspondent for James Gordon Bennett's New York *Herald,* and as an emissary from that city, brimming with news of its late fortunes, promised enlightening company if I could but separate him from his poker-playing companion. Two years had yet to pass before he would find his own place in the columns by approaching a British physician-explorer deep in blackest Africa with the absurd statement that he presumed he was making the acquaintance of Dr. Livingstone.

There were raises all around, and then it was Stanley's turn to fold. Called by the dandy to show his hand, the man from Texas grinned for the first time since he had sat down, displaying an Eldorado of golden incisors, and spread his cards face up on the table. "You're a right judge of horse's asses, Mr. Hitchcock, but you can't bluff for shit. Full house, jacks over deuces."

Before he could rake in the pot, however, his gaudily attired opponent showed four treys.

"The name is Hickok."

The former ranger left the table, clearly in bad cess, but without expressing it. Notwithstanding his ignorance of the other's surname, James Butler "Wild Bill" Hickok's countenance was familiar in the barracks, where a travel-worn copy of *Harper's New Monthly* had made its appearance, complete with his woodcut likeness upon its cover and accounts of his rough-and-tumble adventures on the frontier inside. In particular his prowess with knife and gun was celebrated, as in his one-man destruction of the "McCanles Gang" at the Rock Creek stage station in Nebraska Territory. Before I was very much older, I would learn that the affair was something more on the order of murder from ambush; but then this was the West, where the truth seldom impeded the progress of history in the manufacture.

In any case, skilled duelist or cunning killer, he was no man to question over his card-playing.

Now Hickok's gray eyes fixed upon me for the first time. "It seems we have a vacant chair."

I claimed it. The long months of inactivity had not been for nothing; rudimentary though my poker training was, I had a pocketful of scrip and considered it worth the price of some game-table conversation with Mr. Stanley that might lead to news from home.

"Boss Tweed is no stranger to the *Herald*," he said, when I'd managed by passive means to steer the discussion around to the man responsible for my exile. "He can be reached any afternoon for a quote at Delmonico's, where he eats a simply enormous dinner. His vest would make a suitable tent for several crippled veterans I know who sleep in doorways on the Bowery."

"Then his star has not fallen?"

"Quite the contrary. He's a director of the Erie Railroad now, thanks to some skulduggery he pulled off for Jim Fisk and Jay Gould, and he's running for state senator. The talk is he's got it. Why they're bothering to hold the election come November is anyone's guess. Form, I suppose. The old town's rotten with it. Dealer takes one."

These were unhappy tidings. I'd been feeling homesick of late, and for the first time in two years had toyed with the notion of returning home, for a brief visit at least. However, with Tweed ascendant, and more capable than ever of exacting his pound of flesh for the attack upon his man Brennan, New York was out of the question for me. If Brennan had died of the injuries I had inflicted, the complaint against me would be murder; and even if he had survived, I had only to close my eyes to feel again the heat of his crony's deep-burning gaze and know that I would never be safe inside Tweed's jurisdiction.

I lost the next two hands in silence. Then I shifted my strategy to glean what intelligence I could about my father, the judge. Claiming a slight acquaintance with the family, I asked Stanley if he knew him.

Before he could reply, Hickok uttered a filthy oath and banged his cards to the table. He had made free use of the raw whiskey sold by the sutler, and though his hand and speech remained unaffected, his wagers had grown in proportion to the amount he had imbibed. I had noticed, too, that when either Stanley or I dealt, the frontiersman lost more often than he won, while the reverse was true whenever he had charge of the deck. Since the money signified nothing, I cared not at all, but it occurred to me that the way he played poker, Hickok's skill as a pistoleer was no small asset.

Then the bugler blew Taps, and we were forced to cash in our winnings and retire to our bunks. The march was scheduled to begin at first light, and as silence was strictly enforced in the barracks after the lamps were extinguished, I did not have the opportunity that night to buttonhole Stanley upon the subject of my father; nor did I in the morning, amid the hurly-burly of "Boots and Saddles."

Torches were lit upon the parade ground. In the flickering glow assembled eleven companies of cavalry, all spit-shined leather and glittering brass aboard their curried mounts, the latter assigned by color to their various troops; seven companies of infantry in kepis with rifles upon their shoulders; a battery of artillery, squat cannon pointed rearward upon their axles; a detachment of engineers; the plumed shakos, trombones, tubas, fifes, and snare drums of the regimental band; and, bringing up the rear, the colorful disarray of civilian scouts, Delawares, special correspondents, and teamsters aboard their supply wagons, outfitted according to their own preferences from buckskins to plug hats and ladies' parasols. The air was charged, and for drama, color, and high comedy, the scene compared closely with election eve in Central Park and the Sixth Avenue St. Patrick's Day Parade.

Custer was everywhere: galloping up and down the line astride his white horse, hair and fringes flying, dove-gray campaign hat tilted rakishly, the infamous red necktie knotted to one side, pointing with his saber at this loose cinch buckle or that ex-

posed gallus and yelping orders in his high, excited stutter. He
was as nervous as any bride, and small wonder: After the orgasm
of his triumphs in the late war and the letdown of his inevitable
demotion and a number of petty squabbles with the Department
of the Army that had delayed his reassignment to active duty, he
had to be acutely aware of just how much his future depended
upon the outcome of this, his first campaign against the Indians
of the Plains.

I saw a touching thing. Just before he took his place at the
head of the Seventh, Custer cantered up to the long porch that
ran the length of the married officers' quarters and leaned down
from the saddle to kiss his wife. When the kiss was completed,
Elizabeth Custer—"Libby" to her husband and in the minds of
hundreds of troopers who would never dare to address her so fa-
miliarly; and a better- and more noble-looking woman never set
a daintier foot from civilization to join her warrior-mate since the
Fall of Troy—reached behind her head, tugged loose the pink
ribbon that held her hair in place, and with the dark waves cas-
cading to her shoulders stood upon tiptoe to tie it around his
right bicep. Bearing this prize as proudly as any knight-errant
the scarf of his chosen lady fair, the Boy General wheeled his horse
and galloped over to his place in line, the ends of the ribbon
fluttering. All very picturesque and quite moving, even if the
animal did choose the moment of their parting to unload a pile
of apples from beneath its blond tail.

I was mounted too, aboard Dr. Reuben Samuel's reliable dun
mare, but I was not going along on the expedition. My work for
the army had ended when the last stubborn fife had mastered
the "GarryOwen," and as Custer had made clear that he had
civilians enough on his hands as it was, I was bound for places
more accommodating than the prairie and the garrison, whatever those places might be. The prospect of farewell did not
sadden me. The band director, a former Prussian Army officer
whose pointed beard and Heidelberg accent reminded me un-
comfortably of my tyrannical childhood music tutor, was an
even worse narcissist than the commander of the Seventh. He
accepted my score with the exasperated air of a Fifth Avenue
"swell" placing a copper in a panhandler's palm, then proceeded to trample over all its subtleties in rehearsal, hammer-

ing with drums those notes that should have been tickled with
triangles and burying passages for woodwinds under tons of
brass. Unfortunately, it is his version that survives. To this day
whenever the march is played, usually in tribute to the mar-
tyred Custer, instead of the youthful, impudent preening of the
Irish Fusiliers, I hear a blaring plagiarism of "The Campbells
Are Coming."

That's what I heard that day in the spring of 1867, as the gates
of Fort Riley opened to release the might of the United States
Army in one direction and a lone rider, armed only with a guitar and banjo, in the other. I could hear the whirling and crashing of the cymbals for a long time after we had lost sight of each
other.

CHAPTER TWENTY-SIX

ЛР

On May 10, 1869, with two champing locomotives looking
on, Leland Stanford, president of the Central Pacific Railroad, spat upon his baby-soft hands, gripped the handle of a
sledgehammer, and stepped up to strike the first blow at a golden
spike linking his railroad with that of the Union Pacific at a
place called Promontory in the Mormon territory of Utah. A robber baron's swing being no straighter than his business practices, he missed the first time, hit the spike on his second try, and
passed the hammer to his erstwhile competitor, U.P. President
Thomas C. Durant. Durant pretended the spike was Stanford's
head and so made his first swing count. Afterward the pair
mopped their faces with white lawn handkerchiefs, clasped
hands while the photographer dived beneath his black cowl and
squeezed off a hod heaped with magnesium powder, and went
back to their hotels as the track gang moved in to do the job
right. A lot of idiots in stovepipe hats got their pictures taken
standing atop the engines, and that was that.

Except now a pair of shimmering rails sutured together the recently divided North American continent from coast to coast.
Supported upon oaken cross-ties laid on top of broken pieces of

chat and the bones of untallied numbers of Chinese and Irish laborers lost to brawls, Indian attacks, bad whiskey, and unpredictable charges of explosives, the steel tracks cut the time
required to travel from New York to California from six months
to ten days. Pioneers who a scant ten years before had said good-
bye forever to friends and family to farm the West could get
their beans into the ground, change clothes, catch a train home,
stay for a month, and be back in time to hoe the rows. Elderly
Easterners could for the price of the fare visit grandchildren they
had only read about in letters. Texas cattlemen weary of running
the meat off their steers over the desert country that separated
them from the nearest market could fatten them on grass to the
railhead in Abilene, Kansas, then load them aboard cars and sell
them in Chicago for ten times their investment.

For me, playing the guitar and singing with a cellist and a
three-fingered fiddler in a disorderly house in Laramie,
Wyoming, for bed and board and gratuities, the golden spike
meant New York newspapers in my hands a week after they
rolled off the press. After an absence of six years, my thumb was
once again upon the pulse of my hometown and, consequently,
the world (as well as the *World*).

William Marcy Tweed was a New York state senator now,
without surrendering the city offices of alderman and deputy
street commissioner, which he had held for years. On the first
day of 1869, four Tweed men took office: Oakey Hall, mayor of
New York City; Richard B. Connolly, city comptroller, with both
hands in the treasury; Peter Barr Sweeny, city chamberlain, ju-
diciary watchdog, fully in control of selecting candidates for the
bench; and John T. Hoffman, governor of New York State. His
influence now had spread beyond the city limits. Unchecked, he
might within a few years encompass the nation. Where to hide
then?

The country—no, the globe—was in flux. Ulysses S. Grant,
having traded his soldier's coat for the waistcoat of a politician, was inaugurated president in March. The owner of the
Cincinnati Red Stockings, an Ohio baseball team, commenced
paying his players a salary, thus inventing the professional ath-
lete. Benjamin Disraeli assumed the British prime ministry on
behalf of the Tory Party, and a few months later abolished the
debtors' prisons. Empress Eugénie of France, Napoléon III's

beautiful and iron-willed consort, officiated at the opening of the Suez Canal, linking the continents of Africa and Asia as securely as the railroad shackled together the American East and West.

The "Smoky Hill Expedition," as General Hancock's excursion along the river connecting forts Riley, Harker, and Larned was tagged by the Eastern press, came to little, save entertainment for the plains tribes it was intended to frighten into submission and a meaningless powwow with the few braves who bothered to show up to greet Hancock and Custer outside Larned. Sometime later I heard that the commander of the Seventh managed to shoot his own horse out from under him while hunting buffalo away from the main body of troops. He did himself more credit the following year, when he swept down upon a winter encampment of the Washita River in Indian territory, killing Chief Black Kettle (who had survived the Sand Creek Massacre) and, or so the newspapers put it, "breaking the back of the mighty Cheyenne Nation."

There were laurels enough to go around. In the spring of '69, at a place called Summit Springs in Colorado Territory, General E. A. Carr and five companies of the Tenth Cavalry fell upon a party of Cheyenne dog soldiers and annihilated them at the cost of one trooper killed. A twenty-three-year-old civilian scout earned a line in print for killing the dog leader, Tall Bull. His name was William F. Cody.

I, meanwhile, was stuck in Laramie, living with a whore named Marion and taking long walks while she entertained customers in our room above the Golden Spike Saloon, rechristened from the Powder Horn after Promontory Point. Glumly, I waited out these nocturnal evictions on a bench at the station, where bad as it was the news from New York, arriving by the late train from Cheyenne, represented my lone diversion from a dissipated life.

Frequently, pulling upon the battered secondhand spirit flask that these days was my constant companion, I reflected upon my father's words to me in the only letter I had received from him since coming west: "My sole request is that you conduct yourself in a manner that will not shame you to relate to me upon our reunion." And I welcomed the excuse of a Boss Tweed to postpone that event.

To be sure, the judge would not know me at first, nor perhaps
t second: Twenty-two as of the end of March, I was three inches
aller than when last he'd seen me (although I was not tall as
neasured against the standards of a Bridger or a Hickok, who at
etter than six feet attracted instant notice wherever they showed
nemselves), had grown a beard of which I was somewhat vain,
nd favored the uniform of the "townie"—brushed black bowler,
otched vest, striped suit, and gaiters. The last refinement had
een a birthday gift from Marion, who declared that as long as
insisted upon wearing boots like some untamed mountain man
might at least cover them so people would think I had on a civ-
ized pair of shoes. She had influenced the rest of my outfit as
vell. I was convinced I looked ridiculous, but then she bustled
ne into a photographer's studio, selected a drawing-room back-
rop complete with a bust of Horace painted upon a pedestal,
nd made me stand in front of it while a rodent-faced gent in
irty glasses blinded me with a magnesium flash. When the pic-
ure was ready and I saw myself for the first time as others did,
was appalled. I did *not* look ridiculous, but quite natural in all
he trappings of a city-bred pimp. It was after that I began to
arry a flask.

Over the years I had caught myself from time to time won-
lering what the *real* Billy Gashade looked like—the one who
ad ordered his name printed upon the cards I still carried—and
f by some comedy of errors he had not passed away in Bridey
McMurtaugh's East River Society House, had I seen him on the
treet somewhere? In Denver, say, where I had entertained as
ermin-infested a set of gold prospectors as ever crawled out of
hole in the ground, in a tent stinking of mildew and stale beer?
Or Cheyenne, where I had turned away the amorous drunken ad-
ances of a cow moose named Martha Jane Cannary by telling
er she needed a man more worthy of her, like my good friend
Wild Bill Hickok, to whom I would certainly introduce her when
ll our paths crossed? I felt I'd have noticed Gashade in Dry
Crick, a pestiferous accumulation of mud huts on the North
Platte in Nebraska, where thieves ambushed me in an alley,
nocked out a tooth, broke two ribs, and robbed me of my poke,
orcing me to trade the dun mare to an unsympathetic station-
naster for a ticket on the Overland Stage.

However, since the incident of the photograph, I had stopped wondering. If we were to meet, and I were to see the mirror image of my stripe-suited self staring back at me, I should certainly dive back into the flask until I found oblivion.

I had confronted thoughts of this bleak nature before, in other places, and my reaction was ever the same.

Laramie was no exception. On a splintery night in December 1869, turned out from home once again with a kiss on the forehead and a tug on the scarf from Marion, I steered as always in the direction of the depot, holding down my hat against the wind razoring off the prairie. This time, however, I brought along my guitar and banjo.

CHAPTER TWENTY-SEVEN

Abilene!
The exclamation point this time was warranted; it had not been upon my last visit. Nothing remained of the somnolent log-and-mud farming village where I had spent my first year after leaving the Missouri guerrillas. The buildings I remembered had all been torn down or burned down or rendered unrecognizable by the addition of clapboard false fronts with second-story windows through which blank sky showed from behind. The rutted streets had been graded and squared off into neat grids, hotels had been built, a depot and bank and telegraph office added, and saloons—loud, ugly, dusty, hot, smoky, tinkly, stinking, vomity, beautiful saloons—walled the vast main street on both sides. Even in winter, or so it seemed, a perpetual cloud of golden dust overhung the city, kicked up by the steady traffic of hooves and wheels and high-heeled boots and ladies' patent-leather pumps, never quite settling from the previous day before dawn brought the next day's wind from the prairie, and with it more pumps, boots, wheels, and hooves.

Especially hooves. One word summed up Abilene's change in fortunes from its Civil War languor: beef. In 1867 the Kansas Pacific Railroad had reached town, and within months appeared a sprawl of stock pens, cattle scales, barns, liveries, and offices, all still smelling of sawdust when the first bawling herd of slab-sided longhorn steers arrived from Texas, there to be counted and packed into cars bound for the slaughterhouses in Chicago, and beyond there to a postwar Eastern population starved for meat. Close behind—for animals did not drive themselves—came hotels, bathhouses, gambling hells, drinking emporia, brothels, and all the other establishments that catered to the needs and desires of men who had been deprived of civilization for weeks or months. It was a brand-new industry, the American cattle trade, and the rules by which it was conducted, from rounding up strays to settling upon a price per head (and just what constituted a head), were still being decided upon in January 1870, when I stepped down from a day coach on the east-bound into a manure stench so fresh and warm it raised the temperature ten degrees.

I inquired of a loafer I found leaning against one of the posts that supported the roof of the depot if he knew of a place where I might find a room for the night. He was a lanky specimen in a blue flannel shirt and faded Levi's with the cuffs turned up at the insteps of his boots and a magnificent set of tobacco-stained handlebars whose curlicued tips tickled his ears.

"Wal," said he, tugging with his teeth at the drawstring of a disreputable-looking tobacco pouch, "you might could find a bunk at the Drovers' Cottage . . ."

"Drovers' Cottage." I thanked him and turned toward the platform steps.

". . . but I doubt it. She's full up."

I turned back. "What else is there?"

"Wal, there's the Gulf House, and Mrs. Childress's Boarding-house . . ."

This time I waited while he paused to slide the tip of a gray tongue along the edge of his cigarette paper.

"They're full up too." He rolled the paper and smoothed it between his fingers.

"Is there a vacancy anywhere in town?"

He produced a lucifer from a fold of oilcloth in his breast pocket, struck it against the post upon which he was leaning, and thought while waiting for the sulfur to burn off. Then he shook his head, lighting the cigarette. "I surely doubt it. Shanghai Pierce come in last night with five hunnert head and twenty drovers. That's on top of two other outfits that was already in and a trainload of buyers from Chicaggy. Abilene's a bedbug's paradise tonight."

"I thought all the drives took place in the spring and summer."

"Them Texicans is greedy year 'round. I expect one of these years they'll be pulling 'em in on sleds."

I took my leave of him. I found in his colorful indolence a studied quality that was new to me, but then I'd noticed the fellow had a tattered copy of *Beadle's Dime Library* doubled over and thrust into his breast pocket. These slim, cheap novels printed upon rough pulp paper and bound between cardboard covers had only recently begun making their way west from presses in New York and Chicago, but were snapped up quickly from the feed stores and dry-goods counters where they were offered for sale. I suspected that my fellow pioneers were passing into a period of conscious imitation of the laconic, stalwart Western characters who appeared in them. The curtain had risen upon the second act of the drama—or was it the comedy?—that was the frontier.

As predicted, I found no billet in either the Drovers' Cottage, an impressive three-story frame structure south of the tracks, or the Gulf House, a smaller, newer hotel in town. I decided with resignation to seek a bed in one of the sprawling one-story buildings located north of the city limits where, I was told, the local harlots plied their trade. By now it may be understood that I possessed what is called "a way" with creatures of this description. Whether this was because of my music or my fast-fading lost-waif appearance scarcely mattered; with few exceptions their latent maternal instincts came to the fore whenever I appeared upon their threshold.

I was held up for several minutes by the arrival of yet another herd from the Chisholm Trail: a river of dun-colored, slat-ribbed, vapid-faced steers equipped with murderous long horns measuring at least six feet from tip to tip, bobbing its way straight down Texas Street. Here and there a rider with frost in his whiskers whistled between his teeth and quirted his reins this way and that to keep the dumb brutes from turning against

the stream. A number of other would-be pedestrians were waiting patiently upon both boardwalks for the obstruction to pass,
the women holding lace handkerchiefs to their noses, the men
shifting their plugs from one cheek to the other and stroking the
pocket watches in their palms. Less patient—and loudly vocal
about it—were a number of stubble-bearded men in long buffalo
coats with greasy hair to their shoulders, clustered in front of the
etched plate-glass doors of the Alamo Saloon. These were buffalo hiders, and they held emphatic opinions as to who held deed
to the plains, particularly when the snow was flying and the
hides they sought grew shaggy, and consequently the market
for them more attractive. Cattlemen in their turn resented exposing their herds and persons to Indian braves already angered
by the hiders' wanton slaughter of the buffalo they depended
upon to survive. Brawls between cowboys and "buffler men"
were frequent diversions in saloons from Omaha to the Great Di-
vide.

At length the way cleared and I started across the street, picking my course between disks of cow flop steaming thickly in the
frigid air.

"Billy! Billy Gashade!"

I stopped and peered toward the boardwalk opposite, shielding my eyes against the sun glaring off the frosted rooftops. I
saw a medium-built man in a mackinaw and fur hat of the type
worn by High Plains hunters and trappers, beckoning me with
sweeping motions of one arm. His dark, drooping moustaches
made him appear middle-aged, but when I had mounted the
boards and stood before him, I saw the clear eyes and unlined
face of a contemporary. I recognized him but dimly.

"Mike Williams," he said helpfully, noting my confusion
without rancor. "The Palace Saloon, Kansas City. I tended bar."

I remembered now. The Palace had been an ambitious name
for that rough place, with its green-oak floorboards and litho-
printed boxers torn out of magazines and tacked to the walls for
decoration. Bartender Williams's knack for enforcing order with
a bung-starter and a sawed-off shotgun among the unruly clientele had quickly won him a colorful nickname.

"Iron Mike," I said, shaking his hand. "You spared me a tar-
and-feathering."

"I doubt them ferry fellers would of went through with it, for all their loud talk. You couldn't know 'Dinah Won't You Blow' would set them on the prod so. I just helped them see it before they finished getting your duds off. A thing like that can get to be embarrassing, especially with ladies present."

The only "lady" I recalled had been a three-hundred-pound cigar-chewing soiled dove nicknamed Big Edna, who had cheered on the rowdies with lungs lined with leather; but I was still too grateful for his intercession to correct him. The West was not a place where men rushed routinely into situations that were not their personal concern. "If I'd known there was so much rivalry between them and the railroaders," I said, "I'd have played 'My Gal Sal.' What brings you to Abilene?"

"Money, same as you. These here cowboys don't hold on to their pay any longer'n a double handful of hot coals. I'm getting top wages at the Alamo. Where you staying?"

"I just got in. I thought I'd try my luck north of the tracks."

"The Devil's Addition? That's a far piece to walk just to get your pockets picked by as greedy a bunch in feathers as you'll find this side of a buzzards' nest."

"I'll have to take my chances. There's not a bed to be had in town."

"I can offer the other side of mine." When I hesitated, he flashed his teeth. "Don't shrink up, hoss, I ain't bent that direction. It's just till the end of the season. After the herds roll out and the drovers head for home, you can name your own rate at any hotel in town."

"Maybe just for tonight," I said. "I'm worn out from the train. Tomorrow I can start looking fresh."

He fished a watch from a vest pocket next to the handle of a large revolver and snapped it open. "My shift starts at four. Bed's all yours till two. Come on. I'll introduce you to Mrs. Childress."

"Childress's Boardinghouse?" The loafer at the station had mentioned it. Following Iron Mike down the boardwalk, I began to feel the weight of my guitar and banjo and the satchel containing all the rest of my worldly belongings. My back was sore from the hard seat—Pullman's luxurious salon car had not yet reached that stretch of the Kansas Pacific—and my head ached.

"That's the place. The lady that owns it is stiff as trade whiskey, but she's the McCoy. Just don't stare at her."

I was still pondering the meaning of this advice when we drew up before a whitewashed building, separated from its neighbor on either side by only a common wall. In appearance, however, its isolation was substantial. The windows at ground level were leaded, in contrast to the discolored panes of the saddlery on the one side and the lawyer's office on the other, and the front door painted a pleasing shade of green, with a fanlight on top and carriage lamps mounted alongside. Ornate brass numerals advertised the address from the center panel and a blue-and-white china bellpull announced visitors. Mike employed it.

Presently the door opened the width of a human face, although the face that inserted itself into the gap was scarcely human. Entirely hairless, lacking even eyebrows and lashes, it was as white as paper, with pink eyes and a cleft upper lip that completed its resemblance to a large and vaguely hostile rabbit. The creature, clad in overalls, towered over my companion full twelve inches, and Mike crowding six feet in his stockings.

"Got a boarder for Mrs. Childress," Mike informed him.

The pale giant mumbled something thoroughly unintelligible.

"It ain't for you to say whether she's taking any in," said the other. "Fetch her."

The giant remained immobile.

"It is all right, Chronus. I shall speak to them."

With the eternal slowness of a planet separating itself from its orbit around the sun, the great albino moved to one side, bringing the door with him. Mike stepped past him without another glance in his direction. I followed.

For a time I was blinded. Not so much as a lamp or a candle was burning beyond the door, and thick plush curtains covered the windows. It seemed minutes before my eyes adjusted so far as to discern the smoky outline of the woman standing near the end of the long wainscoted hallway that led from the front door to the back of the house. She was clad all in black, and to her wardrobe had been added a thick veil that covered her disfigurement; but no veil could disguise the measured Grecian tones of her speech. Recognizing me suddenly, she lifted a hand to her mouth, and I saw the familiar garnet ring upon her index finger.

Instinctively I removed my hat. "Good day, Mrs. Patakos," said I. "Or have I now the honor of addressing Drucilla Childress?"

CHAPTER TWENTY-EIGHT

C hildress is not worth discussing," Drucilla informed me. "I married him in Ellsworth for his name and influence—he was a land speculator, and sold his property to the railroad for five times what he paid for it—and left him when he took up with a hotel cook. I understand he lost his money and went to Santa Fe to start over. I do not know what became of the cook."

I expressed surprise that she continued to bear his name.

"Patakos is too closely associated with my former profession, and my maiden name is unpronounceable to Americans. In any case, no decent unmarried woman operates a boarding house. I am the Widow Childress in Abilene. It might surprise you to learn how much better you are treated by clerks and tellers when they think your husband is dead."

Mike Williams having left us to take up his duties at the Alamo, we were alone in the dimly lit but pleasant suite of rooms Drucilla occupied at the back of the house. A spacious kitchen separated them from the dining room, where her cook served breakfast and supper to the boarders, and the parlor, where the guests relaxed and received visitors. My hostess sat in a bentwood rocker, turned from old habit to present the good side of her face to me. My seat was a horsehair sofa upholstered in faded leather, a carryover from the house in Lawrence.

"I suppose the guerrilla raid soured you on your old business," I said.

"I am certain you will not believe me when I say that I have withstood worse. In Lawrence I had an established enterprise and little competition. Out here, anyone with the price of a tent and a string of disease-ridden half-breeds can undercut you. I haven't the energy to scratch for my supper. Meanwhile, everyone needs a roof and a meal, and I no longer have to break up fights or locate a doctor who will perform operations without demanding a partnership."

"I need a roof myself. I cannot pay you until I find a job."

"Mike will find a spot for you at the Alamo. As for the roof, you are welcome to mine for nothing. But for you I would not have had one in Lawrence. The guerrillas would have torn it down brick by brick."

"Still, the result was the same. By the time I found my way back, you and Isabel and the ladies were gone. I was nearly killed by squatters."

"Dear Isabel. She died in my arms of the smallpox in Independence. We were the last to leave the house after the customers stopped coming. It was our decision, however. We made it in our own time, and not at the point of a bayonet. Thanks to you."

"Wherever did you come by Chronus?" The albino had ghosted in and out while we were talking, bringing wood for the fireplace. It was obvious by the way he behaved around his mistress that he was as devoted to her as a child.

"I bought him from a medicine drummer in Ellsworth. He kept the wretch chained to his wagon and made him dance to draw crowds. I dressed him in proper clothes and taught him to speak."

"That must have been difficult."

"Not as difficult as getting him to sleep in a bed. He was accustomed to curling up on a bit of straw in the back of the wagon. I have no idea where he came from or who his people are. The medicine drummer claimed to have bred him from a prizefighter and a she-hare. He is named for the greatest of the Titans, from the stories my father used to tell me about the old gods."

"Is he dangerous?"

"Only to those who would bring me danger. I find him better company than Panama Bob."

"It's a wonder the drummer agreed to part with him, even for a price."

"I drive a hard bargain," said she; and with those words the subject was closed forever. "You have grown, Billy. The beard becomes you. You might reconsider those tinhorn clothes before you show yourself to the cowboys at the Alamo. By the time they are ready to sit down and hear your songs, they have been skinned and skewered by slick gamblers in broadcloth and linen. A buckskin shirt and dungarees will pay for themselves in short order."

I felt myself grinning. "And will you rechristen me after one of the old gods?"

The muscles of her ruined face seemed to shift behind the veil. She might have been returning the smile.

It was a raw town, for all the brass fittings and polished mahogany in the Alamo and feathered hats and fringed white boots of the women who plied their trade along Texas Street; rougher in its way than the log village that had preceded it. Floyd, the counterman of dyspeptic memory (although mine own alone, as no one I asked had ever heard of him), would have shaken his dour head in disgust at the antics of the trail-weary cowboys, who celebrated their holiday by riding their horses into saloons, shooting the glass ornaments off the posts that flanked the entrance to the Drovers' Cottage, and scooping up wasp-waisted young women from the street at full gallop and depositing them with a tobacco-stained kiss upon the porch of some unsavory establishment.

A jail had been built, then rebuilt after rowdy cowboys tore it down. Finding the new construction formidable, with an armed guard stationed in front, the cowboys turned their attention to the mayor's office on Railroad Street, shooting out the windows on their way to the stockyards. Hardworking fellows on the ranch and along the Chisholm, they "blew off steam" in town like children set free from church and seldom damaged anything beyond property and dignity. The trail bosses, notably rough-hewn old Abel H. "Shanghai" Pierce, good-naturedly reimbursed the owners for the former, and after a night or two in jail the hungover cowboys reported with their hats in their hands to apologize to the citizens whose complacency they had ruffled.

Other infractions were less wholesome, and almost invariably committed by persons other than cowboys.

Pistol-packing professional gamblers, outlaws poured white-hot from the crucible of the Civil War, and gunmen hired by the cattle companies to guard against rustlers were a volatile enough mixture to introduce to so tiny a vessel as a frontier cow town. The addition of alcohol, women of easy virtue, and money constantly changing hands made it explosive. A disagreement over cards or the affections of a female that might in other places have ended in a torn lip or a bloody nose commonly overflowed into the street in Abilene, where it was settled with an exchange of bullets or, more often, by the roar of a shotgun fired from cover. A day that began and ended without gunfire and some miserable soul being carried by his friends to a doctor or the undertaker was hailed as a novelty, and celebrated in the columns of the local *Chronicle*.

A succession of town marshals—part-timers mostly, merchants and county sheriff's men seeking to make ends meet—attempted to enforce order, only to be run off or tarred and feathered and ridden out of town on a rail. In practice, this last tradition was a far cry from the picture of fun drawn by those who have never seen it. I had, in Cheyenne and again in Abilene, and had very nearly become a victim myself in Kansas City had not Iron Mike Williams intervened. The targeted individual was dragged into the street, beaten and stripped by a mob, immersed in scalding tar, suffocated by goosedown feathers dumped from pillowcases, and finally hoisted astraddle a section of fence rail supported upon the mob's shoulders, his hands tied behind him and his naked thighs clenching the splintery wood in desperation lest he fall and become trampled, and carried down a public street beyond the city limits, where he was dumped into a ditch or a thorny bramble and advised not to return under threat of death. Humanity was never so bestial as when carrying out this barbaric and thoroughly American ritual. It is no reflection upon their courage that a number of townsmen declined the badge to avoid exposing themselves to it.

True to Drucilla's promise, Mike Williams secured for me a position at the Alamo, playing guitar and banjo, filling in at the piano when the regular player was off, and helping out behind the bar when business was brisk and the staff thin. Although I received no wages, the gratuities were generous, especially after I followed Drucilla's advice and doffed my "city duds" for a shirt of the softest yellow buckskin and a broad-brimmed sombrero, which I properly "seasoned" by soaking it in alkali water and allowing it to dry in the sun. In keeping with the establish-

ment's other appointments—triple glass doors, brass lamps with
white glass shades, red felt-topped gaming tables, fat pink nudes
romping about the walls, and mirrors, mirrors everywhere—I
was offered the use of the stage when it was not occupied by
some traveling troupe, but I turned it down in favor of a spot on
the floor, where I was more approachable and my open cigar box
was within reach of appreciative listeners.

Of these there were many. I played and sang the songs they
crooned to the herds at night when they were skittish—"Beautiful Dreamer," "Old Dan Tucker," "The Night Guard"—and I
sang songs that reminded them of the sweethearts they had left
at home—"Cielito Lindo," "Sweet Betsy from Pike"—and I
taught them the words to new songs that had swept the East
while they were swallowing dust from the Panhandle to the
banks of the Arkansas—"Champagne Charlie," "The Man on
the Flying Trapeze," and "Little Brown Jug," whose unabashed
celebration of the inebriated state never failed to raise whoops
and a cry of "Do 'er agin!" On a good night the box filled
quickly, and Iron Mike took it upon himself to escort me home
to see that I was not waylaid and robbed.

These were my nights. My days were spent at Mrs. Childress's Boardinghouse, where I slept in a large corner room upon
the second floor, comfortably furnished with a brass bed, two
overstuffed chairs and a settee arranged in an intimate sitting
area, a washstand, and a fine steelpoint engraving from a painting by Bierstadt of buffalo crossing a stream, framed in walnut
and hung above the bed. This was the Presidential Suite, kept in
reserve for surprise visitors of steep reputation, and I was
pledged to vacate it the moment word arrived that Ulysses S.
Grant was on his way to Abilene. I took my meals in the com-
munal dining room, served by a garrulous Frenchwoman in her
late fifties who took no heed that her prattle, delivered in her native language (for she knew no English), was understood by
none of her listeners. The food was heavy, and invariably arrived
swimming in wine, but the portions were generous. No one ever
left the table hungry. The living arrangement was the most luxurious I had known since leaving my father's house.

The reader may be surprised, given my description of the
town, that I had been in residence there for some months before
I witnessed my first criminal act. The reason is I spent most of

my waking hours in the Alamo, where order was strictly enforced; fights broke out from time to time, but Mike and his fellow bartenders quickly intervened, often with the aid of a
bung-starter or the sawed-off double-barrel that reposed behind
the bar. On occasion I had overheard gunfire from the street, indicating that the battlers had chosen a new venue and deadlier
means to settle their differences, but I had enjoyed the good fortune never to be present upon the scene. I had seen enough blood
shed for two lifetimes and never felt the urge to fly to a window
when trouble happened.

My luck ended May 14.

It was a Saturday night. The spring cattle season was in full
swing. Sixty thousand head had come through since the last
snow, another twenty-five thousand were fattening on the grass
outside town. Half a million were expected before winter. All the
hotels were packed with drovers and buyers, with the boarders
at Drucilla's sleeping two to a bed, not counting mine and Mike
Williams'. (The bartender had earned special privileges when
he'd evicted a drunken buffalo hider who'd insisted upon taking
target practice in his room.) Players and spectators clustered like
flies around the gaming tables at the Alamo and stacked up six
deep at the bar, inhibiting foot traffic and causing collisions that
would doubtless have led to fights had there been room to swing
a fist. Tobacco smoke hung as thick as moss below the pressed
tin ceiling.

I was singing and playing "Cotton-Eyed Joe" on the banjo,
making little headway against the raised voices and rattling chips
and clatter of the Faro wheel though my throat was raw and my
fingers ached, when catastrophe occurred. It was a warm night
for the season, made more so by the press of hot bodies, and the
doors were propped open to let out the heat and smoke. Suddenly the room was shaken by a horrendous crash. I looked up
to see one of the round felt-topped tables rolling in a semicircle
on the floor like a dropped coin amid the shambles of playing
cards and chips that had fallen from it. Stepping over it gingerly,
like a ballerina avoiding a sandbag dropped in the middle of her
dance, was a tall, scoop-bellied horse colored that mustard shade
that is called claybank, its eyes rolling white with panic, and
aboard it, raking its flanks with his spurs and roundly cursing its
timidity in a voice thick with Missouri, a hunched rider in a

linen duster with slouch hat pulled low and a blue bandanna covering his face. Ducking to avoid hanging lamps, he nosed the claybank through the crowd scrambling to clear a path—hooves clomp-clomping on the hardwood floor—hauled back savagely upon the reins as he approached the bar, and, throwing aside the tail of his duster, swept a nickel-plated revolver out of his holster and "pulled down" on Iron Mike Williams.

"Put the box on the bar!" he bellowed.

Mike hesitated only an instant. The shotgun was at the other end of the bar and the revolver was only inches from his face. With careful deliberation he hoisted the open metal strongbox containing the night's receipts from its shelf below the bar and placed it on top.

The man on horseback motioned him back, then reached down, fisted the paper currency, and thrust it inside his shirt. Gathering his reins, he took aim with the pistol at a lamp hanging from a chain over the bar and fired. The chain parted and the lamp plunged to the floor, shattering and spraying flaming coal oil in every direction. By the time Mike and a handful of cooperative patrons stamped out the fire, the robber had turned his horse and clomp-clomped back out the way he had come in. From the street came the rattle of hoofbeats speeding away.

The county sheriff, a young man grown old in the job, assembled a posse, but there was no moon, and they lost the trail in the darkness east of town. The next day there were fresh cries for law and order, which as usual died down the moment the mayor asked who would come forward to enforce it.

I could not fault my fellow citizens. If the lawless element that claimed the streets was as bold and fierce as the man who had raided the Alamo, the job of eliminating it was far too much for any ordinary man.

For I had recognized the robber.

More specifically, I had recognized his weapon, and thus the hand that had wielded it. Seven years had passed since I had last seen it, and it had been in my possession barely a month, but I knew Corporal Templeton "Tupper" Deane's five-shot European revolver the instant it made its appearance. That, together with the rider's voice, bearing, and pale empty eyes above the bandanna, left me certain he was the man to whom I had surrendered the weapon while Lawrence burned.

Over the years I had found myself wondering upon occasion what had become of Lieutenant John Thrailkill after Anderson and Quantrill fell. I wondered no longer. And then a new question arose: If Thrailkill had come to Abilene, could Frank James and his brother Jesse be far behind?

PART FOUR

Lyric for the Lost

Chapter Twenty-nine

ↄ℩ℙ

The odds being faithless, sooner or later the unluckiest of gamblers must turn up a card that favors him. Abilene's came up on June 4, 1870. On that flyblown afternoon, a square-shouldered, sunburned man of about thirty, with the regular features of an advertising graphic for gentlemen's collars and a meticulously trimmed set of moustaches, climbed the stairs to the office on Railroad Street where Ted Henry, the mayor, conducted his real estate business, and applied for the job of marshal. Henry expressed doubts about the fellow's lack of visible armament but hired him on the spot in lieu of any other applicants. Before he left, the young man handed his new employer a preprinted sign and asked him to post it where he thought best. The sign bore that day's date.

STARTING THIS DATE, CARRYING FIREARMS IS FORBIDDEN WITHIN THE TOWN LIMITS OF ABILENE. VIOLATORS WILL BE FINED FIFTY DOLLARS AND BE ORDERED OUT OF TOWN.

TOM SMITH, TOWN MARSHAL,
ABILENE, KANSAS

Few gave Smith much chance of remaining in residence much past midnight of that first day. The bunch that gathered in Ben Thompson and Phil Coe's Bull's Head Saloon, whose rustic appointments were more friendly to unbathed flesh and stubbled chins than the glitter at the Alamo, were said to have the tar and feathers all ready for the first time the new marshal attempted to enforce the anti-firearms ordinance.

The man was no fool. While his predecessors had patrolled the town on foot, Smith remained on horseback during his rounds, wearing a brace of pistols concealed in shoulder holsters beneath his coat. The first time he came upon a cowboy tearing down one of his signs, however, he left the weapons where they were, leaping off his saddle and thrashing the fellow with his fists. Two or three more of these incidents, followed by a night in jail for the offender and a twenty-dollar fine for defacing city property, and the signs began to stay up. More significantly, the newly installed gun racks in the hotels and saloons filled up with checked weapons.

"They say he's from New York originally," Mike Williams informed me over tea in Drucilla's private parlor one stifling day in July. The afternoon occasions were open to her star boarders only, and although the bartender and I were indifferent to the stiff brew and soapy-tasting lemon cookies she set out, we were rarely absent. It was an hour of repose and intelligent conversation before we reported for work. "Maybe you know some of the same folks."

I was intrigued, for I had not met the marshal yet except to exchange nods when his rounds took him to the Alamo; but I said, "It's doubtful. I understand he's a career lawman. My circles and those of New York's Finest didn't intersect often."

"Well, he wasn't with the police long. I hear he shot a boy by accident and quit. That's why he's the last to pull a smoke-wagon when he's in a tight."

"His reticence will bury him."

We looked at our hostess, who seldom took part in the discussion when it turned to local figures and events; but she went on sipping her tea without elaborating. She had gathered up her veil to drink and nibble, but as always she sat in the chair farthest from the light with her left side toward us.

"It didn't bury him out in Wyoming," Mike said. "Talk is he cold-cocked this pistolero name of Montana Jones with just his fist in Bear River. Dropped him like a turd before he could go for his iron. Your pardon, Mrs. Childress." He reddened at his slip.

Drucilla was unaffected. "An admirable skill, in New York. Perhaps even in Bear River. Abilene is neither of those places. And a bullet travels much farther than a man's fist."

"Not if he makes his move before it's fired. No one ever got killed for moving too fast."

"It's enough for me that he holds Thompson and Coe in check," said I. "Whenever trouble happens it generally starts at the Bull's Head, and I never once heard of either of the proprietors raising a hand to stop it."

Mike slurped his tea. "It'd be closer to enough if Smith shut them down. Why Ted Henry ever issued them two blackhearts a license to run a saloon don't signify."

Ben Thompson and Phil Coe were poor choices to be allowed to operate a drinking establishment, at that: One was a dangerous drunk, the other a cold-blooded killer. The thick-built Thompson, an Englishman by birth with a Texas upbringing, whose speech retained a cockney edge particularly when he became agitated, had been arrested twice for shooting someone, the first time when he was thirteen years old, and had fled New Orleans before the war for killing a Frenchman in a duel. Those were the stories that circulated about him, in any case, and whether they were true or not he dressed the part of the suave duelist in a high silk hat, morning coat, and striped trousers, favoring a game leg with an ebony walking stick. Apart from keeping as much order as he bothered to maintain at the Bull's Head, his sole responsibility to the partnership seemed to be to prevent his associate from losing his temper and hurling someone through a window.

Phil Coe knew no other restraint. A shiftless fool when sober, under the sway of alcohol he flew into towering rages and had come close to killing customers on several occasions when he felt he'd been insulted. Once he was in the grip of these foaming frenzies, the only thing that would stop him was a crack on the skull with the gold head of Thompson's stick. The rest of the time the two saloonkeepers seemed to amuse themselves by feeding whiskey to sullen cowboys and turning them into a destructive mob.

"Thompson and Coe are best left where they are, and the Bull's Head kept open," put in Drucilla. "At least now the marshal knows where to look when something happens. Depriving troublemakers of a place to gather is the same as kicking apart a nest of yellow jackets."

"All the same, I'd admire to see Smith swat one or two," Mike said.

She reached for a cookie. "Bear River Tom Smith will not last six weeks."

It was an uncharitable assessment. Smith lasted six months. Early in November, while attempting to serve an arrest warrant upon a killer named Andrew McConnell in a dugout outside Abilene, the marshal was clubbed from behind by his quarry, and before he could climb to his feet the killer chopped off his handsome head with an axe.

The town seethed. A lynch gang materialized—not surprisingly, at the Bull's Head—but before it could set out after Mc-Connell, news came from Fort Riley that the army had him in custody along with a suspected accomplice and that the pair would stand trial elsewhere to avoid hemp fever. Since their pistols were loaded anyway, the would-be stranglers proposed organizing a citizens' vigilance committee to deal with the inevitable outlaw backlash in the absence of a marshal. A town council was elected. For the first time serious consideration was given the suggestion to tell the cattle companies to bypass Abilene. Ted Henry was ousted as mayor. Replacing him was Joseph McCoy—founder of the local cattle trade, visionary, maker of fortunes, and the inspiration for the phrase "the real McCoy," which ran rampant through the regional parlance. After some deliberation, and over and above the protests of the other men on the council, McCoy selected as Smith's successor a former Indian scout, full-time professional gambler, and until recently the sheriff in Hays City, eighty miles to the west. In the spring of 1871, Wild Bill Hickok raised his right hand and swore to uphold the law in Abilene.

In the history of the frontier, no two peace officers differed in their approach to their duties more widely than Thomas James Smith and James Butler Hickok. Smith had shot but one person in his entire career in law enforcement, and that one by accident; in Hays City alone, Hickok had shot four, killing three. How many others he had accounted for in his checkered past depended upon which tall tale you were listening to at the time. Bear River Tom had dressed and behaved quietly, melding into the background; Wild Bill was partial to low-crowned black hats with dramatic brims, Prince Albert coats, and red silk sashes tied about his waist to hold up his Navy pistols with the butts twisted forward, and conducted himself loudly and obstreperously, especially when he drank or the cards turned against him. Finally, Smith had patrolled the streets at regular intervals, but if you had business with Hickok, you either sought him out at his regular table at the Alamo or you kept it to yourself.

There he could be found day or night, seated with his back in a corner, curly hair to his shoulders, pursing his lips over the hands he was dealt and shoving his chips around with his left hand. His right was always free and rested in his lap near his pistols. Remembering the way his luck had improved whenever he had the deck in Fort Riley, I considered this a wise precaution. However, no one challenged his playing in Abilene.

For a time after he came we exchanged not a word, though night after night we were separated by only twenty feet of floor. Whenever our gazes met, no recognition flickered in his gray eyes, and I supposed he had forgotten our brief acquaintance. However, one night when I was filling in for the regular piano player, Hickok stood, scooped his winnings into his hat, slung it onto his head without spilling a chip, and came my way. He listened for a while, sipping his whiskey—the real imbibers took the stuff in slowly, letting "tenderheels" jerk it down—then placed his glass on top of the upright and asked me if I knew "The Buffalo Hunters."

"I know several songs by that title. It's a popular subject." I tried to concentrate upon my fingering. I was out of practice and his presence unsettled me.

"The one I'm thinking of has injuns in it, and something about hellfire."

"That's 'The Buffalo *Skinners.*' I know it."

He reached into a pocket, walked a silver dollar across the back of his left hand, and flipped it into the cigar box next to his whiskey. "Show me."

> *The water was salty as hellfire,*
> *the beef I could not go;*
> *And the Indians waited to pick us off*
> *while skinning the buffalo.*

We coaxed old Krego to pay us,
but it was no go;
So we left his damned old bones to bleach
on the range of the buffalo.

"It ain't that bad all the time," said he, when I'd finished. "Sometimes it's worse. The work's hard as hell. You get so you don't mind the stink, but it's no fun trying to sleep when your duds are all stiff with old guts."

"You were a hider?"

"You name it, I done it. Well, I wasn't never no streetcar conductor. Shot buff, graded track, farmed, skinned mules, fit injuns, hauled freight, tended stock, kept the peace. Spied for the Union in Missouri. I guess old Sterling Price has reason to ask the good Lord for my damnation."

"I was in Missouri during the war."

Immediately I regretted the admission. The war would never be over in the hearts and minds of many. Not a few of the young men whose fresh graves lumped the hill outside town had gone there over disagreements involving the fundamental principles of North and South, and by all accounts Hickok was not one to forget old animosities. Interested suddenly, he studied me keenly down the length of his bold beak of a nose. Then he retrieved his glass from the piano and helped himself to a long, thoughtful draught.

"Your name's Gashade, ain't it?"

I said it was. I was playing "Jack o' Diamonds"—a simple enough tune, but I gave it all the attention of a funeral mass.

"I had a hell of a time getting shut of this here lady bullwhacker when I come through Cheyenne," he said. "Name of Cannary, though she goes by Calamity Jane. She said you put her up to it."

I nearly dropped a chord. "I might have mentioned your name. She asked me if I'd introduce you. I said I would. She had me in a corner at the time. Her breath was like the alley behind a saloon."

"It is that." He emptied his glass. "Don't introduce me to no more women, hoss. I got all I can handle." He fished out another silver dollar, plunked it into my box, and strolled back to his table.

"That's the truth," said Mike Williams behind the bar, when I related the conversation to him during my break. Resplendent in green vest and sleeve garters with wax in his moustaches, he poured me a drink on the house. "He's living with a woman he knew in Springfield, and there's talk of him and that lady that come through with the circus, and I hear he's romancing that Hazell woman from the Devil's Addition that Phil Coe's sweet on. I reckon they ought to call him Three-Gun Hickok." He grinned lewdly.

I drank. "I'm certain he guessed I was not with the Union. I expected him to make an issue of it, but then he brought up that Calamity Jane business instead."

"I reckon his attitude toward the army has changed. I heard he had a run-in with some drunken troopers from Fort Hays when he was sheriffing in Hays City. Beat blue hell out of a sergeant and shot two others. Killed one. Phil Sheridan put out a warrant on him. That's why he left."

"Some men just draw trouble."

"I disagree. It's been quiet here ever since he come."

"You're just defending him because you were friendly in Kansas City."

"Friendship draws a lot of water with a man like Wild Bill. Just this week he put in a good word for me over at the Novelty Theater. They stuck me in charge of security."

"You're leaving the Alamo?"

"No, it's just part-time. I come running whenever one of them Texicans falls in love with a show girl."

I said, "It's a little more dangerous than that. The Novelty's right next to the Bull's Head."

"That's O.K." His grin was as bright as the glass he was polishing. "I like it various."

CHAPTER THIRTY

☙℘

In the summer of '71, I was privileged to be the only reliable witness to an event that has passed into Western lore. However, my version is not the one you will find there, and few if any credit it.

Among the Texans who swarmed the boardwalks along Texas Street and the Devil's Addition that season was an underweight youth of seventeen or eighteen, with wild eyes and a sallow face broken out in suppurating pimples. His name was John Wesley Hardin, and although according to rumor he was wanted in connection with a number of shooting deaths in Texas, he was in the legitimate employ of one of the cattle companies as a "stock detective"—sanitary terminology for a killer engaged to gun down prospective rustlers. He stayed at the Drovers' Cottage and did most of his drinking and gambling at the Bull's Head. Later I heard that Ben Thompson and Phil Coe put him up to challenging Hickok, toward whom Coe held a grudge because they both shared the favors of a madam named Jessie Hazell; but it is my opinion that the incident I saw was more on the order of a chance encounter.

It was a Thursday night, and slow. The Alamo had closed early, the business being unequal to the cost of the oil burning in the lamps. The town was quiet by the time I cashed in the chips placed in my cigar box by a number of satisfied gamblers and ventured out. Mike Williams having left to attend to his duties policing the Novelty Theater, I was without an escort. I felt restless. Not ready to retire, and knowing Drucilla to be in bed and beyond reach of stimulating conversation, I paused in the shadows of the covered porch in front of the saloon to sip from my flask and contemplate the stars hanging low over the meat market across the street. The street itself was deserted but for two or three loafers like myself leaning against the porch posts and a half-inebriated cowboy making his way down the middle on foot, singing quietly to himself and walking high on his cocked heels. He had on a Sunday suit and vest, pleasantly rumpled, with no collar to his shirt and a pearl-gray Stetson pushed to the back of his head. The rest I have already described. I had no idea at the time that the fellow was Hardin. Indeed, the song he was singing was the only interest he held for me. I was straining to identify it when Wild Bill Hickok stepped out through the door of the Alamo and turned to mount the outside staircase to his room above the saloon.

He was dressed particularly fine that night, in a coat of red crushed velvet that reached nearly to his knees, encircled at the waist by a broad belt with a big square buckle like a bucca-

neer's. Below it a pair of checked trousers were stuffed into tall
boots that gleamed with a blue flame in the light of the street-
lamp. As always, the belt supported the matched Colts and his
hair spilled in perfumed ringlets from under the broad brim of
his flat-crowned black hat. I think that if he had outfitted himself less carefully, the meeting with Hardin would not have happened. As it was, pausing with one foot on the bottom step of the
staircase to light a cheroot, he turned away from the wind to
prevent a spark from the lucifer from burning a hole in his coat,
and as he did so his gaze fell upon the young imbiber singing in
the street.

Shaking out the match, Hickok stepped down from the boardwalk, obstructing the youth's path.

"Warm night," said the marshal by way of greeting. "I believe if there wasn't a breeze we'd all be in our shirtsleeves like
a gang of shanty Irish."

"This ain't warm." It seemed to me that the other swayed a bit
more than his condition warranted. "Where I come from, the
water holes freeze on nights like this. The rest of the time they're
pure steam."

Hickok blew on the match he was still holding, as if without
attention it might rekindle. "I'm thinking your name's Hardin."

"That'd make you Hickok," said the other after a pause. "I
hear how you're all the time thinking."

"*Marshal* Hickok."

The youth smiled slowly. I thought him young to be in possession of so many gold teeth. "How-de-do, *Marshal* Hickok.
I'm *Mister* Hardin."

"Well, Mister Hardin, there's an ordinance against carrying
firearms in town."

For answer, Hardin slowly curled his fingers around his lapels
and spread open his coat. No pistols showed.

After a while Hickok dropped the splinter of charred wood to
the ground and crushed it with the toe of his boot. It must have
been the most thoroughly extinguished match in Abilene. "You
gamble, Mister Hardin?"

"I have been known to wager now and again, yes, sir." He
continued to hold his coat open, like a peddler showing his
wares.

"Bluff much?"

"No, sir, I never do."

"Mister Hardin," Hickok said, "I'm calling the card under your left arm."

For the next twenty seconds—it seemed much longer—nothing stirred in the vicinity of the two men facing each other in the street. A block or two over, a shutter flapped in the wind. It sounded like a pistol shot, yet neither man reacted.

More gold teeth showed then. Hardin released one of his lapels and reached inside his vest with his right hand. Hickok's hand, the one not holding the cheroot, drifted down toward one of the ivory handles above his belt.

It was this hand I was watching when Hardin withdrew a pistol from the sling beneath his left arm. The fingers curled, hesitated, then relaxed. Hickok's whole body began to vibrate. In another moment I realized he was laughing.

"*That's* your ace in the hole?" He gasped for breath.

"Pitiful, ain't it?" Hardin actually sounded sheepish. "I bought it off a fellow in Marshall when I was in a tight. This job come up before I could find one better."

Now I looked at the pistol the young roughneck was holding by the barrel. It was an old cap-and-ball Army Colt, missing its grips and with a twist of rusted wire holding the heavy barrel to the frame. It did not look as if it could fire.

"Ever try to shoot with it?" Hickok asked.

"This greaser vaquero put a hole through my hat on the Chisholm. I kilt him fair and square, but it took two hands. There's a country block betwixt the cylinder and the firing pin."

"Lucky for you Mexicans are slow. Put it up, hoss. I don't need no more sash weights."

That was the end of the historic first meeting between Wild Bill Hickok and John Wesley Hardin, no matter what else you may have heard. The marshal told the gunman to keep his nose wiped and went up to his room. Since then I've heard many preposterous tales about the encounter, told by a couple of dozen men who claimed to have been present. The most persistent held that Hardin offered Hickok a pair of pistols, butts first, then worked the border spin, catching the lawman with his mouth open and two deadly muzzles staring at him. However, if *I* was familiar with that trick, I don't see how Hickok could not have been, given his wide experience. Legends sniff at logic.

The popular account is that the two befriended each other. Although I cannot gainsay the story, I never saw them together after that night. A few days later Hardin left Abilene by way of a window and a handy horse behind the Drovers' Cottage after shooting to death a hapless cowboy who happened to be snoring loudly in the room next to his. In Hardin's defense I must point out that a stray bullet was the cause, fired through the wall to get the wretch's attention. Instead it found his heart.

Mike Williams and I were discussing this incident over tea in Drucilla's parlor when mention of the Drovers' Cottage caused the bartender suddenly to slap his thigh.

"I forgot. Fellow come in the Alamo last night asking for you while you was out taking a leak. Beg pardon, ma'am. He's staying with a pard at the Cottage. You know 'em both, he said. I had to leave for the Novelty before you got back, so didn't get to give you the message."

I knew a chill. My first thought was that Boss Tweed's long arm had reached me at last. The news from the East had not been encouraging. Without coming out and saying it, the Eastern papers had by implication and innuendo managed to suggest that the immigrant ward heeler had every office holder in New York State strung from his watch chain, with one of his stubby fingers dipped in every public project that involved the transfer of money from one place to another. No corner of American politics was so dark it escaped the penetration of those incendiary eyes.

"What were their names?" I asked.

He tugged at his moustaches, thinking. "Bock. He said his pard's name was Howard."

The names meant nothing to me, and Iron Mike's description of the fellow who left them was so general as to encompass every third stranger whose gear found its way into the walnut wardrobes at the Drovers' Cottage. All the way over there I wondered if I shouldn't be heading instead in the direction of the depot, but as always my own curiosity was my lord and leader.

The desk clerk, a tall, balding young man named Mather, who wore his spectacles on a black ribbon clipped to his vest, was known to me. His favorite tune was "Enraptured I Gaze," and because he never failed to place a twenty-five-cent piece in my box when he came to the Alamo to listen to me during his breaks, ill though he could afford it, I felt obliged to play it whenever he was present. For this reason he allowed me to look at the register, where I learned that "J. S. Bach" and "Tom Howard" had checked into room twelve the previous day.

I was close to certain now about the identity of the man who had asked for me at the Alamo, and although I knew no one named Howard I had a fair notion whom the roommate might be. Unlikely as the situation seemed given the news reports I had read recently and the rumors I had heard, it was with the bright anticipation of happy reunion that I bounded up the thickly carpeted staircase to the second story and tapped with my knuckles upon the door marked twelve. The grim note of challenge in the voice that answered sobered me somewhat.

"Name yourself."

"I shall do better than that," said I; for I had recognized the voice. I had brought my guitar, and now I slid it around from behind my back and picked out what I hoped was a recognizable conversion of Bach's *Toccata and Fugue in D Minor.* Half a dozen bars in, the door swung open.

Frank James's appearance startled me. I knew him at once, of course, but at first glance there was nothing in him of the rawboned Missouri plowboy I had last seen behind John Rudd's farmhouse in Carroll County. He had filled out somewhat, less lanky than slender, his hair was longer but well kept, curling at his collar, and the bristly, untrimmed chin-whiskers had given way to a full goatee of which a Southern senator would be proud. He wore a white shirt without a collar tucked into whipcord trousers reinforced with leather for riding. His braces hung and his feet were clad only in stockings, but aside from that he was prepared for visitors: His right hand held a big Smith & Wesson .44 American with the hammer rolled back. When he saw me, the broad bright grin I remembered so well broke across his long, handsome face. He pointed the revolver at the ceiling and let the hammer down carefully.

"Billy! I'll be god-damned!" Thrusting the pistol beneath his belt, he seized my hand in his knuckle-crushing grip and pulled me into the room.

It was a well-appointed chamber, as were they all in that hotel, so elegant in contrast to its tobacco-spewing, dust-slapping, four-times-yearly-bathing clientele: flock-papered and deep-carpeted, with framed lithographs leaning out from the walls and bulbous brass lamps flanking the big four-poster bed. Stretched out upon the mattress, collarless and stocking-footed like his brother, lay Jesse James—more infamous than Frank now due to the coin-flipping myth-making of the Eastern press, wanted in three states, the hero of every cheap novel that did not feature Wild Bill Hickok or Buffalo Bill Cody; the man upon whose head rested a reward (at last count) of two thousand dollars, with or without a bullet in it. That head was visibly older than I remembered it and sported a well-trimmed chestnut beard; no more need to envy my precocious whiskers, as when we were both sixteen.

He, too, held a cocked Smith & Wesson, but was slower to disarm and put it away than his brother, waiting until I was fully inside and he could see me from head to foot. Then he turned over onto his back, slid the weapon inside a fold of the Abilene *Chronicle* resting in his lap, picked up a Bible bound in worn supple leather that he had placed face down beside him on the bed, and began reading. He did not greet me, but there had been no hostility in his expression when he recognized me. We had never had much to say to each other.

Two new features I had noticed, besides the beard: The tip of the middle finger of his left hand was missing, and he had acquired the habit of blinking both eyes rapidly at regular intervals. Given his hunted state, a severed digit and a nervous tic seemed the gentlest on the long list of inconveniences.

"I heard you robbed a train outside Salt Lake City last week," said I as Frank splashed red-tinted whiskey into a hotel tumbler from a dusty quart bottle; the stuff was in such demand all over town the bartenders no longer bothered to clean the vessels before refilling them.

"We stuck up another'n in Little Rock week before that, and a bank in Michigan the same day." He handed me the glass, filled another for himself, and waved me into a tufted chair. "We're busier on vacation than when we're working, if you believe the papers."

"You're on vacation?"

Hitching up his trousers and sitting on the edge of the bed, Frank changed the subject. "When I heard you was playing at the

Alamo, I just had to pay you a call. I figured you'd catch the name I left."

"Not at first. I thought it was 'bock,' like the beer. When I saw how it was spelled in the register I knew it had to be you. No one else out here knows Bach from Stephen Foster. Tom Howard?" I looked at Jesse, who turned a page and said nothing.

"That's just a handle he takes on from time to time. It don't stick in the head and that's good. You know Wild Bill?"

"Not intimately."

"They say he's dangerous." Jesse spoke without looking up.

"It's the best word you could apply to him." Alarmed suddenly, I added, "I wouldn't test it. He's been bitten by fame and he will do anything to make it greater. He would not scruple to shoot you both in the back for the reward and the reputation it would bring."

Jesse turned back a page, paused to read something, then closed his eyes, his lips moving, as if committing a passage to memory. Then: "It's been tried. And yet here we sit."

Frank grinned. "Jess got bit too."

"It's nothing to laugh at. John Wesley Hardin got into a scrape last week right here in this hotel, and Hickok came looking for him with four deputies. He was forced to flee for his life."

"I reckon them Texicans consider four-on-one bad odds." Frank topped off his glass, offered me the bottle, and set it down on the floor when I declined. "Don't bust your blisters, Billy. We done already talked to Wild Bill."

This news staggered me. "You *talked* to him?"

"He paid us a call here this morning. I reckon our disguises ain't so good after all."

"He came alone?"

"I expect he had men posted around the hotel. He ain't *that* wild. Jess and I never let on we knowed what he was talking about, but we got the word. We stick to this end of town, he sticks to his. Oh, and don't rob the bank. He was specific about that."

"I wouldn't trust him to be as good as his word."

"Nobody's as good as his word. We're pulling out at first light tomorrow. I never did like Kansas anyway. Too many Jayhawkers."

"What brought you here to begin with? Abilene is no place to rest, even from robbing banks and trains."

For the first time a furrow appeared between Frank's brows. "We're trailing Johnny Thrailkill, Billy. He turned renegade on us."

In a flash I remembered the robbery from horseback at the Alamo. I hadn't thought about it in months.

Frank was still talking. ". . . had it out with him after Gallatin. It was just this little bank, figured Johnny and Jess and me could take it quick and easy, without Cole and Jim. Johnny went in to change a hunnert-dollar bill—get the cashier to open the box, see. Jess was watching the door, I was on the street. Then the shooting started. That crazy son of a bitch Thrailkill plugged the cashier in the face and lit out with just a fistful of cash. By this time folks was running up to the bank and I had to open fire to back 'em off. Jesse's gray bolted while he was trying to mount and drug him ten yards on his face."

"Still got a pebble or two under my cheek," put in Jesse, turning another page.

"Jess got loose finally and the gray took off. I had to ride back through crossfire to scoop him up. We damn near kilt that mean son of a bitch when we caught up to him. He said the cashier reminded him of that Yankee major that bushwhacked Bloody Bill and stuck his head on a pole. We gave him his split and told him to pull out. Next thing we know he's sticking up banks and saloons in all the places we go to cool our heels. Last winter it was Mineral Springs. This year it's the cow towns, where a man can lose hisself in the dusty crowd if he don't stir things up. Hell, folks are saying it was Jess bust the cap on that cashier. That crazy bastard is costing us all our friends."

"What happens when you find Thrailkill?"

Frank drained his glass. "Well, what would?"

I turned the conversation in friendlier directions. Their mother and stepfather were in good health, Reuben Samuel having recovered from his near-lynching at the hands of the Federal militia. Cole and Jim Younger were resting in Texas, but were expected to rejoin them anytime and bring their kid brother Bob, who yearned for the bandit life. The Union's harsh measures to "reconstruct" the South had converted many a neutral living in the Missouri hills to the cause of the Jameses and Youngers; let the Pinkertons scour the countryside in vain while the gang hid out in corn ricks and laughed at them. I picked up my guitar and played some of the old tunes that had entertained us all that summer of '63 in Clay County. Jesse, perhaps remembering the one that had helped bring him out of his wound-induced coma the following year, lay aside his Bible and sat up to join us in singing "The Hunters of Kentucky." His voice remained sweet and mellow, if halting. His shyness was his central trait, despite the blood-and-thunder tales that were told about him, and could easily have been mistaken for timidity. Years later, when he was hiding out posing as a cattle speculator in St. Joseph, Missouri, I heard he was considered something of a creampuff by some of his swaggering neighbors.

He was anything but, of course; and he showed it as I was nearing the end of the song, when a rattle of gunfire drifted our way from farther up Texas Street. In the blink of a lash he was off the bed and on his feet in an animal crouch, his Smith & Wesson in hand.

Frank moved just as quickly. In an instant both lamps were blown out, and the three of us waited in darkness with the twilight describing a square patch on the floor through the window facing the street. We heard shouts coming closer, and the drumming of feet on the hard earth. Unintelligible snatches of words and names at first, and then a string of information delivered in passing from just below the window:

"Wild Bill just killed Phil Coe and Ben Thompson!"

CHAPTER THIRTY-ONE

As it turned out, that first report was only half right, which as rumors go was at pace with the odds.

Phil Coe was dead, or would be soon, with one of Hickok's bullets in his groin and nothing else to do but bleed to death or succumb to blood poisoning; but his partner, Ben Thompson, was recovering in Kansas City from a broken leg suffered in a buggy accident on the prairie, and had been since before the incident that took Coe's life.

It had started with an attempt by Hickok to close down the Bull's Head for violating the town's anti-obscenity ordinance with a sign displaying a bull clearly in full possession of its genitals, reached boiling point when Jessie Hazell, the marshal's female companion, moved her belongings into Phil Coe's quarters, and came to its bloody conclusion when Hickok, investigating gunfire on Texas Street, found Coe with a pistol in his hand and went for one of his own. Coe, who had taken a drunken potshot at a stray dog, fired first, knocking Hickok's hat off his head. The marshal's aim was lower and more lethal.

The second victim, originally thought to be Thompson, died instantly when he ran up with a pistol in his hand and fell with several Hickok bullets in his chest and stomach. It was Mike Williams, the bartender at the Alamo and special policeman in charge of security at the Novelty Theater, thanks to the recommendation of his friend Wild Bill Hickok.

Iron Mike's death left me empty and Abilene as shrill as it had been following the murder of Bear River Tom Smith. Friends of Coe's and Thompson's, and others who had known and liked Williams, threatened to kill Hickok on sight. The marshal took to carrying a sawed-off Stephens ten-gauge shotgun in addition to his matched Navies and the brace of derringers he was rumored to carry in his pockets. On December 12, some two months after the shootings, the town council met, and at the end of a marathon session during which tempers flared, voted above the protests of Mayor McCoy to terminate Hickok's contract. Debate commenced anew over whether to ban the cattle trade and the trouble that accompanied it from the area, and on February 8, 1872, this remarkable notice appeared in the *Chronicle,* with fifty-eight signatures attached:

TO CATTLE DROVERS.

We the undersigned members of the Farmers' Protective Association and Officers and Citizens of Dickinson County, Kansas, most respectfully request all who have contemplated driving Texas Cattle to Abilene the coming season to seek some other

> point for shipment, as the inhabitants of
> Dickinson will no longer submit to the
> evils of the trade.

Even a dolt could foresee that this meant the end of Abilene as a major center of commerce, and that within a year the community would have reverted to the soporific farming village it had been during the Civil War. By the time the notice had appeared in two subsequent editions, the number of signatures had grown to 366, at which point Ted Henry, McCoy's mayoral predecessor and fierce philosophical opponent, mailed copies to newspapers throughout Texas. Finally, Dickinson's representative to the 1872 state legislature persuaded his fellow public servants to tighten an 1867 law, establishing a quarantine line forty miles west of Abilene beyond which the tick-ridden Texas cattle could not be driven. After three seasons during which one and a half million longhorns had passed down Texas Street, the town's richest period came to a close.

Something in Hickok had changed as well. Even before the council stripped him of his badge, he seemed to have lost all interest in enforcing the law, and for that matter in gambling, which was his first love and sole companion (aside from his propensity to make enemies) through all his incarnations as soldier, plainsman, and peace officer. Day and night he sat glumly at his old table in the Alamo, stirring only to refill his glass and speaking only to order another bottle or hurl vile imprecations at the odd uninformed gambler who came up to challenge him at cards. His appearance suffered. Broken blood vessels turned his slate-gray eyes the color of mud, his chin stubbled over; the celebrated flowing moustaches went untrimmed; his long hair turned dull and lank and looked unclean. He wore the same yellowed shirt for days on end. His nails were bitten and dirty, and he gave off a rank odor like a lion. Of course, no one pointed out these shortcomings to him. There was that shotgun, always in plain view, and he had, accidentally or not, slain two men in as many minutes within three hundred yards of that very spot.

Apologists claimed Wild Bill was in mourning for his friend, and stricken with grief for his part in his death. My opinion was less charitable. His reputation as a great frontiersman was bound to suffer for his lack of judgment in the heat of action, and the thought that the events of a few moments could undo the cultivation of years was eating at him like an ulcer. Conscience and friendship were but abstract concepts to a man like Hickok, as remote as the Milky Way and no more real to him than the Zulu War in Africa.

As for the event itself, I cannot find it in me to blame him. Deadly gunfire had been exchanged, he was surrounded by friends of the man he had shot, and a shadowy figure came racing his way with a revolver. The reflexes and instincts of a life on the plains are not to be overcome as easily as turning out a lamp. I regretted bitterly the loss of my closest companion in Abilene, the man who had helped me find work and protected me from brigands when I carried my earnings home, but he owed his fate to his own overzealousness. "No one ever got killed for moving too fast," he had once said; whether he had had time to realize how wrong he was depended upon how much thinking he had been able to do as he fell.

"No, no sadness," said Drucilla, glancing around at the wooden crates that had taken the place of most of the furniture in her private parlor. Everything else, the items she was leaving behind to be sold or shipped later, was covered with sheets, like shrouded corpses in a mortuary. Only her rocking chair remained uncrated and uncovered, because she was sitting in it. "When you have moved as many times as I have in these past few years, every place looks the same."

She was not the last to leave Abilene, but she was far from the first. With the onset of warm weather, the residents of the Devil's Addition had led the exodus, followed closely by gamblers, barmen, storekeepers, lawyers, and blacksmiths, some of them riding in wagons with the very lumber from which their establishments had been built piled in back, to be reassembled at the end of their journey. Wild Bill Hickok had left—to join his friend Buffalo Bill's theatrical troupe back East, or so it was whispered. Most of Texas Street was boarded up, and over the entire town the dust had settled for the first time in memory, covering it as surely and finally as those sepulchral sheets.

"Where is the next place?" I asked.

"Ellsworth. That's where all the cattle are going next season. Cattlemen, cowboys, buyers, they all need a place to sleep and eat. It is the same, as I said. And where do you go, Billy? I heard the Alamo is closing."

"I haven't given it much thought. West, I suppose. I've had an offer, but I haven't decided yet whether to take it."

She nodded absently, looking away. The untouched side of her face was silhouetted against the light leaking through a space between the curtains. Suddenly she turned it full upon me. The scarred side was barely visible through her veil. "Come with me, Billy."

"What work would there be for me in a boardinghouse?" The response was surprised out of me by the unexpected invitation.

"In my next place I intend to have an organ, or at least a piano. You can entertain the boarders."

"In Boston, perhaps. In Ellsworth they will prefer to mix their amusements."

"Then you will play and sing in a saloon, and sleep beneath my roof. I have become accustomed to your company," she added, turning her head away once again.

My chest grew tight, a sensation I had not known since my decision not to return to New York as soon as I was free of the Missouri bushwhackers. Quickly I said, "You have Chronus, who I think does not approve of me. In any case I have had my life's portion of cow towns. I never did get used to the stench of cattle."

"You will not change your mind?"

"I'm afraid I cannot."

Neither of us spoke for at least a minute. The silence outside was oppressive. Abilene did not seem Abilene without the rattle and squeak of wagons passing by, hammers clattering, saws wheezing, the lowing of steers and cowboys cursing. Then she lifted her white china cup to her lips. "What is the offer you are considering?"

"A party of buffalo hiders wants me to help with the skinning and sing to them in the evenings. I am to take a percentage of the profits in return."

She smiled then in earnest. The expression was necessarily

crooked, but far from unpleasant. When she spoke, her voice was low and mellow as of old, but with a kind of playful melancholy that I had not been aware of before. "And the stench of *cattle* offends you?"

I returned the smile with a shrug. We said good-bye then. There was no place for me to sit, and so I did not have to get up to leave. I could not then guess the circumstances under which we would meet again.

CHAPTER THIRTY-TWO

Oh, it's now we've crossed Peace River,
and homeward we are bound;
No more in that hellfire country,
shall ever we be found.
Go home to our wives and sweethearts,
tell others not to go;
For God's forsaken the buffalo range,
and the damned old buffalo.

My sentiments, after a winter spent on the plains of Nebraska following the southward-migrating herds, were not far different from those of the buffalo skinners of the song; substitute marrow-freezing cold for hellfire, and the least companionable partners I had ever known for hostile Indians, and the lyrics were right on the money.

None of us referred to ourselves as hunters. In truth, I never heard the term *buffalo hunter* until the herds had thinned out to the degree that one actually had to go looking for them. In the early seventies, when a train passing through that Platte River country was forced to wait six hours for a single herd to finish crossing the tracks, the notion of ever having to "hunt" the lumpy, woolly-headed brutes was a supreme joke. Collectively we were "hiders." I was a "skinner," and occupied, with a bald, one-eyed fellow known only as Fetch, a place at the bottom of a special hierarchy. Next came the cook, a black-bearded Scot named Cockerell, with the arms and torso of a grizzly, skinny bowed legs that until his back straightened out late in the morning compelled him literally to support himself upon his knuckles, and a club foot. At the top of our society stood Van Horn, our "runner," or sharpshooter, upon whose keen eye and steady hand depended the success of our venture. A lean, rifle-backed fellow of thirty or so, born in Amsterdam but brought up on a farm in Iowa, he affected the buckskins and shoulder-length hair of the frontiersmen he read about in Beadle's, and during the twilight hours when Cockerell heated his skillet to prepare buffalo steaks seasoned with wild onions and Fetch and I scraped and salted the hides we'd spent all day stripping from the carcasses, he busied himself dismantling his prized Sharp's Big Fifty rifle and cleaning and oiling the parts, wiping them off with a square of soft sheepskin. I suspected he treated the weapon better than he had any woman, and perhaps with good reason. Smaller-bored rifles had little effect upon the thick-hided creatures, and revolvers were useless.

I had been nervous at first about the Indians. For as long as any of them could remember back beyond the time of their great-grandfathers, they had always lived upon the animals we slaughtered for the hides alone, feeding their villages, fashioning their lodges from the skins, and even grinding the bones to make their pottery. (The fact that they would often stampede a hundred buffalo off a cliff to cut out three or four for their purposes was no match for Indian logic; we were white men, we had our domestic cattle and glass plants and textile mills, and hadn't their right to waste buffalo.) I had heard of depredations in the North and South, of much larger outfits than ours shot down and scalped or captured and tortured. Against that risk, the profit we would realize when the hides were sold in Julesburg for between $1.50 and $2.50 apiece seemed tiny. When one afternoon I looked up from the bull I was preparing to skin and saw five men in feathers watching from horseback at a distance of three hundred yards—I feel no need to dissemble in this narrative—I urinated in my trousers.

"I seen 'em," said Van Horn, when I called his attention to these grim spectators. "Sioux, or I miss my guess."

He was sitting on the open tailgate of our wagon, Sharp's resting across his lap while the barrel cooled. We had come upon a small herd of forty buffalo late in the morning and he had shot almost half before the rest spooked. Fierce intelligent creatures when it came to protecting themselves from natural enemies—wolves, blizzards, and the like—they seldom reacted to gunfire, and if they did not catch the scent of blood and none of them bawled going down, had been known to stand around calmly munching grass until the last animal fell. It was the dream of every runner to experience a "stand," and this was as far as Van Horn had ever taken one. His luck had held until he rushed a shot, missing a vital organ, and the wounded cow bolted, bellowing a warning to the others. In another moment they had rumbled away over a rise to the north. Since then Fetch and I had been busy with our knives, slashing the hides of the slain buffalo at the necks and hooves; when that was done we would hitch the wagon with hooks to each and drive the mules forward, separating them from their original owners with a long steady pull. Today it was my turn to slash the more stubborn membranes as the hide came away. The work was odoriferous and filthy, and I was crawling head to foot with the ticks that infested the animals. Christmas had come and gone without notice; I hadn't bathed or slept beneath a proper roof since September. Now, having attracted the attention of the Sioux, I wondered if I ever would again.

"What do you suppose they want?" I asked.

"Meat, I reckon. It's been a hard winter for squaws and bucks."

"Do you think that's all?"

"That, or our scalps. Most like both. If we're all dead they don't have to ask."

I looked again. Sky and earth were white and dazzling. We were all burned nearly as brown as the Indians from the sun coming off the snow. The five seemed nailed to their ridge, only the feathers on their lances stirring in the wind that never stopped, never stopped blowing on the Nebraska plain. Two of them held rifles, the butts braced against their thighs with the barrels pointed straight up, and these, too, were decorated with feathers.

On the other side of the fallen herd, Fetch was at work slashing hides, but I saw him look up from time to time at the men watching from horseback. Cockerell lay snoring in the back of the wagon, wrapped in a blanket atop the stiff hides already stored there. He seemed impervious to the insects and the stench, and slept whenever he wasn't cooking or gathering chips for the fire. He'd have dozed through the Crucifixion, once the dishes from the Last Supper had been cleared away.

"Isn't there something we can do?" I asked then.

"Well, once this barrel finishes cooling I'll pick off what I can. I might get three, this being a single-shot. Wisht I'd bought that Winchester repeater I seen in Fort Kearny coming out. I didn't have the money." He spat into the snow. "I can get the two with rifles, anyways. The rest will turn tail and run."

"What if they charge us instead?"

"Wisht they would. I'd drop all three. They'll run, though. They ain't stupid just 'cause they're savages."

"What harm can three Indians do armed only with lances?"

"Plenty, when they get back to the village and tell the rest what's here. I can't shoot no hundred Sioux braves. They won't stand around waiting for it like buffler."

I watched the Indians absently, wiping the flat of my blade against my trousers, stiff as tree bark with old entrails. "Suppose we give them what they're after?"

"It's a notion," said Van Horn. "I don't think I could get along without my topknot, though. I catch cold easy."

"I don't mean our scalps. I mean the buffalo meat. All we're taking is the hides, and steaks enough for just us four. One of us could ride up there unarmed and make the offer. If they're as hungry as you say, they might let us go."

"Oh, they're hungry. Army's got 'em on the run, and they can't hunt for shit when they ain't concentrating. It is a notion," he repeated, making me think of old Jim Bridger: *Just a dumb notion, mind.* "Question is, which one of us is going to ride up there and probably be the first to give up his hair?"

"I guess I will."

The runner turned a bright eye on me, but there was no admiration there, only wary contempt. It was as if the stranger he had spent most of the night drinking with, thinking him to be of a like mind, had without warning opened his mouth and delivered a sermon against all the things Van Horn stood for. However, he said nothing. He didn't have to; the fresh spittle he shot into the snow at the foot of the wagon was eloquence enough.

I had heard somewhere, perhaps from Bridger, that it didn't do to approach an Indian empty-handed, no matter if you were offering him deed to the whole of North America. I therefore selected a buffalo robe I had pegged and cured myself—my first successful effort, which I had been intending to have made into a coat when I returned to civilization—wrapped it around a hindquarter I butchered myself, unhitched one of the mules from the wagon, and mounted it bareback, laying the bundle across my thighs. As I started toward the ridge, I was aware of Fetch watching me from across the scatter of carcasses, sitting back on his heels with a hand shielding his eyes, and of Cockerell snoring and whistling upon his green hide bed. Van Horn had alighted from the tailgate, jammed into the ground the forked stick he used for a tripod, and fished a paper cartridge out of his pocket, and as he tore the end off with his teeth to pour the powder into the firing pan of the Sharp's, said: "I was starting to get used to having music nights."

I felt neither brave nor hopeful. All I could think of was that it made no difference whether I died upon the ridge with the Indians or down among the buffalo.

The way up the grade was laborious. The snow had drifted, and the mule tried to balk, but I dug in my heels and it lunged through the chest-deep accumulation, wheezing clouds of vapor as thick as milk. The five mounted men watched without moving until I drew within ten yards of them, at which point the one in the center hoisted his rifle horizontally above his head, halting me. A moment went by, during which the icy wind skirled up under the sheepskin lining of my coat. Then they started down toward me, all at once without a signal, as if men and horses shared a single brain.

The one who had raised his rifle stopped in front of me while the others fanned out and around, enclosing me in a ragged circle. Looking into that face, round, burnished, and ageless, with hair gathered into long braids on both sides, eyes the color of smoke from which the lashes had been plucked, and a wide, well-shaped mouth drawn into a permanent scowl, I realized with a sudden dropping of the heart that we had nothing in common, neither language to communicate nor culture to understand nor experience to compare. I knew not how to begin the negotiation I had been rehearsing all the way up to the ridge. Then the leader—for I judged the rider facing me to be the man in charge—broke the silence with one earth-shattering word.

"English?"

I jumped, startling the mule into a snort. "Yes," I said. "My name is Gashade."

He did not introduce himself. I remembered Bridger's telling me that for an Indian to surrender his name was to place power in the hands of the man to whom he gave it.

"Kill buffalo?"

"I skin them."

"Eat?"

"Some." I reached for the bundle across my lap. Immediately I felt the icy touch of the muzzle of the other rifle against the bone behind my left ear. My hands froze halfway.

The smoke-colored eyes flicked to my right. The brave on that side leaned over, lifted the bundle, and unwrapped it, exposing the bloody hindquarter.

"A gift." Carefully, to avoid startling the Indian with the rifle, I raised my right arm and gestured toward the carcasses on the flat, encompassing them with a broad sweep. "All yours. The buffalo robe too."

"Hides."

"Five hides." *Don't be too eager to give things up.* Bridger. *They'll take and take and finish by taking your scalp. It's a bad mistake to think they're not as good as us. It's a worse one to think they're better.*

"All hides."

I shook my head. "Five. We worked too hard for the rest."

I felt a tug that nearly unseated me and thought, *This is it.* However, it was just the Indian behind me, yanking at the strap that held my banjo behind my back.

"Gun?" The leader appeared to have noticed it for the first time.

Again I shook my head. "Musical instrument." Slowly I slid it off my shoulder and held it out. When he made no move to take it, I lowered it and picked out the opening bars of "Cotton-Eyed Joe," a rouser. When I finished, the brave to my right opened his mouth wide and laughed. That astonished me more than anything. Nothing I had heard or read about Indians had mentioned a capacity for mirth. I had thought them humorless and stoic. All around me there was a lifting of the atmosphere.

Now the leader put out his hands, and I placed the banjo in them. He turned it over, studying it from both sides. Stiffly he held it across his body and brushed his fingers across the strings. The strumming noise made his horse snuffle and toss its head. He patted its neck. He was grinning broadly now. I noticed he possessed few teeth, although my impression was that he was a young man.

He appeared to have a sudden inspiration, and held the banjo out to his right. The brave on that side lowered his rifle and kneed his horse forward to take the object. The leader stripped off his coat, a fine woven one with broad horizontal stripes of cream and vermilion. His naked chest was smooth and hairless, the color of an amber bottle. He folded the coat and held it before him across his forearms. Clearly, this was intended as an offering.

"Ten hides."

I regretted the loss of the banjo more than the hides we had worked so hard to acquire. Musical instruments were difficult to come by at that time on the frontier, and I did not expect ever to find a replacement. Yet I agreed to the terms without hesitation, in return for our lives. Moreover, the blanket coat was wonderfully crafted, lighter yet sturdier than the fleece-lined canvas, and stopped the wind more efficiently. We parted then.

It was the work of the rest of the afternoon to finish the skinning, and then Fetch, Cockerell, and I climbed aboard the wagon, Van Horn mounted his Appaloosa (muttering ungratefully about what a poor bargain I had made), and we left by the rusty light of the wallowing sun while the Sioux moved in behind us to harvest their bounty. One of the braves had ridden back to inform the village; women and children swarmed about the carcasses with skinning and butchering tools, chattering happily in their halting, guttural tongue.

I would not have credited it then, but the banjo would make

its way back to me, much changed; by which time I would have changed quite as much. That, however, is a later verse in my ballad. There is a great deal more of it to be sung, with or without banjo accompaniment.

Chapter Thirty-three

It was an old bull, its beard worn short from years of dragging on the ground and its chest and shoulders crisscrossed with old horn scars as thick as hemp, badges of office and trophies won from many challenges to its herd leadership. Although snow was on the ground, its hide was caked with dust, matted from rolling in summer dirt mixed with its own urine, to attract cows with the pungent masculine scent. A bull's bull; Wild Bill Hickok with horns.

Remembering Van Horn's instructions, I stretched out on my chest and stomach on the ground, supporting myself upon my elbows behind his makeshift tripod, gripped the smooth walnut forepiece with my left hand, rolled back the hammer with the other, and snapped the set trigger. Little more than a breath was required now to set the mechanism in motion. I nestled my cheek against the stock, centered the grazing bull in the folding sight, drew in a breath, expelled half of it, and squeezed the rear trigger.

The heavy gun pushed against my shoulder, leaving a purple bruise, though at the time I scarcely noticed the pressure. There was a pause, then a funnel of dust leapt from the bull's coat just behind the left shoulder and it threw up its huge head and rolled over onto its side. Kicked once.

I still regret that old bull. I skinned at least two hundred buffalo that winter, but I personally shot only one, to see what it was like. It was a terrible thing to do to a brute that lived only to graze and shit and make little buffalo.

As the grim winter of 1872–73 howled to a finish, I had a great deal more to feel sorry for, beginning with my decision to come there in the first place. I hated the weather, the exposure, and the hard work. Chief of all I hated my three partners. We spent the whole of a week-long February blizzard huddled together beneath a wagon sheet, subsisting upon buffalo jerky, handfuls of snow to avoid dehydration, and bickering. We argued over everything, but kept coming back to which one of us had suggested preparing and stocking a dugout against just such an eventuality and which had vetoed the suggestion upon the evidence of a mild winter predicted in the pages of the *Farmer's Almanac*.

Van Horn, the aristocrat of our little caste, was the worst complainer. He went on bitterly about the weather, the ten hides we had lost to the Sioux, Cockerell's cooking, the slothful way in which Fetch and I went about our skinning chores, and the long litany of evil tidings that had taken him from his prosperous life in the Netherlands to this God-forsaken spot on the empty Nebraska plain. When sufficiently into the whiskey we passed around to warm the blood in our veins, he lapsed into a slurred patois of Dutch and vernacular American, from which I gleaned intermittent scraps of his life history: Shipbuilders for generations, the family's fortunes were seriously damaged when half the workforce departed for Belgium during the 1830 separatist revolution; the remains of its wealth had supported Van Horn in luxury during his childhood, then when the last of it was gone he had been forced to withdraw from school to work from daylight to dusk on a dairy farm outside Amsterdam in what amounted to indentured servitude. In 1856, at the age of fourteen, he had run away, stowed himself in the lifeboat of an American-bound clipper built by the company his father had once owned, labored in the bilge upon his discovery to pay for his passage, and panhandled on the streets of Baltimore, sleeping in doorways and living upon the scraps thrown out behind the restaurants, until he had assembled enough pennies to cover train fare as far as Iowa, on the border of the frontier and opportunity. There he found himself working on yet another farm, performing many of the same drudgeries he had had to perform back home, until he reached his full growth.

After Fort Sumter he joined the Fifteenth Iowa Infantry and fought at Shiloh, where he was invalided out with a Confederate ball in his hip that still made him miserable when it rained or snowed, as when he was telling the story. Since then he had hauled freight in Arkansas, operated a ferry in Kansas—where no doubt he remembered the much finer water craft constructed by his family in better times—and graded track for the Union Pacific in Nebraska, before deciding there was more money to be made shooting buffalo to feed the track gang. With his wages he bought a Sharp's from a runner who had made his grubstake and was going back East to marry his sweetheart. By this time the traffic in hides was heavier and more lucrative than the one in meat, and a natural talent for marksmanship, discovered in the army, persuaded Van Horn to quit the large outfit he had hooked himself up with and organize his own. That, he now explained acidly, was before he knew how worthless a crew he had assembled. We had given up arguing with him the first day under the wagon sheet, instead possessing ourselves in patience until he passed out, knowing that when he awoke he would begin all over again.

Cockerell, the Scot, held even less regard for Van Horn than the runner held for the rest of us, and never once addressed Fetch or me directly, evidently having made up his mind sometime back that skinners were less than human and less valuable to the expedition than the mules—to whom he *did* speak, if only to damn their absence of a soul whenever they balked or (as upon one memorable occasion) one of them threw a shoe that landed square in his stewpot while he was cooking supper. I understood, mainly through a disparaging comment made by Van Horn, that he had abandoned a wife in Scotland and another in St. Louis, but could learn nothing of his past because he restricted his references to the current situation and his conviction that he would either freeze or starve to death in the worst company he had known this side of the water.

Fetch never spoke except to curse us when we disturbed his sleep or the bottle was too slow in reaching him. No one seemed to know where he had been or what he had done before he joined us, but I for one was certain that he was capable of committing any crime. There was about him an uncleanliness of a particularly vile sort that went deeper than the surface filth of the occupation he and I shared; bathe him, brush him, douse him with scent, dress him in silks and broadcloth, and within minutes his nails would be as black and he would smell as foul as if he had just returned from the killing ground. He secreted the stuff through his pores, directly from the corruption of his soul. The poisonous yellow cast of his bad eye suggested that he had once used it to look at himself in the harsh light of truth, and it had been struck blind by what it saw.

Yes, I earned the good turn Fate presented me at the end of that hellish winter. I am still uncertain as to whether it was worth the cost.

At length the blizzard stopped blowing. It was the work of most of a morning to find and uncover the wagon, after which we donned the snowshoes we'd stowed under the seat and went out in search of the mules and Van Horn's Appaloosa. When the storm had come up—suddenly, as did everything in that country—we had unhitched the team and relieved the horse of saddle and bridle, agreeing that they had a better chance of surviving the blow on the loose than tethered to the wagon. Toward dusk we located the mules, huddled together in an old wallow, emaciated and snowblind but still standing. One died during the night, another the next day. The remaining four were sound enough after three days' rest and grain feeding to return to the traces. We never found the Appaloosa and decided it had either died of exposure and been buried by the snow or stumbled into some other camp and been—well, "adopted" was a more diplomatic term than the ones Van Horn employed. We excavated and loaded the hides we'd pegged out before the blizzard and struck out for civilization, two of us taking turns walking alongside to keep from overburdening the light team.

Julesburg, when we reached it some ten days later, was a riot of activity, nearly all of it directed toward the trade in buffalo hides. There was the Buffalo Trading Post, the Buffalo Saloon— even the Buffalo Clothiers, complete with a three-piece rig and watch chain trapped out on a tailoring dummy in the display window and the name of the establishment painted upon a sign carved into a humpbacked silhouette swinging from an iron post above the door. Wagons piled high with hides jostled one another upon the street, establishments whose advertised business had nothing remotely to do with buffalo had stacks of hides enclosed in stockades built behind the stores, and nearly every pedestrian in sight, man and woman, wore a shaggy coat; at first glance they looked like small buffalo bustling along the boardwalks. The rotting stench, of course, was as much a physical feature of the town as its architecture. I guessed that in warm weather the flies would be plentiful enough to demand the vote, and get it.

My first thought was depressing. With hides in such great supply, the arrival of yet another load must be greeted with all the enthusiasm of a Pullman full of Irish politicians trundling into the New York Central station. As we drew rein before the Buffalo Great Atlantic Emporium and Western Union Office, I reduced my estimate regarding the price our cargo would bring from its early euphoric (and frankly whiskey-induced) high of $4.50 per hide by half, and prepared myself for the disappointment of an offer as low as a dollar. There was a small crowd obstructing the boardwalk in front of the store, shouting and gesticulating; I assumed this was a party of hiders calling the proprietor all kinds of a thief.

I was wrong, as I found out presently. It was not an altercation. It was an auction, and the retailers outnumbered the hiders three to one.

Changes had taken place while we were outside civilization. An Industrial Revolution was in full swing, and tough leather—acres of it, miles of it—was required to make drive belts to operate the great steam-piston machines back East. Fine buffalo robes were the fashion in Boston, New York, and Chicago, just the thing to drape across a lady's lap while riding in a carriage or skating over snow hills in the back of a sleigh: Good quality bull hides suitable for tanning brought between $100 and $175 apiece. Finally, the Department of the Army, having made up its mind to violate the Treaty of Fort Laramie and lay claim to all the Indian lands from the Black Hills to the South Platte, had decided that its best interests lay in depriving the Plains tribes of their main staple and thus shatter their fighting spirit, and in a hundred little ways encouraged the slaughter by hiders. Thousands of surplus Sharp's rifles, long the favorite of runners the frontier over, were pulled out of government warehouses where they had been gathering dust since Appomattox and dumped on the market, selling for as little as a dollar apiece. (The fact that this unfair competition employing its own product forced the manufacturer into receivership was of little interest to Washington.) Large hunting parties were offered military escort through Chief Red Cloud's Bozeman country to ensure their safety from raids by hostiles. The price of a Sharp's 420-grain cartridge, in-

undating the market in thousands of case lots from the same
army shelves where the rifles had been kept, fell from a quarter
to a dime; and to reduce even further the initial outlay by hiders
planning extensive expeditions, ten cents were exchanged for
each spent shell brought to post traderships at all the military
forts. Never in human history had an animal been cheaper to
stalk and more profitable to slay.

Between November 1872 and February 1873 we had collected four hundred hides, of which we had cured and treated
twenty for robes and preserved five with the heads for mounting.
The proprietor of the Buffalo Emporium, having lost out in the
bidding on a big shipment of a thousand hides, intercepted us on
our way into the store. Accompanying us to the wagon, he inspected five or six hides at the top of the stack, peeling them
apart from the rest like sheets of tin, ran his fingers through his
full white beard, and offered us six dollars for each green hide,
$150 for the mountable skins with heads attached, and twenty
apiece for the robes.

"I guarantee you won't get better anywhere in Julesburg," he
said. "If you like, I'll give you a letter, and if anybody in town
tops it and will put it in writing, I'll match his offer. I'm sick of
pretenses and dickering. I can't keep a hide in stock."

"Done," said Van Horn, without bothering to consult the rest
of us. I decided against objecting. The total came to $3,400. I
had ridden into Julesburg filthy and penniless. On my way to the
bathhouse I carried a poke containing $850 in paper and silver,
my quarter of the winter's bounty.

That night, stretched out upon my hotel bed—my first of any
kind since before Thanksgiving—smoking a twenty-five-cent
cigar and digesting oyster stew and half a ham, I spread open the
first of a bale of old New York newspapers I had bought for a
penny from a merchant who used them to wrap purchases and
read about the fall of Boss Tweed.

At the height of its power in 1870, the Tweed Ring pocketed
sixty-six and two-thirds cents out of every dollar paid by the
county and city to their vendors. Upon one day in April, it was
estimated, between fourteen and fifteen million dollars in fraud-
ulent bills were plundered from the city treasury, with the bulk
of that amount divided among Tweed and his circle of cohorts
and the rest banked by Tammany for the payment of bribes.

Construction of a new county courthouse, projected to cost three million, came in at twelve; the remaining nine million was booty. During Tweed's first trial for embezzlement in 1872 (it ended in a hung jury), a bill to the City of New York for ten thousand dollars in office supplies was broken down as follows: six reams of foolscap; six reams of notepaper; three dozen boxes of rubber bands; two dozen pen holders; one dozen sponges; four bottles of India ink.

The *Times,* freed from shackles suddenly by the death of a Tweed man on its board of directors, lunged in snapping. It was fighting the Tammany machine, squads of waterfront toughs armed with revolvers and blackjacks, and Tweed's own enormous personal popularity, purchased from his illiterate constituents through years of glad-handing and charitable donation; but once it got its teeth into his fat calf—as it did with the help of a satchel full of ledgers spirited away by a disgruntled county bookkeeper named O'Rourke—it proved the most persistent of bull terriers. As the Boss's cronies fell one by one to indictment and conviction—Chamberlain Sweeney, Comptroller Connolly, Mayor Hall—the newspaper's cartoonist gleefully dipped his pen in acid and drew bloated caricatures dressed in stripes with big black iron balls chained to their ankles. In a very short time, the signature he placed upon these mean-spirited little windows into the back rooms where big-city politics were conducted would add a new adjective to our language. His name was Nast.

Tweed would stand trial again. Meanwhile the list of the incarcerated grew. It was so long, and the print so gray and smudged, that I almost missed a name at the bottom of one dense column:

Michael J. Brennan, assistant city fire commissioner; four counts, embezzlement; two counts, conspiracy to commit grand larceny; sentence, 3–5 years hard labor.

So Jehosophat had survived. I was not a killer.

My conscience was numb. Save for a sickening lapse when I awoke in the East River Society House, I had never once felt guilty for my actions on behalf of a fallen police officer and then myself. The news that I could not be arrested for murder, and that the one man who would have bothered to pursue the matter was too busy preventing him*self* from going to prison, affected me in a way far more profound. It helped me come to a decision that had begun to form the moment I learned that I was no longer a poor itinerant musician. I was going home.

CHAPTER THIRTY-FOUR

I t was a good year to have money.
Every year is, of course—"I've been rich and I've been poor, and rich is better," Sophie Tucker once told me, then repeated it for a journalist, though she stole it from Nora Bayes—but in 1873 this was especially true, because almost no one else did.

In September, the bottom fell out of the New York Stock Exchange. The banks in the city, fearing a "run," closed their doors. As always, the experts had reasons to offer: the sudden halt in the flow of money to, from, and through Tammany in the wake of Tweed's collapse, the shooting death by a rival the previous year of notorious stock manipulator Jim Fisk, the ouster two months later from the directorship of the Erie Railroad of Fisk's partner Jay Gould by stockholders, creating a vacuum that was filled all too quickly by chaos—any one of these incidents was sufficient to sow fear. All at once was the stuff of mass hysteria, which if you're in the habit of reading your history with a magnifying lens for the footnotes you'll see went down as the Panic of '73.

Wars, elections, and sexual indiscretions receive much more attention—squalor and despair don't offer painters much opportunity to employ cadmium red, nor writers their favorite punchy adjectives—but financial failures are far more devastating, and the ripple effect much broader. This one affected the whole of the continent, and by reflection the rest of the civilized world, for four dismal years. Independent banks collapsed. Mortgages were called in. Farms went on the block. Families separated. Heads of families committed suicide. Children were swallowed by orphanages and factories. Eggs sold for three cents the dozen.

I was aware of none of this when I took a train east from Julesburg toward New York. With money in my pocket I journeyed by Pullman salon car with arrangements for a sleeping compartment, and within a few miles determined that, fortune willing, I would henceforth travel by no other method. When it pleased me to be sociable, I joined my fellow passengers in a coach equipped with deep mohair-covered seats, room to stretch one's legs, and a footrest that swung up and out of the way when it was not desired; or I could repair to the bar or the dining car. When I wished to retire, an accommodating Negro porter would materialize outside my compartment, key at the ready to unlock and pull down a berth that was altogether more comfortable than either my lean-to at Fort Riley or the wagon sheet in Nebraska. There I lay in my nightshirt, allowing the motion of the train to rock me into a doze and wondering if that hot, dusty ride I had taken in the other direction ten years before were not just some troubling dream remembered from childhood.

New York had awaited my return for a decade. I saw no reason why it could not wait another few weeks while I took in the city of Chicago.

Upon my last trip through, I had been too young, too limited in my finances, and too distracted by my situation to appreciate any of the features the great Midwestern juggernaut had to offer. In truth, harnessed by wartime shortages and surviving almost exclusively upon its reputation as a produce-shipping center, it had borne little promise of the grand metropolis it would become following the Union victory and the ravenous craving for Western beef that swept the East in the years succeeding.

The Great Fire, two years in the past now, was a black memory to those who had lost friends, family, fortune, and that crucial intangible sense of personal security to the flames, but five million in donations from America and Europe, poured over two hundred thousand in damages, had gone a long way toward eradicating its more visible legacy. Most of the rubble had been cleared. In its place had sprung a fireproof city of brick and steel and mortar, great spreading factories with tall chimneys in rows like rifles on parade. In the center beat its virile heart: the long barns, squat packinghouses, pens, maze of wooden chutes, and multitiered slaughtering floors of the Union Stockyards, where workers in blue overalls trotted bawling steers in one end and workers in white aprons carried sides and quarters still bleeding out the door. From there the beef was hung from hooks in freight cars packed with dry ice and sent north to Milwaukee, east to Detroit, Cleveland, New York, and Philadelphia, and south to Richmond, where carpetbaggers sold it for pirate prices to gentry in frayed cuffs sipping green whiskey in the empty rooms of plantation houses in need of shingles and paint. A black pall of coal smoke, locomotive exhaust, and coke residue, thick and gritty, overhung the vast gray sprawl on Lake Michigan like God's brow over Sodom.

Paradise, for a healthy twenty-six-year-old male with jingling pockets, no attachments, and a winter of hardship behind him.

I checked into the Palmer House—plush floral carpets, brass bedsteads, a separate bath on every floor—reported to Marshall Field's to be measured for a new wardrobe, made an appointment at a photography studio to have my picture taken when the clothes were ready, and bought a ticket for that evening's performance of the first play I had seen since coming west, a thing called *Scouts of the Prairie*, featuring none other than William F. "Buffalo Bill" Cody, Hickok's friend and the celebrated slayer of Tall Bull, the Cheyenne chief, whose infamy seemed to have increased since his death at Summit Springs. After a dinner in the gaslit hotel dining room of roast duck and red wine, topped off with a delight called Iced Cream, I hailed a two-wheeler and alighted at Nixon's Amphitheater just in time for the overture.

I daresay that proscenium, hung with olive curtains and broken out in gilded cherubs, death's-heads, angels with trumpets, and the obligatory masks of Comedy and Tragedy, never saw anything to compare with *Scouts of the Prairie* since the fire. Penned, the rumor went, in an alcoholic three hours by a scoundrel operating under the alias Ned Buntline, the play consisted mostly of windy campfire monologues by its star player Cody, another lanky authentic frontiersman named Texas Jack Omohundro, and its paunchy author, decked out in buckskins and a preposterous wig. These were punctuated by the odd Indian attack and romantic interludes between Texas Jack and a "Cheyenne princess" identified in the program as "Mlle. Mor-

lacchi." Of course it was all claptrap, and its hero a humbug, but
the snapping and blue flame of the blank pistols shook the audience out of the torpor created by the overheated poetastry of
the dialogue, and when the savages seized, bound, and stood
Buntline over a genuine smoldering fire, the delirium was electric. A New York house, I thought, would have applauded good-
naturedly, laughing behind its programs. At the Novelty Theater
in Abilene the liquored-up cowpokes would have whooped and
fired their pistols into the ceiling, provided they could be re-
strained from taking potshots at the actors. In Chicago, the
crowd of Friday-nighters stamped, whistled, pounded their
hands, and demanded curtain call after curtain call until the proprietor came out to announce that an additional performance
had been appended to the Saturday schedule. More cheers
greeted this announcement, and then the chattering, rib-nudging
exodus was under way.

As it turned out, I was wrong about the New York audiences.
When the show toured there, the Broadway columnists were
disdainful, but the theater was sold out for its entire run. It
seemed the farther one traveled from the actual arena, the higher
grew the level of interest in the doings out West. Cody himself,
pale-faced with stage fright while taking his bows but looking
very much at home in his exaggerated fringes and ten-gallon
hat, appeared overwhelmed, although that far into the production
he might have been expected to have grown accustomed to it.
Recalling that impressive figure in his long chestnut locks and
the reaction to his ridiculous little melodrama, I was not greatly
surprised a dozen or so years later when his Wild West extrava-
ganza swept across Europe like Napoleon's Grand Army.

Outside, it was a pleasant autumn evening, with the gas lamps
aglow and a smell of burning leaves in the stiff breeze coming
off the lake. I ignored the horse cabs drawn up before the theater
and began walking toward the hotel. I wore my striped suit from
Laramie, somewhat the worse for wear but freshly brushed and
pressed, and I was approached three times by panhandlers within
five blocks. One I assumed was a veteran, displaying the iron
hook he wore in place of his right hand, but the others appeared
whole and healthy despite their dirty faces and shabby dress;
one was younger than I. I gave each a coin, for I had known their
misery once. Farther on I saw shapeless figures heaped in door-

ways, and when I passed a small fenced-in park I noticed that every bench was occupied by a supine form. These were sobering indications of the grim economic period through which we were passing. I wondered, with so many so close to desperation, if it had been a wise choice to walk, and began looking for a cab.

No sooner had I developed this course of action than someone came up quickly from behind and slid an arm inside one of mine. In self-defense I turned—and found myself looking into an enormous pair of blue eyes ringed in artificial shadow and overhung by a charming hat, slanted steeply to one side and trimmed with ostrich plumes and lace. The dress the creature wore was just as becoming, snug at the waist, open to the collarbone, and decorated down the front with velvet frogs in imitation of military fashion; not that any gouty old general ever cut a figure as fetching as the tiny specimen of femininity clutching my arm. She was five feet and ninety pounds, not an inch nor a grain more, under thirty, with golden tendrils framing her face, and it occurred to me that if she were not careful with the white lace parasol that rested upon her shoulder, the wind would pick her up and carry her all the way to Des Moines.

Which, I decided, would be tragedy for me.

Naturally, she was a harlot. There was, however, a world of difference between the women who quartered the streets of that city and those who hiked their skirts for every hider and saloon swamp in the territories. Out there, where men outnumbered women twelve to one, being female was the only criterion (and I had been to places where even that was waived under certain circumstances); bad teeth, prominent moustaches, and surplus flesh lay outside the notice of a man who had spent the last six weeks in the company of unshaven drovers and ticky cattle, or one who had just stumbled blinking into the sunshine from an underground shaft with only a whiskey glass full of gold dust to compensate him for ten months of heartbreak. Chicago, for all its cattle stunners, boat-pullers, barrow-bellied police officers, and robber barons, was a woman's town, with ten gorgeous, buxom, salon-coiffed, Paris-gowned females hanging upon the arms of every monopolist. The plush parlors in the Loop daily turned away women who could set all of Denver scrambling to carry their hatboxes, had they but known it. The fishing in pub-

lic waters was not as costly as in the private ponds, but the catch
was not much less impressive.

Thus I spent my first night in the Windy City.

There is a trunk in storage in San Francisco, if it has not been
sold to pay for the rent I owe upon it. Buried inside, beneath a
moth-eaten striped suit, stacks of yellowed song sheets, and a
woven coat of Indian manufacture wrapped carefully in blue tissue and sprinkled with camphor, is a photograph still in its cardboard studio frame. The model is a wicked-looking young blade
in full evening dress complete with tails, posed incongruously
before a sylvan backdrop with an empty two-seater glider hanging from an apple tree branch. A silk hat is cradled in the crook
of one arm, while his other hand clutches a pair of gray kid
gloves upon the silver crook of a brand-new cane. His hair is
longish, although not so long as an Indian scout's or a Wild West
show entrepreneur's, his beard is trimmed into a neat Vandyke,
and there is a youthful arrogance about the way he stares fixedly
at the camera, as if to say that he has money or that he has recently slept in the arms of a desirable, naked woman.

Both statements are true. Yet there is something else about that
young fellow that disturbs me greatly in my old age, and that is
that I don't know him, not from Adam, and although I can guess
what thoughts are passing through that slick head, I cannot
fathom why he harbors them, or what makes him reckon them
worth holding on to. At the time the picture was developed I remember being quite pleased with it—certainly more so than I
was with the one I'd had taken in Wyoming—but I'd choose
the other over it now, if only because what it showed about me
had had the power to upset me. That's why the Chicago photo is
in storage, and if it's gone at auction, whoever bid upon it is
welcome to do his own guessing.

I had intended to stay three weeks, then press on east. I stayed
six months. Had my money held out, I might have stayed
even longer, for I had discovered an indolent streak, and was
curious—that old bugbear—to see where it would lead.

My guitar gathered dust upon the top shelf of the wardrobe in
my room at the Palmer House; I had not sat down at a piano
since Abilene. Others could entertain me. I attended Wagner's
Tristan und Isolde at the Opera House, in which Christine Nils-

son sang the female lead, heard Sarasate play with the Symphony, returned to *Scouts of the Prairie* and saw an entirely different play with the same performers portraying the same roles, and became something of a connoisseur of the better brothels along Fifth Avenue, which in 1870 had been rechristened from Wells Street to spare the memory of Captain Billy Wells, an early local martyr to the Indians who had originally settled the lake basin; the women at the Metropole were better-looking, but the ones at Madame Fleauville's were more well mannered, and the cigar-chewing Negro who played the piano at the Dearborn House was the most accomplished musician I had ever seen, performing exercises upon the keyboard that my old dragon of a tutor had insisted were "impossible, *jung Meister;* concentrate upon the things of this world, and leave the fantastic to *Herr* Robert-Houdin." The man's mastery, beside which I was a backward student, made me sick at heart, all the more because it came to him naturally; he admitted to me that he had never learned to write his own name, let alone read music.

In this manner, along with meals, my hotel accommodations, cigars, and whiskey, my funds drained away at a rate that fascinated me. Although I supplemented them from time to time with winning wagers at the racetracks outside town and a plethora of gambling halls—banned, by order of the city fathers, but easy to find, and still easier to get into, provided one had cash to show—I celebrated my twenty-seventh birthday in the bar of the Palmer House with a glass of whiskey I bought out of the last of the original $850 I had carried away from Julesburg and studied the train ticket that would take me back West in the morning. I had pawned my new clothes and some odds and ends of jewelry I had acquired—ruby stickpin, platinum watch and chain, gold ring—and pocketed enough to set myself up for a few weeks in whatever town was printed upon the ticket. The whiskey had not been my first of the evening, and reading was something on the order of a chore.

Needless to say, I felt low. Money stuck to me no better than it did to those poor wretches who begged coins from me whenever I went out in my city finery, and I hadn't a crippling injury or a nationwide depression to hold responsible. Indeed, if I clung to any sort of pride, it was my refusal to blame my financial condition for denying me a reunion that season with my father and mother in New York. If I had a thousand dollars, if I had ten thousand, I should have spent it on anything but a ticket home. The manner in which I had conducted myself during my brief prosperity had demonstrated that I was not the kind of man with whom my father would choose to associate, much less have for a son. I had stared into this abyss before, of course, but then I'd had my music for compensation. Now, having seen and heard what a genuine artist could accomplish, which practice as I might I could never hope to approach, I doubted that I would ever again find the courage to take up a musical instrument. I would tend bar for my living, or hand out towels in a bordello. It was high time I took up a profession in keeping with my low character.

"Mr. Gashade?"

I looked up from the bottom of my glass—swam up would be a more appropriate description—into a round, hairless face beneath a soft hat, with an egg-shaped pair of spectacles straddling its nose and a Pickwick collar tickling the largest and fleshiest earlobes I had ever encountered. Their owner stood at my elbow, both hands clutching a dilapidated leather portfolio in front of him like a bird balancing itself upon a telegraph wire.

"I have that honor," said I. "May I stand you to a libation? Today is the anniversary of the day of my birth."

"Indeed, sir? Many happy returns. Unfortunately, I must decline your generous hospitality. I am a man of temperance." He cleared his throat, a demure ripple. "The desk clerk told me I might find you here. I left my card upon two previous visits, with a note asking you to pay me a call. My name is Whitstead. I am the bookkeeper at the Cook County Fairgrounds."

I remembered the name. I had supposed he was a creditor. "You have an excellent racetrack. I have made down payments upon a number of horses there."

"That brings me to the reason I am here. There is a matter involving a wager you placed last fall."

I reached the end of my tether. Placing my back against the bar, I snatched my old cowhide poke from my pocket and spread it open under his nose. "Take it all, Mr. Whitehead; the poke too. It is not enough that I have squandered a small fortune at your facility. Since you must hound me at my place of residence for more, you may as well own that you are a thief and pick my pocket." There was no cash in the pouch. I did not feel the need to mention the grubstake I had in the hotel safe.

To my astonishment, the bookkeeper thrust his portfolio under one arm and took the poke. "Whitstead is my name, sir. This is what I need to see, if you have not—Ah!" He separated a cardboard stub from the jumble between the folds. "Here it is, October twenty-fifth, sixth race, horse number nine: Buffalo Skinner. It paid twenty to one." Keeping the stub, he returned the pouch. "Normally, we at the fairgrounds consider an unclaimed ticket to be the bettor's responsibility. However, because there is a substantial sum involved, unlikely to be overlooked indefinitely by the winning party, and because it is essential that our books balance at the end of the fiscal year—"

"How did you find me?"

He had untied his portfolio and was rummaging inside. "Your calling card stuck to the banknote with which you placed the wager. Because of the amount, I inquired at all the best hotels." He withdrew a check and placed it on the bar. It was made out to me in the amount of four hundred dollars.

" 'Entertainments,' " he mused, while I studied it. "Are you in the show business, Mr. Gashade?"

"No. It was a bad joke."

Wishing me a pleasant birthday, he left. I felt nothing. What value hard work and probity in a world that rewarded indolence?

". . . help overhearing your glad tidings. May I interest you in a proposition?"

I looked into the pleasant, ruddy face of the stranger who had inserted himself into the space next to me. He had black side-whiskers under a bowler hat and prominent front teeth that clamped his lower lip like a hasp.

"I'm not interested in purchasing any gold bricks today." I folded the check into my poke.

His chortle, like his accent, was distinctively British. "I am not a confidence man, but a purveyor, and at the moment I am without a partner. If you will allow me to serve you from the bottle at my table, I shall explain myself."

"What happened to your partner?" I was mildly amused. He reminded me of a caricature of a Limey in a variety house in Brooklyn.

"He was arrested." The hand he offered was freckled and soft, with pink skin showing beneath the nails; there was none cleaner west of Albany. "Delmar St. George Dibble. All my partners call me Del. I should be honored, Mr. Gashade, if you would follow their example."

CHAPTER THIRTY-FIVE

𝄢

Del Dibble claimed to be sixty, but I didn't credit it any more than his insistence that he'd served under Lord Cardigan in the Crimea—as quartermaster, of course. Although he might have dyed his hair and muttonchops, the rest of him would have had to have been preserved in the same vinegar that pickled his heart. More times than I can count I saw him spring aboard a wagonload of contraband to test a knot or adjust the sheet, all in one motion from ground to tailgate, while I at twenty-seven made use of the sideboards to pull myself up.

On the other hand, threescore years seems scarcely enough for anyone to have grown so wicked.

Forty or sixty, he's dead by now—hanged, shot, or (as seems most likely) gone in his sleep with that same contented half smile he shone upon me that day in Chicago, while measuring me for a square yard of stone floor in Isaac Parker's dungeon in Fort Smith. In that hole I cursed him by the day, yet from this distance I bear him no grudge. If he was the instrument of my fall, no one put my thumbs in a screw to persuade me to take him up. Shark that he was, he cruised the waters of the bars, brothels, and elevated railway of the city, moving in swiftly the moment he smelled blood.

"The procedure is simple, and you won't even need a map to get where you are going," said he, over a bottle of aged and mellow whiskey at his corner table; perhaps the best that can be said of him is that his taste in the finer comforts was irreproachable, and that he was not stingy in sharing them. "I have an arrangement with the proprietor of the House of Lords Saloon in Fort Smith. He needs only to see my face to turn over his inventory—that, and a hundred fifty dollars American."

"Arkansas?"

"That's just the jumping-off point. After we say good-bye you will drive the wagon along the South Bank of the Arkansas River into the Indian Nations, then follow the Canadian when it forks to the south. Three days after that you will be in Indianola, where Ed White Turkey will give you three hundred in gold for the cargo. I shall be waiting when you return to Fort Smith with the empty wagon. The profits will be divided down the middle."

"What's the penalty for transporting liquor in the Indian territory?"

"My friend, there is none. The federal court in Arkansas is a political boondoggle, as crooked as any man in Grant's cabinet. Most of the marshals traffic in liquor on the side. If you are stopped, the chances are they will confiscate the shipment and turn you loose."

"And if they don't?"

"Even better. Judge Story peddles dismissals at a fixed rate. For a little more he may even return the liquor."

"Still, the risk seems steep for seventy-five dollars."

"It's one hundred percent profit. Those Creeks and Cherokees are starving for whiskey; Ed White Turkey will take as much as we can supply. You can make six trips in a season. That's four hundred fifty dollars, and you won't have to peel hides or worry about your scalp. The Five Civilized Tribes have worn trousers and spoken English for forty years."

"If it's so simple, why don't you drive the wagon?"

"I am too old. I can barely handle a one-horse buggy. You took your turn with a six-hitch team in Nebraska. In any case our little enterprise requires someone with an established reputation to show himself in all the respectable places in Fort Smith. How would it look if Cornelius Vanderbilt were seen mounting to the cab of Old Number Nine, wearing a cap made of ticking with a red bandanna dangling from his hip pocket?"

I don't know now if Del Dibble actually saw himself as a robber baron on the grand scale of a Vanderbilt. It's not impossible. The most successful confidence men begin by selling themselves their own bill of goods.

It doesn't signify, as they used to say in Missouri; I became his creature. To give him his due, I must point out that throughout the first summer and autumn of our association, nothing transpired to dispute what he had told me of Fort Smith and the Indian Nations.

I have not visited there since long before it became the State of Oklahoma, but from stories I hear, admission to the Union has not changed the place demonstrably. In my time it was the home of domesticated Indians, outlaws on the run, and human predators not far removed from our animal ancestors. Only last year, federal agents cornered bank bandit Charles Arthur "Pretty Boy" Floyd, an Oklahoma native, in a farmer's field in Ohio and shot him to pieces, exactly as U.S. marshals hunted down and destroyed Ned Christie in the northeastern section of the Nations a generation earlier. Both were accused of the ambush murders of federal men. The territory was set aside by Andrew Jackson for members of the Cherokee, Chickasaw, Choctaw, Creek, Quapaw, and Seminole Nations—the so-called Five Civilized Tribes (plus one)—who were torn from their homes and prodded over the Trail of Tears, conveniently out of sight of white society. Governed by the federal court in Fort Smith, Arkansas, its seventy-four thousand square miles were patrolled by a handful of native peace officers and an even smaller number of deputy United States marshals, making its rocky hills and tangled forests a haven for every blackguard and brigand with a price on his head and a rough idea of its boundaries. No one will ever know the full extent of the crimes and depravities that took place there. Most of the ones we know about were too despicable even for the dime novels. The motion picture industry will not touch them.

The musical profession is different. I heard three separate ballads about Ned Christie's vendetta the first year following his demise; and I understand my old friend Woody Guthrie is composing one about Pretty Boy Floyd.

Music was beyond my ken in the Year of Our Lord 1874. I had pawned my guitar in Chicago along with my jewelry and wardrobe—not for the two additional dollars it brought, but with the air of a man ridding himself at last of a pious and quarrelsome companion—and for the first time in ten years I decamped for the sparsely populated regions without so much as a harmonica for my personal amusement. I hoisted my single portmanteau into the brass rack above my Pullman seat, swung down the footrest, and stretched out, waiting for the regret. I waited all the way through Illinois's furrowed fields and while changing trains in St. Louis; gave up waiting somewhere among the steep green hills of the Ozarks, and by the time the car in which I was riding swept through a ravine and the whistle blew for the Fort Smith station, I had forgotten I ever knew F major from a sixbrace.

I made eight trips between Fort Smith and Indianola throughout June and November. My traveling companion was a half-Creek, half-Negro murderer (I was convinced) named Charlie Stone Bucket, flat-faced and dusky-skinned, with dead black hair worn long and chopped off square at the corners of his jaw and across his forehead, like an Aztec warrior in an old woodcut. He wore smoked glasses to protect his weak eyes and rode next to me with a ten-gauge shotgun across his knees for close work and a big Remington rolling-block rifle behind the seat for use at a distance. Del Dibble said Charlie was there to secure the shipment from highwaymen, but I suspected he was guarding it from me as well, lest I decide to set myself up in competition with my partner.

The half-breed was poor company. Journey after journey he wore the same calico shirt, corduroy trousers, broken-down Wellingtons, and stained Yankee kepi, and the continuing decrepitude of trousers and shirt suggested he had not had them off between trips. He emitted an eye-watering odor of stagnant sweat and rancid bear-grease—the latter to ward off mosquitoes, or so he claimed. Certainly it repelled almost everyone with whom he came into contact, although I myself was immune thanks to my recent occupation in Nebraska. His sole topic of conversation was the legions of women he had known, with and without their consent. I loathed him, and he in turn distrusted me. Camping along the Canadian, whenever I returned from relieving myself in the woods I found him sitting up in his bedroll with his shotgun in both hands, eyes glittering in the moonlight.

Three times we were waylaid.

The first was by a party of deputy U.S. marshals escorting a wagon containing a half-dozen men with their ankles bound and their hands tied behind their backs. It was my impression that federal law enforcement appointees had to be in top physical condition, but the spokesman was morbidly fat, sunken in rings

of suet like a raccoon aboard his big shaggy chestnut, with a
filthy bowler jammed down to his ears and a stout cigar screwed
into a corner of his mouth. His badge, a small silver star in a circle, sagged from one pocket of his flannel shirt with a thick fold
of arrest warrants thrust inside. It was clear from the way his
muck-colored gaze kept sliding toward our cargo of barrels that
he coveted it; but when Charlie Stone Bucket, fingering the ten-
gauge in his lap, informed him that we were about Del Dibble's
business, he nodded, puffed at his cigar, and snarled to us to
stand aside for officers of the court and their prisoners. Obvi-
ously, Dibble had made prior arrangements.

Another time, while we were picking our way down a rocky
grade, three horsemen burst from behind a nearby stand of
sycamore, plainly bent upon stampeding our team and upset-
ting the wagon. However, when a blast from Charlie Stone
Bucket's shotgun carried away the lead rider's left sleeve and
most of his ear, he and his companions fell into confusion. I un-
furled my bullwhip over the heads of our horses and we rattled
down the rest of the grade and away, losing two barrels off the
back. I kept up the pace for two miles, but we were not pursued.

We were not so lucky the third time. Admittedly, upon this occasion our vigilance slipped. We had left the Arkansas River
ferry only that morning and were not four hours into the Nations;
consequently we considered ourselves relatively safe when I
drew rein to give the road to a group of drovers evidently bound
for the saloons and brothels of Fort Smith. My companion, who
dismissed all "cow-scratchers" as beneath contempt, pulled out
the tail of his disreputable shirt to wipe his glasses as they
passed. Suddenly there was a rattle of forestocks and a crunch of
hammers, and we looked around to find ourselves inside a semicircle of revolvers and rifles, all pointed at us.

"What's in the wagon?" one of them demanded, in a tone that
told me he knew the answer.

"Flour," I replied. Indeed, that was what was stenciled upon
the lids of the barrels.

One of the riders near the back of the wagon leaned out of his
saddle and gave one of the barrels a shake, sloshing the contents
around inside. "I got sad news for you, peddler," said this one.
"Your flour done got wet."

Another rider thought this was the funniest thing he had ever heard. His laugh was a high hard bray.

I don't know if Charlie Stone Bucket tried to make a fight. I was busy looking at the man who was doing most of the talking when one of the others swept his rifle stock across the half-breed's face, shattering his nose and his glasses. He clutched the seat to keep from falling while the man who had assaulted him grasped the shotgun by its barrels and slid it off his lap. Charlie Stone Bucket kept still after that, covering the lower half of his face with both hands to control his nosebleed.

"You want the same or worse, peddler," said the one with the words, "you go right on staring."

I lowered my eyes. I *had* been staring at him. He'd filled out some, grown a sparse beard and his fair hair to his shoulders, but it would take more than that, or the broad brim of the black hat he wore with an eagle feather in the band, to prevent me from recognizing John Thrailkill. Even had I failed to note the deadness of his eyes—blank buttons, doll's eyes—I could have picked out the shiny, slim-handled revolver he held from a pile of similar weapons. He had used it in Abilene when he stuck up Mike Williams at the Alamo Saloon, and had carried it all through the war after taking it away from me in Lawrence.

Now he reached over, grasped my chin with his free hand, and turned up my face. Looking into the empty holes through which he saw, I tried to keep my mind empty, lest it communicate anything about our past association. I saw puzzlement cross his features, an attempt to remember. Finally he let go and leaned back.

"All you whiskey peddlers look alike," he said, but he sounded unconvinced. "I got good news. You boys are walking back to Fort Smith."

"Aw, shit." This from the man who had struck Charlie Stone Bucket. His face was narrow and rodentlike, with a predatory nose and boils in his beard. "Cain't we at least take target practice on the breed?"

"We can't risk the shots this close to town. Them marshals'd shoot us all trying to escape for a load half this size."

We alighted from the wagon, my companion glaring murder over his hand with blood welling between the fingers. Looking down at me from horseback, Thrailkill said, "Was you in the war, peddler?"

"No, I was too young."

He stared at me hard for another moment, then shook his head. "Get to walking. First one of you turns his head carries it back."

I have never taken a longer walk in my life than the one that carried me around the bend and out of John Thrailkill's sight behind a stand of hardwoods. At any moment I expected him to remember the youth who had humiliated him before his fellow Missouri raiders with the border spin, and put a slug between my shoulder blades.

Fort Smith was a quiet place to spend the winter. The cattle drives were over, the steamboats put in less often, and all thirty saloons hunkered in for the long dead spell before spring. The Fort Smith *Herald* occupied itself with reports of suicide on First Street—locally referred to as "The Row"—where the harlots found time at last to take stock of their lives and decide whether they were worth the trouble of continuing, and the periodic arrival of a wagonload of prisoners from the Nations bound for the courthouse attracted curious crowds, but for these diversions the place might have been Abilene before and after the boom. I took a room in a boardinghouse—clean, with a hearty breakfast and dinner provided, but the proprietess, a hefty Scotswoman whose skinny, put-upon husband chopped firewood out back and carried it to the rooms, was no Drucilla; her conversation was even more limited than Charlie Stone Bucket's, and scarcely as entertaining. Charlie himself wintered somewhere in the Nations and Del Dibble returned to Chicago.

Accomplished liar that he was, he had told the truth about the law in Fort Smith. John Sarber, the United States marshal appointed by President Grant to enforce the law in the Indian territory, was a sloth and probably corrupt, taking no official interest in the larceny that ran rampant through his deputies. District Attorney Newton J. Temple, it was rumored, had been subpoenaed to testify in Washington about irregularities in the system by which certificates of payment were issued to jurors (and not paid), and while the reports were probably untrue that Judge Story kept a list of bribery amounts for certain offenses posted in his chambers like a restaurant bill of fare, it was widely accepted that dismissal of charges for any crime including murder was merely a matter of negotiation in the Fort Smith court.

He, too, was under investigation; but the local wisdom was that things had always been this way and were not likely to change, regardless of who wore the robes.

I whiled away the cold months along the Row and in the saloons, where I ignored the piano players and guitar pickers, drinking alone and catching up on the news of the world as it was reported off the wires in the columns of the *Herald*.

Boss Tweed had exchanged his table at Delmonico's Restaurant for a cell in the New York County Penitentiary on Blackwell's Island. Although he had originally been sentenced to serve twelve years, the Court of Appeals had ruled that although the defendant had been convicted on 204 counts of criminal fraud, no punishment in excess of that prescribed for one offense could be inflicted. However, the State of New York had announced its intention to bring suit to recover six million dollars of the plunder that had been traced to Tweed, and when he was released in January 1875, he was rearrested and confined in the Ludlow Street Jail in lieu of three million dollars' bond. Manipulate how he might the system that had made him rich beyond all pretense of decency, Tweed's reign was clearly over.

That same month, acting upon information that Frank and Jesse were inside, Pinkerton agents surrounded the Clay County, Missouri, home of Dr. Reuben and Mrs. Zerelda Samuel. When their demands for surrender went unanswered, a detective lobbed a cast-iron device, shaped vaguely like the base of a lantern, through a window. Moments later a tremendous explosion blew out all the panes, carrying away Mrs. Samuel's left arm below the elbow and the life of Archie, her nine-year-old son by the doctor.

Pressed by reporters, a Pinkerton spokesman identified the device as a smoke bomb intended to drive the occupants outside; it had evidently exploded when someone swept it into a fireplace, igniting the kerosene. The spokesman's name was Captain John Terrence Fabian, my old acquaintance from Abilene and before that the train station in Indianapolis.

Frank and Jesse had been nowhere near their mother's house at the time of the raid. The Pinkertons had hoped to take the James boys away in chains and thus bring them down to human size for those who would erect statues of them. Instead they managed to strengthen even further the Jameses' support among the Yankee-hating hill people of Missouri.

I thought of that remarkable woman, correcting her grown sons' English and calmly describing her husband's lynching by the federal militia. I doubted the mere loss of an arm would quench that fiery spirit.

Change was abroad in Fort Smith as well. Under threat of impeachment, Judge Story resigned, and for his replacement the president turned to a thirty-six-year-old former United States congressman from Missouri. Although Isaac Charles Parker had a reputation as a teetotaler and an ardent supporter of Indian rights, the general opinion around town was that he would prove to be as corrupt as his predecessors, or at best ineffectual. The federal bench in the Western District of Arkansas, with jurisdiction over the Indian territory, had a reputation for grinding a man's resolve down to pebbles.

This was the atmosphere in which I set out, in May of 1875, to deliver the first load of whiskey of the season to Ed White Turkey in Indianola. With me, nose decidedly askew but brand-new shotgun in place and a host of new female conquests to share, was Charlie Stone Bucket.

I found him easier company, for all that. I was both rested and restless after the long hiatus. The sycamore were heavy with leaves, the birds and frogs were in full voice, and a warm breeze was puffing up from Texas, combing my beard and bringing with it the scent of blue lupine and morning glories. I had the strongest possible dose of spring fever.

In my euphoria, I felt no great alarm, shortly after crossing the tracks of the Missouri, Kansas, & Texas Railroad—affectionately known in those parts as the Katy Flyer—when two riders came into view a hundred yards down the road and, spotting us, drew rein. They wore the tall-crowned hats of drovers, but neither had been among John Thrailkill's band the previous autumn, and in any case the scattered buildings of Indianola were visible behind them. Civilization was too close for an ambush.

It was a great surprise, then, when lifting his shotgun into a wary position, Charlie Stone Bucket was thrown over the back of the seat by a blast from the rifle of the man mounted to the right, and quick as thought his partner bounded ahead of him and leveled the barrel of an enormous Colt at me across his forearm.

"Stand still for arrest!" he bellowed through his handlebars.

I raised my hands. "I work with Del Dibble."

The handlebars formed a grim line. "Well, fancy that. *I* work with Judge Parker, and you'll meet him in Fort Smith. That is, if you don't jerk a piece like your friend and save me the freight."

CHAPTER THIRTY-SIX

✥

The federal courthouse was a two-story brick building set at an eccentric angle to the Arkansas River and partitioned into a courtroom, jury rooms, and offices for attorneys, clerks, and U.S. Marshal James F. Fagan, who had succeeded the indolent John Sarber during the housecleaning that took place in the wake of Judge Story's resignation. It was an official-enough-looking building, wainscoted in golden oak and lit by lamps in bowls suspended from the ceilings, with only the bars on the windows in all rooms and corridors accessible to prisoners to remind the visitor that it was a place of justice in a land that regarded the law as something to be ignored or eradicated.

Below ground level, the genteel trappings vanished altogether. The basement was eight feet deep, stone-paved, and separated by a solid stone wall into two compartments, each twenty-nine by fifty-five feet. Chains were stapled to the walls at ten-foot intervals, a kerosene barrel cut into two halves served as bathtubs, and buckets stood in the bases of the old chimneys for purposes of sanitation. This was the federal jail, where some prisoners were interred awaiting trial, others awaiting execution. It was my home for five months.

I was not chained, but assigned to a filthy straw pallet teeming with vermin. At first I avoided it, but the stone floor was clammy and hard, and after two nights I no longer paid attention to the bites and itching, although they troubled me fresh after my monthly bath. By then I had grown accustomed to the hideous stench of the place, an evil mix of offal, urine, perspiration, mildew, and despair. Each day I asked the guard who brought food and water (about which the less said the better), a heavy-shouldered brute armed with a short truncheon, when I could expect my case to come to trial. His reply was ever the same: "You got about six dozen rapists and murderers ahead of you. Wait your turn." After a month I stopped asking.

I wasn't lonely. At any given time I had eight to ten inmates with whom to converse upon my side of the partition, some of them quite personable, including two or three who were considered enough of a risk to chain to the wall. They came and went, however: acquitted, remanded to a court in a different jurisdiction, convicted and sent north to the Federal House of Corrections in Detroit; or, as in the case of six men at once on September 3, declared guilty and suspended by their necks from the infamous Fort Smith gallows.

Although there was a room upstairs where prisoners could confer with their lawyers, I never saw it. I had no attorney, and Del Dibble never offered to provide me with one, and for that matter never visited me. Incensed at first, I eventually came to realize that nothing had been said about what might happen in the event of my arrest, and that no promises had been made. He had probably left for Chicago within a day of my incarceration, and was even now haunting the city's drinking establishments in search of a new associate. Had my predecessor been rotting away in this same dungeon as we were sealing our partnership? It seemed likely. If I had not asked the questions I should have when it counted, it wasn't because they hadn't occurred to me. I simply had not wanted to hear the answers.

In August, I think it was—I reckoned the passage of time by information carried by fresh inmates—a fanfare of blows and curses announced the arrival of additional company. A new prisoner had tried to push his escort off the top of the stairs and been soundly trounced by two guards with their fists and truncheons. By the time they dragged him into my half of the basement and fixed the shackles to his wrists and ankles, he was unconscious, his face a mass of bruises, and his long fair hair streaked with blood. I knew him instantly, however. The Great West was vast, but it seemed it was not so large I could wander in it for long without encountering John Thrailkill.

Several yards separated us, and at high noon the dugout windows near the ceiling allowed only gray twilight into our world, and so I was not greatly concerned that he would recognize me, having failed to do so in broad daylight on the other side of the Arkansas River. As the days passed and he recovered from his injuries in so far as to engage some of the other prisoners in conversation, I learned that he was under a charge of murder and rape. The murder victim, a white farmer living in the Cherokee Nation with his Indian wife, had shot and killed one of Thrailkill's companions during an attempted robbery along the Canadian River. Thrailkill boasted that he had tracked the man to his cabin, lured him outside by gobbling like a wild turkey, and shot him from ambush. Then he had gone into the cabin, pistol-whipped and raped the widow, and left with eighty-six dollars he found stashed in a tobacco tin behind the cookstove. "Parker's marshals," as the deputies working under Marshal Fagan were coming to be known, caught up with him on the road and surrounded him.

He stood trial shortly thereafter—I envied those arrested for capital crimes only because justice came to them more quickly than to a lowly rumrunner—and was sentenced to hang. As the last of the first half dozen condemned by juries since Parker's appointment, he was scheduled to join the other five in a swift gesture of official retribution.

Such a burden would have been impossible for any ordinary gallows to accommodate. For Fort Smith, this was operating at only half capacity. The scaffold was eighteen feet long, with a single trap running its entire length, and had been designed to suspend twelve men at a time. It was the talk of the West; some said it had been inspired by the efficiency with which the pack-inghouses in Chicago dispatched, quartered, and packaged cattle even before the life heat had passed from the carcasses. Until now it had been little more than a curiosity, receiving infrequent use, and then only to hang one man at a time.

That was about to change. No more momentous marriage was ever engineered than the one that united Isaac Parker and the Fort Smith gallows.

Thrailkill seemed unaffected by his sentence. If anything he became more loquacious, striking up spirited conversations with some of those scheduled to join him upon the scaffold, notably Daniel Evans, who had shot a nineteen-year-old boy through the head for his horse and saddle, then had the temerity to wear the boy's fancy high-heeled boots throughout his trial, and James Moore, a horse thief who had killed eight men in the course of his career, the last a deputy marshal. They seemed to consider themselves charter members of an exclusive club.

Which, in a way, they were; for from the moment they dropped through the trap, Congressman Parker of Missouri would cease to exist and the legend of the Hanging Judge would be born.

I did not, of course, seek Thrailkill's attention. Neither did I avoid it, knowing furtive action to be the surest way to shine a beacon upon oneself. He did look my way upon occasion; however, having learned by way of the grapevine the nature of all the infractions that had brought our little community together, he made no attempt to draw me into conversation, doubtless considering a mere whiskey runner to be no fit company for a murderer. Once or twice, stirring from a doze, I opened my eyes to find him gazing my way pensively through the gloom, yet I had no way of knowing if he was sorting through his memory for my features or simply brooding upon his fate, and staring at me in lieu of the wall opposite. I had the misfortune during one of these episodes to be asked by a wife-beater with whom I had become conversant, Alvin Sixkiller by name, if from my vantage point I could see where the sun was in the sky, and to be addressed as "Billy" within Thrailkill's hearing; but as he showed no reaction I assumed his reverie was impenetrable.

Two nights later I awoke strangling, with a chain around my neck and John Thrailkill's voice whistling in my ear. "What good's your border spin now, you Yankee pissant?"

Sliding my way across the floor, he must have found just enough slack in the chain that married him to the wall to sling it over my head. I clawed at it with both hands, but the iron links were biting into the skin. I couldn't get my fingers underneath.

"Guard! Gua—" The chain tightened, sealing off my croak.

"Go ahead and holler," said he, but he made no attempt to loosen the bond. "Time it takes to bash in my brainpan with their damn clubs, you'll be done for, and I'm dead either way."

I felt my face swelling with blood. Black checks obscured my vision.

"I knowed it was something about you when I put the bulge

on you across the river. You growed up some. I should of tied you up and cut off your business and fed it to the magpies."

His words thrashed inside my head, tangled with the blood surging in the arteries at my temples. I heard shouting, blows struck, but it was all very far off. They might have been re-membered sounds, flying away from my memory as it tore loose and spun through my skull. New York, fire bells and chopping axes; Lawrence, cries and shooting; Pilot Knob, pounding hooves and sabers clashing; Cheyenne, Laramie, Abilene, the buffalo range, Julesburg, Chicago, the Nations. Fort Smith . . .

"—choke you all over again in hell, you Jayhawking son of a—"

I fell in darkness.

"How does the defendant plead?"

I stood before the high oaken bench, hands folded in front of me as if for protection. I had on a cheap new flannel shirt, scratchy but clean, and an old pair of patched overalls donated by the Fort Smith Ladies' League, of which Mrs. Parker was a prominent member if not its president. My worn old boots were the only items on my person that belonged to me.

The room was done all in oak, from the picture rail near the ceiling to the railings that enclosed the jury box and separated the court from the spectators' gallery, and the pewlike benches beyond, where some of the curious had gathered to see what Parker was about this day. The effect, enhanced by the strong to-bacco odor that permeated the place, was of standing inside a gi-gantic cigar box.

"Guilty, Your Honor," I said.

It was October. John Thrailkill was as dead as Bloody Bill, as dead as Quantrill and the Southern Confederacy; as dead as his heart, which had been buried with the woman he had intended to marry before hell came to Missouri. On the third of Septem-ber, 1875, he had joined the five other men whose hearts had been interred long since, dropping through the twelve-foot slit behind the courthouse into eternity. There had been talk of a postponement after a gang of guards had seized his limbs and swung a truncheon square across his face to separate us before I finished strangling; but as announcements had already gone out and Parker's views were clear upon the "cruelty" of false stays, he had appeared before his Maker upon the appointed day with his nose broken and swollen and a black eye upon either side.

Later, when jail trusties came with lanterns and a mop to tidy the area he had occupied, they found a mural meticulously rendered with a stub of gray chalk upon the stone wall that supported his shackles. The former artist had sketched in silence while the rest of us slept, unaware of the work of art taking shape within arm's length. Summoned down to take a look, Parker had ordered it to be scrubbed off immediately. The glimpse the picture offered inside the mind of its creator, of scaly, half-human demons feeding upon (and copulating with) decaying corpses in a craterous battlefield, was disturbing by any standards, particularly those of the judge's stern Methodism; yet I believe I was the only one who noted the resemblance between the features of both the ghoulish victimizers and their hollow-eyed victims and those of the artist himself. A short drop at the end of a stout rope, a few swipes with a wet mop, and a lifetime of self-violation disappeared as if it had never been.

As for me, two days' rest in the Fort Smith infirmary and I was declared recovered sufficiently to resume my incarceration. However—in deference, perhaps, to my ordeal, or simply because it served to remind someone of my existence—a date for my arraignment was fixed shortly thereafter. Even so, I am told that five months awaiting disposition of my case was far from the record for that overworked court.

A tall man, Judge Parker looked taller still behind his elevated bench, broad across the chest in his pleated black robes, with his chestnut hair brushed to a sheen and threads of wiry gray in his chin-whiskers and moustache, although he was just in his middle thirties. He had strong bones and chilly blue eyes, like silver coins in the bed of a clear mountain stream. His lids were heavy, his voice low but not unpleasant; it was said he could be heard clearly above the dozens of worshipers who sang "Praise God from Whom All Blessings Flow" every Sunday.

"Have you anything to say in your defense before I consider your sentence?" he asked.

"No, Your Honor."

"Have you a permanent address in or near Fort Smith, Mr. Gashade?"

"No, Your Honor."

"Honest employment?"

"No, Your Honor."

He fingered his whiskers. "You place me in a difficult position. After nearly half a year in confinement, you oblige me to return you to jail until sentencing. An unemployed transient is scarcely a fit candidate to be released upon his own recognizance. My views upon the certainty of punishment are well known."

"I am sorry, Your Honor."

"You are convinced there is no one to claim responsibility for your conduct pending a date for sentencing?"

"I have no friends in Fort Smith." *Or anywhere else*, I added silently.

"Very well." He raised his gavel. "This court orders the defendant to be returned—"

"I'll look to him," someone spoke up from the back of the gallery. It was a strong female voice.

CHAPTER THIRTY-SEVEN

☙

Her name was Alma Barnstable.

She was small and slight, but wiry strong within the limits of her unpredictable fits of energy; I saw her go as long as fifty hours without a break, and flag soon after rising from a full night's sleep. She was extremely fair—her skin was almost blue, with the shadowy veins visible beneath, like one's own fingers behind a fine china plate—with pale green eyes, a long, straight nose as delicate as stem crystal, and blond hair cut boyishly short and worn in bangs across her high forehead. She was twenty-two when we met. She looked younger and seemed much older. I never saw her wear anything but the same ivory-and-black high-topped shoes, worn at the heels but always freshly polished, an unadorned white dress that hung from her collarbone to her toe-caps with only a hint of waist, and a lace-trimmed bonnet to prevent sunburn, of which she was in great danger after only a few minutes' exposure; not that it prevented her from venturing out often for many hours at a stretch as she pursued her special calling. The bonnet didn't go with the dress, nor the dress with the shoes. I'm convinced that had she been informed of this, she would have changed nothing. She cared less about what people thought of her than most women I've known, and any man.

She was the daughter of Christian missionaries sent by their church in Maryland in 1860 to minister to the faith of the Five Civilized Tribes. Her father, a practical man, as adept with a hammer and plane as he was with a hymnal, and her mother, a trained nurse who set the arms of Choctaw and Cherokee women broken by their drunken husbands and stitched and bandaged their sons' knife wounds suffered in brawls outside the establishments where liquor was sold, had operated a combination meetinghouse and infirmary on the other side of the Arkansas for four years, then died of the cholera within ten days of each other. Orphaned at eleven, Alma was taken in by a Seminole woman who operated a laundry in Fort Smith. From her, the young girl learned the ancient Creation beliefs that still wound their way among the Christianized standards of the peoples whom her parents had regarded chiefly as converts and patients; discovered the healing properties of yarrow, snakeroot, and elderberry bark; and, helping the old woman peg shirts and suits of underwear to the clothesline behind her ramshackle house, listened to stories of brutality and depravity from white and Indian households upon both sides of the great river that would have drained the blood from the face of a longshoreman in Baltimore. By age nineteen, at which time the old woman died after a lengthy decline, Alma retained few illusions about the enlightened nature of the human spirit.

Why she chose to accept custody of a confessed rumrunner had, I suppose, something to do with this altered awareness. In any case, the decision was in keeping with the methods by which she had conducted her life in the three years that she had been on her own. That those methods had established a reputation in the community was evident by the deference with which Judge Parker addressed her in his court that day.

"Miss Barnstable?" It seemed the jurist raised himself slightly from his seat behind that high bench to locate the sparrowlike creature who had spoken from the last row of the gallery.

"Yes, Judge."

"Miss Barnstable, everyone in Fort Smith is aware of your altruism. However, the defendant is not an underage orphan in need of nurturing and moral guidance. He is an adult, and by his own admission he is a criminal. To offer to take him in as if he were some stray—"

"Judge, who is in need of moral guidance if not a criminal? Anyway, you asked for someone to claim responsibility. I am claiming it."

Stern lines fissured his face. "It is not seemly for an unmarried woman to share quarters with an adult male. Furthermore, it is not legal."

"If that is the case, Judge, I know of eight citizens of this community who should be in jail."

In all his twenty years on the Fort Smith bench, I doubt that anyone else—lawyer, supplicant, or witness in the dock—got away with addressing Parker by any other title but "Your Honor." It was not that Alma didn't respect him; it was merely her way to confront everyone, panhandler and prince, eye to eye. As for her declaration, the ripple of gasps and titters that swept through the gallery indicated that many of those present were aware of the identities of the eight citizens to whom she had alluded.

Parker gaveled for silence, then delivered a brief lecture upon the subject of immorality versus the appearance of same, but the argument was clearly over. He set a long date for sentencing, waggled a finger at me to remind me that abuse of my freedom would be a far more serious crime than the one to which I had confessed, and remanded me into "the good, but, this court is convinced, misdirected custody of Miss Alma Barnstable, of this city," snapped his gavel again, and called for the next case.

"Miss Barnstable," said I, when the two of us were alone in the corridor outside the courtroom, "I don't—"

"My name is Alma. And you will be Billy. Do you know how to chop wood?"

"Chop wood? Yes."

"I don't require anyone for that. Elmer is good at it, and one or two of the others are of age. I only asked because a man who knows how to chop wood is usually good for most of the chores that need doing. I intend to put you to work, Billy. If that doesn't

suit you, the jail will continue to accommodate you. I'm not operating a hotel for loiterers."

"What *are* you operating?"

"Behind schedule," said she, consulting a tiny brass watch
pinned to her bosom; she wore no other jewelry. "Come with
me." She struck out for the stairs at a masculine pace, obliging
me to trot to catch up.

"I have possessions," I protested.

"I'll send Elmer back for them. It's time for Coral's lesson."

Grateful as I was to be free of that dungeon, I felt that I had
been manipulated into indenturing myself as some kind of unpaid servant, and wondered if my diminutive keeper made a
habit of recruiting her household staff from the arrest rolls. Her
brusque manner was not far removed from that of the guards,
and as she paused outside to retrieve a lace-trimmed handkerchief from the tiny reticule she carried on a loop around her
wrist, I was somewhat surprised not to see at least a small pistol inside.

The house to which I accompanied her, half a mile or so from
the courthouse, was large by local standards, with a long porch
in front furnished with rocking chairs, and smelled of pine sawdust and fresh whitewash. A pair of girls, aged about ten and
fourteen, were sweeping the porch and front steps with home-
made brooms; at Alma's approach they stopped and curtsied,
pulling out the hems of their dresses as decorously as if they
were at dancing school.

"Come inside, girls," said Alma. "I'm calling a meeting."

Inside was a parlor, airy and comfortable-looking, although
shabbily appointed: The rug was threadbare, the upholstery
patched, and the curtains were made inexpertly from flour sacks.
Sewing baskets littered the room and an Autoharp, the one visible nod away from the raw basics, leaned in the corner by the
fireplace. There a boy around sixteen clad in overalls was sweeping the hearth. I felt a pang of lost youth. He was the age I had
been when I came west.

"Elmer, where are James and Otis?"

The boy grazed me with a look that fixed me somewhere
below the level of the ashes in his dustpan, then slanted his head
toward the back door. "Jimmy's out mending fence like you
said. I don't know where the hell Otis is."

"Say that again, please."

Her tone was deadly calm. To my astonishment, this young hulk, who was nearly twice the woman's size, ducked his head as if he'd been struck. "Sorry, ma'am. I don't rightly know where Otis is. I think he's upstairs loafing."

"Find him, will you, please? And please call James and tell him I wish to see him. I want to talk to all of you."

He stood his broom and pan against the mantel and went out through the back.

"Elmer's father was hanged last year," Alma said. "Teaching manners to an angry boy is difficult."

I said I didn't mind.

"I wasn't apologizing. I was explaining."

Presently we were in the company of five youngsters. Aside from Elmer and Otis, a younger, less fully developed boy who shared the other's thick brown hair and hooded eyes, I could tell at a glance that none of them was related to the others. Coral, the youngest, was thin, black-haired, and chewed her nails all the time she was in the room. The other girl, Augusta, was hefty, with red in her hair and that troublesome look of a child who is close to becoming a woman and growing impatient with the wait. James, twelve or thirteen and towheaded, with the remains of a recent sunburn flaking away from his cheeks and the bridge of his nose, was a big-knuckled, scrawny outdoors type who would probably have climbed a tree as readily as any of the rest of us would walk through a doorway.

Alma's speech was brief. "I want you all to meet Billy. He'll be with us for a while, so you're not to go treating him as a guest."

Coral took her fingers from her mouth long enough to ask where I would sleep. Alma said there was a mattress in the attic and no one would have to give up his or her room.

Elmer evaluated me once again, coming up with the same low figure. "I look after the young ones," he announced.

"That's our agreement, whenever I'm out," Alma assured him. "This won't change that."

Otis said, "He's old."

James peeled a large patch of dead skin from below his left eye. "Was your daddy a law or a jailbird?"

"You shut up!" snarled Elmer.

Grinning, James closed his hands around his neck, crossed his eyes, and stuck out his tongue as if he were choking. Elmer lunged toward him. Alma stepped between them with the reflexes of a trained referee.

"James, finish fixing that fence. Elmer, go out on the porch and move the rockers so Augusta can finish sweeping."

Augusta said, "What about Coral?"

"It's time for her lesson."

"I ain't through cleaning the fireplace," Elmer protested.

"It will still be dirty when you get back."

The two would-be combatants went their separate ways.

"Otis, your brother said you were upstairs resting. Are you ill?"

"No'm." The boy stared down at the scuffed toes of his shoes. They appeared to be two sizes too large.

"I'm glad to hear that, because the cistern needs filling."

He shuffled out. Watching his back, Alma shook her head slightly.

"James's father was a deputy marshal," she said. "A squatter shot him as he was entering a cabin to get in out of the last big snow up in the Winding Stair Mountains. He thought the shack was abandoned. James suspects everyone who ever spent time in the Fort Smith jail. He will come around to you in his season."

"I think I can defend myself from a boy."

"Don't be too sure. I've been missing a butcher knife for a month." Her eyes were cool. "It isn't you I'm concerned about, although I may be when I know you better. James's father would not want him to walk off Parker's scaffold."

The subject needed changing. I asked her if the house was an orphanage.

"It is a place of reclamation."

Before I could inquire into that, she said that I must be hungry and that I would find a loaf of fresh bread in the pantry and a pot of beans warming upon the stove in the kitchen. Then she told Coral to find her slate.

The girl's lesson, overheard from the kitchen, was arithmetic; but there was no mention of apples or of trains approaching each other from distant stations. Alma was teaching Coral how to make change. During later lessons, the girl would learn how to calculate percentages by figuring out the shipping fees in a harness manufacturer's catalogue.

"This will all go to waste if Coral marries an Astor," said Alma when I inquired about her methods. "In case she does not, she will be able to support herself as a clerk. If Greek and Latin had a practical application in today's world, I would teach her those as well."

The house was indeed a place of reclamation. I never knew whether Alma during the many months she spent nursing the dying Seminole woman had thought consciously of how she would spend her life; but immediately after the old woman was buried, the room in which she had expired was occupied by the six-year-old daughter of a man who had been sent to the Detroit House of Corrections to serve twenty years for attempting to rob the Fort Smith post office. After eight weeks the girl's aunt and uncle arrived from Ohio to claim her, but by then two more children were living in the house. One, the fourteen-year-old son of a horse thief hiding out somewhere in the Nations and his Indian mistress who had died of consumption, ran away. The other was Augusta, whose father had slashed her mother's throat with a bowie knife before plunging it into his own breast in a tiny cabin on the Canadian.

Little Coral was the only resident whose parents were both still living, or believed to be. While traveling by train from North Carolina to California, the couple had quarreled bitterly over who was responsible for the child's bed-wetting, and achieved peace by leaving the sleeping girl on a bench in the Fort Smith station when they moved on.

"She's forgotten them now," Alma said; "and she hasn't wet the bed since her first week in this house."

The house was not the one where the Seminole woman had died. A year later Alma had pestered and shamed the community into pooling its resources to build a more spacious and comfortable place in which to shelter the disenfranchised. Now she supported herself and the children through donations, gifts of food and clothing, and odd jobs taken on by the boys, who pocketed a percentage of their earnings and turned the rest over to the household account. "I've tried to teach the girls sewing for the same reason, but I never acquired the knack for it myself. My parents were too busy converting the pagan. The old woman mended some of the shirts she washed, but I suspect she never taught me because she was afraid I'd set myself up in competition."

"I have to ask why you choose to sacrifice yourself for the children of strangers," said I. "Most people would not, particularly for the offspring of criminals."

She was silent long enough to convince me she had never before taken time to contemplate her motives. Finally she said, "The law is an imposing machine, especially with men like Judge Parker at the controls. The gears are too big. Things—people fall between the sprockets. Who will reclaim them if I do not?"

I slept in the attic, dined in the kitchen upon meals prepared by the girls (which were barely adequate, cooking being another skill that Alma lacked the ability to pass on), and did whatever work required a man's strength: rehung doors, unstuck windows, dug the well deeper when it went dry, moved furniture so the girls could sweep under it. Someone was always sweeping somewhere. When the cistern was full, the grass trimmed, and the windowpanes sparkled, there was always something to be swept. During the hours of daylight, no one sat in the house except to eat or take lessons.

I worked as hard as the lot of them and was never commended until the day Alma rose from the gallery in Judge Parker's courtroom and told him how valuable I had become to her household. Parker listened, his face as unreadable as a cedar Indian's. Then he read out my fate.

"For the crime of transporting and selling liquor in the Indian territory, this court sentences the defendant to serve twelve months at hard labor." He lifted his gavel. "Paroled in recognition of time served." Bang.

As relief flooded into my extremities, he waggled a finger at me. "You, Mr. Gashade, will remain in Miss Barnstable's charge for the seven months remaining in your sentence. If during that time you violate any law, or leave this jurisdiction without the permission of this court, your parole will be revoked and you will serve the full twelve months in Detroit."

In Alma's company I walked out into the blustery air of December a free man by most standards. I did not consider myself such. After two months beneath the same roof, I was in love with my warden.

CHAPTER THIRTY-EIGHT

1876.
The year cries out to be pounded through the skulls of imbecilic schoolchildren as relentlessly as 1066 and 1492; perhaps more so, for those dates introduced but a single Norman invasion and the mere discovery of a New World, while the Year of the American Centennial bulged to bursting with momentous events that have been reenacted, argued over, wagered upon, and fought for the honor of across poker tables and over fences throughout our continent every day for nearly sixty years—and will be, I suspect, for sixty more.

Who but a tenured professor can tell you the age of William the Conqueror when first he set booted foot upon English soil, or Christopher Columbus's response when the cry "Land ho" boomed out above the mutinous mutterings of his verminous crew? Conversely, who does *not* know the significance of Northfield, the reason for Jack McCall's infamy, or the images connected with the oxymoronic name Little Big Horn? None of these appellations was familiar to the public at large in 1875; by 1877 they had become fixtures in the historical mosaic.

Each of them touched me personally, and perhaps uniquely, for I really believe that I alone could claim close acquaintance with the principals involved in all three events. However, 1876 affected me upon a level entirely more visceral. I began it as a criminal, under threat of the penitentiary, and ended it as the man I am now, older and less certain that there is order to the universe, sadder but at peace.

When I fell in love with Alma is a question of no consequence, even were I able to provide an answer. Irritated at first by her cool manner, representing as it did the assumption that I would carry out all the menial tasks with which she greeted me each morning; I came grudgingly to admire her for her very self-assurance, to marvel at her single-minded determination to bring her charges through one more day, and yet the next when that day was done, and finally to appreciate the beauty of her person, within and without. When, as happened infrequently, she was late rising, or excused herself to her room when dusk was barely upon us, I found myself strangely bereft, precisely as if a heavy curtain had been drawn between myself and the sunlight. Gradually, I began to notice her lithe silhouette beneath the white dress when she passed before a bright window; the delicate line of her throat when she raised her head to see why one of the girls was taking so long beating the dust out of the rugs in the backyard; the way the lamplight wrapped itself around the bones of her face when she turned up the wick in the evening. She was by every standard a handsome woman, and though she scarcely required adornment, would draw every male eye and no small amount of female envy in a Chicago restaurant the moment she crossed the threshold in silks and feathers and with a light application of paint.

At these times I looked at her with the wonder of discovery, pride in our acquaintance, a measure of masculine lust, and, particularly when my bones were weary from a day of exertion and I felt the weight of my twenty-nine years, curiosity over what our children would look like. The first time this occurred to me I realized what I suppose I had known for some weeks without bringing it out for study, that I was in love for the first time in my life, and probably the last.

It was on a dismal day in late January that I told Alma how I felt. Late in the morning one of those freak blizzards that catch Arkansas by surprise once every two or three years had passed through like an enormous flour sifter, flattening fences, heaping roofs ill-prepared to support the weight of a heavy snow, and sweeping eight-foot drifts against the walls of barns and houses and arbitrarily along ridges so slight one scarcely noticed them when stepping over them in mild weather. Night had fallen, the doors and shutters were barred against the gales that came in hinge-rattling gusts first from this direction, then that; the children were asleep beneath heavy counterpanes sewn by the Fort Smith Ladies' League; and the pair of us were sharing a pot of tea at the scarred and much-repaired table in the kitchen before retiring. The tiny flame in the lamp upon the table flared and dimmed with the passage of the razorlike drafts that found their way through flaws in the siding, painting crawling shadows upon Alma's unlined face. She was looking away when I spoke.

"That pane needs putty," she said when I finished. "One good blow from the northeast and it will pop out."

"Alma—"

She stood. "The snow will stop soon. You'll want to rise early to shovel."

"Alma, did you hear what I said?"

"I have no such feelings for you." She gave me the coolness of her gaze for a beat, then turned and left the room.

I did not speak of the matter again that winter.

The snow did not stop soon, but continued to fall for two days, by which time Fort Smith was paralyzed. For the first time since his appointment, Parker suspended testimony in a trial while waiting for witnesses bogged down in their journey from the Nations. Upon the afternoon of the second day, unable to venture outdoors and having exhausted all inside chores for the time being, I picked up the Autoharp out of boredom and laid it across my knees. Rusty as I was and unfamiliar with the idiosyncracies of the instrument, it took me some time to master the scale. By accident I found the opening bar of "Bringing in the Sheaves," and so I continued it, employing the triangular guttapercha pick that rested atop the mantel. When I looked up, Alma was standing in the kitchen doorway watching me.

"It belonged to my mother," she said. "No one's played it since she died."

"I'm sorry." I got up to return it to its corner.

"I didn't mean that. I tried to sell it, but Fort Smith is a poor market for unnecessary merchandise. It's been the only item in this house that served no purpose. Until now."

Thus another duty was added to my roster. As the snow receded and the first green shoots appeared among the tangles of brown grass, I entertained the household in the evenings. It seemed everyone had a request except Elmer, who sat glum and unresponsive through the recitals until one night I asked him if there wasn't something he wanted to hear that he hadn't heard in a long time.

"No." He stared at his hands folded in his lap.

"I know one!" James's face lighted with evil glee. " 'Hing, hang, hung!' "

"You shut up!" Elmer leapt to his feet.

" 'Hing, hang, hung,' " James sang, " 'see what the hangman done.' "

Elmer lunged. I slung out one arm, grasped him from behind by his overalls, and told him to sit down.

" 'Hung, hang, hing, see the bad man swing.' "

I let go. Elmer closed the distance in a stride, fell upon James where he sat on the patched settee, and the two of them tumbled to the floor grappling.

"Otis! Girls! Stop them!" Alma was glaring at me.

Otis grabbed his brother by the shoulders and Augusta and Coral got hold of James and separated them. One of Elmer's shoulder straps was broken. James had a bloody nose.

"Why did you let them fight?" Alma demanded.

I started another tune. "The only way to stop a fight is to let it be fought. This one has been building up too long. If you don't let them use their fists, someday it will be done with guns."

"This evening is over. I want everyone in bed in five minutes."

For the rest of the week Alma did not speak to me except to tell me what work she wanted done. As time went by, however, and there were no more incidents between James the lawman's boy and Elmer the son of a condemned criminal, I sensed a softening in her silence more eloquent than anything she might have found to say. Not that the taunting stopped; but a lighter note of good-natured teasing had appeared in James's offhand comments, and Elmer was learning to banter back. It was armistice of a kind, as much of one as boys—or even most men—were likely to acknowledge.

One evening, quite by accident, I discovered the piece Elmer wanted to hear, a sprightly reel from the Scots Highlands that his late father had been wont to hum when occupied with some labor in the days before life went sour. The boy confessed this to me in private after he had left the room blinking hard the first time I played it. After that I made it a fixture. It never again made him cry. Sometimes he smiled, and I knew he was remembering something specific.

"I didn't know you were a musician," said Alma one night, when the children had been shooed off to bed and I was putting away the instrument.

"I am not, although I thought I was for most of my life." I told her about the colored piano player in Chicago, omitting the nature of the establishment in which he played.

She was not taken in by the subterfuge. "You're probably the only patron who appreciated him. Meanwhile, you have brought a measure of happiness to a boy who has known nothing but misery for two years. Who is the greater musician?"

"Elmer is not a typical audience."

"In every audience there is at least one Elmer. You have a God-given gift. It's a sin to conceal it."

"If it is a sin, it's one of my lesser ones."

"Don't be bitter, Billy. You haven't the right."

"You don't know that. You know nothing about me."

"I love you."

She said it on her way to her room. Her back was turned, and I spent the rest of that night arguing with myself over whether I had heard her correctly. In the morning, she was as she had been every day since we'd met, and there was no asking her about what she had said. I decided to wait until the moment returned.

And if it did not—what?

The columns of the Fort Smith *Herald* fed me news from both coasts and the great space between. In December 1875, Boss Tweed, who had enjoyed the privilege of a daily supervised visit to his Manhattan mansion to soften the rigors of life in the Ludlow Street Jail, had disappeared. Broadsides were issued throughout the United States and Canada offering a reward of ten thousand dollars for his delivery to the authorities. That night I had a nightmare: Tweed—noose-shaped beard, burning eyes, diamond stickpin, and all—appeared upon Alma Barnstable's doorstep, his heavy stick raised to thrash the assailant of Jehosophat Brennan. With dawn the apparition vanished, and I knew him to be cowering in some secluded room eight hundred miles away, awaiting clandestine passage to some latitude from where he could not be extradited. However, the fact that I had been troubled by him at all demonstrated clearly that all my old ghosts were with me yet.

Six months later, nearing what appeared to be a moderate-sized village of renegade Indians among the swells of the Little Big Horn Valley in Montana Territory, Lieutenant Colonel George Armstrong Custer divided his Seventh Cavalry into three units to surround the lodges. Charging what he believed to be the end of the camp, he found instead that he was attacking the center of a community of some fifteen thousand Sioux, Cheyenne, and Arapaho, which bent in the middle to encompass his two hundred cavalrymen and swept them from the face of the earth. As details attending the death of one of America's anointed heroes filtered eastward, I learned that upon this occasion the Boy General had left the regimental band behind at Fort Abraham Lincoln; still, as from beyond a distant hill, I heard the whirl and crash of the "GarryOwen," and saw the flicker of interest in the gray-blue eyes of the young commander the first time he heard it, surrounded by his soporific greyhounds at Fort Riley.

Had his hemorrhoids troubled him to the end?

In August, while James Butler Hickok was playing poker in a saloon in Deadwood, Dakota Territory, a cross-eyed saloon swamp named Jack McCall crept up behind him and punched a pistol ball through that head of splendid curls. According to later accounts, the hand held by Wild Bill contained a pair of aces and a pair of eights. I wondered if at the moment of death he had been cheating.

Then came September, and Northfield, Minnesota.

Frank and Jesse James, accompanied by the three Younger brothers and sometime companions Bill Chadwell, Clell Miller, and Charlie Pitts, raided a bank in that prosperous farming center and stirred up a hornets' nest. When the shooting was over, Miller and Chadwell were dead and the wounded Youngers were in jail. The Jameses alone managed to slip through the various posses who winnowed the countryside and were believed to be in hiding somewhere in Missouri, or Texas, or California. A rumor circulated, gaining momentum as time passed and no further robberies occurred bearing the distinctive James stamp, that Jesse was dead.

I doubted the rumor. He had been wounded several times in the war, twice badly enough to be despaired of by his doctors, and he had survived a dozen years of national notoriety without spending so much as a day behind bars. It was not in Jesse's cards to pass out of existence quietly. As for Frank, it was the

central truth of his nature that no one with whom he traveled
would come to harm so long as he was able to place himself between it and his companion. Separate from him, one's chances
were no more than equal; with him, they automatically improved
fifty percent. If Jesse was dead, so was Frank, and Frank James
dead was a situation ludicrous to contemplate. It would take
more than the Pinkertons and the authorities of four states to
extinguish that broad guerrilla grin.

I devoured each fresh journalistic speculation in the only waking hour I had to myself, by the lamp in the kitchen after the rest
of the household had retired. One night toward the end of my
court-enforced stay, I was climbing the stairs to my attic cell, my
head filling with the latest report that Jesse was in Colorado
posing as a mining engineer, when I heard the unmistakable
sounds of sobbing. The house was full of children who had lost
their parents, and it was nothing unusual in that hour when one
is most alone to overhear an expression of grief. This was no
child crying, however. The sounds were coming from Alma's
room.

CHAPTER THIRTY-NINE

♪♫

Her bedroom, I was surprised to note when she opened the
door at my knock, was the largest in the house, although
scarcely better furnished than any of the others. There was a
fine old four-poster bed with a feather mattress, but the washstand needed a new finish and age cracks checked the basin.
Framed miniature portraits of a woman in a high-necked blouse
and a man with a full beard encircling his jaw—her parents, I
assumed—hung upon the wall opposite the bed, and a lamp and
Bible and the schoolbooks Alma used to educate the children
stood upon an unremarkable chest of drawers. There was no
other furniture, not even a chair. The message conveyed was
that the room served no other purpose than a place to sleep.

One look at Alma confirmed that she had not been sleeping.
Dark thumbprints showed beneath her eyes and she appeared

gaunt, almost transparent, with the lamplight seeming to shine through her from behind. She had thrown on a white cotton dressing gown over her muslin nightdress and thrust her tiny feet into a pair of satin slippers that were anything but new, and probably acquired secondhand. Her eyes and nose were red.

"I wondered if you were all right," I said.

"I need to sleep. So do you." She started to close the door.

"Are you ill?"

The door stopped eight inches from the jamb. Her eyes were luminous in the gap. "Yes."

I knew then: her periods of exhaustion, her sometimes erratic hours. A faint medicinal odor reached my nostrils from the depths of her bedroom. "Should I get a doctor?"

"No. I have seen enough of doctors to last me"—she laughed shortly—"the rest of my life."

The floor seemed to open beneath my feet. I pushed at the door. She let go, and as if she had lost her balance she fell against me. My arms closed around her. A great shudder racked her body. When at length she pulled away, her features were composed. Her will was iron from first to last.

"I have a disease of the blood." Her tone was the one she used to explain a new chore to one of the children. "None of the doctors I've seen know much about it. They agree on one thing."

"It's that bad?"

"Yes."

"There are specialists in Chicago—" I began.

"Not in this."

A moth flung itself against the window. "How long?"

"That's one of the things they didn't agree on. According to the least hopeful, I am already in the churchyard." She placed a hand upon my arm for support. "I need to lie down."

I closed the door behind me and helped her to the bed. She lay on her back beneath the covers, staring up at the canopy. "I sent away for medical journals. Half the articles claim it's caused by a poisonous miasma. The other half say it grows from inside, like a carbuncle. They will have to come to some sort of conclusion before they can begin to treat it. Someone who isn't born yet may benefit."

Suddenly I was filled with rage. "You're twenty-two years old!"

"I turned twenty-three last month. What is that? My mother and father were thirty and thirty-five."

"People live to be eighty. Useless people. Wicked people."

"Good people too. It's not a question of arithmetic."

"It's not fair!" Her calm acceptance drove me to fury.

"I said the same thing when they told me. It is fairer than you think. I might have been run over by a wagon, and then where would the children be? This way I have had time to make the necessary arrangements. Mrs. Parker and the Fort Smith Ladies' League will take over the operation of this house when I am gone."

"Do the children know?"

"Yes."

That surprised me. "Even Coral?"

"I think you'll agree they all have a closer acquaintance with death than most children their age."

"When were you planning to tell me?"

"I wasn't."

I let my next question pass unspoken.

"You're leaving at the end of this month. Judge Parker himself has said you will be free to go then. You are not a child in need of care and guidance. What would have been the point?"

"Love. We love each other."

"I don't love you."

"You said you did. Did you think I didn't hear?"

"Go away, Billy. Leave this house tonight. Go away from Fort Smith. Judge Parker won't send anyone after you for the sake of a few days. Not to bring back a simple rumrunner."

"Who will take care of you if I go?"

"The same person who has taken care of me since the old woman got sick. Her disease required a good deal more attention than mine. Augusta is the same age I was then. She will see to my needs when I can no longer leave this bed."

"You're a fool."

She smiled up at the canopy. She did not smile often. When she did she lit the corners of the room untouched by the lamp.

"Every beast recognizes its own kind," she said. "What were you planning to do when peddling whiskey lost its romance? Would you hold up banks and trains like your heroes Frank and Jesse?"

I was caught off-guard. "What do you know about Frank and Jesse?"

"I am not blind. I've seen how you sit up straight whenever you come upon a reference to them in the newspaper. Leave it there, Billy. Life on the scout is not for you."

I was standing over her. She was as pale as the pillow upon which her head rested. "You don't know as much about people as you think you do, Alma Barnstable. I have been on the scout since I was Elmer's age."

I told her my story then, all of it. She was silent for a time after I finished.

"We're both fools. You are the greater one. Go home, Billy. Talk to your father."

"What shall I say? 'Good day, Judge. I have whored and drunk whiskey and run with bad men and broken the law of the land. Is my old room ready?' "

She looked away. "I'm sorry."

"Please don't be."

"I'm not sorry for you." She looked back at me. "I'm sorry for your father. He can't be much of a judge. Even Parker, who hangs men five and six at a time, does not expect perfection. To lack compassion is a serious failure in a jurist."

"My father is a great man."

"Great men are not always good men."

"He is the best man I've ever known. If I were as good I'd never have left New York. If I were half as good I would not hesitate to return."

"I need to sleep now." She closed her eyes. In a moment the even rise and fall of the counterpane told me the conversation was indeed ended.

The next day she was up before me, and the routine was as always. It was as if the subject of our discussion had never arisen. The children sensed a difference, however. Not so much as a word was spoken of the matter, but whenever Elmer's gaze met mine I felt an arc of understanding, and when I asked Augusta to fetch water from the well so I could wash the window in Alma's room, her reply that she would do it right away carried a tone I had not heard before. I had never before sensed such a matter-of-factness concerning death in the company of people so young, and hope never to sense it again. They were incredibly

old, these children, most of whom had not been born when first
I laid eyes upon a poor corpse dangling by its neck from a rope
above a street in Manhattan; in their eyes and upon their faces
could be read the tragic wisdom of centuries.

Alma began to fail at the same time as the leaves upon the
trees that grew along the Arkansas. The mornings when she was
unable to descend the stairs grew together. The time between
these late descents and her early retirements narrowed, then disappeared entirely. Two days, three days, a full week she spent in
her room, where Augusta brought her meals and carried out her
chamber pot. A week became two. The doctor, a tall, stoop-
shouldered fifty-year-old who had signed many a certificate of
death so that Judge Parker's condemned could be cut down and
carted away, came and went. No one else saw her but the daughter of parricide and suicide, who merely shook her head when I
asked if I could visit. Yet the routine of the household went on.
Augusta never came downstairs without bearing instructions for
each member. Alma seemed determined to remain in charge, if
in fact it was not just habit. Either way it was unnecessary. Her
influence was so much a part of the residents' lives, and every
task had been carried out so many times before, that the work
would have proceeded on schedule if she never said a word.

Then came the day when each of the children was summoned,
one by one, to climb the stairs. Each visit consumed no more
than five minutes, and then a congested and contorted face
would reappear upon the ground floor and another name would
be called.

Coral was the last child to emerge from her room. The muscles of her face were working, but she did not cry, nor did she
speak. Her eyes sought mine. I nodded and ascended the stairs.

"Please open the curtains."

The room was indeed dark, and reminded me of Drucilla
Patakos and her eternal twilight. When I spread the curtains,
coppery autumn light spilled in.

"That's much better. The doctor closed them, I can't think
why. I will have my fill of darkness soon enough."

I was surprised to see that she was sitting up slightly, a pillow
wedged behind her back for support. She wore the white cotton
dressing gown. Her pallor now was marblelike. The dark
smudges were gone from beneath her eyes, which had acquired

a wonderful luminescence. She was beautiful, achingly so. My throat closed. I could not have spoken even if I could think of something to say.

"Your sentence was over last month," she said. "Did you forget?"

I shook my head.

She looked beyond me, toward the window. "Winter will be here soon. I hope it's milder than the last one."

"I'll help the children through it," I managed to say.

"That's exactly what I don't want. It's why I asked you up here."

She was looking at me now. I waited.

"The Ladies' League will find it difficult enough teaching the children to recognize their authority without another adult around to confuse them. Every time the children are told to do something they'll look at you for confirmation."

"You're asking me to leave."

"It's only a matter of time before Mrs. Parker or someone else tells you to leave. My way is more polite, but my reasons are the same. You will be doing the children a favor. Their loyalties have been jostled around enough." She closed her eyes. The counterpane rose and fell. Plainly the effort of speaking was claiming all her strength. "Promise me you'll go."

"I promise." I waited again, but she did not speak. "Is that all you wanted to see me about?"

"Of course not." Her eyes opened. "I need you to promise something else. I think you know what it is."

"My father."

"No, that's something you must decide to do for yourself. If I force you, you'll resent it, and that will poison the reunion."

"My music."

She smiled faintly. This time she failed to light the room's corners. "How possessive you are. Music belongs to everyone. I'm referring to your gift. I want you to use it. The Autoharp is yours."

I hesitated.

"Don't thank me," she said. "You know how I feel about having unnecessary things around. Once you're gone it will collect nothing but dust."

"It's a difficult instrument to travel with."

"You won't have to carry it far. Mr. Cooper at the general merchandise thinks he has a customer for it. He has a guitar someone gave him to settle a credit bill. I spoke with him last month. He will accept the Autoharp in trade for the guitar."

After a moment I smiled. "It seems I have no choice."

"The last choice you made did not serve you well." She glanced away then; her eyes had started to fill. "I'm so frightened, Billy."

I sank down on my knees beside the bed, embracing her for the second and last time.

〽〽〽〽〽〽〽〽〽〽〽〽〽〽〽〽〽〽

PART FIVE

Rebel's Requiem

〽〽〽〽〽〽〽〽〽〽〽〽〽〽〽〽〽〽

CHAPTER FORTY

✧

I played the Autoharp once more only, leading the mourners at Alma Barnstable's graveside in the Fort Smith Cemetery in "Bringing in the Sheaves." The turnout was large, including the mayor, who had celebrated the life of the deceased in full, rounded phrases at the funeral in the Methodist church; the re- doubtable members of the Ladies' League, black-cloaked and -hatted against the first icy breath of winter; and Isaac Parker, who stood a little apart from his wife wearing a caped overcoat and holding his soft hat before him in both hands. I could not help thinking that a donation of a dollar from each of those pre- sent would have elevated the standard of living of all the mem- bers of Alma's household; but respect costs nothing in dollars and is always in ample supply for the dead.

The children wept quietly and undemonstratively, in contrast to a number of women in the group whom I had never seen within five hundred yards of Alma's house. Upon her death it had sud- denly become the fashion to claim intimacy with her. A column in that day's *Herald* had celebrated "the good Christianity of Fort Smith's late lamented citizen." There was talk of erecting a statue before the courthouse, dedicated to her memory and bearing the legend "The Angel of Fort Smith" chiseled into the base. I never found out if anything came of it.

Eustace Cooper, behind the counter at the general merchandise, was an honest man. For the Autoharp he traded a guitar that had seen better days and made up the difference in cash, with which I purchased a ticket on the next train west. I told the children good-bye and rolled out at nightfall.

My heart was a stone, its weight pulling me farther into the interior of the continent, whose great spaces separated the fleeing from the sadnesses and mistakes of the past. I seldom spent more than a week in one place. Often I was gone the next morning without having unpacked my threadbare valise. I played in saloons whose names I never bothered to learn. I was as a man on the run.

Weeks, months, seasons tumbled into the gap between my heels and the last town: winter in Fort Worth, where the gaunt, whiskey-flushed faces of cowboys beseeched me silently for a tune that would play in their heads when the blizzards found them riding the fenceline; spring in Dodge City, where I saw a buffalo hider disembowel a cowboy in the Lone Star Dance Hall during a dispute involving their respective occupations. The proprietor, a self-styled dandy in a figured vest with tobacco spittle glittering on one lapel, continued dealing faro without making a move toward the shotgun leaning in the corner at his elbow. After thrashing around for a while in bloody sawdust, the injured cowboy was removed by his friends to a doctor's care, whereupon the fellow at the faro table directed his bartender to mop up the mess. (The proprietor's name was Masterson. I understood he was a sometime peace officer, celebrated for the wisdom of his reticence.) Summer in Denver, and a short stint at the piano on the ground floor of the Rocky Mountain Hospitality House, operated by a cheroot-chewing harridan who called herself Colorado Jo, but owned by the county sheriff, three hundred pounds of tax-supported corruption with a bad case of gout and a habit of laying harlots open to the bone with a horsewhip when he suspected them of pocketing the house receipts. A brick supported one corner of the piano where the leg had been shot from under it by a drunken miner.

A great gift, music. It was forever placing me in high company.

October found me in Nebraska. There I stopped at Fort Robinson after revisiting a portion of my history on the plains. Those long silken grasses grew now through the bleached rib cages and empty eye sockets of a million buffalo, scattered across the prairie like pieces of broken crockery. The great herds were thinning out at a rate that seemed marvelous; already the concept of a train being forced to wait a day for a slow-moving river of humps and horns to cross the tracks recounted like a tall tale told by toothless old men.

The post trader, a sallow-faced cadaver whose tuft of gray chin fuzz reminded me of cheese mold, demanded twenty-five percent of my gratuities in return for his consent to let me occupy a stool in the corner of his establishment. I agreed with a sigh. The congressional decision to replace the old sutler's system with post traderships overseen by the local fort commanders had ushered in a new era of greed. "Liquor's extra," he added, almost as an afterthought.

"I don't drink." It was not a falsehood. I had not tasted liquor since my arrest in the Indian Nations.

He spat, though he wasn't chewing. "Penny a cup for coffee."

Raising my eyes in exasperation, I noticed a familiar-looking object lying atop a high shelf behind the counter. "Is that banjo for sale?"

He turned to look up at it, as if surprised that such an object could be in his possession. He turned back with an expression of disgust.

"That was in some truck General Crook brung in with a Sioux buck last month. Buck got hisself bayoneted trying to escape. The army took his guns."

I felt a tingle. "May I see it?"

"It's all junked up."

"I'd like to look at it anyway."

He scratched his head, delaying. His natural instinct to make money was at odds with his unwillingness to climb the ladder that leaned against the shelves. Finally he expelled a great lungful of stagnant air and dragged it over.

When he alighted, I resisted the urge to snatch the instrument from his hands. It was painted all over with spiritual symbols in primary colors, the catgut strings had been replaced with sinew, and the parchment had been torn and then patched with a square of animal membrane and some kind of native glue. However, the changes could not disguise an object I had carried for years. Instantly I was transported to a ridge three days' ride east of Julesburg, where the gift of a banjo had made the difference between safe passage for myself and my partners and our scalps hanging from a pole in a Sioux lodge. I saw again the interest in a pair of smoke-colored native eyes when callused fingers brushed its strings.

"Five dollars gold," said the trader.

"All I have is silver."

This put him out as much as the notion of having to scale the ladder. "I should of stood in Cincinnati," he whined. "I can't get ahead out here. This here's genuine injun workmanship."

"A moment ago you said it was all junked up."

"You want it or not?"

I gave him five silver dollars. In Chicago, banjos were selling fresh from the factory for two apiece, but I'd have paid fifty for that one and considered it a bargain. I strummed it once. Although it needed tuning, I was surprised by the mellow tone the crude strings offered. I thought of a question.

"What was the Indian's name?"

"Crazy Horse."

I didn't hang around Fort Robinson long. The Department of the Army was engaged in a full-scale campaign to round up the Plains Indians. There would be no more nonsense about sovereign nations or noble savages or ignorant children in need of spiritual guidance from the Great Father in Washington; it was hem them in, shoot their horses, burn their lodges, imprison or hang those who could definitely be identified as participants in the Custer massacre, and pen the rest up on government reservations. The spectacle of those arrogant bands reduced by starvation and bombardment to crawl to the fort under military escort, weaponless, dragging all their earthly possessions behind them upon travois, was too painful for one who had seen them in their full-blown pride. I thought of that long-ago party of horsemen, balancing a worn old banjo and a small stack of hides upon the one hand and the lives of a handful of interlopers upon the other, and deciding for whatever reason to let them go on living. It wasn't because of the offer I had made; they could have slain us and taken everything, including our horses and weapons. Their kind had done as much or worse upon other occasions, as had ours. I liked to think there was a spark of humanity in their leader that made him say that for this day at least, the killing would stop. Whether he was indeed Crazy Horse, the great Sioux general who had sent Custer to his grave while Sitting Bull claimed the credit, or (as seemed more likely) he was just some anonymous minor chieftain whose musical prize had made its way from one red hand to another until it wound up in the leader's possession, was immaterial. A spirit that was capable of mercy in a savage season was too great to see laid low by a column of illiterate troopers.

In truth, the man who gave him that instrument would not have felt this way. Still congratulating himself upon his savvy horse trading ("Think of it; three thousand in hides for a broken-down banjo. Stupid heathens!"), he would have stayed to see the show. I was not that man, merely a distant relation. He had never lain in the dank of Judge Parker's dungeon, listening to the *squee-thump* of the gallows trap dumping open under the feet of six of his fellow transgressors, nor held the head of a nearly grown boy to his chest in the night when the boy awoke from a frightening dream, calling for his executed father. He had not known himself for a coward, afraid to present his own father with the image of the man he had allowed himself to become. Certainly he had never loved, nor been forced to stand by watching while the woman he loved faded from this life. I was a more solemn man, but an improved one. Like my banjo I wore indelibly the markings of my passage; the music I made was more mellow.

The next year I was in New Mexico Territory, playing and singing in a general store in Lincoln owned by a lawyer named McSween. The lawyer's partner, an expatriate British rancher by the name of Tunstall, had been slain in a dispute with his rural neighbors. Tension was thick in the store whenever employees of rival cattle companies were present. Upon these occasions I selected music of a neutral nature, evoking pastoral memories of times a century removed from the current troubles, of countries a hemisphere away. They had their effect upon my listeners, or seemed to. No incidents took place upon the premises when I was there to witness them.

Once indeed, John Chisum, an oak-hewn old rancher, erect as a fence rail tamped squarely into the center of the affray, snapped a nod of approval in my direction when he paused at the counter to order nails by the keg and ammunition by the crate. He had with him a willowy youth scarcely over five feet tall, buck-toothed and talkative, attired in a plug hat creased upon one side of the crown and a heavy ribbed sweater tugged down over his waist in an unsuccessful attempt to conceal the pistol he carried upon his right hip.

This fellow took a liking to my music and came around often after that, sometimes upon a ranch errand, but usually just to pull up a stool and listen. His name was William—Billy to his friends, who, in order to avoid having both of us turn our heads when only one of us was hailed, took to calling him the Kid. I was fond of the young man, despite his larcenous streak; more than once I saw him slip some unimportant item from the counter where it was displayed into his sweater pocket when he imagined no one was looking. It seemed a minor failing on the part of one so good-humored and charming. I confess I doubted the speaker when the story reached me, a month after I made his acquaintance, that the Kid and his cronies had just gunned down the county sheriff and one of his deputies in the street.

I left soon after. The Lincoln County War was then in full cry, I had seen and heard enough of battle to last me all my days, and the gratuities were not likely to continue flowing as long as customers were afraid of being chopped to pieces by bullets the moment they showed themselves out-of-doors. I heard later McSween was killed in a siege upon his home from which the Kid shot his way out. This was the beginning of his notoriety, which even so would not spread much beyond New Mexico for another dozen years, long after he was in the ground.

In the fall of 1879 I took my first vacation ever, hiring a horse and trap in Socorro and heading south into old Mexico, where I spent two weeks drinking lemonade in the shade of an adobe cantina in a place called Casa Negrita and reading month-old newspapers from the States. Jesse James was not dead, it appeared; he and Frank had been positively identified among the men who held up a train in Glendale, Missouri, in October, pistol-whipped a guard, and vanished into the hills with six thousand in cash and securities. Pinkerton Captain Jack Fabian discounted earlier inflated estimates of the amount and reported that the reward for information leading to the capture of Frank and Jesse had gone up to five thousand dollars apiece, with a matching sum offered for the conviction of each.

I worked my way north to Tucson the next year, then followed the circuit down to Tombstone. Playing guitar there in the orchestra pit of the Birdcage Theater, I learned Billy the Kid had been killed by a man named Garrett, but by then I was packing once again, and too preoccupied with where I should go, to give him anything more than a passing reflection. So many had died since making my acquaintance that if I dwelt upon the subject I might have condemned myself for a Jonah: Jim Bridger, infirmity and old age; Wild Bill Hickok, an assassin's bullet; Quantrill and Bloody Bill Anderson, fire from ambush; John Thrailkill, a long drop at the end of a short rope; and now Billy, the youngest of all. Boss Tweed, the ogre of my exile, was gone, dead of his own enormous appetites in a guarded bed following his recapture in Spain. The news left me feeling strangely detached, as if my old music tutor, bane of my childhood, had succumbed, far too late to bring me any joy.

Tombstone, rich in silver as it was, had become too various for me. One of my strings had broken at a crucial point, causing Eddy Foy to miss a step while dancing onstage, which prompted a sardonic comment from a drunken cowboy in the audience. A sometime dentist and full-time gambler named Holliday, also drunk and watching from a box, told him in a loud voice to shut up. One of the cowboy's friends produced a pistol and fired it toward the box. The dentist drew his own weapon, but before he could return fire another man in the box grasped his arm and escorted him out. I believe the man was one of four brothers, gamblers who sometimes kept the peace, but whether it was James or Virgil or Wyatt or Morgan I cannot now say; all those Earps looked alike.

I rode the next day's stage back to Tucson, and there caught the first train heading east. It happened to be bound for Missouri.

CHAPTER FORTY-ONE

St. Joseph was as prosperous a city as existed in the beleaguered State of Missouri. Built of brick and frame upon orderly streets facing the great river, surrounded upon three sides by a green-and-yellow checkerboard of dairy fodder and wheat, it sheltered some forty thousand souls, who visited its shops and gathered at the quay in neckties and bright bonnets to see what and whom the great stacked steamboats brought down from Omaha and up from Joplin. Its room rates were too steep for a poor itinerant musician, and so I commuted by means of an aging mare I had bought in Platte City between the public house where I performed and my room upon the second floor of a farmhouse in what was called the Crackerneck section of Clay County, less than an hour's ride from the James-Samuel farm of misty memory.

Passing the cutoff that led past the farm, I thought invariably of that strong woman, rearing her sons and caring for a husband broken by his brush with death, steeped in her hatred of the Union but maintaining her good humor throughout. She would be elderly now, doing her chores one-handed, embittered further by the loss of an arm and her youngest son to a Pinkerton bomb. I knew not if she would welcome me now, with my Northern origins still so plain upon my countenance and in my manner; but it was more than this uncertainty that prevented me from taking that side of the fork. Going back was not in my nature.

The public house—or so I continue to call it, for its quiet, shaded atmosphere of male companionship put me more in mind of what I had read about the taverns of London than the smoky, noisy saloons of my past experience—was a place of hanging oil lamps and framed steelpoint engravings upon the walls of prize-fighters in tights, of captain's chairs around dark oak tables with initials carved into their tops, and billiards in the back room. It was cool and pleasant, smelling of spilled beer and cigars and the gamey musk of the mounted elk's head moldering above the stone fireplace. There were times when even the gentlest of music was an intrusion. At these times I filled my coffee cup from the pot simmering on the heating stove behind the bar and took it to a corner table to sip and reflect. I think it was the very Englishness of the place that drew a large young man into it in the damp spring of 1882, wearing a flamboyant coat trimmed in purple velvet and his hair to his shoulders. Inside the door he struck a pose with one hand upon his ample hip, making eye contact with each patron who raised his head to stare at the new-comer. Spying me sitting with my coffee, he strode over, swinging his stick with the confidence of a man approaching the very fellow he had come there to see.

"I beg your pardon, old sport, but would you mind terribly if I joined you?"

"There are empty tables," said I, for I had been thinking of Alma and did not much care for company. His Irish accent scarcely endeared him to me. It reminded me of Jehosophat Brennan.

"Empty heads as well, I fear. I find both depressing. You hold it in your power, sir, to spare me a fate worse than indifferent tailoring. Yours is the only cultivated face upon the premises. If I hear the words 'Howdy, stranger, take a load off and hunker down hyar' one more time, I shall scream."

I sat back, mildly interested. His face was heavy and his lips were thick, but he seemed to consider himself uncommonly handsome, a difficult combination that required years of effort. He might be diverting, at that. I inclined my head toward the chair opposite. He scraped it out and threw himself into it as if he had been on foot for a week. "I am in your debt, sir. May I buy you a whiskey?"

"Coffee's my drink."

"My compliments upon your abstemiousness. As for me, I can resist everything except temptation. Innkeeper!" He thumped his stick. "A fresh pot for my friend, and a bottle of bourbon for myself."

The bartender, a horse-faced crank named Cy who suffered from shingles, thumped down a bottle and a glass and topped off my cup from the evil-looking pot. The Irishman paid him and he hobbled away upon spraddled legs.

My benefactor lifted his glass. "To your president, whoever he may be at present."

"To your queen." I drank from my cup.

He emptied the glass in a long draught, then refilled it. "Ah, yes, the queen. Had she given me the chance, I'd have voted for her." His lively eyes alighted upon my guitar and banjo leaning in the corner. "Are you a musician?"

"For want of a more precise title."

"A difficult art. If one plays good music, people don't listen, and if one plays bad music, people don't talk." He held out a large and meaty hand, beautifully manicured. "My name is Oscar Wilde."

"I know." I shook it. "Billy Gashade."

"Am I so famous, then?" He appeared delighted.

"I read in a broadside that you were lecturing in Leavenworth. The moment you walked in I said to myself, 'This must be Wilde.' No other man in this part of the country would have the nerve to wear that coat in public."

His laugh was loud and booming, a surprise in view of his reputation. I'd expected a titter. Abruptly he stopped, studying me over his drink. "I sense you also are not from this part of the country."

"I was born and raised in New York."

"New York, yes. I approve of the place. The hotels are above reproach and the morals are beneath contempt. Also my lecture there was a sellout."

"If I thought I would be received as warmly, I would return," said I.

"How long have you been away?"

"Nineteen years."

"All the more reason to go back. All your enemies are likely dead. I have always said that a man cannot be too careful in the choice of his enemies."

"It is not my enemies I fear."

"Your friends, then. That I cannot help you with, having none myself."

"I am speaking of my parents."

"I regret that I can offer you no sympathy. To lose one parent may be regarded as a misfortune. To lose both seems like carelessness." He drained his glass again. Again he refilled it. "Forgive me. I am not a facetious man by nature, merely by experience. I would hear your story."

It was my turn to study him. He had a guileless look, for all his pretension. I suspected the show of arrogance concealed a fragile spirit.

"Have I your word you will not use it in your fiction?"

"Certainly not! What earthly good is a conversation off the record when material is so hard to come by?"

We shared our secrets then, Oscar Fingal O'Flahertie Wills Wilde and I; or as many as anyone does with a stranger, which amounts to more than he will confide to a companion of long-standing. Nothing important, of course—our respective darkest demons remained securely locked in their cages—but enough that we came away with a better understanding of each other than I warrant we had of ourselves. Years later, in his time of trouble, when his very name was spoken in vile whispers like that of some loathsome disease, I thought of that conversation, and hoped he remembered it and found in it some measure of the solace I felt at the time. It is the supreme tragedy of the human condition that we are so quick to crush the beauty from the butterflies in our midst.

While we were talking, the room had begun to fill. Dusk was upon us. Cy, waddling beneath the burden of his painful affliction, lit more lamps and served the newcomers from a tray bristling with glasses and bottles. Beyond Wilde's shoulder I observed a pair of men in business suits and bowlers enter and sit down at a table in the opposite corner. The older of the two wore a chestnut-colored beard neatly trimmed after the fashion of physicians, and when he removed his hat and placed it on the table I saw that his hair was receding at the temples. He blinked rapidly while giving his order to the bartender, as if to accustom his eyes to the artificial light.

I drank the last of the coffee. Wilde was speaking; I waited for him to pause. "Would you excuse me for a moment? Someone just came in whom I haven't seen in years."

"Go to him, by all means. The only way to get rid of a temptation is to yield to it."

As I approached, the bearded man saw me and leaned back in his chair. His right hand rested upon a folded copy of the *St. Joseph Gazette,* or rather inside it. The click of the hammer was smothered by the din of voices that filled the room. Alerted, his companion twisted to face me, groping inside the side pocket of his coat. He was a pale young man, dark-haired, with shifting eyes and the kind of schoolboyish good looks that certain women find difficult to resist, even as their purses are being rifled.

I stopped, holding my hands out from my sides. "This is no way for old friends to greet each other." I forced a smile.

The bearded man blinked. "Billy?"

"Have I changed so much?"

"Is this a wrong fellow?" The younger man possessed one of the less fortunate regional accents, thin and twangy. His eyes remained upon me.

"Have a seat, Billy. I hardly ever see any of the old outfit these days."

I borrowed a vacant chair from a nearby table and sat. The strangeness of the situation was like a fourth member of the party. Here he was, the most wanted man in America, sought by the authorities from Boston to the Barbary Coast, calmly conversing in a place of public commerce less than a day's ride from the farm where he was born. The years of gun battles and midnight rides, of suspicion and months spent in hiding, showed in the lines of his face and the threads of silver at his pink temples; at thirty-five we were the same age, but he could have been mistaken for a man in his forties. For all that he looked to be in good condition, flat-bellied and sinuous in his movements.

"Is it still Tom Howard?" I asked Jesse.

"It is. The name has brought me luck and I see no reason to change."

"How is Frank?"

"I don't see much of Buck these days. He is playing farmer and reading Shakespeare."

"You left Abilene in such a hurry we never got to say goodbye."

"The place was becoming various. We were supposed to be on vacation." He leaned forward then, removing his hand from the newspaper. "Billy, this here is Bob. Bob Ford, Billy Gashade."

To my surprise, a broad grin lit the young man's face and he offered me a slender hand. "Did you and Jesse ride together in the war?"

"We rode in the same direction at the same time," I said. "However, I was no guerrilla."

"Those must've been some times. I wish I was old enough to run with Bloody Bill."

Cy appeared then, with beers for Jesse and Ford, and we stopped talking. Jesse raised his eyebrows in my direction, but I shook my head. He paid for the beers. When we were alone: "You're working in Saint Joe?"

"Now and again. I take it you live here."

"I got me a little place on Woodland. You ought to stop by.

Zee gets restless with just me and the children to talk to. Zee, that's my wife. I'm a family man these days."

I congratulated him. I felt uneasy. Here was an affable Jesse I had never seen. Except for brief moments when I was playing one of the tunes he remembered from his mother's song sheets, I had never known him to lay down his guard so completely. It occurred to me that he was growing weary. A hand can bear the weight of a cocked pistol only so long before it begins to weaken.

"You know Buck's married too," he said. "Nice girl."

"I hear that's the best kind."

Now his forehead wrinkled. "I reckon you're still unhitched or you wouldn't still be on the move. You ought to find someone."

"I did."

"Well, hooray!"

"Then I lost her."

"I'm sorry. Truly I am. There are other women."

I shook my head, smiling. "I never thought I'd live to see the day I'd be getting advice to settle down from Jesse James."

Bob Ford shushed me, but no one could overhear us in that buzzing room.

Jesse scowled down at the newspaper in his lap. "I've been at this twenty years almost. I can't hardly remember why I started, except every time I go to visit Ma she reminds me. I think if I was to retire she'd take my place. She always did have more rebel in her than Buck and I put together." He sipped his beer. "You get tired. You get the awfullest kind of tired."

He was staring at the opposite wall, or rather through it. I thought I knew at what. "I read about that business in North-field," I said.

"That was Cole's idea from the start. 'Them scandihoovian farmers got more money than they can carry in two buckets,' he said. 'We ought to ride on up there and give 'em a hand.' Every gun in that town was on us when we come out of the bank. They chopped Chadwell and Clell Miller clean to pieces. The Youngers too, only they survived. Not that they'd want to, rotting in a Minnesota pen for life." He moved his shoulders. "Never stick up a place you don't know. You can tell 'em Jesse said so."

"They'll never get you, Jesse." Bob Ford was beaming.

"They wouldn't have much if they did. Not no ten-foot-tall desperado with Colts growing out of both fists like they expect."

The company was depressing me: an aging bandit afraid of his shadow, and his callow companion, fairly slobbering for a pat on the head from his god. I pushed back my chair.

"Good luck to you, Mr. Howard. Give my regards to your brother."

"I don't see much of Buck these days. You know he's married now."

I looked at him closely, suspecting some of that Missouri humor that so often escaped a listener from the East. There was no light in his eyes. In that moment he reminded me of no one so much as his stepfather, defeated so many years before by forces he didn't understand. I wanted to warn him, *Go to Frank; there is safety.* Instead I said nothing.

Oscar Wilde had made serious inroads upon the bourbon in his bottle when I rejoined him. However, his eyes were clear and his voice steady.

"Doubtless an old friend. They insist upon coming back despite our best efforts, like the detachable collar."

"Just someone I'd heard was dead," I said.

And I had heard right.

Our conversation wandered. After ten or fifteen minutes, Jesse James and Bob Ford got up from their table and left. As they passed a man seated near the door, Ford glanced his way. Immediately the man shifted positions and spread his copy of the *Kansas City Times* in front of his face.

That face troubled me. If it was him, he had put on considerable weight, becoming absolutely stout, and grown a crepey beard. However, Jesse James and Captain Jack Fabian in the same room at the same time was too great a coincidence to accept.

The next day I was playing "Londonderry Air" for an Irish laborer when someone burst through the door with news. Jesse James dead . . . right here in St. Joe . . . his own parlor . . . back of the head . . . Bob Ford.

I had never composed a song. That night, lying against the pillows in my Clay County bed with my guitar across my lap, I began picking out the bars of a standard ballad, the words dropping into place as I sang them, as if from a great height:

> Jesse James was a lad
> who killed many a man.
> He robbed the Glendale train . . .

CHAPTER FORTY-TWO

New York had changed, perhaps as much as I.

I was prepared for physical growth. The seven-story city I remembered had stretched upward and northward, bumping the sky with great Gothic spires and creeping up past the forties and fifties, encompassing the wilderness that had become Central Park, with no sign that it would quit before the tip of the island forced it to do so. All this I had heard about or suspected, but nothing I had read or imagined could embrace the noise of the place as it charged into the last two decades of the nineteenth century. The rustling of the crowds upon the sidewalks, the jangling trolleys, the brisk trotting of horses pulling hansoms and four-wheelers, the braying whistle of the elevated train as it roared overhead, releasing a gusher of sparks and cinders to the pavement—the very earth vibrated beneath the din. My head was splitting long before I alighted in front of the familiar old brownstone on Fifth Avenue and paid the driver his exorbitant ransom.

The building appeared unchanged, although it seemed to have grown smaller after all those blocks of skyscrapers, and oddly provincial, having been the center of my world for so long. I climbed the front steps, took a deep breath—and turned and nearly left, seized suddenly with a panic I had not known since that interminable trek from the buffalo camp to the ridge where a band of Sioux sat considering the fate of the trespassers. I turned back and tugged at the bell before I could change my mind again. The door was opened after a moment by a man in overalls whose gray, drawn face I had never before seen.

"Nobody by that name living here," he said when I inquired for my father. "They cut this place up into apartments five years ago. I don't know who owned it before that, nor where they went."

I tried two other doors in that block. The liveried maid who answered the next was ignorant as well. When no one answered the fourth time I rang the neighboring bell, I started to leave. I came back when I heard the door open.

Instantly I recognized the old woman who asked me what I wanted. She was whiter-haired, perhaps, and more shriveled than I remembered, but she had been ancient for as long as I had been aware of her. The lace at her throat was costly and the diamond upon the wedding finger of her left hand was the size of a thirty-two-caliber bullet, the band sunk deep into the old flesh. She was hard of hearing and almost blind, but nothing was wrong with her memory.

"Your father lost everything in the Panic," said she, once I'd succeeded in convincing her of my identity. "He sold the building to pay his debts. Had to resign from the bench then, because he didn't have a residence in the city. I heard he and your mother moved in with his brother on Long Island."

I winced at the bitterness of the situation. At the time I'd left home, my father and my uncle had not spoken to each other for years. They had broken over the latter's unethical business practices.

I took the train to Long Island. I had not been there since I was a child, but I remembered the big house and fourteen-acre estate at Southampton. The footman, whose powdered wig and silk stockings told me his employer had surrendered none of his conceits, took me to my uncle, a short, bald man with massive side-whiskers, who looked me up and down suspiciously, fired off a series of questions designed to trip me up over vagaries in the family history, harrumphed over the correctness of my answers, rang for the butler, and instructed him to take me to my father.

"What about my mother?" I asked.

"Dead these three years. I told him he'd never amount to anything, married to a sickly woman."

I bridled, stung by grief and his callous attitude. "A district judge doesn't amount to anything?"

"Pah! A public servant is still just a servant. He isn't even that any more, just a burden on the brother he was too good for when he was riding high."

Fearing that I would be ejected without being allowed to see my father, I held my tongue and accompanied the butler to a hall bedroom, where a nurse with a wart on her chin informed me that the judge had suffered a stroke some months before and was unable to speak, although she believed he understood things that were said to him.

I scarcely recognized him. He looked as small as Alma in a wheeled bath chair with a rug drawn across his knees; withered, white-haired, and vacant-eyed. The right side of his face was slack. I told him who I was. He showed no reaction. I told him again, this time grasping the pale, spotted hand that rested atop the rug. It seemed I felt a faint pressure. When I identified myself a third time, his eyes rolled my way and appeared to fix themselves. I recognized then the directness of the old jurist. He opened his mouth and tried to speak. Plainly the effort excited him, for he was trembling. The nurse took his pulse and asked me to come back later.

My uncle, it developed, had been divorced from his first wife for many years. The woman to whom he was now married was half his age, a pleasant solidly built woman with black hair and great sympathetic brown eyes, who told me her husband was not as bad a fellow as he seemed to want people to think him. I was still upset and replied that he must want people to think him very bad indeed. At this point she excused herself, and I thought I had offended her. Presently, however, she returned to the spacious living room, whose windows looked out upon the Atlantic, and handed me a bundle of papers five inches thick, bound with faded blue ribbon.

"They are letters from your father. He kept on writing, even though he didn't know where to send them when they started coming back."

The one on top bore an 1863 date. My throat closed. "He might not want me to read them. I'm not the same person he addressed them to."

"Read them. I've had the north room aired out and the bed made. Of course you're staying."

I stayed, and I read the letters. When I had finished, I returned to my father's room. The nurse, who was capable of greater human feeling than her appearance indicated, left us alone, and there in the gray silence I told my father everything that I had done and seen since the day I left. I do not know how much he heard or understood. He lay in bed, his eyes open. When the nurse came back, I rose and touched his hand again. Again I felt a faint squeeze.

He died the second week in December, in his sleep, without having said a word to me in nearly twenty years. I felt, however, after reading his letters and presenting my life to him with all its many shortfalls, that we stood upon the same level.

I declined my uncle's halfhearted offer to bear the cost of his burial. Instead I used the last of the money I had saved to purchase a walnut casket with a gray silk lining and arrange for a modest service at the Marble Collegiate Church at Fifth Avenue and Twenty-ninth Street, just down the street from our old home. It was attended by a number of Father's legal associates and fellow club members, a small group of less than two dozen. He was interred in the churchyard beside my mother, beneath a granite headstone I had ordered bearing his name and the dates of his birth and death, together with this inscription:

"For this my son was dead, and is alive again; he was lost, and is found."

—LUKE 15:24

My song is almost ended. Yet there are a few more verses to be sung.

The era of the New York music hall was then just beginning. On the basis of the popularity of "Jesse James"—crude ballad that it was, it swept through the Midwest from saloon to saloon like a brand of cheap potent whiskey, and had been heard in San Francisco—I obtained a position as house lyricist with the Mellow Memories Song Sheet Company, three flights up from Forty-fourth Street at the corner of Broadway. Very soon I learned I could supplement my income by selling work on commission to my employers' competitors. My career as a full-time freelance composer began when Mellow Memories discovered my duplicity and fired me. When the royalties began coming in I moved out of my uncle's house into an apartment on Forty-second. There, the cacophony of a hundred pianos clattering out a hundred parlor tunes day and night prompted deafened local journalists to dub the neighborhood Tin Pan Alley.

I was working steadily and making more money than I ever had in my life, but something was missing. I found it when I walked into a dank, brick-walled drinking establishment in Greenwich Village one Saturday night and talked the proprietor into allowing me to play and sing a few of my songs in the corner by the stove, where patrons never sat because the heat was oppressive. The audience response, modest though it was, fed an appetite I hadn't realized I'd acquired all those years I sang for my supper in every watering hole between St. Louis and Cripple Creek. I came back the following Monday and every night after that. When new people began coming in because they'd heard there was music, the proprietor put me on salary, on top of which I was free to claim all gratuities.

Since Jesse's legendary death, the James brothers were front-page news even in New York. Frank surrendered himself to Governor Crittenden of Missouri six months after St. Joseph. Tried three times for robbery and murder and acquitted, he walked out of an Otterville, Missouri, courtroom a free man in February 1885. He was never again to my knowledge associated with any criminal activity, and died a respectable farmer in 1915, leaving behind a tidy nest egg contributed to by his personally guided tours of the James farm at fifty cents a head. Bob Ford and his brother Charlie, who had conspired with the Pinkertons to kill Jesse, were convicted of his murder and sentenced to hang, only to be pardoned immediately by Governor Crittenden and set free with five hundred dollars of the promised reward of five thousand in their pockets. Four years later, Charlie committed suicide. In 1892, after being hounded through the West, it was said, by the line in my song, "that dirty little coward, that shot Mr. Howard," Bob Ford was cornered in his own saloon in Creede, Colorado, by a James admirer named Ed Kelley, who blew his head off with a shotgun.

About this time I was moved to visit the site of the East River Society House, where nearly thirty years before I had recovered from injuries sustained in the draft riots while Boss Tweed's men were scouring the city for Jehosophat Brennan's assailant. The building was gone, the lot where it had stood surrounded by a ten-foot board fence behind which a construction crew was laying the foundation for yet another skyscraper. A policeman I spoke to on the corner informed me that the old building had been demolished after the roof collapsed during the great blizzard of '88. He had been on the beat only three years and had never heard of either Bridey McMurtaugh or Templeton "Tupper" Deane of the Invalid Corps.

Relaxing at home on a Sunday, I read in the *World* that a company formed by Thomas A. Edison was at work in the New Jersey countryside, photographing models in action for the new motion-picture process invented by the company's founder. These "photoplays" had started to pull in nickels from candy stores where they were projected upon bedsheet screens and from hand-cranked viewing machines installed inside smoke shops and soda fountains, and public demand for complete and coherent stories had prompted Edison to re-create daring exploits from the West for the camera. My old curiosity intact, I journeyed out there the next weekend, only to be told by a harried employee in riding breeches carrying a megaphone that motion-picture-making being a silent process, the company had no need for a musician.

I discovered, however, that a rival company was shooting in the area. The man I spoke to there was intrigued with the concept of providing music on the set to establish the proper mood for the models, whom he referred to as actors, and put me to work on the spot. His employers were so pleased with the results that within a month I found myself the director of a quartet including a violin, a bass fiddle, and a spinet piano.

One morning I reported to the barn outside Union City where the equipment was stored and copies of the day's shooting schedule were given out, only to find the door padlocked and a notice tacked up explaining that the building and its contents had been confiscated by the county sheriff. The Edison Company, which claimed exclusive patent to the motion-picture process, had filed infringement charges against all its competitors; any further violation would result in arrest for each member of the offending company and destruction of its equipment.

At the end of that week, a meeting was convened in the downtown office of the company's owner, who announced that the operation was moving to California, outside the reach of Edison's long arm. The sleepy residential community of Hollywood, located just outside Los Angeles, had been selected, and any member of the company who cared to relocate was invited to come along. That weekend I closed out my apartment and gave notice at the saloon in the Village. I had been in one place far too long as it was for a man who had spent most of his life wandering.

The train ride through the country of my awakening was uneventful. Electric fans cooled the cars, train changes were efficient and infrequent, the sleeping berths were a good deal more comfortable than many I had been forced to put up with for months at a time. I was growing into a time of life that celebrated the convenience, but I was still close enough to my youth to decry the loss of a sense of adventure. If the mechanics of travel continued to improve, I postulated, one would soon cross the continent as easily as he crossed the street, without reflection upon the men and women who broke their hearts and lost their lives during the same journey.

Hollywood, a sun-washed section of reclaimed desert made up of small stucco-and-tile houses on streets lined with palms and orange trees, had begun to bustle: Other outlaw production companies had preceded us, and dusty cowpokes from all over the West had set up camp outside town as casting calls went out for extras, wranglers, and stunt riders to enliven the backgrounds of westerns being shot. As the great ranches broke up and cow work became scarce, the news of opportunities for employment had made of this unlikely place a boomtown every bit as raw and wild as Abilene in its heyday. A few weeks after I had settled in, I stepped outside my rented bungalow in time to see a foreman employed by William Ince shoot down a stand-in with the Griffith company in the middle of La Cienaga Avenue. During the inquest that followed, testimony revealed that bad blood had existed between the pair ever since they had fought over a lower bunk at the King Ranch in Texas.

That aside, I was working hard and enjoying myself, but I craved recreation. An Essanay extra with whom I'd been friendly in Fort Worth when he'd worked for Shanghai Pierce told me of an establishment in the San Fernando Valley that specialized in female escorts who bore a close resemblance to well-known motion-picture queens. "You could have you a fine time, if the old lady that runs the place don't put you off your feed."

The house, a cool, sprawling mansion of timber-reinforced

adobe with a red tile roof, occupied twelve acres of an old Spanish land grant dating back to King Philip. Mary Pickford, attired only in a big hair bow and a diaphanous peignoir, was entertaining a pair of moguls-in-the-making on the sofa in the front parlor, and Mabel Normand and the Gish sisters cruised the halls and staircases in brassieres, panties, and garter belts studded with rhinestones. They were close matches to the originals, provided one didn't stare too hard through the careful makeup.

I became bored with the conceit quickly and sat down at the piano in the parlor to play some tunes I was in danger of forgetting. I had been at this for some time when a huge Negress in the black dress and white lacy apron and cap of a housemaid tapped me on the shoulder.

"Beg pardon, mister, but the lady of the house say she'd admire to speak with you upstairs."

She escorted me up the sweeping carpeted steps to the second floor and rapped lightly upon a door at the end of the hall.

An instant before a voice answered from inside, I had a premonition. "The lady of the house" was known to me.

The dimensions of the room were difficult to determine in the gloom created by the thick curtains that covered the windows. The voice that greeted me from somewhere near the back, however, was as clear as if the speaker were standing at my side.

"Well, Billy, you are getting quite gray."

"I wish I could claim it's premature," said I.

A small electric lamp came on with a snap upon a plain writing table ten feet away. She, too, had aged. Her hair was entirely white, and a mass of wrinkles marred the hand that wore the garnet; but the undamaged side of her face, turned toward me, was largely unchanged. An extra line here and there could not affect the handsome bone structure I remembered so well.

I said, "I see you've given up the boardinghouse business and returned to the basics."

"The rents here are too cheap. I cannot compete. You might be surprised to learn how many famous and desired people make use of my services, when it seems they could have anyone they wanted without paying a fee."

"Perhaps they prefer your Theda Bara to the real article."

"I have a Ramon Novarro as well, and a Francis X. Bushman. My clientele is nothing if not diverse. Are you revolted?"

"A frontier town is a frontier town. None of the old rules apply when the money's standing around in bushels and the Mexican border is so close."

"You are growing tolerant in your old age, Billy."

"I've lived some since Abilene."

"Any regrets?"

"Almost nothing but."

She nodded slightly. "This is good. I do not trust the man who says he would live his life the same way if he had the chance to repeat it. And there is hope in the 'almost.' As for me, I would change everything."

I shook my head. "If you did that, I would not have the 'almost.'"

"Perhaps there is hope for me also," she said after a moment.

"There's always hope." I spread my arms, smiling. "Isn't that what this is all about?"

The shadow of the ghost of a smile touched the one visible corner of her lips. "Good-bye, Billy. Enjoy the hospitality of my house tonight. I should be very disappointed in you if you choose to come back."

"Not even to visit you?"

"Especially not that. I am your past. You cannot visit the past, only live there. To live there is to die. Remember that as the last counsel I will give you."

She snapped off the lamp.

The motion-picture industry has changed nearly as much as the American West, and I was there to see it happening. Talkies came in, and after a period of jabbery "message" pictures and tinny musicals, the camera learned to move again and westerns came back, with the bonus of loud gunfire, hammering hooves, and singing cowboys. The money's not so good now: A Depression is on, and as I approach my ninth decade I have to submit my work through younger songwriters of indiscernible talent, whose names appear in the credits identifying them as the authors. Arthritis in my hands keeps me from playing my own compositions. Myra, the landlady's daughter, finds the chords I want on her mother's piano and writes them down for me— when she isn't out with some producer who will never give her a speaking role, not even if she performs an unnatural act upon him during the lunch rush at the Brown Derby.

I pawned the guitar last year, but I've made arrangements to leave the banjo to Myra, along with a letter authenticating it as one of the items found in Crazy Horse's possession when he was killed. A wealthy collector of western memorabilia may pay her enough for it to finance her own studio.

I've changed my thinking since my final meeting with Drucilla Patakos. I don't regret much. I've known some of the best and worst men of my time, survived events that sent better men than I to their graves more than half a century ago, and, as I was told by one of the strong, intelligent women who have charted the course of my life, I have my gift. Unlike its composer, the song I wrote fifty-three years ago grows stronger each year. A month hardly passes that I don't hear it on the radio or in a supper place with a live performer, usually at the request of one of the patrons, even if whoever sings it usually leaves out the last verse:

> *This song was made by Billy Gashade*
> *Just as soon as the news did arrive.*
> *He said there was no man with the law in his hand*
> *That could take Jesse James when alive.*

Not a bad epitaph for either of us, if I do say so myself.

B.G., Hollywood, California,
April 3, 1935